To Judy:
Enjoy this
word. &

Amazon.com
Barnesandnoble.com

Hearts of Gold

Frank P. Whyte

Frank P. Whyte

August 2003

PublishAmerica
Baltimore

First printing

ISBN: 1-59286-568-2
PUBLISHED BY PUBLISHAMERICA BOOK PUBLISHERS
www.publishamerica.com
Baltimore

Printed in the United States of America

For Archie Y. Hamilton, M.D.
While we conducted the business of death, you
managed to teach me a good deal about living.

ACKNOWLEDGMENTS

The road to publication has been a long one and I have been helped and influenced by many people along the way. I would first like to thank the staffs and physicians of the Sacramento, California County Coroner's Office and the Oregon State Medical Examiner's Office. Chief among these individuals were Pierce Rooney MD, Larry Lewman MD, Ronald O'Halloran MD, now the Ventura County, California Medical Examiner, and William Brady MD. I would also like to thank investigators Patrick Chamberlain and Robert Felton for unselfishly sharing their knowledge when I was a fledgling deputy coroner.

I would also like to thank Terrence Williams MD for allowing me into his open-heart surgery suite, on several occasions, in order that I might become more familiar with cardiac bypass surgery. That experience was invaluable in this work. I am also indebted to cardiologist Bruce Fleishman MD who reviewed this work for technical authenticity. I tried to incorporate his suggestions into the text, and if any errors were made, they are mine, and not his.

This book is dedicated to Archie Hamilton MD, an individual of most unique character. More than anyone else in my life, he taught me about living and about life. His sense of humor, while occasionally morbid, was most often timely and appreciated. I left his employ a changed man, some changes good, some not so good, but my awareness of the human experience had been granted a depth that I would not have otherwise known without him. Thank you, Archie.

Of course, any acknowledgment statement would be incomplete without recognizing the support of my daughters, Lindsay and Andrea. I want the two of you to know that you can accomplish anything. This book is proof of that. I also thank Lori Cleverley for her support during the embryonic stages of writing this book.

And finally, and with the deepest of love and respect, I express my gratitude to my wife, Kitty. Your support and unending faith in my ability, as well as your perspective, and help with typing on the rewrites, gave me what I needed to see this thing through. Thank you, I love you.

CHAPTER 1

Portland, Oregon is known as the City of Roses. Once nestled, now sprawling, it occupies that portion of the Willamette River Valley that is closest to the Great Mother River - the Columbia. It arose from timber, fishing, and trade. It grew from industry. It is now another large city, but one with a face that is its own. It is a face of culture, of flavor, but it also is the face of urban decline that plagues every other metropolitan area in this country.

On a sunny day, there may not be any more beautiful city on Earth. But sunny days are few. More often, the clouds fly low, the winds blow cold, and the rain falls in sheets as the mighty Pacific conjures and sends its wrath inland. For no other reason than that of sustained torrent and darkness, a deviancy of the human spirit seeps into the souls of men. Depression is common and suicides are many. But eventually, the sun does come in all of its glory. The tall fir trees sway gently in the prevailing winds, the flowers bloom, the children play, and the people come to know why they have endured the many nights of cold, wind, and rain. Such is the City of Roses.

* * *

Ike Paponis stood with his hands resting slightly on the mahogany railing at the top of the curved staircase. This vantage point allowed him a full view of the huge and elaborate ballroom below, which was filled with the many guests who had accepted invitations to this party. Rarely had anyone declined an invitation to an affair hosted by the heart surgeon turned politician. Ike had power in Portland - probably more power than any other man.

He was beginning to enter the other side of middle age, but Ike still managed to remain young at heart. His vitality easily matched that of a man half his age. Intellect and experience allowed him to exercise that vitality with a keen discretion.

He was not becoming frail in middle age. He exercised regularly, although swimming laps in his indoor pool had replaced the wretched ten mile runs that had been the morning ritual for most of his adult life. In fact, the wisps of gray at the temples, contrasted with the tanned olive skin that spoke of his Grecian heritage, were the only indications that the man was aging at all.

From his vantage point, Ike Paponis could see his beautiful young wife.

Sharon Paponis was a lithe blonde with a quick wit, charm, and a mental acuity that rivaled that of her husband. He had married her ten years earlier, when at the age of twenty-eight, she had fit his needs quite nicely. She now seemed to enjoy her position in life, for being the wife of Ike Paponis could certainly be classified as being a full-time job.

But the benefits of the job could not be replaced by other employment. She had virtually everything that she needed and nearly everything that she wanted. Sharon's wardrobe and jewelry collection were extensive. Their posh Lake Oswego estate, its furnishing, their automobiles, and private plane, all provided more that the typical comforts.

Sharon Paponis was the ambassador for the powerful cardio-thoracic surgeon who had managed to build an empire in Portland. The empire had one primary function which was to buy influence. Ike Paponis had managed to control local politicians, wealthy businessmen, and members of the United States Congress. His petitions were commonly heard in the Oval Office of the White House, and frequently deference was granted his wishes.

Ike had originally formed a consortium that had consisted of him and his two closest friends. But now, the three were no longer partners. It had been a fruitful venture for all three men. They had amassed what could only be described as a fortune, and they had used that money for whatever causes that they had deemed to be important. Impressive results were achieved, but as is true in most human endeavors, the ultimate objectives had been by no means altruistic.

As Paponis surveyed the well-dressed and socially-acceptable crowd below, be saw that Sharon was having a discreet conversation with Allan Spandell Jr., a young attorney. Although Ike had maintained his vitality, he knew that it was necessary for his wife to have youthful friends. He could offer her love, but he and his wife had come from different worlds. Ike's childhood had been marked by street smarts and poverty. Sharon had been groomed by the socially elite.

Allan Spandell Jr. was the son of one of Ike's partners. Spandell Sr. was a probate attorney and a key cog within the corporation when it had all started many years ago. The surgeon had considered forming an alliance with the younger Spandell, who was following in his father's footsteps, but in the end, he had decided that he would never be able to share some of the secrets involving the group.

Paponis also felt that the junior attorney lacked the shrewd business sense necessary for some of the more intricate aspects of the operation. His father had been tactfully ruthless. He had been able to cross the ethical boundaries when the situation had dictated it. Ike Paponis doubted if there were many men left like he and Allan Spandell Sr. Men were no longer made of the same fabric as he and his partner had been. The surgeon felt that men today lived with a sense of fear. They lived within the confines of political correctness. Ultimately, even Spandell Sr. had succumbed to this weakness. They lacked soul and were unable to make the tough decisions necessary to achieve the greater good.

Paponis and his friends had been products of a different world, a different America. Their parents had known what it was like to be poor, and they had been adept at being resourceful enough to provide for themselves and their families. These had been stern-willed men and women with strong value systems.

The conversation between Sharon Paponis and Allan Spandell appeared to be slightly more than cordial. Ike knew that Sharon was fond of the young attorney, and he also knew that if he were to lend himself to jealousy, he would certainly be jealous of the liaison. He didn't know if the two were sleeping together, and he didn't really care. He knew that his wife was intelligent enough to know that discretion was of the utmost importance. But such were the perils of relationships with passionate women.

The heart surgeon decided to leave the responsibility of entertaining his guests in the capable hands of his young wife. It was already eleven o'clock at night, and he needed to be out of bed by three for a four o'clock procedure.

* * *

There was a flurry of activity in the heart room. Ike Paponis M.D. walked through the door to the operating suite at exactly four a.m. Both his equipment and his patient were ready for surgery. The man on whom he would be operating this morning was a fifty-five year old white male who had complained of chest pain earlier in the week.

The man had come to the emergency room, and he had then been admitted to the cardiac care unit. A cardiologist had performed a cardiac catheterization, and found that two of the vessels supplying oxygenated blood to the heart were almost one hundred percent blocked. The cardiologist had attempted to open the vessels using a small balloon within the arteries, but the effort had been unsuccessful. The man was a walking time bomb, and without open heart surgery, he would certainly die within a matter of weeks.

9

Paponis was the only surgeon at the Health Sciences Medical Center to begin his operating schedule so early in the morning. It was just one of his personal habits. In reality, however, it was probably nothing more than a power play. The surgeon truly enjoyed disrupting everyone's schedule. He liked the idea that the nurses and technicians were jumping through hoops in the middle of the night just because it was his personal whim to operate at these God-forsaken hours.

But those who prepared his patient and his instruments knew that the job had better be done properly and on time. Paponis had a propensity for the public humiliation of those who had failed to adhere to his meticulous requirements. A quiet word from his mouth had been sufficient to terminate the employment of more than a few nurses. His verbal tirades could be endless, and God help those who dared to challenge him.

Paponis was a great source of revenue for the Health Sciences Medical Center, and the hospital administration would never dare to cross him. He had national renown, and his connections went deeper than any of those who knew him would venture to guess. Nobody had the courage to confront him, for they were all familiar with the fates of those who had tried.

The lights were bright in the operating room. The patient had been intubated with a plastic tube that went down into his lungs. This was connected to a ventilator that breathed mechanically for the patient. The entire body had been covered with sterile blue drapes, with the exception of the chest, which was the color of the red-brown Betadine solution which had been used to cleanse and disinfect the skin. Infection was one of the biggest concerns during the recovery period, and every effort was made to avoid it.

Intravenous lines had been started, and another line had been inserted into an artery in the wrist to monitor arterial pressure. The anesthesiologist had already administered doses of Ativan and Arduan. The patient was paralyzed by the effects of the Arduan, and would have total amnesia regarding the procedure due to the effects of the Ativan.

The heart-lung bypass machine stood at the ready. It was this machine that made open heart surgery possible for the masses. A perfusionist waited for the order to go on bypass. At that time, the patient's heart and lungs would be bypassed, and the blood would be oxygenated by this large mechanical device. This whole procedure was necessary to provide life-giving oxygenated blood to the tissues of the body, while the heart was at standstill for the operation.

Without a word to his crew, the surgeon stepped up to his place next to the operating table. He was immediately handed the small electocautery pencil that had replaced the scalpel for most surgical incisions. The current that went through the device helped to create a near-perfect incision while stopping most of the associated bleeding at the same time.

He made the longitudinal slice downward from between the clavicles to the base of the sternum. He then took the electrical saw in hand and made a perfect cut through the bones of the sternum. Heavy metal spreaders were used to pull the bone apart, exposing the organs of the chest.

As the heart surgeon methodically performed his duties, the young surgical resident was busy retrieving a portion of the saphenous vein from the patient's leg. This segment of vessel would be used to bypass the blocked sections of the coronary arteries. The body was cooled to twenty-eight degrees centigrade, and only then was a dose of very cool, highly-concentrated potassium solution delivered directly into the heart. The potassium solution so disrupted the concentration of the ion within the heart that it effectively caused the organ to come to a complete halt.

The sight of the non-pulsatile heart within his patient's chest had never ceased to amaze Ike Paponis. This was ultimate power. This was the power over life and death. Without his skill and willingness, the man would surely die.

The flow of adrenaline caused by this realization encouraged the surgeon's hands to move rapidly. He found the sections of blocked artery, took the portion of the vein removed from the patient's leg, and sewed one end of it into the hole he had punched into the aorta just a fraction of an inch above the heart. He then sewed the other end into the coronary artery in the heart just beyond where it was blocked. This procedure would give the gift of life to this man.

He could still marvel at the modern advances that newly developed technology had provided for him. Paponis was second generation. Those who had come before him had been a breed apart. They had, for the most part, been driven men obsessed with the theory that lifesaving surgery could be performed on the human heart.

The first such procedure had been performed by Dr. John Gibbon in 1953, and he subsequently became known as the father of open heart surgery. The truly phenomenal development, however, had been credited to Dr. Michael De Bakey, who had conceptualized the heart-lung bypass machine. It was this device that had allowed the practice of open heart surgery to become a viable alternative to death from massive heart attack.

These men had been pioneers, cowboys, men of vision. Paponis, and many of his second generation, were politicians. He worked his rich network of professional associates in search of new referrals. He was a man of blatant opulence and already in possession of an unparalleled ego. He lived in a big house, drove a fast car, had a pretty wife, and never hesitated to step on whomever was in his way. For Ike Paponis, it had always been that way, and it was not likely to change now.

CHAPTER 2
August, 1980

Ike Paponis, Allan Spandell, and Martin Spencer were seated at their table in the luxurious dining room of the Lake Oswego Country Club. The three were the newest inductees into this exclusive fraternity of Pacific Northwest elite. There had been twenty-four applicants, but only the names of Paponis, Spencer, and Spandell had been approved for membership.

It was a feather in the cap of each of the young professionals. There had been more prominent names on the list seeking membership, but the committee had seen something special in each of these three men. They had vitality, intelligence, and a will to succeed that was difficult to mistake.

Paponis was a young heart surgeon, Spandell, an attorney specializing in probate law, and Spencer, a medical examiner, who had just accepted a position with the Multnomah County Medical Examiner. They would all have influence in Portland. It was just a matter of time.

The three men were already quite at home in their new environment. It was nothing less than each had expected of themselves, and even though they were all in their early thirties, each had already plotted his own course. Membership in the Lake Oswego Country Club was merely one of the initiating first steps.

"Congratulations, gentlemen. It's good to see that the club we have selected had the good sense to recognize potential when they see it." The words had been spoken by Ike Paponis. He raised his glass in mock salute as he spoke the words that bore the flamboyant self-assuredness that was his most notable characteristic. His two companions raised their glasses as well.

"Did you really have any doubts?" asked Allan Spandell sarcastically. He had graduated from McGeorge School of Law in Sacramento, California several years earlier, and he had spent the last three years as a deputy district attorney in San Francisco. Spandell was tall and thin with high cheekbones that spoke of aristocracy. He had chosen probate law primarily due to the relative scarcity of probate lawyers in his native Portland. His talents were actually better suited to the energetic cross-examination of the criminal trial, but Spandell was out to make a buck, and he couldn't think of any better way to do it. There would always be wills to be prepared and estates to be settled, and these would always involve paying customers. Criminal law might be more exciting, but it would never be as lucrative as Spandell needed it to be.

Martin Spencer watched and listened as the other two men bathed in the glow of their recent success. He was happy to have been inducted into the club, but he was not nearly as pretentious about it as were his two companions. The truth be known, Spencer was actually surprised that he had survived the selection process.

Marty Spencer had recently completed a fellowship in forensic pathology at the medical examiner's office in Dallas, Texas. In addition to his forensic practice at the M.E.'s office, he also intended to have a clinical practice at a local hospital. There he would diagnose tumors and other unusual disorders. While the pathologist was not as ostentatious as his new friends, he did have the same desire for personal wealth.

"I'm glad that you guys were so confident, but I'm pretty darn glad for the break. I never expected to get in. Now all I have to do is figure out how I'm going to pay the dues."

"Don't worry about that. There's more money in this club than anywhere else in the entire Northwest. You'll make so many connections here that you'll be well on your way to being a rich man inside of a year." Paponis knew why he had joined the club, and he was only sharing his personal views with the pathologist. He fully intended to work every angle of this membership. He would be the heart surgeon to the rich and famous. One successful operation would lead to ten more, and the fees would be enormous.

"That's easy for you to say. You're a surgeon who's going to have a private practice. I'm going to be a county employee on salary. Sure, I'll scrape together a few extra bucks at the hospital, but my earning potential still won't be near either of you."

"Don't sell yourself short, Marty. You've got to be able to think creatively. If we all stick together, I think we'll be able to help each other make our fortunes. It's the eighties, man. We can do anything." The alcohol had only served to enhance Ike's usual bravado.

Marty Spencer was more than a little amused by these two men. He had become a medical examiner strictly by design. He was a handsome man, but shy by nature. He had never felt confident that he would have the personality to handle daily interactions with patients. There was a good deal of solitude to be found in performing autopsies. He would not have to be subject to the pain of his patients. His would be a cold and analytical practice - devoid of the lucidity of human emotion. There would be others who could talk to the families and console the widows. He could just tuck himself away in the

14

morgue and laboratory where he felt most comfortable.

The three men had several more drinks and left for their homes. If they were to be successful in their endeavors, they would at least have to project the image of sobriety. And each of them had every intention of being successful.

* * *

The months went rapidly by, and the three newest members of the Lake Oswego Country Club became Wednesday afternoon fixtures on the golf course. Ike Paponis regularly invited local family practitioners and internists to join him and his friends for lunch and a round of golf. It was the heart surgeon's way of rounding up business, and it had proven to be quite effective.

Paponis wined and dined the physicians, and he impressed them with his style and grace, all contrived, mind you, but what did they know? The five handicap didn't hurt either. It was the ideal set up. The physicians evaluated their patients and sent them to Paponis for surgery. He was able to perform two operations daily, received between three and five thousand dollars for each procedure, and he still had ample time for afternoon office hours, except for Wednesdays, which were reserved for golf at Oswego with his two friends.

Allan Spandell had opened his own firm in downtown Portland. He had leased a spacious suite of offices on the eleventh floor of a large building, and already his business was supporting itself. It had been a risky venture initially. Spandell had considered joining an existing firm, but his membership at Lake Oswego had changed all of that.

The Lake Oswego Country Club was the most exclusive club of its kind in the Pacific Northwest. The membership was extremely wealthy, and for the most part, elderly. It was a probate attorney's dream. The elderly members of the club had all been quite taken with the young trio and made every effort to help them succeed in business.

Marty Spencer had arrived at the Multnomah County Medical Examiner's office having bright hopes of being able to practice his specialty while staying out of the limelight. At full staff, the medical examiner's office would have employed three full-time medical examiners. But when he had shown up for his first full day, there had only been two. The workload had been heavy, but Spencer had been happy to have the opportunity to gain the extra experience.

What he had not counted on was that his superior, Dr. Anson Baxter, would suddenly decide to resign his position and move to Florida. The county board of commissioners had appointed Spencer to fill the vacated position of Chief Medical Examiner, and in addition to expanded duties, he found himself responsible for the workload of three full-time pathologists. Again he didn't mind, because he was able to avoid some of the more high-profile tasks such as playing politics and dealing with the media. All of the activities that Marty Spencer had tried so desperately to avoid had suddenly been dropped in his lap ten fold.

He was now unable to moonlight at the local hospital due to time constraints and possible ethical impropriety. This forced him to try and survive on the fifty thousand dollar annual salary that he was being paid by the county. Given the circles that he was traveling in these days, that was not an easy task.

Marty surprised himself, however, by growing nicely into his new job. He had more of a penchant for dealing with the politicians than he would ever have expected, and the media clamored to have the handsome young medical examiner on the evening news. It seemed that the viewing public could not get enough of their new medical examiner describing the gory details of each new murder.

Ike Paponis was acutely aware of his friend's financial difficulties, but he was more aware of Spencer's position and newly found public appeal. It was a friendship that he was glad he had developed, and he knew that he would continue to nurture the relationship. He had several ideas about how he could help his friend to be financially secure, but it could be politically touchy arranging the details.

The medical examiner was busy in the morgue when Paponis strolled through the doors early one afternoon. The heart surgeon was suddenly startled by the carnage before him. He was not a stranger to the human body, or even to death, but the sight of ten naked bodies, in varying states of disarray, and lined up on the stainless steel gurneys, was astonishing to him.

Marty Spencer was methodically making his way down the line. A microphone was suspended from the ceiling over each of the gurneys, and there was a foot pedal to operate the dictation system on the floor next to each of the stretchers. Spencer was able to move quickly from body to body, as morgue attendants had removed all of the vital organs prior to his examination. He merely needed to collect samples of suspect tissue, dictate his report, and move onto the next customer. He looked up from the body of a young black male, who had been racked by gunfire, to see his friend's smiling face.

"Ike, what the heck are you doing here?"

"I had to see just exactly what it is that you do for that paltry salary that the county pays you." Paponis's tone was cordial and not at all condescending.

"Well, I'm afraid this is it. This is a pretty typical day for me."

"You know, I never really imagined that it could be like this. I had to do the obligatory pathology rotation in med school, but those autopsies were a heck of a lot different than the mess you've got here. Shoot, we could spend days on the same body and still not find the cause of death."

"Unfortunately, I don't have the same luxury. If I ignored this place for two days, I would be so inundated with bodies that I would never be able to dig myself out."

"When are you going to get some help down here?"

"I've got a couple of guys coming in for interviews next week. Or should I say, one guy and a young lady. The problem is that this job doesn't pay much. There just aren't enough doctors specializing in forensic pathology these days. I'm hoping that at least one of these folks will meet my needs, though. Preferably both. God knows there's enough work to go around."

"Look, Marty, the reason that I stopped by is that I've got an idea for a new business venture. With all of the family practice offices springing up, the hospital labs have so much work that it's taking days to get results. I'm convinced that the wave of the future is in private laboratories picking up the slack for the hospitals. You know, Marty, there's going to be a heck of a lot of money in this – I'm convinced of it. All I want to do is to get in on it early."

"So what does all of this mean for me?"

"I think that you're just the guy to head up an operation like this. What do ya say?"

"What are you asking me to do? Do you think I would need to quit my job here? I don't know how I would ever have enough time to manage something like that in addition to my duties here."

"Hell no, I don't want you to quit! Your position here will give the whole operation credibility. If we're going to make this thing go, we're going to have to keep you in the public eye. Marty, you're a celebrity. The people love you. That tells me something. When a guy who makes his living cutting up dead bodies can become as popular as you have become, then I know I've got the guy I want to head up this operation. We'll make a bunch of money." The surgeon had great business sense, and he knew that he had a winning idea.

"Ike, I hate to rain on your parade, but I'll never have time to do justice to a venture like that. I'm more or less drowning here already. I'm afraid that I wouldn't be much good to you. And besides, I'm afraid that this would be a big-time conflict of interest. The county commission would never stand for anything like it." Spencer had hated to make the pronouncement. He knew that a venture like this could be his ticket to some of the wealth that his friends seemed to be enjoying.

"Don't worry about the politicians, Marty. I'll take care of them."

"Since when do you have so much pull with the politicians?"

"Since I did open heart surgery on Sam Berry's wife."

Sam Berry was the chairman of the board of the Multnomah County Commissioners, and Ike Paponis had become well acquainted with him while he had been caring for his wife. He had shown extra attention to the commissioner, because he had somehow known that the time would come when Berry would be able to return the favor.

"I still wouldn't have the time, Ike."

"Do you intend to waste your whole life down here working for scraps? You'll have plenty of help in this venture, and I don't suspect that it will take much of your time. I just need your name on the letterhead, and some of your management skills to get the project rolling. After we get it set up, it'll probably run itself. I'm telling you, Marty, this is going to be a gold mine."

"Check into it a little further, Ike. If you find that I can do it without getting into any legal trouble, then we'll talk more about it."

"Don't worry about legal trouble. We'll have Allan handle that end of it."

CHAPTER 3

Sam Berry sat at the desk in his office in the county courthouse. He had been a fixture on the county commission for the previous sixteen years. He wielded his power as he saw fit. There had never been any questions regarding contracts that he had authorized, and his "at will" hiring and firing of many county employees had not even raised an eyebrow. Sam Berry administered his position according to his own liking, and it was the rare individual who dared to challenge his authority.

In recent years, however, Berry had become his own worst enemy. He had always been impressed with his position, but unfortunately, the financial rewards had never been in keeping with a man of his station. The difficulty rested with the fact that he associated with some of the most powerful business brokers in the city, but he had never felt like he was one of them. In many cases, he did their bidding, helped them to amass their fortunes, but he had never been able to reap any of the financial rewards.

Berry was frequently a guest at social gatherings attended by the powerfully elite. He had been invited to the Lake Oswego Country Club for rounds of golf, and his wife had been included in many of the activities of the wealthier women in the community. But Sam Berry never felt quite like he was good enough.

In the past two years, he had invested his life savings in a series of risky financial ventures, and today he was broke. Far worse than that, he was heavily in debt, and in danger of losing his home. His wife had recently undergone open heart surgery, and the insurance company had only picked up eighty percent of the tab. Now he owed Health Sciences and Dr. Ike Paponis and additional twenty-five thousand dollars. It was no exorbitant sum when talking of his wife's good health, but it was nearly the straw that broke the camel's back.

Sam Berry had tried to cover his losses by secretly borrowing form his campaign chest, and if this fact were ever discovered, he would face the loss of his position and maybe even criminal prosecution. He was a nervous wreck, and had even been having some vague chest pain of his own. But he also knew that he couldn't afford to see Ike Paponis when he still owed him so much money. And none of those other butchers were going to touch him.

For some reason that Berry had been unable to fathom, Paponis had called his office this morning and asked for a meeting. The commissioner couldn't imagine the surgeon coming in to shake him down for the delinquent bill. But he also couldn't come up with another reason that Paponis would be calling on him. The whole thing was making Sam Berry just a bit uneasy.

Ike Paponis walked through the door to Sam Berry's office with the warm affect of an old friend even though the surgeon and the politician were only casual acquaintances. Berry thought that he was powerful, but when he caught sight of the composed and well-dressed surgeon, he was able to easily see who possessed the true power at this meeting.

"Dr. Paponis, how nice to see you. To what do I owe the pleasure of this visit?" Sam Berry had been politically successful largely as a result of his ability to hide his true emotions, and this was nothing more than an exhibition of that art.

"Sam, I just wanted to talk privately with you about a business venture that I have in mind. I thought that you might be just the man to help me get over some of the hurdles. How's your wife by the way?"

"Have a seat, Doctor. She's doing fine. Better than I've seen her in years. You're quite the miracle worker, you know."

"You're probably exaggerating, but I certainly enjoy the flattery." Paponis took a seat in front of Berry's desk.

"Sam, I've got an idea for a new business venture that I think will be a real money maker. I do have a few obstacles, though, and I just wanted to run some things by you to see what you think."

"You know that I'll do what I can. Shoot, I owe my wife's life to you, and I'd love to be able to repay at least a small part of that debt."

Paponis could only smile. He had no intention of showing his hand just yet, but he was certainly pleased that Sam Berry was aware that he owed a large debt. Ike was well aware of the large sums of money that Berry owed, but if any discussion of the debt could be averted, it would actually be a more powerful tool.

"Sam, I would like to start a nationwide chain of private laboratories. I'm convinced that there's a need, and I'd like to build my first one right here in Portland."

"It sounds like a great idea, but I don't see what you need my help for." Berry was cordial, but he was also looking for the strangle hold that was sure to follow.

"My problem is that I need a pathologist to head up the operation. Marty Spencer and I are friends. I trust his judgment. I want him to be the active director of the project, but he's concerned about a possible conflict of interest."

"That shouldn't be a problem. We'll miss him, but as a favor to you, I would accept his resignation in the interest of him furthering his career."

"I'm afraid that's not what we had in mind. I feel that it's imperative that Dr. Spencer is able to maintain his position as the county medical examiner. That will give us a certain credibility that we feel will be quite important - at least initially. Perhaps after we're established, it may become prudent for Dr. Spencer to resign his position as medical examiner, and we'll certainly be willing to entertain those thoughts when the time comes."

Sam Berry's expression had become one of concern. He felt Paponis closing in for the kill but he was committed to standing his ground.

"I don't think that you understand, Dr. Paponis. It just isn't ethically possible for Dr. Spencer to function in both capacities. In addition, the county has very specific statutes forbidding this very kind of conflict of interest."

The commissioner was cut off in mid-sentence by the heart surgeon. "Mr. Berry, I am afraid that it is you who doesn't understand. I am not here to negotiate with you. I expect your compliance in this matter. I will also expect several zoning concessions for the actual physical structure." Paponis maintained his composure. He was still smiling, but the implied threat was not lost on the commissioner.

"I'm sorry, Doctor, but my hands are tied. You're asking me to do something that is not within my power to do. If I could help you, I certainly would, but I can't."

"Mr. Commissioner, I've done some checking on your financial status. You've covered your tracks pretty well, but I have to tell you, I've found some very damning information frighteningly close to the surface. You're in way over your head. And we both know what you've been doing with that campaign chest of yours. You could go to jail, Sam. And I could help to make that happen. You're also in to me for a lot of money, and I would be well within my rights to pressure you for that. I could make things tough for you, Sam. But that's not what I want to do." Paponis began to smile effortlessly as he changed his tack. He had been able to unnerve the commissioner at no expense to himself. It was a wonderful feeling.

"Sam, I really didn't want this conversation to go like this. I actually came by here to tell you that I could help you with your problems. I could absolve your debt to me, and I could compensate you for your help with my, shall we say, tribulations."

"Dr. Paponis, I've been offered bribes by many people before you, and I've yet to be bought."

"Sam, you just go ahead and take a little while to think about this. I don't see where you've really got much choice, but I'd like you to have the opportunity to look at this from your own angle. I'd like to think that this was more a matter of friends helping friends. I'm talking about a lot of money here. This could be your ticket to a comfortable retirement. I could offer you enough money to take care of all of your financial obligations right now, and there could be plenty more down the line. Just think about it. Without the deal, you're finished. Humiliated. Help me out with these two small details, and your troubles are over. It doesn't sound like a very difficult decision to me, but you just go on and give it a little thought."

Ike Paponis arose from his chair and left the county commissioner's office unceremoniously. He knew that he had made his point, and he really didn't care if he had been successful or not. If Sam Berry chose to reject his offer, he would crucify him politically. At that point in time, he would merely post a similar offer to Berry's successor.

By the time that Ike arrived at the Lake Oswego Country Club, Marty Spencer and Allan Spandell were already nursing cocktails. The attorney was glad to see his friend arrive because they had business to discuss.

Spandell's practice was growing by leaps and bounds. The very best move that he could have made was his decision to apply for membership at Lake Oswego. The members of the club had begun to utilize his services almost exclusively, and the referrals had kept him so busy that he found it necessary to expand his staff.

The attorney had also been surprised by the generosity that many of his clients had shown. They had asked him frequently about charitable organizations that he recommended, and then dedicated portions of their estates to those charities. Initially, Spandell had nothing but the nationally known organizations to offer. The whole process had made him think, however. How could he initiate a charitable fund that would benefit the citizens of the city where he lived? Why not just start such a fund? It would be a boon to his own political stature if he could administer a fund that would provide college scholarships for needy youngsters, fund medical aid clinics for indigents, and clothe and house the homeless.

Ike Paponis walked directly to the bar, ordered a double scotch with a single ice cube, and joined his friends at the table.

"It's about time you showed up. Any later and we wouldn't have been able to have lunch before teeing off," teased Spandell.

"I'm sorry, guys. I had a meeting with Sam Berry this morning, and I got caught in traffic between here and the courthouse."

"What kind of business did you have with that old bastard?" asked Spandell with curiosity.

"Just that deal to have Marty head up the lab project that we talked about."

"Darn it, Ike. I really wish you wouldn't push this thing so hard. There's no way the county commissioners are going to go for a deal like this. They want me tucked away in the morgue where I belong." Marty was clearly concerned.

"Don't sell yourself short, Marty. I fully expect to have the approval of the full commission by sometime tomorrow."

"How did you manage that?" queried the medical examiner.

"The secret, my friend, is to have some sort of leverage. Fortunately for us, Sam Berry has several very untidy skeletons in his closet, and a little investigation told me all about them. He'll either consent and give us his full support or I'll ruin him. It really makes no difference to me either way." Paponis gently rolled the scotch in his glass, and he concentrated on the fluid motion of the liquor as he spoke. Marty Spencer could see the cold resolve in his friend's expression, and he could only wonder how a man who was sworn by oath to the art of healing could be so utterly ruthless.

"You know, Ike, that sounds a little like blackmail, and I thought blackmail was against the law."

"Correction. It sounds a lot like blackmail, but it's only a problem if you get caught. I've got Berry by the balls. You've got to decide right here and right now if you're going to ride the train with Allan and I. I play hardball because it's the only way I know how to play. We either beat these bastards at their own game, or your future consists of dicing up those rotting stiffs down at the morgue for the rest of your life. And don't tell me that minuscule salary they pay you has purchased your undying loyalty. If that's the case, then you have sold yourself far too cheaply, my friend."

"That's not what I meant, Ike. Sam Berry has been in office for a long time. I figure he's got to know how to manipulate people or he wouldn't have lasted this long. I just don't want to get my neck so far out on the block that Berry and his buddies can lop my professional head off. They may not pay me much right now, but it's all I've got."

"Not for long, Marty. Not for long. This lab deal is going to make all three of us rich. Just hang in at the medical examiner's office for two years, and you can thumb your nose at whomever you want – Sam Berry included."

"Allan, did you get those contracts drawn up like I asked?"

"I've got them in my briefcase right now, Ike. The contracts establish you, Marty, and me as a corporation. They can be filed as soon as I get the appropriate signatures. The initial outlays will be borne by you and me, but the profits will be split equally among the three of us. As soon as you've secured the ten acres on the north side, I'll start taking construction bids. Marty will have to be responsible for acquiring all of the necessary equipment, and the architect needs some input from him too. I figure, that if all goes well, we'll be operational inside of a year."

Marty Spencer had listened intently to what had been said, but he still couldn't believe what he had heard. What he thought was a newly developed concept was actually a well developed plan. He also knew that the time for hedging his bets was over. Either he committed, or he divorced himself entirely from the scheme. The problem was that he really liked the idea of establishing an independent laboratory, he welcomed the opportunity for additional income, and he also enjoyed the prospect of wielding enough influence to shake up the established political order. He didn't know where these thoughts were coming from for they were contrary to his nature. But they were there, and it was time to quit whining and commit.

"Marty, I know you're concerned about bucking the system, but you already know that a little of that is necessary in any endeavor. You've just got to be aware that the politicians will chew you up and spit you out if it serves their purposes."

"Don't worry about me, Ike. Heck, I'm just glad that you've invited me in. That's really very generous given that I'm the resident poverty case."

"That's no big deal. We're in this thing together," said Allan Spandell before raising his glass for a toast. "To S.P.S. Laboratories, Inc. Would anyone care to join me in a drink to our future?"

Spencer and Paponis joined in the toast and the deal was sealed. After the toast was completed, Allan Spandell began to speak once again.

"You guys wouldn't believe what's been going on down at my office. Nearly everyone of these old guys at this club," and he gestured with his eyes around the crowded dining room, "wants to donate a sizable portion of their estates to charity. Some want to give to universities, others to libraries, the American Heart Association, you name it. I'm talking millions of dollars. I started thinking that if I could establish some sort of fund to benefit the local community, these guys would jump at it."

"That's a great idea, Allan. A social commitment like that would only enhance our professional standing. And the thought of controlling that much money sends chills up and down my spine. Heck, set the thing up as the Portland Fund and start taking in money. I'm sure we can find some appropriate way to spend it."

Golf was a pleasure that day. They had tied themselves together in a long-term business relationship, and they were preparing to leave their mark on the community in which they lived.

At nine o'clock the following morning, Ike was handed a message that instructed him to stop by Sam Berry's office at his convenience. He had just completed his first bypass of the day and was preparing to go back into the operating room for the second procedure. He was miffed that Berry didn't handle the matter over the phone. But he would go. He would dance. He would play the game. To a point, that is.

He dropped the top on his Carrera and started down the hill from Health Sciences at exactly one o'clock. It was only a short drive to the courthouse, but at least he had the opportunity to breathe something other than sanitized hospital air.

Sam Berry was the very picture of graciousness when the surgeon walked through his office doors. He quickly rose from his seat behind the desk and moved around the corner of his desk to greet Paponis.

"It was so nice of you to make time for me. Have a seat. Have a seat. Can I get you a cup of coffee" A little nip of something, perhaps?"

"I'll have a glass of scotch if you've got any handy." The commissioner moved behind his desk and opened the bottom drawer. He kept a bottle of double malted there for just such an occasion. He poured two generous portions and handed one to the surgeon.

"Doctor, I thought we should meet privately to discuss this issue. I've come up with a couple of ideas, and I think that we can come to some sort of mutual agreement on this."

Paponis could tell that he had shaken the man yesterday. Berry had on his best political face and seemed eager to please.

"I knew I could count on you, Sam."

"I've talked to the other members of the commission, and I've told them that we were in danger of losing the services of Dr. Spencer. Nobody wants that to happen. I told them that I didn't think it was reasonable for us to expect that we could retain a quality forensic medical examiner on the salary that we pay him. I also explained a little bit of our conversation yesterday, and they all agreed that if Dr. Spencer can continue to do the fine job that he has been doing, then none of us would interfere with what he does in his spare time. We just don't have the money to pay him what he's worth, so this is probably a good solution to everybody's problems. Shoot, his office is already short of help and having trouble attracting qualified applicants. If we were to lose him, then I just don't know what we would do. So the bottom line is that I think we can help each other out."

"Sam, you've done a good job with this. I've got some papers for you to sign, and after that, you'll be on your way to financial security. We'll handle that very carefully, though. I told you that I'd look out for you, and I fully intend to hold up my end of the bargain. As of this moment, you can consider your debt to me as being absolved. I really appreciate what you've done. If there is anything that I can do for you in the future, don't hesitate to ask."

Ike Paponis produced the documents that Allan Spandell had prepared, and Sam Berry put his signature to them. He also signed off on the zoning concessions. Paponis had triumphed in his first tussle with the politicians, and the experience had left him with a thirst for more of this kind of activity.

"Remember, Sam, if you need me for anything, please call."

"Well, Doctor, to be perfectly honest with you, I've been having some chest pain lately. It comes and goes, but it really has been bothering me. I've wanted to come to see you, but with that big debt, I just couldn't bring myself to do it."

"Don't think twice about it, Sam. I'll see you in my office at noon tomorrow. It's the least I can do to thank you for your help."

Paponis was pleased with himself when he left the county courthouse. Everything was falling into place. He knew that the next few months would put a strain on his already demanding schedule, but the additional profits would surely make the effort worthwhile. And now, Sam Berry was coming to him for help. Within a few short years, he would own this town.

CHAPTER 4

Ike Paponis and Sam Berry arrived at the surgeon's office at nearly the same time. Paponis had just completed his second open heart procedure of the day. Berry looked like he needed one before the day was out.

Ike had a trained eye, and his first glance told him that the commissioner was not well. His complexion was an ashen gray and the nailbeds at his fingertips were nearly purple. The man was sweating profusely, and his shirt was nearly soaked through with perspiration.

"Sam, you don't look so good. How long have you been like this?"

"About an hour, Doc."

"Are you having chest pain right now?"

"You bet. This is about as bad as it's been."

"Lois, get an ambulance," called the physician to his receptionist, who set about immediately to complete the task.

"They're on the way, Doctor."

"Just lay down on the couch here, Sam. The medics are on their way. Look, I need to know right now. If we get to the point where I think we need to do surgery, do you want me to do it?"

"I've got no way to pay you. You know what condition I'm in financially." Berry's words had been halting and almost inaudible.

"Don't worry about that, Sam. Your debt to me is paid. You should have come to me sooner."

The ambulance arrived, and the paramedics quickly placed the commissioner on the stretcher. They started intravenous lines and attached a cardiac monitor to electrodes that they placed on his chest. Ike could tell by the wave form on the monitor that Berry had suffered some heart damage already. He also knew that chances were good that he would be taking the man to surgery soon.

"Sam, I've got to get you to the hospital quickly. From what I see here, I'm probably going to have to take you to the operating room. I'll get a cardiologist to do a quick test where we insert a catheter into the artery at the top of your leg, and then we'll advance it up toward your heart. We'll inject some dye and see what kind of circulation you've got going through your heart. My guess is that it's not going to be too good. I think you know that it's too late to turn back now. But don't worry, I'm going to take good care of you."

The conversation had taken place while the commissioner was being wheeled to the waiting ambulance. As the ambulance pulled away with lights flashing and sirens blaring, Ike jumped into his Porsche and raced toward the hospital. While en route, he called a cardiologist friend of his, Curt Pifer, and asked him to meet him at the ER.

Ike arrived at the emergency room just as Sam Berry was being transferred onto the stretcher in the department. He ordered a quick electrocardiogram, and then he assisted the nurse and orderly in wheeling the commissioner to the cardiac catheterization lab. Curt Pifer was there to meet them, and he wasted no time getting the patient prepped and the procedure started. It wasn't long before both physicians knew that their patient needed to go to the operating room. The crew was summoned and hasty preparations were made.

"Sam, I'm afraid we need to go to the OR. I'm sorry that we have to do this under emergency circumstances, but I'm afraid that we don't have any choice. Do you want me to call your wife?"

"No, Doctor. Don't do that. Wait until it's all over and then call her. I don't want her having anything else to worry about. You know her health hasn't been good, either."

Several operating room technicians and nurses began to set up the suite as rapidly as possible. They opened sterile packages of instruments and tossed the wrappers toward the trash bins, leaving them on the floor if they didn't reach their destinations. Monitors were turned on and checked. Soon, the patient was brought in and prepped for surgery.

Open heart surgery was anything but routine, but emergency circumstances such as these, served to energize the crew even more. Medical personnel could endure hundreds of routine operations or diagnostic procedures just waiting for one case such as this. The adrenaline that coursed through their veins served almost as an aphrodisiac and delivered almost sensual pleasure. The rewards for being part of saving a life could be personally measurable.

Sam Berry was placed on the operating table and was immediately hooked up to the heart monitor. Having been given a preoperative sedative of intravenous Valium, he was still conscious and alert, but his senses were dulled. He could hear the high-pitched beep of the monitor, and somewhere in the drug-induced haze, he found comfort in the steady regularity of the sound that he heard.

The arm boards were attached to the operating table, and additional intravenous lines were inserted. An arterial line was placed using a long catheter that was placed into the radial artery in the left forearm. This line served several purposes; it provided an accurate measurement of arterial pressure, and it provided an expeditious source of arterial blood to test the content of various blood gasses such as oxygen and carbon dioxide.

Vital signs were recorded. Sam Berry was then anesthetized, intubated, and placed on a ventilator. His color seemed to improve almost immediately with these procedures. The ashen-gray color gave way to a warmer pink that indicated more efficient oxygenation of the blood.

A small nasogastric tube was inserted through the nose, and it was pushed down into the stomach. The tube would decompress the stomach by draining any food material or gas from it. This same tube would serve to hold a temperature probe that would measure the core esophageal temperature. This would be important as the body was cooled for surgery.

Ike Paponis walked into the operating suite amid the flurry of activity, and everyone came to a halt expecting the usual verbal tirade from the surgeon. But he was different today. The nurses and technicians could see the change in his eyes that shown above the mask. They were almost sparkling, and there was even the hint of humor where none of them had seen it before.

"Do you think we could have some music today?" Ike never operated to music, and this was yet another deviation from his usual routine.

"What would you like, Dr. Paponis?"

"Mozart, I think, don't you? That should make things nice."

Ike stepped up onto the stool next to Sam Berry's body. He made a linear incision directly down the center of the commissioner's sternum. He then used the saw to cut through the bone and then the heavy metal spreaders to spread the bone apart.

Skillfully, the surgeon removed all of the tissue from around the heart itself, and then stood quietly to observe the beating action of the heart within the politician's chest. He could tell by the motion of the heart wall that there had been significant damage already done to the muscle. He wasn't sure how effective his bypass effort would be, but he would give it his best shot, and hopefully, give Sam a new lease on life.

He used a pair of very sharp scissors to cut through the pericardium, the tough sac that surrounds the heart and then inserted the tubes that would be connected to the heart-lung machine. He filled the chest with crushed ice to cool the body to the desired temperature. Good surgeons were patient when cooling the hearts of their subjects, and Ike was, by all rights, a good surgeon.

29

All of the tubes were connected for total heart-lung bypass, and the machine was turned on. The tubing of the large apparatus was made of silicon elastomer, and had a large internal diameter that allowed it to deliver six liters of oxygenated blood per minute. The machine was operated on non-pulsatile roller pumps that propelled the blood through the system in such a way as to provide the least trauma to the cells. In addition, all of the blood was routed through large buckets of ice to further cool it.

As Paponis gave the order to go on bypass, the cardiotomy sucker began to draw blood from the heart. It was then filtered in such a way that it was not traumatized and did not froth. It was also important to keep all free air out of the system.

When the core temperature reached twenty-two degrees centigrade, Ike gave the order to administer the potassium-rich cardioplegic solution. A total of four CCs of the solution was delivered directly into the heart, and within his chest, Sam Berry's beating heart gradually ground to a halt.

Ike knew from the cardiac catheterization that the blockage was in the left anterior descending coronary artery. Therefore, he would be retracting the internal mammary artery, and he would use that vessel to bypass the blockage.

The surgeon was nearly giddy as he held the county commissioner's stilled heart within his hands. Only yesterday, Berry had thought that he held all of the cards. He had acted as if he could dictate to the doctor and his partners. He had the audacity to suggest that Mary Spencer would be prohibited from participating in the laboratory venture.

But now, Ike held the man's very heart within his hands. Should he decide, Berry might never awaken from the anesthesia. There were any number of things that he could do operatively that would allow his patient to survive anywhere from a week to a month. He could use dissolving sutures that might last only for several days. He could single stitch the graft, and the first episode of elevated blood pressure could break it free. He could make a tiny incision into the wall of the ventricle, that would later weaken and form an aneurysm. In that event, Sam might live for two months.

Yes, there were any number of fatal outcomes that the surgeon could engineer for the good commissioner. And the cocky politician certainly deserved any one of them. But Sam Berry just might prove to be a good ally at this point in time. The saving of his life should, and most certainly would, buy his loyalty.

Paponis completed the graft and left the closure of the wound for the surgical resident. He grasped the spoons that represented the internal defibrillator, placed them in contact with the stopped heart, charged the paddles to ten joules, fired it, and watched the heart begin to beat once again.

"Ladies. Gentlemen. I thank you for your assistance."

Paponis was relaxed. He was in a good mood. The operating room crew did not know what phenomena that this could be attributed to, but they were not about to question their good fortune, either.

Sam Berry would survive. And Ike Paponis would insure that he did not forget the debt he owed. Certainly the saving of a life, the commissioner's own life, would command a hefty price.

CHAPTER 5

Nineteen eighty-four was a year of great prosperity for many in the United States. And so it was for S.P.S. Laboratories and for the three men who ran it. Their operation had grown to twenty-five facilities and plans were in the works for even more. While they were not getting overtly rich for their involvement in the venture, they were utilizing profits to expand the operation. It was a forgone conclusion, that in the near future, they would be taking in untold wealth.

The Lake Oswego Country Club was still the Wednesday afternoon destination, and families and children had not altered the ritual over the years.

"Gentlemen, we need to talk." As usual, Ike had been the last to arrive, and he expected that the world stop and take note of the occasion.

"Sit down, Ike. Have a drink." Allan Spandell had already had two martinis and was feeling relaxed.

"I know that we generally try to avoid shop talk out here, but we've got problems." Ike had a strained look on his face, and this was unusual.

"Ike, we are running an independent business operation that is valued in excess of fifty million dollars. What could possibly warrant that look of consternation?"

"Guys, we're broke. We're worse than broke. I knew that we were probably a little ahead of ourselves with the last five labs, but I never thought it would be enough to bring us down."

"What are you talking about?" Marty Spencer had not a clue.

"What I'm talking about is that if we don't come up with ten million dollars in the next forty five days, then we're totally screwed. We could lose every damn lab that we've got out there."

"Ten million dollars!" Allan nearly choked on his martini.

The financial aspects of the lab operation had been handled by a private accounting company that had been overseen exclusively by Ike. The surgeon had divulged only peripheral details of their joint venture. This was partially a matter of control, but Ike also had several other purposes.

Allan Spandell's law practice had skyrocketed, and his work with the Portland Fund was taking up an increasingly larger portion of his time. Marty Spencer was handling the day-to-day operations of S.P.S. and was still the Multnomah County Medical Examiner. His duties at the M.E.s office were mostly that of a figurehead, but after nearly five years in the position, it had become a way of life for him. He was the Multnomah County Medical Examiner. The people of Portland expected him to maintain the position. His clout within county government had allowed him to increase his budget and to hire adequate support staff. Heck, the place more or less ran itself. All Marty had to do was make an occasional appearance on the evening news.

S.P.S., however, was another matter entirely. There were constant problems with personnel, equipment, and quality control. While he tried to delegate some of the responsibility, he still did not want to relinquish managerial control of the labs. They were his babies, and he wanted to keep it that way.

But he had also not been aware that they had been financially strapped. He had never thought to question Ike about it in view of their rapid and progressive expansion. Apparently, he had made the fateful error in thinking that everything was okay.

"Ike, just how in the world do you propose that we raise ten million dollars in forty-five days? Will we have to sell off some of the labs?"

"I'll be damned if I'll give up one inch of what we've earned. I refuse to sacrifice one lab to the bankers." Ike was irate that Marty had even suggested such a solution.

Allan was the soothing voice of reason. "Ike, nobody means to tick you off. But we've got to look at this thing realistically. Ten million dollars is a lot of money. If we are mortgaged to the point where they are calling in our loans then we've got real problems. We're going to have to come up with some way of retiring this debt, or we're going to lose everything. Maybe we really do need to look at selling a few of the units, or maybe we could even go public. We can work this out. But we'll probably have to be creative."

"Like I've told you already, we're not going to sell one laboratory while I'm still a part of this corporation. Am I clear on that? Creativity? I'll grant you that. What I need to know is whether or not you two have got the balls to carry out what I've got in mind."

"I suppose that would depend on what kind of mischief you've got in mind. Just what are your ideas, Ike?" asked the probate attorney.

"Allan, how much money do we have in the Portland Fund right now?"

"Wait a minute, Ike. We can't even consider that money for our personal use. That would violate at least thirty local, state, and federal laws that I know of, and I'll have no part of it."

"That's crap, Allan. I'm not talking about pilfering the money. I'm merely talking about floating a loan to the corporate fund for long enough to let some of our profits catch up with our debt load."

"We don't even have ten million at our disposal. And to tell you the truth, even if I was inclined to get into this in a limited sort of way, I would never consent to bankrupting the fund for any extended period of time. That could raise too much curiosity."

"What's the bottom line, Allan? How much usable cash do we have at our disposal?" Ike was leaning over the table now, and the expression on his face couldn't have been more serious. He glanced to his left and to his right to insure that nobody else in the room was listening.

"I'd have to check to be sure, but I think our current operating capital is at approximately seven point eight million. I do have several outstanding commitments right now. I could stall those donations temporarily, but any long-term delays would raise too many eyebrows. You know, everybody wants their money. Even if the worst thing that happened was that rumors got started, it would still probably put a big damper on our donations, and then we'd be totally screwed."

"Well, that's a start." Ike was eager now.

"I didn't say that I would consent to this, Ike." Allan still hoped for an alternative solution to the problem. His stint as a deputy DA had ingrained in him a true respect for the law, and what Ike was suggesting was clearly against the law. Despite all of this, he found himself being drawn to the proposal, and that was a bit scary.

Marty had been listening intently to the exchange, and he too was concerned by what Ike was suggesting. He was a public official, and while the loss of that salary wouldn't cripple him financially, his departure from the office, under conditions such as these, would be a scandalous affair that he'd like to avoid.

"Just where do I stand in all of this, Ike? I want you to know up front that I'm against this. We set up this fund so that we could make a positive social contribution, not so we could bail ourselves out the first time we got into trouble. I think we should explore some other possibilities."

The surgeon could actually feel the reluctance that was being expressed by his partners. Manipulating people had always been his greatest talent, and now was the time for a little of that. It would have been his preference to tell Allan and Mary to go to hell and do things his own way. But they were in this together, and by bringing them in as deeply as he would be, might prevent betrayal later. He also knew that the two men were approaching ethical boundaries that neither man wished to cross, but what they didn't know, was what he really had planned for them would make this seem like child's play.

"Guys, I understand your apprehension. I really do. What I'm proposing that we do poses a risk. I know that. We just have to make sure that we don't get caught. If you remember correctly, you were both apprehensive about getting into the lab project in the first place. We've not been in any financial crisis before this, and we've all had a very comfortable living from the profits that we've turned so far. So we're a little overextended right now. No big deal. If we can manage to figure a way out of this, then there will never be a financial institution anywhere that will refuse us backing. This is a make or break, guys. This is the test of our corporate stability that we all knew we'd have to face sooner or later. We either gracefully resolve this dilemma, or we cave in right now. Personally, I'm not willing to go down without a fight."

Marty and Allan had listened carefully, and they knew that much of what Ike said made sense. They still weren't able to embrace the utilization of funds that were supposed to go for charity, but they also knew that the plan had merit – it could save their butts.

"Allan, how much money can we get our hands on right now?"

"I suppose that increments of three to four million every couple of weeks might not raise too much suspicion. That would still leave us a shortfall of approximately three million dollars. Are you sure that you really want to do this?"

"Give me a better solution, and I'll take it."

Allan appraised the other two men closely. For a moment he looked like he might speak, but then thought better of it. He just smiled and shrugged his shoulder in acquiescence.

"One more question. What is the status of our pledged funds?" Ike couldn't even look the attorney in the eye. He just swirled the swizzle stick around and around in his cocktail.

"Shoot, I've never even considered that. I suppose somewhere in the neighborhood of eighteen to twenty million dollars. Why do you ask?"

"Just out of curiosity, who is the largest donor?"

"I guess that would be Bill Evans. His contract is for six point eight million dollars. And his wife, Helen, died last year. So there's no interim stopping point for the money."

"I know Bill. He's a patient of mine. Nice guy…"

Ike was reflective, and while Allan could easily have guessed why his partner had posed the question, he consciously repressed all of the possibilities that his mind would have otherwise considered.

Marty Spencer left the Lake Oswego Country Club after their round of golf. He navigated his Mercedes 300DL to his home in an older section of Beaverton, a more upscale section of Portland. His Tudor home was in a near-perfect state of repair, and his yard was decoratively landscaped and carefully manicured.

Dr. Martin Spencer, the Multnomah County Medical Examiner, was not at all comfortable with the plan that had been proposed by his friend, Ike Paponis. Marty Spencer was well off, and his county salary was paltry when compared with what he made at S.P.S. But he was concerned with the direction that his professional life was taking. He had merely deluded himself into thinking that the labs were his responsibility. He now knew that was a joke. He who controlled the purse strings, controlled the enterprise, and he obviously didn't control the purse strings.

As he tried to analyze the situation more carefully, he realized that he was the most out of the loop of the three partners. Allan controlled the Portland Fund, and Ike controlled Allan. He was becoming unnerved by his vulnerability, but he also knew that there was very little that he could do about it.

If the truth were to be known, Marty was just a bit afraid of Ike. He had seen the outcome of too many scrapes that the heart surgeon had been involved in over the years. He knew that to tangle with Ike meant certain professional destruction. That realization aggravated him, because he knew in his heart, that if push ever came to shove, Ike would hang him and Allan out to dry.

Marty walked sullenly into his home. He could smell the aroma of dinner being prepared as soon as he opened the door leading from the garage to the house. Sally, his wife, was busy in the kitchen, and the medical examiner noticed that she was pouring two glasses of wine as he came through the door.

"How was your game, honey?"

"Not too bad. Ike won again, of course."

"You can't let him bother you, Marty. He's so competitive about everything he does. Typical surgeon."

"I know. But just once, I'd like to kick his butt."

"Don't let it get you down. You play golf for enjoyment. If he feels like he has to win every week, then he can't possibly be getting much relaxation out of it."

Marty kissed his wife on the cheek, picked up his glass of wine and the day's mail, and made his way into the study. The world was weighing heavily on his shoulders, and this fact wasn't being lost on his wife. She followed him into the study a short time later.

"Is everything okay with you?"

"Sure. Why do you ask?"

"I don't know. Just a feeling. You can't be married for as long as we have been and not know when something is wrong."

"I guess I'm a little down. It's nothing I can really put my finger on though," he lied.

"Well, if you need to talk, let me know."

"I will, honey. Thanks for being there for me."

Allan left the country club knowing in his heart that everything Ike wanted him to do was against the law. He also knew that he would do it without question. He had a great law practice, and his firm made a good deal of money. But his involvement with S.P.S. was so intertwined with his personal and business finances that any failure on the part of S.P.S. would cripple him financially. Tomorrow morning he would begin making arrangements for the transfer of funds, and he would just have to trust fate and good luck to protect him.

Ike went directly from the country club to his suite of offices. When he entered, he turned on only a single light. He knew that it could be viewed as unusual if he were to be noticed in his office at this our of the day. But maybe that was just his own paranoia.

He went directly to the file cabinets that housed the medical charts of his patients. Quickly he retrieved the chart of one William Evans. The chart was informative. It was complete with several electrocardiograms, lab work, reports of stress tests and cardiac catheterizations, and his own notations that had been collected over the past several years.

Reviewing the chart, he reacquainted himself with the medical condition of Mr. Evans. Moderate atherosclerotic coronary artery disease. Mild diabetes that had been controlled with diet modifications. A history of atrial fibrillation that had been pharmacologically controlled with Digoxin. In his own notes, he could see that he had recommended that the patient return twice annually for reevaluation. That would put his next visit at just over a month from now.

Ike sat at his desk and smiled to himself. He left a note for his receptionist to call Bill Evans and schedule him for an appointment sometime in the next several days. He turned off the light in his office, locked the door, and left the building. As he turned the key in the ignition of his Porsche, he considered going directly home but changed his mind. At home he would be alone, and tonight he wanted company.

Ike had not yet married. In fact, he didn't know if he would ever marry. But he did have a healthy sexual appetite, and he didn't hesitate to satisfy it.

Rachel Roxbury was a local artist of some renown. The surgeon knew her to be someone he could enjoy physically, as well as intellectually, without the usual pressure to settle down. Put simply, Rachel Roxbury liked to screw, she didn't give him any crap, and she was no air head.

When he arrived at the artist's home, he quickly noticed that she was entertaining several guests. They had barbecued dinner and were enjoying cocktails when Rachel answered the door.

"Ike, you should have called. What are you doing?"

"I played golf this afternoon, and I couldn't get you out of my mind." He took her in his arms and kissed her passionately.

"I've got some friends over. Do you want to come in and have a drink?" He kissed her once more on the lips and followed her into the living room.

Ike hated modern art, and Rachel's house was full of it. Incomprehensible prints and formless sculptures. And her friends were not much more defined than was her art. They were left-wing socialites who thought that justice could be effortlessly legislated, social consciences with human form, pipe dreams with skin. Rachel was a social animal.

"Everybody, this is Dr. Ike Paponis. He's a friend of mine. Ike, this is David, Becky, Steve, and Sharon."

Ike knew that he would never remember these people's names beyond this evening, and judging from their appearance, the less contact that he had with them tonight the better. He would just stay close to Rachel, and hopefully, they would all leave soon. But this was not to be the case. David, a slender man with long hair, unrestrictive clothing, and frameless glasses, was the first to speak.

"So Ike, what is your Ph.D. in?"

"I don't have a Ph.D. I'm a medical doctor," you nitwit. But David was duly impressed.

"Oh, I'm sorry. A medical doctor… do you specialize?"

"I'm a heart surgeon. Or more correctly, a cardio-thoracic surgeon," you moron. Ike had managed the perfect smile of a diplomat through his condescending hatred of the man. The answer, however, had drawn the attention of the other members of the group.

Sharon Burch was an athletic appearing blonde, who was reserved, and just a bit out of place with this liberal group. As soon as Ike laid his eyes on her, he knew that he had to have her. The mere expression on her face told him that this was a woman of perceptive intellect. It would be touchy arranging a liaison with her without hurting Rachel's feelings, but Ike had no doubts that a relationship would develop.

Sharon did not speak, but Ike knew that she had understood him perfectly. She understood every word that had been spoken or intimated. Every subtle nuance. He also knew immediately that she felt the same way that he did.

Rachel brought him a glass of scotch with a single ice cube and led him by the hand to the back yard. There was a swimming pool and hot-tub all surrounded by redwood decking. There were exotic plants and soft lighting. All in all, it was a very romantic atmosphere.

"I sure wish you would call once in awhile." It was a gentle rebuke without malice.

"I'm sorry, Rachel. You know my schedule. Between surgery, office hours, and the lab business, I usually don't know if I'm coming or going."

"I know. I'd just like to see a little more of you. I need at least one conservative Nazi type in my life for variety." Ike smiled because he knew that he was well to the right of most of Rachel's friends. That realization caused him near elation.

"Well, anyway, you seem like you're in a good mood. What's been going on with you?"

"Nothing special, really, I played golf with my friends today, and I didn't have to worry too much about business. I'm sitting here with you, drinking a cool glass of good scotch, and your communist friends are in there, and I'm out here. I'd say that's enough to put me in a good mood."

"I think Sharon likes you," said Rachel matter-of-factly.

"What would make you say something like that?"

"I don't know. Maybe the way she looked at you." Rachel had not seemed to be put off by the observation, and Ike moved closer to her. He took her in his arms and kissed her with an exploring tongue. The skin on her back ignited into goose flesh with his touch. Rachel was a good woman, and Ike appreciated her willingness.

As he embraced her, holding her firmly in his strong arms, he happened to glance toward the sliding glass door that opened onto the patio. Sharon was staring unabashedly at the couple on the bench. Ike could see that the look on her face was one of curiosity. She seemed to be studying his moves, the way he kissed Rachel, the way he held her in his arms. It was a look of pure appraisal. Without warning, she smiled and turned away.

Rachel turned her face toward Ike and initiated a warm kiss, but the moment was gone. The lust that Ike had felt for Rachel now belonged to Sharon. He kissed her lightly and turned away.

"Don't you think that you should be getting back in to your friends?"

"Don't worry about them. They're old enough to take care of themselves."

"I'm just sorry that I dropped in unexpectedly. I feel bad about messing up your evening."

"Since when have you dropped in any other way? Look, Ike, we're way beyond this. You don't have to make excuses to me."

"Let's just go in for awhile. We'll have some time alone after your friends have gone."

They went back inside, and Ike refilled his glass with scotch. He was doing his very best to mingle with Rachel's friends when she approached him suddenly.

"Ike, is there any way that you can give Sharon a ride home? I hate to even ask. I'll make it up to you tomorrow, though."

"What's the matter with Dave or Steve?"

"Sharon and David really don't get along too well. I think they might have had some problems in the past. Steve and Becky are together, and Steve drives an MG, so there's no room for Sharon. Please, would you do this for me?"

"I'd do anything for you, but I was hoping that we could spend the night together."

"I told you that I would make it up to you tomorrow." Rachel stood up on her tip toes and kissed him on the cheek. Ike could see that her eyes reiterated her promise.

He opened the door to the Carrera, and Sharon slid into the seat as comfortably as if it had been her own vehicle. Her beige skirt was cut well above the knee, and when she took her seat, it hiked up revealing shapely yet muscular quadriceps. Ike thought that he caught a glimpse of lace, but he also knew that could be his imagination.

Sharon was quiet on the way home – answering questions with primarily yes and no answers. She lived in an exclusive apartment house downtown, and he soon guided the Porsche into the parking lot.

Sharon had not done or said anything to enamor herself of the physician, and Ike was on his best behavior. As soon as he turned off the engine, he got quickly out of the car and went around to open the passenger's door. She rose from the car even more seductively than she had entered it. As she stood up, Ike was so taken with her beauty that he was compelled to take her in his arms. Their lips met passionately. There was something extra in this union – something special. There was a fire that Ike had never before felt.

He was a man in the throes of middle age, and yet he once again felt like a teenager. Sharon unceremoniously reached for his trousers, unfastened his belt and pants, and carefully unzipped his zipper. She took him in her hands firmly and realized that it would not be necessary to work at a response. He was ready.

With her one free hand, she tore her lace panties free from her waist and laid across the hood of the Porsche. He needed no prompting as she failed to relinquish her hold on him. She guided him directly into her, and she pulled him deeply inside. As he felt her clench around him, he thought that he detected the faintest wisp of a smile on her face.

"I've always wanted to do this," she half stated, half moaned.

"Then I'm glad you chose me."

There was no verbal response from her now, only the rise and fall of her hips and buttocks, the insistence that he felt in her hands. It had been slow when it had started, but it had rapidly accelerated to a heated fury. Her back arched and virtually every muscle within her body became taut. There was no crying out. She was far too controlled for that. There was only a low guttural moan that signified her satisfaction.

The intensity of the experience was more than Ike could bear, and he reached orgasm with her in unison. Ike came in rhythmic thrusts, and then his body went limp. Sharon nibbled on his neck, and she lightly stuck her tongue into his ear in an effort to revive him.

"Come on Ike, walk me upstairs."

CHAPTER 6

The call had been disconcerting. Why had the office of his heart surgeon called to make an appointment a full two months ahead of schedule? Bill Evans had complete faith in his physician, but he just couldn't understand what could possibly be so medically pressing. Yes, the call had been disconcerting indeed.

But Ike Paponis had been emphatic. Mr. Evans needed to come to his office at his earliest convenience. The heart surgeon had even checked with his receptionist several times to insure that the appointment had been made and confirmed.

As scheduled, Bill Evans arrived at the office of Ike Paponis. He was asked to have a seat in the waiting room and was ushered into an examination room ten minutes later. To have been taken back any sooner would have seemed unusual to this patient.

"Bill, good to see you. Thanks for coming in on such short notice."

"I'd have to be a fool to ignore my heart surgeon's request to come in for a check up. What's wrong, anyway?"

"Bill, I'm going to be honest with you. The last couple of times that I've seen you at the club your color hasn't been good. You also seem to be losing a lot of weight. I don't think that's a good sign either."

"What do you mean, my color has been bad?"

"It's nothing that I can really put my finger on, Bill. You've just been a little pale. At times, you almost appear cyanotic. That is, you have an almost ashen hue. This tells me that you're not getting good oxygenation. It makes me wonder if your heart is functioning as effectively as it could be." The surgeon's expression was one of true concern. It was a look that he had perfected long ago.

"Actually, it's interesting that you've asked me to come in. I haven't been feeling well lately. Haven't had much energy. I thought that it was just a letdown after Helen's death. You know, I was depressed. But I suppose that if I was to tell the truth, I've been getting short of breath too. A round of golf totally wipes me out."

"That's what I was afraid you'd say, Bill. After I noticed the change in your condition, I took the liberty of going back and reviewing your chart. Bill, I think we've got some problems. Six months ago you had a seventy percent

43

occlusion of your right main. In addition, your circumflex was more that fifty percent blocked. You were doing well then, so I thought we could buy some time. I think the clinical picture has changed since then, and I think it's time we start to consider some definitive therapies."

"Definitive therapies?"

"I don't want to alarm you, Bill, but I think that it's time we discussed surgery."

"Open heart surgery? I don't even want to think about that. What with Helen gone, I'm not even sure that I want to prolong my life. I don't want to put myself through all of that."

"I understand what you're saying, Bill. And I'll certainly respect your wishes. But the bottom line is that what I'm offering you could be a new lease on life. I'm not proposing that we prolong your life without giving you the means to enjoy it. I can give you, realistically, ten to fifteen more years of quality life. You'll have more energy to do the things that you love to do. If you want to travel, you'll be able to. If you want to play golf everyday, then you'll be able to do that without risking your health. It's your call, Bill, but it makes sense in my mind."

"You make a pretty strong case, Ike. I imagine that I'm going to have to think about it for awhile though."

Ike felt himself losing the sale. He needed to convince Evans that surgery was necessary. But the last thing that he wanted to do was to appear desperate. And desperate he was. He couldn't believe that he was asking the man to consent to being killed. But kill he would, purely and simply.

As he considered it, it didn't feel much like murder. There was something about the operating room – the sterile environment that would not let something as vile as murder enter it. No, this would merely be a scheduled death. William Evans would just be dying at the precise moment when he could do the most good for the Portland Fund and S.P.S. Laboratories. Ike Paponis, M.D. knew that he needed to close the deal.

"Bill, I encourage you to think about this. Go ahead and get a second opinion if you think you need to. But what I want to caution you against is taking too much time. I think that right now you are doing as good as you will do. You're a cardiac disaster waiting to happen. The sad truth is that you could die at any moment. Either one of those arteries in your heart could become clogged at any time. If that happens, the likelihood is that you'd be dead within the hour. If that's what you want, if you're prepared to die now, then so be it. All I'm trying to tell you is that I think I could change all of that.

It's got to be your call, Bill, but it's not one I'd put off making for too long."

Faced with what appeared to be the absolute reality of his situation, Bill Evans really had no choice. Along with everybody else, he suffered from the basic instinct for survival. Despite his inescapable loneliness, he was unable to relinquish his hold on life willingly. If Ike Paponis could offer him life then that would have to be the option that he would choose.

"Ike, go ahead and make the arrangements. I guess I'm not as ready to die as I thought."

"Bill, I really encourage you to get a second opinion. If it will put your mind at ease, then by all means, do it. I certainly won't be offended if you do."

Evans was calm, and there wasn't the slightest trace of fear in his eyes. He had made his fortune largely as a result of his ability to size up a man. The sad reality on this morning was that ability was failing him. And more sadly still, it would be a fatal mistake.

"Ike, I've known you for more than six years. I've watched your practice grow, and I've watched you mature. If I can't trust you, then how am I going to be able to trust somebody else? Just do what you think you have to do. My heart is in your hands."

"We'll take good care of you, Bill. I'll have my staff make the necessary arrangements, and we'll be in touch soon."

Things were falling into place. Ike didn't let the problem of needing the ten million dollars trouble him too greatly. He just set about doing what he felt that he had to do. That was the only way to solve problems. What was he supposed to do? He couldn't just sit around and complain about his problems?

One day later, and much to his surprise, Bill Evans was notified that arrangements had been made for his admission to the Health Sciences Hospital. He had hoped for a bit more time to put his affairs in order, but if his condition really was an emergency, then it was probably better to face this ordeal as soon as possible.

He did not see or talk to Ike Paponis again until he was laying on the stretcher in the preoperative prep room. Something did not feel quite right, but he couldn't put his finger on just what it was. In actuality, he thought that this was probably a normal reaction to what he was facing. He knew that his heart would be stopped during the operation, and he equated that with being dead. He was just afraid that maybe Ike would not be able to bring him back.

The patient thought back to the days when he had been an army paratrooper. He could still remember standing in the door of the C-119 for his first parachute jump. He had looked down at the patchwork below and realized that he had been afraid. It had been one of those occasions when you had to make peace with your God. Today was the same.

He found that peace more easily than when he had been an eighteen year old boy. He had lived a good life. Helen, God rest her soul, was gone. Nobody wanted to die, but should that happen, he felt ready.

He felt the warmth of the anesthesia as it coursed through his veins. He tried to move but couldn't, and that frightened him. In one instant he had his terror, and in the next moment, he was gone.

The crew set about their business after the patient was anesthetized. The chest was scrubbed and opened. The lines were hooked for heart-lung bypass. The surgical resident harvested a section of the saphenous vein.

Ike stopped the heart and methodically began to search for areas of occlusion. The businessman truly did have heart disease, but it certainly wasn't bad enough to warrant surgery. He knew that he must be meticulous in his search. To do less would arouse suspicion.

After the appropriate amount of time, he stated, "Here it is. I think we've got it. Do you have that section of vein ready? Right main is nearly one hundred percent occluded. Come on people, let's get moving."

Ike poked a small hole in the aortic arch and stitched the section of saphenous vein in. Normally he would have tied a series of multiple single knots to secure the graft, but not today. He simply wove the suture through. In and out. He completed the procedure by tying only a single knot.

Shelly Grayson, the head scrub nurse on the open heart team, casually noticed the deviation from standard procedure. She knew better than to challenge the surgeon, but she carefully catalogued the event in her mind. She had never known Dr. Paponis to be so obviously remiss in his practice, and she couldn't figure out why he was doing it today. Maybe this was a new technique. She would have to inquire about that later.

The procedure was completed, Bill Evans's heart was easily restarted and his chest was subsequently closed. He was then taken directly to the cardiac care unit where he would be recovered slowly. It would be nearly a day before he would be allowed to awaken.

The patient progressed as nicely as anybody could have hoped for. Only Ike knew, however, that Bill Evans was merely waiting to die.

CHAPTER 7

Senator Talmadge Hyle was a closet homosexual. The senior senator from Oregon had the picture-perfect family, adoring wife, and two beautiful daughters. But this was just for the picture.

He had a long history of sordid affairs with multiple young men, but such was his power in the Senate, that his private affairs remained just that. There had been rumors, none substantiated, but his ability to squelch the talk had been nothing short of amazing.

The biggest problem that Talmadge Hyle faced was that of a changing world. The press lived to expose flaws in their political leaders, and a penchant for sex with young boys was not a quality that the public would find endearing in their elected officials.

Publicly, Talmadge Hyle was pro-life. He was a defense hawk. He touted himself to be for smaller government and campaign finance reform. He was anti-pornography, especially in neighborhoods, and he had sponsored several anti-abuse laws. He was a strict Christian. And he slept with young men.

The senator sat on the powerful Senate Finance and Appropriations Committees and the Intelligence Committee. His counsel was often sought by more junior members, and he was often invited to White House meetings.

He was popular at home and rarely received any real threats to his re-election bids. But times were changing, and Talmadge Hyle found himself taking his lifestyle more deeply under cover. He maintained a private residence in Alexandria while his wife and daughters remained in Portland. For the most part, as long as he remained discreet, the senator was able to conduct his private affairs in the comfort of his own home.

Jason Riley was a young Washington reporter. He was a graduate of the University of Notre Dame, and he had every intention of becoming a powerful newspaperman. He was not disillusioned by the small desk in his tiny cubicle at the Post. He knew that he had to pay his dues. Washington was a tough town and journalism could be a brutal business.

The Notre Dame education was prestigious. The campus in South Bend, Indiana promoted optimism by its very nature. The domineering football program, the measurable successes of past graduates, the legends of Knute Rockne and Ara Parseghian, the look of confidence on the faces of the students, made the graduates of Notre Dame truly believe that all things were possible.

Jason Riley did not get good assignments at the Post. He was relegated the mundane tasks of sitting through the long and boring sessions of the Senate Finance Committee. His articles did run in the paper, and they were always technically correct. Occasionally, they were even interesting. But rarely were they truly noteworthy.

Jason knew that for him to make it to the top of his profession, he would have to personally uncover some horrific scandal. He knew that it would have to be a previously undiscovered piece of information about a powerful Washington figure.

That was the problem with the Washington elite. Whenever they accomplished something newsworthy, there were press releases and news conferences. Any minor achievement could be enlarged until it was bigger than life. They dealt in images, not in reality. It was the reporter's job to sift through what was real and what was hype. The newsman must always avoid being led in the direction in which the politician would lead him.

The reporter had watched Talmadge Hyle for quite some time. At fifty-nine years of age, the senator still had a full head of black hair. He wore dignified reading glasses that rode low on his nose whenever he was conducting official government business. Talmadge Hyle mastered whatever he endeavored to understand.

Jason had heard all of the rumors regarding the private life of the senior senator from Oregon, and quite honestly, he had a difficult time believing them. It simply did not fit into the hierarchy of reason, that a man of such power and stature, would allow his position in life to be endangered by a sexual deviancy. Well, a deviancy to some.

In addition to unbridled optimism, the cloister of Notre Dame also engendered a certain amount of naiveté. And Jason also felt that if there were any truth to the rumors, the tabloids would have been all over the story. It had been his experience that folks like that lived for trash like this. And if they were unable to substantiate it, they would create it.

Curiously, though, there were no rumblings about the senator from Oregon. That fact alone stimulated the creative juices of the young reporter. Why was the riffraff of the journalism world so afraid of this man? They attacked all vulnerable targets, and perhaps therein lay the key. Maybe Talmadge Hyle was for some reason not vulnerable. The other thing that he had to consider was that perhaps there was no truth to the rumors.

The reporter sat and watched as the senator conducted the meeting. He observed for telltale signs of character flaw, and he saw none. What did he expect? Did he think that a man such as Talmadge Hyle would just hand over his career? Hardly. If there was dirt to be found, then a careful search would have to be conducted.

"Senator Hyle. Senator Hyle." The senator stopped and directed his gaze toward Riley. That was all the opening that the reporter needed.

"Senator, what are the latest reports of campaign fund violations from a laboratory consortium in your state?"

The blood seemed to drain from the senator's face, and his usually stoic demeanor was now one of trepidation.

"Who are you, son, and who do you work for?"

"Jason Riley, sir. I work for the Post. I'd like to discuss this with you further if you can find the time." The conversation had already become a private one as the senator was quickly trying to size up the young man. He needed to know what Riley already knew.

"Mr. Riley, I appreciate your concern, but this is really an accusation without foundation. Dr. Paponis of S.P.S. Laboratories, to whom I think you are referring, is a personal friend of mine, who has also been a loyal political supporter. I assure you, however, that everything has been quite legal, and beyond that, ethical as well."

"I accept your word, Senator. But the actual list of contributors that was released by your own office seems to suggest otherwise." Riley had apparently done his homework.

"Mr. Riley... did you say it was? Why don't we have some lunch? Do you have plans? We could have something brought into my office, and we could discuss this further there."

"I don't have anything planned."

"Splendid. It's eleven thirty right now, and I have to meet with some constituents. How does one o'clock at the Russell Building sound?"

"I'll be there, Senator. Thank you."

Jason couldn't believe that he had been asked to lunch by the senator. It also made him wonder if the hospitality didn't mean that perhaps Senator Hyle did have something to hide after all.

This was developing into a near-perfect scenario. Riley never imagined that he would be able to trip the senator up on the campaign finance issue. As was generally the case, a lot of money in these "war chests" was technically obtained in a manner that was contrary to the letter of the law. But there were so many loopholes that it would take an absolute fool to find himself in legal trouble for campaign fund violations. That is not to say that an occasional fool cannot be found in Congress, but Talmadge Hyle was no such fool.

The constituent that Talmadge Hyle was meeting with that day was none other than Dr. Ike Paponis. The heart surgeon was a loyal supporter whose contributions earned a good bit of personal attention. Considering the young reporter's question, however, this wasn't exactly the best time to be having a meeting with Ike. The senator could not allow the reporter to establish any basis for a quid pro quo between the senator's campaign funds and any political favors being granted to the surgeon.

"Ike, how the heck are you? Come on in and have a seat." The expansiveness was not feigned. After all these years, it had become an actual part of his personality.

"Thank you, Senator. And thank you for seeing me on such short notice."

"Ike, you're a true friend to this office. You know that. Anything that I can do to help you, you should know that I'll do it."

"I know that, Senator, and I appreciate it. But the bottom line is that I'm a supporter of what you do, and what you stand for, and that is why I'm loyal to your office." And now that the obligatory crap was out of the way, he could get down to business.

"I appreciate your loyalty, Ike."

"I know you do, Senator. The reason that I'm here today, is that recently I've been getting some alarming inquiries into my business practices by at least one member of the United States Senate."

"I haven't heard anything about this," said the senator, playing the role of the genuinely uninformed.

"I have to tell you, Senator, this is all a bunch of crap. My idea for a chain of private laboratories was merely an idea that was before its time. Fortunately, for myself and my associates, we have been able to accrue our resources to the point where we are a nationwide chain. The accusation that we have attempted to form a monopoly doesn't have any foundation."

"Have you been led to believe that you're in legal trouble?"

"I think that's an understatement, Senator. Wilson, from Minnesota, I think you know him, has been conducting an investigation into our operation. The damn democrats can really be pains in the butt when they want to be. They can't police themselves, but they can sure try to dig up the dirt on everybody else."

"So there's no substance to the allegations," asked Hyle as he peered over the top of his glass frames.

"None whatsoever. We're a group of businessmen engaged in the enterprise of capitalism. To the best of my knowledge, we haven't done anything that would impede anybody from purchasing or developing a similar business. And that, Senator, is the honest truth."

"I'll tell you what, Ike. I'll look into it. Graham Wilson shows a lot of promise, but he does seem to let his concerns turn into crusades. You know the type. I think that, perhaps, intervention on my part might serve as a learning experience for the man."

"Thank you, Senator. It's hard enough to try to keep our fiscal head out of water, without having to worry about some zealot in search of a cause."

The two men shook hands, and the senator assured the surgeon that he would be in touch. The politician knew that it would be a situation that would be easily resolved. He was glad for that. For him to become too involved in the affairs of even his most ardent supporters, detracted from his ability to pursue his own causes.

* * *

William Evans rose from bed on the same morning that Ike Paponis went to Washington to meet with Senator Talmadge Hyle. He still could not get used to the absolute silence in his home since his wife had died. Helen had been everything to him.

He found himself turning on the morning news program just to create some background noise. But it was to no avail. Sound loud enough to shatter his eardrums would still not allow him to escape the deafening silence.

His routine had become somewhat regimented since his release from the hospital. He would arise in the morning, slip into a comfortable sweat suit, brush his teeth, walk briskly for three miles, and then come home for two cups of hot herbal tea.

This was the part of the day that Bill Evans enjoyed most. Since he was forced to live alone, this was the one part of the day when he could exalt in his aloneness. He appreciated the sweet smell of the flowers, the striking hues of the green grass, the leaves on the trees. And it was during these walks that he frequently reminisced about his life with Helen.

Bill Evans tried to walk fast enough to derive some aerobic benefit from his exercise. But he was also cognizant of the effects of the vigorous motions on his body. He knew that he should be careful not to overdo. Ike Paponis had told him to exercise, had told him that it was integral to his recovery, but he had also warned him about trying to do too much too fast.

The morning was beautiful. The rising sun had already begun to warm the air. Bill Evans knew that his life would never be the same without Helen, but he was still glad to have another day of it, even if it meant being alone.

He began to lengthen his stride as the small beads of perspiration began to break out on his forehead. The elderly gentleman could tell that his strength was returning. He knew that in just a few short weeks he would be able to swing a golf club. And if he had one pleasure left in life, it was playing golf.

That thought alone caused him to push himself even harder. He was breathing harder, and focused his concentration on the massive form of Mt. Hood in the distance. He could feel the sweat as it ran down between his shoulder blades. He could feel his heart beating faster and faster. Bill Evans was beginning to feel fit again. That Ike was some kind of a miracle worker, wasn't he?

The exercise caused his blood pressure to rise. The elevated pressure, in turn, filled his ventricles more than they normally would be at rest. The Frank Starling Law of the Heart dictated that the more full the ventricles, the greater the force of contraction of the heart.

The uppermost suture of the bypass graft began to tear – slowly at first. The nylon threads were pulled taut. But all of this was happening without any appreciable pain. Bill Evans pushed himself harder, and when the pressure became great enough, the thread broke, and the single stitch unraveled like a dropped spool of kite string. His heart continued to pump for several more long moments, but no blood was being returned to it.

He fell to the ground in an instant, and it was in that same instant that he knew he was dead. As his head struck the sidewalk, he felt the pain, but there was no way for him to react to it. The sensation of dying was not exactly an unwelcome one. He believed that he would soon be reunited with his beloved wife. That gave him peace, as life quickly drained from his body.

* * *

Jason Riley arrived at the offices of Talmadge Hyle at precisely one o'clock. This was going to be a special interview for the junior reporter. In his several months covering the Finance Committee sessions for the Post, he had often had the opportunity to publicly question the senators and their staffs, but he had never been invited to a private meeting. He had a sneaking suspicion that Hyle had something to hide. Why else would he have invited him to his office?

Hyle's secretary was a handsome blonde of approximately thirty years of age. She was attired in conservative business clothing, and her smooth straight hair was pulled neatly into a bun. Her desk was stately by secretarial standards, and she was the picture of composure behind it.

"Jason Riley to see the Senator, please."

"Yes, Mr. Riley, the Senator is expecting you." She depressed a button on her telephone and spoke into the receiver.

"Mr. Riley is here to see you, sir. Yes, sir, I will." She rose from her desk and moved toward the elaborate wooden door to her rear.

"If you'll come with me, Mr. Riley, the Senator will see you now." She opened the door and ushered the reporter into the spacious office.

Talmadge Hyle was on the phone, but rapidly concluded his conversation with the junior senator from Minnesota. He rose from behind his desk, and adorned his face with the most genuine look of congeniality that he could muster.

"Mr. Riley, I applaud your punctuality. That's a quality I admire in a man."

"I appreciate the opportunity, Senator."

"Can I get you a drink?"

"A bottled water would be great, if you have any. It's a bit early for anything else."

"So it is," he said as he produced a bottle of Evian.

"Have a seat, Mr. Riley. Lunch will be along shortly. Now what was it that you wanted to discuss with me?"

"Senator, I'm sure that you're aware that Senator Wilson is conducting an investigation into the business practices of S.P.S. Laboratories of Portland. I'm sure you also know that this business is headed by a Dr. Ike Paponis. I believe that he is one of your more generous supporters. This is technically the target of my inquiry."

"So what exactly are your concerns, Mr. Riley? Anybody can open an investigation at any time, for any reason. That doesn't necessarily mean that there is any truth to the allegations. That requires proof, son."

"Senator, I've examined the records of contributions to your campaign fund. It didn't take much to see that the Portland Fund has been your largest contributor."

"And you think there is something unusual in that?"

"Not other than the money that you have taken in from the Portland Fund clearly exceeds the amount that you can receive from a single source. My biggest concern, is that Ike Paponis and his two partners have been making illegal contributions in return for your intervention on behalf of their various business concerns."

Talmadge Hyle did not change his expression, but he did change his attitude.

"Mr. Riley, do you think I'm some sort of damned fool? I've held this office for a good number of years. I sit on two of the most powerful committees in this esteemed body. Do you think that I would in any way jeopardize my position for a few measly dollars? Your little inquiry should have shown you that I haven't even come close to utilizing the sum total of my available funds in the past several elections."

"But sir, the figures that I have reviewed indicate a clear violation of the statute."

"Son, please don't take this the wrong way, but I'm going to give you a little lesson in political science." His tone was clearly patronizing. "I don't make the rules, Mr. Riley. In order to get elected to any political office, one needs to spend money. I wish the system were set up differently. Then I wouldn't have to spend so much of my time trying to raise money, and I could spend more of my time doing the job that I have been elected to do. The good people of Oregon have the right to expect as much."

"Fortunately, I have friends like Ike Paponis. They contribute large sums of money, and this decreases the countless fund-raising activities that I would otherwise have to endure."

"But, Senator, Surely you are aware that the amounts that they are contributing exceed the legal limits."

"Mr. Riley, surely you are aware that the Portland Fund is merely administered by Dr. Paponis and his associates. The fund itself, represents donations from many people, from many walks of life. If you were to account for each of these individuals, you would find that legal limitations have in no way been exceeded. I understand your concern, but hopefully, you understand a bit better now."

Riley felt stupid. Humiliated. Naive. "I'm sorry, Senator, I didn't consider that. Now that I do, it makes sense."

Riley was rescued by a young man with a dining cart.

"Well, if we've concluded our business, perhaps we could enjoy some lunch." The senator stood and inspected the food on the cart as the waiter dismissed himself silently.

"I hope you like venison, Mr. Riley. It happens to be one of my favorites." They filled their plates and sat at a small table at the far side of the room.

"I appreciate being invited here, Senator."

"Think nothing of it, son. I'm happy to have the opportunity to put your concerns to rest. So tell me a little about yourself, Jason. I hope you don't mind me calling you Jason? Do you have a wife? Children?"

"I don't mind you calling me Jason. And no, I'm not married."

"Surely a good-looking man like yourself has got a beautiful woman tucked away somewhere?"

"I wish I could say that was the case, but I can't. In all honesty, most of my time has been consumed trying to build a career for myself at the paper. I haven't had much time for relationships." Jason could feel the inappropriate sense of familiarity that the senior senator from Oregon was beginning to display toward him.

"Young man, you've got to realize that there's more to life than climbing the corporate ladder. Slow down and smell the roses, son."

"You're probably right, sir. But surely you must have some idea of what it's like to start at the bottom."

"Indeed I do. Things haven't always been this way for me. Why, I can remember… Well, there's no need to get into all of that. I'll tell you what I'm going to do for you. I've got two tickets for Phantom of the Opera at the Kennedy Center next week. If you're interested, I'd like you to be my guest. It won't do your career any harm to be seen with me, and quite frankly, I'd like the company. As you may know, my wife and daughters maintain a residence in Oregon, and it does get lonely for me here from time to time."

"I'd be honored to be your guest, Senator."

"Fine then, Jason. I'll have one of my aides contact you when the appropriate arrangements have been made."

The two men finished their lunches, and the senator then cordially ushered the young reporter from his office. Jason knew that he would accomplish his mission only if he created the proper scenario, and only if he didn't scare the senator away. He could tell that Hyle was interested in him, and while that thought sickened him personally, it excited him professionally. He would have to pursue this very carefully. Talmadge Hyle was no fool.

CHAPTER 8

Despite all of his experience and seniority, Marty Spencer had never found a way to exempt himself from the clinical aspects of his practice. At least two days a week, he still found himself in the autopsy room doing the job that he had been trained to do.

The cool temperature in the dissection room, coupled with the bright neon lights, created an environment that could not be mistaken for any other. The bodies were carefully lined up on their individual gurneys, awaiting Dr. Martin Spencer to cut them from stem to stern. He would carefully describe, weigh, and dissect each of the major organs. He would incise the scalp, remove the face like a mask, and saw through the skull to expose the brain. And just as if it were any other organ, the brain would be weighed and dissected.

There was nothing that could be described as romantic in this business. The blood flowed freely, there was a wide assortment of foul odors, and the survivors of the victims were many times more difficult to deal with than was the actual labor. But for Marty, his fascination with the work had remained intact for all of these years.

When he walked into the autopsy room, he surveyed a scene that would keep him busy for most of the day. There was a total of eight bodies, but two of those were homicides. Detectives milled about and drank coffee from Styrofoam cups. Photographers from the State Crime Laboratory snapped photos every few seconds. And a deputy prosecuting attorney looked as if he would be sick at any moment.

"What have you got for me, gentlemen?" The M.E. walked into the room and donned his rubber apron without fanfare.

"It's a simple mom-shot-pop," said the detective from the sheriff's office.

"We've got a dead hooker, Doctor." The city's detective chimed in a short time later.

"Well, who's first?"

"We logged in at two thirty a.m.," said one of the sheriff's department detectives.

"Yeah, but our gal was discovered dead before yours was," replied one of the city investigators.

"Yeah, well that's crap. Just because we can process a scene faster than you, doesn't mean that we should be penalized for your ineptitude.

Marty Spencer could feel the tension rising between the representatives of the incorporated and unincorporated area.

"Calm down, boys. Why don't we just toss a coin? County, you guys call it in the air."

"Tails!"

The quarter hit the medical examiner's hand, fell to the floor, and rolled on its edge across the room. The coin then hit the wheel of another stretcher and fell flat on the floor. Marty moved across the floor to determine the results and to retrieve the coin.

As he bent down to pick it up, he was startled to see that the body on the stretcher was none other than that of Bill Evans. He carefully surveyed the mid-line incision on the man's chest, and nearly lost his own breath. He was sure that if he were able to see a reflection of his own face, he would see that the pallor matched that of the dead man on the stretcher.

"Heads," he stated barely above a whisper, as he struggled to regain his own composure. All he wanted to do, but dreaded doing, was to get inside Bill Evans's chest to see what the heck had happened. But that would have to wait until he finished with the two homicides. He would just have to keep it together long enough to get the cops out of there. The sad truth was that he already knew what he would find when he dissected Bill Evans's heart.

He forced a smile, and returned to the corner of the room where the detectives congregated.

"It looks like the city takes honors, fellas'. Let's get started."

He stepped up to the body of the young prostitute. He looked carefully at the external surfaces of her body and began his dictation by depressing the foot-pedal underneath the gurney.

"The body is that of an adolescent female, appearing consistent with an age in the late teens to early twenties. The head hair is an auburn color, shoulder length, and moderately curly. The irides are blue. The bulbar and palpebral conjunctivae are free of large hemorrhages, but do exhibit multiple small petechiae. The face and scalp are free of any grossly visible contusions, abrasions, or lacerations. But the face is once again remarkable for the presence of multiple small petechial hemorrhages overlying the maxillae and zygomatic arches bilaterally. Period. Paragraph."

"There are marked, but early, areas of red-purple contusing to the anterior surfaces of the neck. When palpated, the cricoid cartilage is found to be abnormally friable and appears to have sustained a crushing injury. Period.

Paragraph."

"The chest, abdomen, back, and upper and lower extremities are grossly unremarkable."

Marty then expertly swabbed the oral, vaginal, and rectal cavities of the victim. The swabs were rolled onto a microscopic slide, allowed to air dry, and then fixed with an aerosol fixative. Scrapings were taken from under the fingernails and were given to the criminalists from the crime lab.

He opened the body using the standard Y-shaped incision. The soft tissue was reflected back, the rib plate was removed by using a scalpel to cut through the soft cartilage in the front part of the rib cage, and finally the organs of the chest and abdomen were exposed.

The medical examiner pulled down on the lungs by grasping them above the apices, and making a horizontal incision through the trachea, esophagus, and aorta, he began to reflect the tissues downward. After reflecting the diaphragm, the organs of the chest could be removed in block. The procedure was called a Rokitansky maneuver.

After examining the internal organs, Marty carefully dissected upward to remove the organs of the neck. It was important that he not make any holes in the skin of the neck, or cut either of the carotid arteries, or there would be a funeral director out there who would be more than a little upset with him. Holes in the neck were nearly impossible to conceal when it came time to view the body.

"The neck organs are removed intact, and are found to be profoundly injured. There is gross hemorrhage involving the strap muscles bilaterally. The hyoid bond is remarkable for several gross fractures. The areas of injury are accompanied by marked swelling and edema. Period. Paragraph." Making these observations, and coupling them with the hyper-inflated state of the lungs, Marty was able to make his diagnosis.

"Cause of death, asphyxiation due to manual strangulation. That is the end of this dictation. Thank you."

"So you don't think any ligatures were used, Doc?"

"I'd testify against it. There was too much random damage to the neck tissues. Injuries from a ligature would be more confined. No, your hooker was strangled by the hands of a fairly powerful guy."

"Anyway to tell if he was right or left handed?"

"Not based on what I see here."

"Okay, Doc. We'll got out of here and let you get to the rest of your work. Thanks."

Marty completed the autopsy of the elderly gentleman that the sheriff's office was interested in quickly. It was a simple gunshot wound to the chest that transected the aorta, and caused the man to bleed out. The word was that the man's wife had been threatening to kill him for a long time. She had finally gotten angry enough, or bored enough, that she went ahead and did it. Open and closed case. Ain't love grand?

The police officers and criminalists took their own good time leaving. It was a full half hour before Marty was left alone with his own private nightmare.

He moved as quickly as he could to the body of Bill Evans and began his dissection even before dictating an external description. His scalpel was moving faster than it ever would have on a routine case, and they were all routine cases anymore. Every cut was designed to get him to the dead millionaire's heart that much more quickly.

He found that the pericardium, the tough sac surrounding the heart, was adhered to the heart itself. This would be the result of the recent open-heart surgery. He scraped away the fibrous tissue, and eventually, he was able to see the uppermost portion of the graft. Actually, it would have been hard to miss because it was hanging there freely. How could the darn thing have torn free? But in his heart, Marty knew the answer. As he attempted to put the graft back into place, he saw that it had been straight stitched. Bill Evans was dead because Ike had wanted him dead.

Marty felt physically ill immediately. No longer was he just a part of misappropriating funds. He was now indirectly involved in murder. Unless he reported this crime to the proper authority, he would be guilty of complicity in the crime.

Less than was his usual meticulous manner, the medical examiner quickly completed the remaining autopsies. He felt somewhat guilty about rushing his work, but it was really of no matter anyway. There is no way that he would have been able to concentrate on his work. He was merely going through the motions.

After completing the last case of the day, he went to his office and closed the door behind him. He unlocked the bottom drawer of his file cabinet and removed a small bottle of bourbon. He had only drank liquor in his office once before, and that had been the day he and Sally's first child had been stillborn. He felt much the same as he had on that day.

The sick feeling in the pit of his stomach would not go away. He was trapped, and he couldn't think of anything that he could do about his current situation. And make no mistake about it, he was extremely angry with Ike.

He poured a full glass of the sour mash, and drank half of it in a single gulp. The liquor burned his esophagus but only seemed to warm his stomach. He stared blankly out of the window of his office at the bustle of the city below him. He poured his second glass of whiskey and knew that he was going to have to confront Ike. Anything less would be the reaction of a coward. And he was no coward.

The drive to Ike's office was a bit more eventful than he would have liked it to be. The alcohol had made him lightheaded, and these effects, coupled with his racing thoughts, created a near inability to concentrate on his driving. He went left of center several times, and he nearly rear-ended another vehicle at a stoplight.

Not bothering to find a parking place, he came to a stop at the curb in front of the door at Ike's office. Barreling through the front door, he was temporarily waylaid by a highly-skilled receptionist.

"Can I help you, sir?" She had made her living studying faces, and this one concerned her.

"Dr. Martin Spencer to see Dr. Paponis."

"Is he expecting you, Dr. Spencer?"

"He'll see me."

"He's with a patient right now. If you would just have a seat in the waiting area, I'm sure he'll be with you as soon as he's able."

"You can do better than that, lady. He'll see me now." The intensity frightened the receptionist to action.

"Just a moment, sir. I'll tell him that you're here." He stared at her with a stone face that didn't even acknowledge that she had spoken.

She knocked on the examining room door, and stuck her head in. "Doctor, there's a Dr. Spencer here to see you. I think he's the medical examiner."

"That's fine, Lois. Tell him to have a seat in my office, and I'll be right there."

"I think you should come now, Doctor." Ike excused himself and left the examining room. As he did, the placating expression on his face was replaced by one of rage.

"Lois, since when are you incapable of taking directions? You know that I don't like to be disturbed when I'm with a patient."

"I know. But I think he's been drinking. He's really angry, and he scared me a little."

Ike motioned Marty into his office and asked, "Marty, what brings you here at this hour of the day?"

"Cut the crap, Ike. We need to talk." Ike quickly surveyed the waiting room and patient care area to insure that nobody had overheard Spencer's comments. Satisfied, he quickly whisked the medical examiner into his office and closed the door.

"Marty, I don't appreciate you coming into my office and making a scene like this. What's gotten into you? Are you drunk?"

"Cut the shit, Ike. I know you killed him, you bastard. None of it's enough for you, is it? Why did you have to kill him?" Marty was on the verge of losing control if he hadn't crossed that line already.

"Killed who? What are you talking about?"

"Boy, if this isn't a typical Paponis response. Never lose your cool. Never admit to anything. Never apologize. What happened to your conscience, Ike? Or did you ever have one?"

"Marty, I still don't know what you're talking about," pleaded Ike, his composure intact.

"Bill Evans is dead, you son of a bitch! I just did his fucking autopsy, and I can tell you that it didn't take a fucking rocket scientist to see that you straight-stitched his graft."

Ike knew that he wasn't going to be able to lie his way out of this. He sat down at his desk, pulled a rare cigarette from the top drawer, and lit it. Each time he tried to speak, he stopped himself. He stared directly into the medical examiner's eyes, and for just the briefest of moments, Marty thought he saw a trace of guilt. But then it was gone.

"Marty, I'm not going to lie to you. I did straight-stitch the graft. I wasn't sure how long it would last, but to be perfectly honest, I thought it would take just about this long." Ike was somewhat contrite, and Marty had never seen him this way before.

"Marty, he didn't want to go on living anyway. His wife died about a year ago, and he has just been kind of marking time until it was his turn. You're right, I shouldn't have done it. But I was desperate, and he practically begged me to do it. You know what kind of financial trouble we're in. You know that we needed a miracle to bail ourselves out. Bill Evans was our miracle. I didn't know what else to do."

"What you did was wrong. How can you not see that? This is first degree murder, premeditation and all. And if that wasn't enough, you technically defrauded him to the tune of six point eight million dollars. I'm going to have to notify the authorities. You can't get away with what you've done. You're not God."

Marty's words seemed to roll though Ike, and every accusation seemed to incite him to a greater level of anger. By the time the medical examiner was finished, Ike was poised like a cat.

"So who the hell are you to point the finger at me?" Ike was on his feet, and had adopted a fighter's stance. The upper body was squared off and taut. The jaw was fixed.

"You're in this as deeply as I am, Marty. So is Allan. Don't think that you can run to the cops with your little story and then get off Scot free. It's just not going to work that way. I swear that I'll take you down with me. We started this thing together, and that's how we'll end it - together. I will not be your patsy. You agreed to the use of those funds, and you know damned good and well that would be enough to finish your career. And if I go down, S.P.S. goes down. Then you and Allan are broke. And Allan would probably end up disbarred. Then it's over for all of us. You go ahead and do what you think you have to do, but just try to remember the price that you'll be paying. How are those cute kids of yours going to go to college? You think about it, Marty."

Ike knew that he had just struck a nerve, and he just stood and watched his friend wilt before him. Ike knew that both Allan and Marty were tied to their possessions, and neither man would part with them willingly.

"Ike, you can't just go around killing people."

"Come on, Marty. It's not like this has happened before. I wouldn't be much of a surgeon if it happened all the time. But desperate circumstances demand desperate measures. You've got to have more guts. It's not going to do any of us any good if you cave in."

Ike was upset with Marty, but he didn't want to further aggravate the situation. This was definitely a time for diplomacy. He didn't like the idea of having to look over his shoulder, but he felt that both Allan and Marty feared him to some degree, and that wasn't all bad.

"Marty, we've been friends for a long time. I don't want that to change. And we're partners. Virtually everything that we have is intertwined with one another. But there is something that you need to know about me. Neither you, Allan, nor anyone else, will ever bring me down. You can take that to the bank."

"Is that a threat, Ike? You tell me that we're friends in one breath, and then you threaten me in the next? How am I supposed to feel about that?"

"I'm just trying to be honest with you. I know myself pretty well, and I also know what lengths I would go to if I was threatened with the loss of the business. I certainly don't like doing it, but I think you know what I would do to protect my interests."

Marty could feel the icy-cold hostility. The eyes are the windows to the soul, and the medical examiner saw everything he needed to see in the eyes. He felt a cold chill run through his bones, and he knew that now was not the time to push the issue further. Ike Paponis could destroy him, and he knew without a doubt that he would surely do it.

"Marty, you've got to be willing to make the hard choices. You and Allan are too soft. You've got your cushy little homes and your fancy cars. Your families have everything they want. Do you guys think money grows on trees? Well, it doesn't. My butt is the one that's been on the line. I'm the one who's set up to take the hits. You two continue to soak up the bucks, but my rear end could be in the ringer. I'm tired of it. You're either with me, or get the hell out of my way. It's that simple."

Marty was seized with a myriad of emotions. They included fear, guilt, loathing, and just a smattering of loyalty. He felt trapped, and he knew that, for now, the only thing he needed to do was to get away from Ike Paponis.

"You've got me in a really tight spot, Ike. I'm not going to pursue this any further, but I don't want to see anything like this again. If we end up tangled in the legal system, none of our efforts are going to matter much anyway. You've accomplished what you set out to do, so how about just laying low and letting some of this blow over?"

"Don't worry about a thing, Marty. Just go home to your sweet little wife and leave the dirty work to me."

"I wish I could do just that. Unfortunately, you've brought me right into the middle of this. Do what I said, Ike. I don't want to see another case like this in my morgue."

Marty left the office without shaking hands or saying goodbye. Ike watched him leave, and as the door slammed closed, he smiled. He had heard the warnings, but they hadn't troubled him. Neither Allan or Marty were his match, but to their credit, they knew that as well as he did.

Marty pulled into his driveway and quietly opened the front door to his home. He could hear his wife in the kitchen and his two children playing at the back of the house. He went directly into the den and sat in his favorite black leather chair where he was able to contemplate his lawn.

His shrubbery was trimmed to perfection, and the grass was a rich shade of green. The flower beds, filled with roses, added bright color to the suburban scene. Marty was suddenly struck by the fact that he had done nothing to contribute to the beauty of his lawn.

The yard was maintained by landscapers. His house was cleaned by maids, his laundry was cleaned at the dry cleaners, and his automobiles were serviced by mechanics. How dependent he had become on these people and the money that he paid for their services. He knew that he was happy, and he also knew that he did not want to change his lifestyle. But he also knew that he couldn't live with himself if Ike continued with his acts.

He picked up a copy of the Oregonian that sat on the end table next to his chair. He went directly to the obituaries, and the small article that notified the city of the death of William Evans. The entry was unflattering for a man who had accomplished so much in a single lifetime. Two paragraphs. No survivors. Estate to the Portland Fund. Goodbye, Bill, we'll miss you.

Marty dialed Allan's phone number and felt fortunate that he had been able to reach him at work.

"Marty, what can I do for you?"

"Allan, I need to talk to you. Is there any way that you can drop by on your way home from work?"

"Sure, Marty, what's this about?"

"We'll talk when you get here. Thanks, buddy."

Allan was troubled by the call so he wrapped up things as quickly as possible. He suspected that it had something to do with Ike, but he wasn't sure.

Marty walked out to the driveway when Allan arrived and Allan could see the strained expression on his friend's face.

"Thanks for coming. I didn't know who else I could talk to."

"No problem, what's going on?"

"Come on in, I'll get you a drink."

Sally was in the entrance hallway when Marty opened the door. "I didn't even know you were home, Marty. Allan Spandell, I haven't seen you in months."

"Hello, Sally. You're looking as beautiful as ever."

Sally Spencer was a self-assured woman, but the compliment still made her blush. Marty kissed his wife on the lips, and asked if she could get drinks for Allan and him. She retreated down the hallway, and Allan and Marty went into the den. Allan took a seat on the couch, and Marty walked over and stared out the front window.

"Allan, Ike is out of control."

"What are you talking about, Marty?"

Sally brought drinks in and saw the pained expression on her husband's face. One glance from him, however, told her that now was not the time to inquire further, and she left gracefully.

"What are you trying to tell me, Marty?"

"Did you see the obituaries today? Bill Evans is dead. Did you know that?"

"Sure I did. I'm his attorney, and he donated all that money to the Portland Fund. They called me less than an hour after he was pronounced."

"Did you know that Ike did surgery on him a few weeks ago?" Marty had turned away from the window and was looking directly into Allan's eyes.

"Yeah, Bill contacted me beforehand. Said that in case anything went wrong he wanted me to know what was going on. He didn't have any family, you know."

"Allan, do you remember the conversation we had with Ike at the club awhile back? The one when he told us the corporation was in financial difficulty?"

"Yeah."

"Do you remember Ike asking who the biggest contributor to the Portland Fund was? You told him it was Bill Evans."

"I remember, Marty."

"Well, newsflash, Allan. I did Bill's autopsy a few hours ago, and it was perfectly obvious to me that Ike didn't do that operation anywhere close to the way it should have been done. What's worse, from everything that I could tell, Bill Evans never needed surgery in the first place. Ike just killed him so he could get his hands on the money." Allan could see that Marty believed everything that he was saying. And that was important, because the story would certainly have been unbelievable to any rational mind.

"Have you thought about what you're saying, Marty? These are some pretty wild accusations."

"I don't have to think about it. I saw it with my own eyes. I'm a forensic pathologist, Allan. This is what I do. I know what I saw. Ike killed Bill Evans just as surely as if he had put a pistol to his head."

"Have you talked to him?"

"I went directly to his office when I finished the autopsy. He didn't even deny it, Allan! He more or less told me that it was nothing more than the price of doing business."

"It sounds more like murder. What are you going to do about it?"

"Probably nothing. What can I do about it? We're in this up to our eyeballs, Allan. He knows that, and he's banking on it. He doesn't care about us. If I go to the police, we all go down."

Neither Allan nor Marty saw the Porsche cruise slowly by the house. The driver of the car knew that it didn't take a superior intellect to know what the conversation in the house was about. He had them right where he wanted them. He depressed the gas pedal and sped down the street faster than he should have.

"Tell you what, Marty. Let's just ride this out. Hopefully, it was just a one shot deal. Our only other choice is to blow this sky high, and I don't really want to do that. Damn, I don't like being put in this position."

CHAPTER 9

The sleek looking limousine pulled up directly in front of Jason Riley's townhouse. The windows of the vehicle were darkly tinted, and even though the reporter could not see inside the passenger compartment of the car, he knew the senator was waiting for him there.

Riley was dressed in a rented tuxedo, and he locked the front door of his home before walking toward the car. As he did, the chauffeur walked around the rear of the car and smartly opened the door for him. "Good evening, Mr. Riley." Jason nodded at the man's courtesy as he slid into the seat with a modicum of difficulty.

"So good to see you, Jason." The reporter felt the senator's appraising eyes on him as soon as he was inside the car. He was temporarily amused by the thought that he was possibly going on a date tonight. But he approached his task dutifully and realized that things were unfolding just as he had hoped.

"Thank you, Senator. I've never been picked up in a limousine before. I'm not accustomed to such style."

"This is a special night – Phantom of the Opera. Have you seen it before?"

"I hate to admit it, Senator, but I've never seen a Broadway show of any kind. I'm afraid that when it comes to the cultural arts, I'm rather a heathen. It's usually just football games for me."

"Then I'm glad to have the opportunity to expose you to some of the best that the city has to offer." Hyle pulled a bottle of champagne from a bucket of ice and carefully poured two glasses.

"To our evening out." Jason touched his glass to the senator's and then drained it. He was appalled by the man's gall, and he eagerly drank the alcohol to hide his disgust. He knew that the entire evening was a product of his own design, but the senator was so blatant in his intentions that Jason found the entire situation to be embarrassing.

He had considered long and hard what his response would be if the senator made a sexual advance, and he was sure that the sexual advances were drawing ever nearer. But he still didn't know how he would react.

He knew that he had to play the game this evening. That would be difficult because he already found himself sickened by the images that were flowing through his brain.

"I'm so happy that you were able to accept my invitation. The long months in Washington get quite lonely with my family in Oregon. And nobody seems to understand when I attend an event with a female escort."

"As I told you, Senator, it really is my pleasure. You are treating me to something that I would not otherwise have been able to do, and I appreciate it." Jason was adopting a demeanor that was categorically effeminate. He knew that to catch the big fish one must use the appropriate bait.

The limo pulled directly up to the immense front doors of the Kennedy Center. The chauffeur got out and opened the door for his passengers. The senator and his guest then went into the ornate hall. Their overcoats were taken from them by a teenage boy who greeted the senator by name.

Seats were in the front row of a private box, and the vantage point was unbelievable. Ordinarily, Jason would have hated something like this, and he was disgusted with himself for accepting the invitation. But the potential story showed great promise.

Talmadge Hyle was enraptured by the show. He rarely spoke to Jason except to bring his attention to some aspect or subtle nuance of the performance. Jason was very tuned in to the way the senator was touching his arm. They had seemed to be innocent brushes, but they had caused Jason's heart to beat wildly.

The sensation was probably fear. Or maybe it was excitation. But excitation would be only about the possible story, and not arousal.

When the show was over, the urgency of the senator's movements suggested that he was eager to be out of the theater, and the two men walked out to the waiting limo.

"Did you enjoy the show, Jason?"

"I'm not sure that I would want a steady diet of it, Senator, but it was very interesting."

"Where to now?" asked the senator, as if any suggestion Jason were to make would be acceptable.

"If it wouldn't be too much of a bother, there is a club that I wouldn't mind stopping by on the way home." Hyle sat forward and gave directions to his driver before readdressing his attentions to the passenger in the rear compartment.

Ciro's was a fashionable club on the D.C. circuit that attracted a wide variety of patrons. The reporter marveled at the diversity of the crowd. There were straight couples as well as those with alternative lifestyles. There were odd but fashionable hair designs. And the clothing and other adornments were obviously being worn to attract attention.

Jason wished that he could feel comfortable with such people, but he couldn't. His conservative Catholic upbringing, and his years at Notre Dame, had enlightened him, but had also instilled a conservative moral code. Almost immediately, he found himself stereotyping nearly everyone at whom he looked. His senses were so alive with the sights and sounds that he almost felt as if he was in a dream state. And the senator was looking at him appraisingly again.

"This is an interesting place, Jason. Have you been here before?"

"No, I haven't. I had just heard about it, and thought it would be an interesting place to try. I hear all sorts of people come here."

"And the word is, at least in political circles, that this is a safe place to come and be yourself. I'm afraid that I've never really found anyplace where I could be that comfortable, but that's the word around town anyway."

"So, Senator, what you're telling me is that there's really nowhere that you feel free to be yourself."

"I wouldn't go that far. But there aren't many places."

"What would it mean for you to be yourself, Senator?"

Hyle looked directly into Jason's eyes. "I'm gay, Jason. Did you know that about me?"

The reporter was caught off guard by the statesman's frontal approach. He had hatched this entire scheme in the hope of breaking a sensational story, but he had never really resolved exactly what he was going to do if it actually happened.

"I have heard rumors, Senator, but I also knew that you have a wife and two daughters back in Oregon. To be quite honest with you, I never really put much stock in rumors and especially rumors of this nature. I guess that I've always felt that whatever a man's sexual preferences are, they're his own business."

"How very progressive of you, Jason. In this day and age, it is so difficult to find someone without a critical opinion. We are all different, but that is our right. It's what makes the world such a wonderful place. You know that I'm attracted to you, don't you, Jason?"

Here it was. What did he say now?

"Senator Hyle, I don't know what to say. I've never been involved in a homosexual relationship. I guess I've never even considered it. Are you saying that you're interested in me… sexually?"

The senator scooted across the vinyl seat of the booth until he was in very close proximity to the reporter. Once again, he placed his right hand on the inner aspect of Jason Riley's thigh. The young reporter once again experienced the dichotomy of emotions that both excited and repulsed him simultaneously. He found it immediately strange that he had never examined his own sexuality more closely. Here he was, trying to expose the senator for his aberrant behavior, and he didn't even know how he felt himself.

"Jason, I've been attracted to you since the first time I saw you. I tried very hard to resist it, but in the end, I found that to be impossible."

Jason felt the air being sucked from his lungs – such was his astonishment.

"I don't think that I'll be able to do this, Senator."

"Please, Jason, call me Talmadge."

"Talmadge, I've never seen myself as being homosexual. I don't think I can do this."

"I don't want to rush you, Jason. I can be patient. Anything worth having is worth waiting for. All I ask is that this remain between the two of us. I know that you're a young reporter, and a story like this could send you to the big time. All I can tell you, Jason, is don't even consider it. If this affair would happen to find its way into the papers, you have to know that I have enough clout to destroy you."

"What are you trying to say?"

"Jason, I care about you. I can give you the big story that you need so desperately. Just don't do anything distasteful, or you'll be ruined."

Jason knew that he was being threatened. It wasn't even a veiled threat. He also knew the senator was capable of doing exactly as he had threatened to do. That reality sent a cold chill down his spine.

"I would never do that, Senator. But I'm not ready for a romantic affair with a man either."

The two men finished their drinks and left the club without further talk of romance.

* * *

Ike, Allan, and Marty sat at an isolated table in the restaurant at the Kaneeta Indian Reservation resort in eastern Oregon. They had dined on stuffed game hens that bad been baked in clay for most of the day and were then dipped in huckleberry sauce. Currently, they were in the throes of heavy drinking. There had been no talk of the death of Bill Evans, and the three men, had in fact, been getting along better than ever.

The trip had been Ike's idea. Relationships among the three men had become strained in Portland, and given their integrated dependence on each other, he knew that something needed to be done to get them back on even keel.

Kaneeta was the perfect place. Not far from Portland, over Mt. Hood, and into the near desert of eastern Oregon, it boasted peace, booze, and natural hot springs. It would be a good place to relax and rekindle their friendships. Families and obligations were left behind, ostensibly to tend to business, but the sole purpose of the trip was to play in the sun for a few days.

"Gentlemen, I've been saving the best news for just the right moment. Our financial troubles are over. We are once again financially solvent." Ike motioned to a waiter across the room who quickly brought a bottle of expensive champagne.

The presentation was made to Paponis, and the glasses were poured. Ike stood and raised his glass.

"To brotherhood, and to the success of S.P.S. To our success." They toasted one another and drank down the champagne. Allan and Marty had enough alcohol in them that they were truly able to enjoy the moment without all of its implications. For the first time in months, they were able to put their fears behind them.

Marty Spencer had not divulged the true results of the autopsy on Bill Evans. And there had been no inquiries anyway. The Portland Fund had received the money that Evans had designated, and Ike had used it to bail out S.P.S. Laboratories. The company was now stronger than it had ever been. Everything had gone exactly as Ike had said it would, and nobody outside of their tight little circle was any the wiser.

Marty had begun to put the intentionally botched surgery out of his mind. He had rationalized that it all truly was for the greater good. In addition to that, his fear of Ike had diminished somewhat, and this was a much better disposition of affairs. They were once again a closely knit group of friends.

"Gentlemen, I know that the past several months have been difficult for all of us. A good many things have happened, and we've all been second guessing each other. We almost lost everything that we had worked so hard for. But that is all behind us now. We have turned our deficit into a surplus, and it's high time we gave something back to the community."

Marty could not believe what he was hearing. What was Ike going to propose?

"Guys, what I'd really like to do is to open a free medical clinic in downtown Portland. I've always told you that I wasn't as hard as you thought

I was. I just wanted us to be able to get far enough ahead so that we could do something that would truly make a difference."

"That's a great idea, Ike. Are you talking now or sometime in the future?" Marty was immediately excited by the idea.

"I want to get started right away, and I want your names all over the project. It'll be great PR."

"Ike, I'm sorry that I doubted you. I can't thank you enough for doing this. It'll make all the difference in the world to me."

* * *

While Ike and his buddies were bonding in the desert of eastern Oregon, operating room nurse, Shelly Grayson, was continuing to be haunted by what she had seen in the operating room that day. She had considered talking to the hospital's nursing administration, or even to one of her close friends, but at this point, she didn't even trust her own instincts.

Had she really seen what she had thought that she had seen? Surely Dr. Paponis would not have deliberately bungled his patient's heart graft. She knew that the surgeon could be a difficult man to deal with, but to suggest that he could do anything of this magnitude was nearly unthinkable.

Why was she the only one who suspected that something had been amiss? Surely the anesthesiologist, Dr. Able Samson, would have noticed if something about the procedure was other than it should have been. There were perfusion techs in the room, and neither of them had suspected anything.

Shelley Grayson knew that she was on her own. If she said anything, it would be her word against Dr. Paponis. She knew whom the hospital administrators and other authorities would believe, and it surely wouldn't be her.

She was torturing herself and it had to stop. The only way was to confront Dr. Paponis directly. She had witnessed his tirades on more than one occasion, but he didn't scare her the way he did other people. She knew that she would just have to bide her time, and wait for the appropriate time to talk to the surgeon. Until then, she had to keep her mouth shut and her ears open.

* * *

After returning from Kaneeta, Allan and Marty set about making plans to open the aid clinic. Allan handled the details pertaining to building acquisition, and Marty began to assemble the necessary equipment and personnel to staff the facility. It was proving to be a catharsis for both men.

They had been so emotionally burdened by the grave potential outcomes of Ike's deeds that the opportunity to perform a task that would truly benefit the community was a welcome relief. They could not have felt better if this was the very penance given them by a priest in the confessional.

Even Sally Spencer noticed the immediate improvement in her husband's attitude. She worried about him, if only by virtue of his occupation. She knew that being surrounded by violence and death weighed heavily on his soul. She watched closely for the telltale signs when Marty drew inward, when his sleeping or eating habits changed, when he began to drink too much.

In recent weeks, however, he had seemed to be more well adjusted. He was happier and didn't seem to be so troubled by his work. He had also shown excitement when talking about this new project. Sally truly believed that her husband had a good and giving heart. She regretted that his chosen specialty in medicine gave him so little in the way of human contact. He would have made such a wonderful family practitioner, or perhaps a pediatrician.

Sally also like Allan, and she was glad that he would be working with her husband on this new project. She was also glad that Ike would be minimally involved. She didn't care for the heart surgeon, and she liked even less that Marty was so professionally tied to him. Ike Paponis was just a little too slick for her liking.

But Ike was in the height of his glory. Nobody but he would ever know the true financial miracle that he had managed to pull off. But Ike knew, and he was his own biggest fan.

He no longer had to worry about his two friends. The men had proven to be loyal even though he knew that they both had serious ethical misgivings. Yes, thought the surgeon, everything was shaping up nicely. Marty and Allan were all wrapped up in their little do-gooder project and were feeling great about themselves. But Ike was only beginning to set his plan in motion.

CHAPTER 10

Richard Cranston was the popular mayor of Portland, Oregon, and he was also a fan of Ike Paponis. Like he had for Talmadge Hyle, Paponis had nearly financed Cranston's bid for office with donations from the Portland Fund.

Ike was very intent on influencing the national political scene, but he was not about to let loose of his strangle hold on local politics either. Ike didn't like Dick Cranston, and he had no respect for the man, which was worse. But he didn't have to like or respect him, he only had to use him.

The building that housed the Multnomah County Medical Examiner was in a desperate state of repair. Were it to be inspected, it would most probably have to be shut down. Ike wanted Marty firmly in his corner in the future, and it was his contention that securing a new facility for the M.E. just might accomplish that.

Mayor Cranston had been happy to receive the invitation for a round of golf at Lake Oswego. He knew better than anyone else that keeping Ike Paponis in his corner would prove to be an invaluable asset to his career.

Ike had been very careful to insure that only he and the mayor would be playing golf together on this occasion. It was time to call in a couple of markers, and that was always something that was best done privately.

Dick Cranston had driven his Lincoln Town Car to the club. He was grateful to have the afternoon off away from the media and his inescapable entourage. He liked all the attention, but he also liked to be left alone occasionally. As he walked into the dining room, he could see Ike sitting at a table on the far side of the room. The surgeon stood to greet him.

"Dick, so good to see you. I hope this isn't interrupting your schedule too much." Ike offered his hand, and the mayor shook it firmly.

Dick Cranston was not the picture of a big city mayor. His six-foot frame was muscular and tan. His black hair was becoming gray at the temples, and he looked more the type for the board room than the smoky political back room.

"To tell you the truth, Ike, you've interrupted my schedule in a big way. I just haven't quite figured out how to thank you for it."

"I'm glad to hear it."

Ike ordered beers for both men as he played the role of a gracious host.

"How are things going for you down at City Hall? Is there anything I can help you with?"

"I appreciate the offer, Ike, but everything is going well. If I could just reign in that council a little, my life would be a little easier. I have to tell you, though, I do like that idea of yours for the medical clinic for the indigents downtown. The local hospitals have been all over me for city funds for treating the homeless. We just don't have the money."

"Would you like to be a part of the project, Dick?"

"Sure, what could I do?"

"Not much, really. Just commit some of the city's resources, on a limited scale of course, and I think that would be enough. I'd like for this to be a joint project."

"It'd be great PR for me too. That's just the kind of exposure I need," said the mayor with enthusiasm.

The beers came, followed shortly by lunch, and the two men enjoyed some casual conversation before making their way out onto the golf course.

Ike could have destroyed the mayor on the golf course, but he deliberately held back. He played well enough to impress Cranston, but not so well as to embarrass him. When they reached the fifth hole, they were forced to take a seat on a bench to wait for the group in front of them who were playing more slowly. After sitting in silence for a few moments, Ike began to speak.

"Dick, what I really wanted to talk to you about today was a new building for the Medical Examiner's office. That place is a rat trap you know."

"I hate to admit it, Ike, but I didn't know that. I don't think I've ever even been down there. Dead bodies and I just don't get along. I guess I'll just have to take your word for it."

"As you probably know, Marty Spencer is a good friend of mine. He's been doing an outstanding job for this jurisdiction for years, and he's never asked for a darn thing. I think it's high time that the city and the county get together, and get him out of that abomination that you call a morgue and get him a decent facility to work in."

"That's a great idea, Ike, but we flat don't have the money. That I know for a fact."

"That's a bunch of bologna, Dick." Ike made the statement as he was addressing his ball on the tee. He then made a perfect back swing and drove the ball straight down the fairway for a very long distance. It was just the kind of swing that let Cranston know that the surgeon had been sandbagging. Ike had done it in just such a way, as to say, I've got you outclassed, Dick, and you know it.

"That was some swing, Ike."

"Just got lucky I guess."

Cranston executed a mediocre tee shot, and the two men made their way down the fairway.

"Dick, when was the last time that you were in to see me?" Watching the mayor light his fourth cigarette in an hour had prompted the surgeon to ask the question.

"I suppose that I'm about due."

"I thought you promised me that you would quit those damn things," said Paponis as he gestured toward the lighted Marlboro.

"Easier said than done, my friend."

"Well, how have you been feeling?"

"To tell you the truth, Ike, I've been getting short of breath when I exercise, like when I climb a flight of stairs. I've tried to ignore it, but even that is getting harder to do."

"You probably ought to make an appointment to come in to see me early next week."

"I'll do that, but if my opponents get wind of me having heart trouble, they'll be all over me about it."

"It'll just be between me and you, Dick. I don't have any interest in divulging any of your medical problems, and besides, I'm sworn to protect your confidentiality."

"So you really think that we ought to build a new morgue?"

"Let me put it this way, Dick, I would consider it a personal favor if you were able to make this happen for me."

"I'll see what I can do, Ike. In the meantime, keep up the good work with the medical clinic. Send me over a list of whatever you think the city can do to help, and any good press that you can send my way would be greatly appreciated."

The two men finished their round of golf without further talk of any official business. And Dick Cranston promised to call the office to make an appointment for the following week.

* * *

"God, I thought you'd never get here. You really shouldn't keep me waiting, you know," said Sharon as she opened the door wearing a sheer negligee. She had curled her lower lip outward as if to pout, and the look made Ike forget virtually everything else that was going on in his life. He feasted his eyes on her, and tried to overcome the urge to take her immediately. He wanted to drink in her beauty and intensify his already overwhelming desire.

"You look beautiful," he stated unabashedly, as she moved across the room to pour two glasses of wine. The soft light accentuated her alluring attire.

Ike had not been able to stay away from this woman since the first night that he had met her. She was beautiful, intelligent, and a dynamic lover. She had not been demanding of him, but for the first time in his life, Ike had found that he was treating her as a good woman should be treated. He respected her needs, and he had done nothing to abuse the relationship.

Rachel Roxbury had given them her blessing. Sharon was her friend, and she bore Ike no ill will. The two seemed to be in love, and she merely accepted the change in her role from lover to friend.

"How did your golf game go?"

"I played with the mayor today. I made sure that I didn't beat him too badly."

"You mean you didn't let him win?" she asked teasingly already knowing the answer.

"I never let anyone win. If you don't know that about me by now, then I suggest that you make note of it."

"You're such a tough guy, Ike," she cooed as she touched her forefinger to his neck, her tone slightly mocking.

"You know it, baby."

"Tough with everyone but me."

"I don't know what it is about you, Sharon. You make me feel human. I guess that's a weakness that I'm just going to have to get over."

"Take you time, tough guy. I like you just the way you are." She nuzzled close to him and draped one of her thighs across his legs. He felt the warmth emanate from her body, and he was no longer able to contain his desire.

He took her fully in his arms and kissed her deeply. This attention was all that was needed to unleash her pent-up desire. She covered his face and neck with a flurry of brief but intimate kisses. Her tongue lingered at his ear, as she pulled upward on his polo shirt to remove it from his muscular torso.

She traced a line down his chest with her tongue and totally enveloped his left nipple in her mouth. She then skillfully undid his belt and the clasp of his trousers and carefully unzipped the zipper.

Ike could wait no longer and pulled her onto his lap. He controlled his urgency and entered her gently, but as soon as he was in, he could control himself no longer. Her cries were loud and her movements were focused. He was totally enthralled with the rise and fall of her breasts beneath the sheer nylon.

When he glanced at her face, it appeared as if she were miles away, when in truth, she couldn't have been closer to him if she tried. At that moment, Ike surrendered to the fact that he loved this woman. And if history bears the truth, he knew that it was unlikely that he would ever love another.

He felt her body tense, then stiffen, while failing to relinquish the rhythmic motion. When Ike realized that he had satisfied this woman, he could postpone his own pleasure no longer. Her body collapsed against him as the well-achieved fatigue consumed her. She moaned lightly as she nuzzled her head into the crook of his neck. They rested quietly in each other's arms and enjoyed the utter peace of the moment.

"Sharon, what would you say if I asked you to marry me?" Ike had startled even himself by asking the question.

"I'd say the sex was even better than I thought."

"I'm serious, Sharon. Don't joke about this," he said with an intent look on his face.

"You don't want to marry me, Ike Paponis. You don't want to marry anyone."

"I suppose that it's my fault that you think I feel that way. But I really do want to marry you, Sharon."

"Okay, mister, I'm going to take you up on this. Or maybe I should say, I'm going to call your bluff. No fancy wedding though. If you want to do this, we get on a plane for Vegas right now. But you better be sure of yourself."

"I've never been more sure of anything in my life."

Sharon detached herself from her future husband and retrieved the two half-finished glasses of wine. She handed one to Ike.

"For better or worse, Ike. Don't ever forget that. I always swore that I'd never get married. I'll do this, but don't bullshit me, Ike Paponis."

"I couldn't do that, Sharon. I don't exactly know why, but I could never do that."

"You call the airport right now. If we're going to do this, we're going to do it right now."

Ike made the call to the airlines, and the two packed suitcases for their trip. He called his secretary and made arrangements to clear his calendar for the next several days. Fortunately, he was only scheduled for office hours and had no surgical procedures planned. They drove to the airport for the trip to Las Vegas.

CHAPTER 11

Marty Spencer loved his work at the medical clinic. He was practicing medicine as any family doctor would, and for a forensic pathologist, whose days consisted of performing autopsies and examining microscopic tissue samples, the experience was a true pleasure. He didn't get into anything really serious. Cases such as those were referred to one of the local emergency rooms. But he was able to treat colds and sprains, and he often spent time just talking with mentally ill patients who had been forced onto the streets by political budget reform.

It gave him a sense of warmth that he had not felt since his days as a medical student. For the most part, the clinic was staffed by volunteers who had practices in the more-affluent areas of town, but Marty donated as much of his time as his schedule would allow. Even Sally was putting in long hours at the clinic, and the experience was drawing them ever-closer together.

It was early autumn, and the temperature had begun to fall. If he had forgotten, this was the time of year for respiratory ailments of every sort. He found that some of his patients were desperately ill. They were desperately ill, but he could make them better. He felt good knowing that he was making a difference.

All of the beds in the clinic were full when the black limousine pulled up in front of the free clinic. Senator Talmadge Hyle had come to visit his constituency, and he had Mayor Cranston in tow. There was also the usual entourage of aides, security personnel, and the obligatory representatives of the press. Jason Riley had been invited along on the trip to Oregon, and he made occasional notes on his legal pad.

Marty held his stethoscope to the back of one of his patients, and listened to the wheezing that characterized the man's respiratory effort. He heard the commotion outside and looked up just in time to see Dick Cranston come through the front door. They mayor's eyes met those of the medical examiner, and he began to move directly toward him. The entire crew moved closely behind. Cranston had no medical experience, and therefore did not know that it was in bad taste to interrupt a physician when he was with a patient. In addition, the mayor was out to impress the senator, he just couldn't imagine that anything would take priority over that.

"Marty... Marty Spencer." The mayor moved ever closer as a

photographer began to snap photos. He was careful to seek angles that would place the senator and the mayor in photos with Dr. Spencer and his patient.

"Mayor Cranston, to what do I owe the pleasure of this visit? Senator Hyle." Marty nodded his head in deference to the senator and managed to conceal his displeasure with the uninvited interruption.

The mayor was the first to respond. "Marty, we've been getting word of the good things you're doing down here, and we just wanted to witness it firsthand."

The photographer motioned the senator and mayor to move in closer. "Senator Hyle, Mayor Cranston. Could I get a shot of the two of you with Dr. Spencer?"

"Sir?" and he motioned to the disheveled-looking patient who appeared to be elated by all of the attention. "Let's see if we can get you into the picture as well."

Marty was immediately put off by the intrusion, but he was astute enough not to object. And from the looks of things, objections wouldn't do any good anyway. After the photo opportunity was exhausted, the mayor gently nudged the medical examiner over to the side of the room.

"Marty, I just wanted you to know that I'm looking into what I can do to get you a new facility."

Spencer appeared confused. "Dick, we just moved in here. I don't think we have any need for a new facility yet."

"I'm not talking about this clinic. I'm talking about a new building for the Medical Examiner's office."

"You're considering building a new office for the M.E.? What prompted all of this?"

Now it was the mayor's turn to look confused. "Well, Ike Paponis just talked to me about this the other day. I had just assumed that you knew about his proposal."

"He hasn't said anything to me about it. I guess I don't know why that should surprise me, though. Ike does whatever Ike wants to do, and he only informs the peasants if he feels like it. What would be his interest in a new building for the M.E.?"

"I haven't the slightest idea, Marty, but I just wanted you to know that I was looking at it, and I'll see what I can do."

Marty was more than a little aggravated with Ike. Every time he started to feel good about their relationship, Ike would go and do something like this behind his back. He was well aware that he did need a new facility, but he didn't like the idea of Ike being the prime mover in the whole affair. He knew, or at least he thought he knew, that his friend had good intentions and that did serve to soften the sting of being left out of the loop.

Senator Hyle was the next to address the medical examiner. "Martin Spencer, you're the medical examiner, aren't you?"

"That's correct, sir."

"That's what I thought. How does it feel to be working on live people?" The question had been childish, but the senator seemed to be truly amused with himself. He acted as if he had been the first one to ever have made such a joke. The fact was that it was just the kind of truly tasteless remark that the medical examiner heard on a near-daily basis.

"I'm enjoying myself, Senator. It's an opportunity to practice medicine like I never have before."

"Have you ever considered doing this on a larger scale? I've been thinking about this a good deal lately. Have you ever considered forming a team that would respond to natural disasters such as earthquakes or hurricanes?"

"That really sounds more like a governmental task. No, to be perfectly honest with you, I haven't had any time to think about anything but this clinic, my job, and the labs. Fortunately, my family can help out around here, so I get to see a bit more of them. But I don't think I have the time to become involved in any other projects.

But the senator had seemingly already lost interest and was moving away. As an afterthought, he said over his shoulder, "You just think about it, Dr. Spencer. You're doing a lot of good here, and you could be doing so much more."

"Thank you for your interest, Senator." Marty quickly put the visitor out of his mind and got back to his patient.

Richard Cranston had heard the interchange between the senator and the physician, and he knew that Hyle was merely trying to capitalize on the goodwill of the volunteers to further his own causes. Once again, the mayor interrupted Marty and his patient.

"Marty, I'm having a little reception for Senator Hyle at my home tonight. If you and Sally are free, I'd like to have the two of you stop by."

"I'll talk to Sally, and we'll give you a call later. Is Ike coming?

"You mean you haven't heard?"

"Heard what?"

"Ike's in Vegas getting married."

"He's doing what?"

"Rumor has it that he's in Vegas getting married. You mean you didn't know anything about it?"

"I had no idea."

"Just like Ike, isn't it. He has to keep everybody in an uproar. Anyway, try to make it tonight if you can."

* * *

Marty and Sally Spencer arrived at the home of Mayor Cranston just in time for drinks. The physician had been caught completely off guard by the news of Ike's sudden decision to get married, but he had become more comfortable with the idea as he had considered it over the past few hours. It was probably just what he needed to provide a little stability in his life.

The gathering was informal. Senator Hyle was present with his wife and two daughters, but he seemed to be spending most of his time with the young reporter who had come with him from Washington.

Dick Cranston moved expertly through the crowd doing what he did best – sucking up. He made sure that the drink glasses were kept full and that the snack trays made rounds regularly.

Marty Spencer's powers of observation had improved due to his recent interactions with live patients, and for his money, Dick Cranston did not look well. Most worrisome was his ashen-gray color. But beyond that, Marty noticed that the mayor was sweating profusely and cradling his left arm as if it were in an invisible sling.

He knew that Dick had a history of heart problems, but he had never seen him look so bad. Just as he pondered the implications of what he was observing, Dick Cranston went down.

"Call an ambulance," screamed the physician, as he pushed his way through the crowd who had surrounded the fallen man. Cranston was still breathing on his own. That was a good sign. He was sweating enough to have soaked his clothes, and his skin was pale as a ghost, but for now he was alive.

"Dick, are you having chest pain?"

"I don't know if I would call it pain. It's more like a heavy pressure. It's almost like a steel band is squeezing my chest tighter and tighter." His words were feeble – almost inaudible. Marty had to lean very close just to hear what the man was saying.

"Dick, does your pain go anywhere?"

"Yeah, it's weird. It goes down my arm and into my jaw. I can even feel it in my back."

The medics arrived quickly, and Marty started an intravenous line as the paramedics were hooking him up to a cardiac monitor.

"Dick, I think you're having a heart attack."

"I could've probably told you that an hour ago, Marty."

"I wish you would have."

The mayor was loaded onto the cot and was headed toward the door. Marty jumped into the back of the ambulance and stared at the crowd of people who stared into the vehicle in disbelief. The sensation was different from any the medical examiner was used to. He was locked in a life and death struggle to keep the mayor of the city alive. The adrenaline rush was incredible.

The reflection of the red flashing lights could be seen on the objects outside the vehicle. The wail of the sirens was deafening even inside of the van. The high-pitched beep of the heart monitor was irregular, echoing the struggle of the mayor's heart to stay alive.

The ride to the hospital was a short one, and the mayor was in the emergency department in only a matter of minutes. There was a large contingent of Portland police officers in the parking lot, and the uniformed men provided a protective vanguard as the medics and their patient had flowed through the doors to the hospital.

Marty was immediately relegated to the role of spectator, and while he had enjoyed the rare medical challenge, he was more than happy to relinquish the responsibility to more capable hands.

"Get me a couple more lines. What have we got for a rhythm? I need a nitro drip... now! Has anybody got a pressure yet?"

"Pressure's eighty-four palp. Looks like sinus brady with a lot of PVCs."

"Okay, hold the Nitro. We've got to get his pressure up. Slam some fluids, people. Get the external pacer over here." There was a flurry of activity around the mayor's stretcher, but even the best efforts of the emergency department crew seemed to be falling short.

The emergency physician's face was drawn, but his eyes were fiercely alive. These were the situations that he hated the most. They were also the ones that gave him a reason to live. Everything that he did on this night would be scrutinized. If he were successful, he would be a hero. To fail would make him the goat. To him, it was of no consequence that it was God's hand that really mattered. He had to find a way to cheat death. And he was also relatively certain that God was not feeling the pressure right now.

"Give him an amp of Atropine. Is the Lido going yet? If not, hold it until we get his rate up. Is the pacer ready?"

"His rate's coming up, Doctor."

"What have you got for a pressure?"

"It's up to ninety-eight, Doctor."

"Good, good. Let's get some TPA going." TPA was the clot-busting miracle drug that was saving a lot of lives.

"Mayor Cranston, do you have a cardiologist whom you see regularly?" Cranston was more alert and his color was improving. And his brain seemed to like the improved circulation that it was getting.

"I go to Ike Paponis."

"But he's a surgeon. Don't you have a cardiologist?"

"No, Ike's the only guy I see for my heart."

"Jackie, get Ike Paponis on the phone," said the ED doc with a sense of urgency.

"He's out of town. In Vegas getting married. Just my luck, huh?" The mayor's voice was still feeble.

"Try his office anyway. See if there's anybody taking call for him."

"Mayor Cranston, I think you need to go to the cardiac catheterization lab so we can see what's causing you all of these problems. If we can't get hold of Dr. Paponis, is there another physician who we can call?"

"Shoot, I don't know. I guess Paul Switzer would be my second choice," he said as the nurse returned to the room.

"Dr. Jenkins, they expect Dr. Paponis back sometime tomorrow morning. Dr. Pifer is taking his calls until then."

"Never mind. Go ahead and get Dr. Switzer on the line. Tell him we need him in here pronto to do an emergency cardiac cath. Tell him his patient is the mayor. That'll get him moving."

"You know, Doc, I sure wish you would just call me Dick. I think the time for formalities has long since passed." The statement had seemed to exhaust the mayor, and he was becoming more lethargic.

"Dr. Switzer will be here in ten minutes. He said to get the mayor packed up and down to the cath lab right away."

Portable monitors replaced the hardwire that the mayor was connected to, and the IV bags were transferred onto a pole on the moveable stretcher. The emergency room doctor accompanied the patient on the trip to the cath lab where he was transferred to another table and prepped for the procedure. Paul Switzer burst through the door to the cath lab looking like he had just been roused from sleep, which he had.

"What have we got going on here?" the cardiologist asked the emergency department physician hurriedly.

"Well, you'll probably recognize the mayor laying on the table over there. I think he's having an anterolateral infarct. Ike Paponis has been following him, but Ike is out of town, and the mayor asked for you."

"Oh shit. Paponis will lose his mind if he finds out that I've been involved with one of his patients. He can't stand me. Who's taking his calls?"

"Dr. Pifer is taking his call, but the mayor asked for you specifically. At this point, this is a medical rather than a surgical problem. I think you are well within ethical boundaries at this point. What else can you do?"

"I can get the hell out of here. Paponis will have my butt." There was true concern in Paul Switzer's eyes. He definitely did not want to cross Ike Paponis.

"Dammit, Paul, we haven't got any choice. We're running out of time, and how do you think Ike would react if he thought you let his patient die?"

"I guess you're right. Pretty sticky situation you've gotten me into, Dr. Jenkins."

"Just do what you've got to do, Paul. If Paponis throws a fit, I'll take the heat for you."

"I just may have to take you up on that." Paul Switzer donned his lead apron and moved over toward the patient's bedside. He explained the procedure to the mayor and then further prepped his right upper leg with Betadine.

Sterile instruments were arranged on the table, and television screens that doubled for fluoroscope monitors were positioned around the room. Later, when the dye was injected, the cardiologist would be able to see areas of blockage on these screens.

"Dick, I'm so sorry that his happened tonight. I'm going to do a heart catheterization, and hopefully, we'll be able to get the problem fixed. I looked through your old record, and I saw that you've had this done before."

"A couple of times," said the mayor trying to conserve energy with an economy of speech.

"Dr. Paponis is the only physician that you see for your heart?"

"Yes."

"I understand that he's out of town. Just out of curiosity, why did you select me?"

"I heard you were good."

"I appreciate the compliment, but you have to know, Ike Paponis and I don't get along very well."

"That's tough. It's my call."

"Okay, none of what we're going to do here should be any big surprise to you. We're going to insert a long wire catheter into the femoral artery at the top of your leg. We'll advance it up through your aorta to your heart. Once we get there, we'll inject some dye to see if we can find the blockage that we already know is there. I'll then inflate a small balloon to see if we can get the artery to open back up. If we can't manage to do that, you'll probably need to have some surgery."

Dr. Switzer began his procedure, and Dick Cranston squirmed a bit on the table with the initial discomfort. The cardiologist depressed a foot pedal and the fluoroscope screens came alive. This allowed him to observe the wire as it coursed toward its destination. Once in place, the physician injected a small amount of dye, which rapidly flowed into the coronary circulation. The sounds in the room were those of huge machinery taking radiograph images in rapid-fire succession.

It didn't take long to see the nearly one hundred percent occlusion of the left anterior descending coronary artery. This was the main vessel on the left side of the heart, also known as the widow maker, that carried oxygenated blood to the left ventricle. Paul Switzer knew that if he was unable to get it open with the balloon, then a large part of the muscle of the left ventricle would die, and so probably, would Dick Cranston.

"That's a big occlusion you've got there, Dick. I'm going to take a shot at getting it open with the balloon right now."

"Do what you can do, Doctor."

The physician guided the small inflated balloon into the blocked artery, and when he had it in the proper position, he ordered it inflated. The vessel sprang immediately open, and Switzer let out a sigh of relief.

"I think we may have gotten it, Dick. I'm just going to back the catheter out slowly, and we'll see what happens."

As he withdrew the catheter, the artery appeared to stay open. He pulled out the entire length of the wire and held firm pressure to the insertion site.

"Am I going to be okay?" asked the mayor still sounding somewhat feeble.

"We'll keep our fingers crossed, Dick. And we'll have to keep a close eye on you for the next several hours. But I'm optimistic."

"Thanks, Doc." And with the immediate worry over, Dick Cranston drifted off to sleep.

"Get him to the unit immediately. And I want to know right away if his status changes."

The cardiologist went to the waiting room to speak with the crowd who had assembled there. He saw the idiot with the television camera right away. He realized that it was six o'clock in the morning and knew that his announcement would be just in time for the morning news. He also saw Talmadge Hyle standing in one corner of the room.

This was all he needed. He was about to give a press conference regarding the patient of a man who hated his guts. What a way to start the day.

* * *

Ike and Sharon Paponis arrived at the Portland International Airport at five a.m. having taken the red-eye back from Las Vegas. Ike had managed to get an hour of sleep on the plane, but he in no way felt rested. They took a cab home, and upon entering the residence, he automatically picked up the remote control and clicked on the television.

At first, he was stunned by what he saw. Paul Switzer was on the morning news flanked by Senator Hyle. What was that asshole doing on the morning news with Talmadge Hyle?

Ike hated Switzer with what he thought was good reason. Switzer was cocky. He thought he could cure everybody with that little balloon of his, and he had publicly demeaned Ike on several occasions. He had the audacity to suggest that perhaps some of the surgeon's procedures had not been medically necessary. Ike could have crushed his head and not thought twice about it. But what was this all about?

"Mayor Richard Cranston suffered a heart attack at his residence last evening. His condition was initially grave, but he has since been given blood thinning medication and has undergone successful angioplasty. While he is still considered to be in critical condition, doctors now say that he is stable."

Ike was livid. What was that idiot doing taking care of his private patient? Curt Pifer was supposed to have been taking his calls, and he should have been the one to treat Dick Cranston. He was barely even able to hear the words that Paul Switzer was babbling – something about the mechanics of a heart attack.

"Sharon, I've got to get to the hospital. The mayor is having a heart attack, and somehow, Paul Switzer has maneuvered his way into taking care of him.

Dick is my private patient. For God's sake, you can't even leave town for a couple of days, or something like this is what happens."

"I guess this is my first taste of what it's like to be a doctor's wife." She moved close and kissed him on the lips, but she could tell that his heart was already at the hospital.

Ike jumped into his Porsche and sped up Sam Jackson Boulevard toward the Health Sciences Medical Center. He knew that he would never be given a speeding ticket for racing to help the mayor, especially when the poor man had an idiot taking care of him.

He parked his car in the physician's lot, and he literally ran to the third floor, which housed the cardiac care unit. He went to the nurses' station and found Paul Switzer drinking coffee and joking with several of the nurses. To his amazement, he also saw Talmadge Hyle sitting there.

"I want to know what the hell is going on, and I want to know now!"

"Settle down, Ike. Settle down." Paul Switzer was on his feet but in a non-confrontive posture. But Ike could see that the blood had drained from the man's face.

"Don't you patronize me, you son of a bitch. Curt Pifer was taking my calls. Dick Cranston is my private patient. Dr. Pifer should have been taking care of him."

"Come on now, Ike." Talmadge Hyle had his best political smile on.

"Talmadge, this is none of your business."

"Now just a minute, Doctor."

"No, you wait just a minute. I don't give a shit if you're the damn president. This is between Dr. Switzer and myself."

"Ike, Ike, Ike, Dick asked for Dr. Switzer to care for him."

"That's right, Ike. Lord knows that I wouldn't have otherwise been near one of your patients."

The high-pitched squeal of the heart monitor alarm went off just as Paul Switzer was finishing his statement. All conversation ceased as everyone directed their attention to the monitor.

"That's Dick Cranston," said Switzer as he moved rapidly toward the bedside.

"I'll handle things from here, Dr. Switzer." Ike's tone left no room for argument.

"Ike, his heart rate is thirty-two, and he's having a bunch of PVCs. His ST segments are off the chart. I've got to get him back to the cath lab to get that vessel opened back up. He had an occluded left main that I was able to open with a balloon a couple of hours ago."

"If he's re-occluded after you've already ballooned him, then he needs to go to surgery."

"Ike, I don't think surgery is warranted here. I can drop a stent into that artery and fix him right up. Besides, he's not stable enough to go to surgery."

"That will be all, Dr. Switzer. This is my patient," said Ike dismissively.

"Whether you like it or not, Dr. Paponis, I have a professional liability here too."

Ike walked over to his colleague and grabbed him by the front of the shirt.

"Dr. Paponis, I hope you know that his constitutes assault, and I will file charges."

Ike drew back his right hand, and let go with a right hook to the cardiologist's chin sending the man sprawling to the floor. Ike then strode over to where he was laying, stood over him, and looked him in the eye.

"Now it's assault and battery. Go ahead and file charges. I don't give a shit."

Talmadge Hyle nearly ran to restrain Ike.

"Come on, Ike, you're way out of line here."

"Senator, get the hell out of my way. I've got a patient trying to die in there, and I don't give a rat's ass about what any of you have to say about what just happened here."

Ike then addressed his attention to the nurses who were standing and staring in shocked amazement.

"Alert the operating room that we'll be coming right over for an emergency bypass graft. One of you get in there and give my patient an amp of Atropine. NOW! Pack him up and get him to the OR. I'm going to go scrub."

Having given the order, and considering the graveness of the situation, automatism took over, and the CCU nurses began to swing into action. They quickly packaged their patient and transported him to the operating room.

Paul Switzer picked his stunned body off the floor and gently massaged his chin. He was alone except for the companionship of Senator Hyle.

"Don't mind Ike, Dr. Switzer, He's just strung a little tight. That's what makes him such a good surgeon."

"That's a matter of opinion, Senator. But I guess I might as well get out of here. There's nothing left for me to do."

"Don't worry about this, Doctor. It'll blow over."

"It will not blow over, Senator. But thanks anyway for the reassurance. I appreciate it." Paul Switzer was a good man, and he got out of the hospital as quickly as he could that morning.

The mayor was sedated and chemically paralyzed. The breathing tube was then placed for surgery, and he was attached to a ventilator. All of the intravenous lines were placed, and the chest was prepped with Betadine.

Shelley Grayson walked hurriedly toward the physicians' lounge to alert Dr. Paponis that his patient was ready for surgery.

"Dr. Paponis, we're ready for you." Ike didn't speak to her, and her many years of dealing with temperamental surgeons had taught her not to press the issue. She was quite familiar with this particular surgeon's bad temper, but he appeared to be in a particularly foul mood this morning. She had heard about the incident with Dr. Switzer in the CCU, and while she was appalled, she was not surprised.

Ike strode into the operating room suite. He had already placed his surgical cap and mask, and as soon as he walked into the room, a nurse stood waiting with his sterile gown. She pushed it up onto him, fastened the Velcro fasteners, and held the midline cinch as Paponis slowly turned in a circle to bring the strap around his abdomen. Having completed the move, the nurse tied the knot, securing the gown in place. She then held open the size eight sterile gloves, and Ike forcefully inserted first the right then the left hand into them.

"Doctor, I'm having a hard time keeping your patient's heart rate up. I think he could code at any minute," said Able Samson, the open-heart anesthesiologist. Ike just stared at the man for a long moment with eyes that bore holes into him.

"Of course he could code at any moment. He has a totally occluded left main. That's why we're here." More than what he had said, but the way in which he had said it, unnerved the operating room crew.

Ike quickly opened Dick Cranston's chest while the resident began to harvest a section of the saphenous vein. Ike was livid that Paul Switzer had treated his patient. That son of a bitch had been a thorn in his side for several years, but this definitely took the prize. Ike would not have let Paul Switzer treat his dog.

But more than anything else, Ike was upset with Richard Cranston. How could the mayor have seen fit to betray friendship, political support, and financial support, and allow that idiot to treat him. The mayor had made a bad call, and now Ike knew that he would face all sorts of grief for having punched Switzer in the face.

Ike began his search for the occluded portion of the vessel. It wasn't hard to find. The whole damn thing was diseased. The team went on bypass, and Ike began to complete the graft. But he could not control his rage. Dick Cranston had betrayed him. It was true that he had never held the mayor in very high regard, but Cranston didn't know that. As far as the politician knew, Ike Paponis was his best buddy.

Very subtly, Ike used his scalpel to make a small incision into the lateral surface of the patient's left ventricle. He knew that a small aneurysm would now form on the mayor's heart within weeks. He was certain that the man would be dead within a month. He knew that these were rugged consequences for the mayor's breech of loyalty, but there was a bottom line. Cranston had screwed up.

Ike attempted to close his patient fast enough to conceal his deed, but he was not fast enough. Shelley Grayson was nearly in a state of shock. The surgeon had to nearly yell at her to get the pack of suture that he needed to close the tissue. She had been busy trying to assimilate and catalogue everything that she had seen. One thing she knew for sure – Ike Paponis was way out of control.

CHAPTER 12

Miguel Dominguez sat with his back propped up against a tree as he cleaned his M16A1 assault rifle. The weapon had been given to him courtesy of the United States Government. Dominguez was the leader of a group of outlaw bandits who involved themselves in everything from gun running to the illegal exportation of gold and silver.

Dominguez, and virtually every member of his squad, had been members of the Nicaraguan Resistance, or Contra effort, as it had been popularly known. Now that the Sandinistas, the bloody Communistas, had been defeated, more politically than militarily, Dominguez and his men had been warriors without a battle to fight.

He had ridden through the streets of Managua in triumph when free elections had replaced the Communist rule of Daniel Ortega and his ruthless junta. La Prense, the most widely read newspaper publication in the country, was once again a free press and no longer just a mouthpiece for Ortega.

In many ways, Dominguez and his men were heroes. They had helped to liberate their homeland, and many of their comrades had died in the process. They were indeed heroes, but their country was still racked by unemployment, poverty, and political turmoil. The few jobs that were available paid only the salary of a peasant.

Miguel had done the only thing that he had known how to do – survive. He was a highly-experienced jungle warrior, and despite the woes of a country with a poorly managed economy, there were still great riches to be had by men who were still able to use a little old-fashioned ingenuity. Today, Dominguez had large stores of cash and precious metals. He had also done many favors for powerful men in his country, and soon he would be able to retire as a powerful man himself.

He and his men were camped near the Boca River, just north of Mt. Kilambe and south of the city of Bana. As usual, they were in hiding. They were in hiding, not from the squads of government forces, but from assassins of the Medellin drug cartel of Colombia.

During the past month, Dominquez and his men had confiscated four plane loads of cocaine from the Colombians. The guerrilla leader hated drug use. He thought of it as a curse on the physical vessel of the spirit that had been given by God. But the drug trade would continue with or without him, and Miguel Dominguez had a very special agenda in mind for his future. It was merely a minor obstacle that the agenda would require a great deal of money.

Dominguez and his men still had access to weapons and ammunition that had been supplied to them by the Americans during the Nicaraguan civil war. Many of these caches were still kept in Honduras very near to the northern border of Nicaragua, and that is why his men were camped in this area. Should they be attacked by the Colombians, they would have ready access to their weapons.

"Jorge, come and sit with me for a while. We must talk." Miguel was calling his younger lieutenant to join him.

Jorge Delgado was a strapping young lad who could easily have graced the cover of Soldier of Fortune Magazine. His jet-black hair was shoulder length and pulled into a ponytail. He wore the black and green jungle boots of an American soldier in a tropical climate, as well as camouflage fatigue pants. Even in the relative security of the encampment, he still wore two bandoleers of seven point six two ball ammunition for his M60 machine gun, crisscrossed over his head and shoulders. He wore no shirt beneath them, and his darkly pigmented skin glistened with sweat. The younger man moved toward Dominguez with the deference that is usually granted to good leadership.

"What would you like to talk about, esse?" he asked as he slumped onto the ground next to his comrade.

"Jorge, we need to make arrangements to transport the drugs out of the country where we can sell them. Of course, the obvious destination is America, but all of this is new to me, and our connections are limited." Miguel had been looking toward his rifle as he spoke. He had removed the cotter pin from the bolt assembly, removed the rear bolt extractor, and then tapped free the firing pin. The long piece of silver metal made a tinkling sound when it struck the inside of the bolt, as it fell free.

"Miguel, we need to think of those who were with us during the conflict. Many of them were CIA, but there were others who were nothing more than mercenaries looking to make a fast dollar. I think that we could do business with one of those men."

"This is the same as what I have been thinking, Jorge. Do you know of any of those men who are still in our country?" asked Miguel as he continued to scrub the burnt carbon from his weapon.

"I have heard that Ben Harris is living in an old hangar at the Bonanza airfield. I have been told that he flies an old Beechcraft into the jungle for several mining companies. He must be able to shave some gold and silver off for himself or he would no longer be here."

"That is true. Most of the Americans who are still here are thieves of one sort or another."

"Ha! And now we are thieves ourselves." Delgado's response had been a little too lighthearted for his commander who was quick with a rebuke.

"Taking drugs from the fornicating Colombians is not theft, Jorge. Maybe if we capture enough of their planes and their murderous cargoes, then they will find another country in which to refuel. I don't want their stinking drugs and drug money in our country."

"You are right, Miguel. I was only laughing about our current situation. We have gone from Freedom Fighters to drug runners. I would have thought the results of our patriotism would have been far different. Maybe we should even just destroy the cocaine."

"You are probably right, Jorge. I have never seen any good come from these things. But the lure of the drug money is strong. What we have seized from the Colombians will bring us many millions of American dollars – enough Cordobas for all of us to retire to large estates with grand haciendas."

"Maybe we should wait, Miguel."

"No. The Colombians will be searching for their product. I do not fear them, but if we are able to do this thing, then we should do it quickly."

"Perhaps you are right. The sooner that we are free of the drugs, the sooner we can relax, eh, Miguel?"

Miguel Dominguez had never feared any man. But, at forty-six years of age, he had begun to tire of his struggle. Despite the rigid regimen of activity, he had still begun to put on weight around the middle. The bullet that he had taken to his right knee several years earlier had been repaired in crude surgical fashion and had left him with a pronounced limp. He was beginning to learn what other wise men of his age had come to realize – a man's most valuable weapon is his mind.

The fire still raged in his own eyes. He had been fiercely dedicated to the fight for freedom, and he was eager for his countrymen to taste the fruits of prosperity. But the Sandinistas had so decimated the economy, and will of the people, that the road back would be a long one.

"To relax is a dream of mine, Jorge. A dream that still seems so far away." Miguel stopped cleaning his rifle as he pondered his last statement. The older man's desire was so intense that Jorge could almost feel it.

"You and Emilio go to Bonanza this afternoon. Find Ben Harris for me. If he is amenable, bring him here to me."

"Do you wish us to fly, Miguel? Dominguez's greatest treasure was a helicopter that had been given to him by U. S. Soldiers. Only Miguel and Jorge were trained to fly it.

"No, if we were to take the helicopter into the sky now, word would spread through the countryside like wildfire. The Colombians would find us very quickly, and we would face the risk of losing our fortunes. That, my friend, is a risk that I would rather not take."

"You are right. We will take a Jeep."

"Thank you, my friend. And remember, no word of our mission to Mr. Ben Harris until he is brought here to me."

"No worry. After all of these years together, I know how you think."

Miguel rapidly assembled his now immaculate rifle, and used it to raise himself from the moist ground. Delgado and Emilio Vega were anxious to leave the encampment. The inactivity of the past several days, coupled with their fear of being discovered by the Colombians, had caused them to become a bit stir crazy. They loaded up their gear and began the trip to Bonanza. If they were lucky, there would be time to spend with a woman.

The road to Bonanza was not unlike any other dirt road through the mountains of Central America. Farmers could be seen lazily tending their crops or animals on the distant hillsides. The hills and meadows were a lush green, but the sun was oppressively hot.

Jorge and Emilio felt immediately happy as they drove toward the airfield at Bonanza. Even though they were no longer engaged in a rigid military regimen, they were still responsible to their leader, Miguel Dominguez, and this temporary escape had made them almost giddy.

Both men knew Ben Harris. They also knew, that if crossed, Ben Harris was a man to be feared. Generally, though, he was a congenial sort whose experience and expertise had been invaluable in the war against the Sandinistas.

As the sun began to set in the western sky, Emilio and Jorge found themselves on the runway at the Bonanza airfield. Far away from the newer buildings, that represented the twentieth century, there was a very old and disheveled hangar that was surrounded by several Quonset huts. The two men knew that this is where they would find Ben Harris.

Harris had been with the CIA during the Viet Nam Conflict, and he had been an effective counter-insurgence expert. He spoke five different languages, and the darkly pigmented skin allowed him to feel at home in any number of Third World countries. He had been drummed out of the CIA in the mid-eighties, during a time when the agency had been going to great lengths to clean up its image.

Now, Harris was a consultant. That was simply a euphemism that stated, that whenever there was some particularly abhorrent mission to complete, Ben Harris was the man for the job. For now, however, the ex-agent was content to operate his charter flight service into the jungle. He didn't ask many questions of his clients, and they didn't offer him much information, either. It was a cash for services operation. Thank you very much.

Ben had not had a flight in days, and he had been drunk for a like amount of time. He was expecting a client tomorrow for a flight into the Cordillera Isabelia, northeast of San Pedro Del Norte. He had flown the guy in before, a doctor from the states who owned, and was developing a gold mine. Ben had been amazed at the amount of money that the guy had soaked into the place, and as of yet, there had been no strike.

As he sat at the cheap wooden table, drinking a warm bottle of beer, he heard a knock at the door.

"Señor Harris, are you there?" Ben had picked up on the Spanish accent, and he answered the men in their native tongue. He figured that it was just a couple of the vagrants who hung out around the airfield and frequently hit him up for booze or money.

"Get the hell out of here. Leave me alone."

"Señor Harris, it is Vega and Delgado. We bring you a message from Miguel Dominguez." The pilot jumped to his feet and opened the door. Perhaps the visit held the hope of work, excitement, something…

He embraced the two Nicaraguan Freedom Fighters as soon as he had opened the door. "Jorge, Emilio. My brothers, how are you? Come in. Have a drink."

These three men had shared the best and the worst of what it is to be a warrior. They had lain in wait to spring ambushes on the hated Sandinistas. They had fired door-mounted machine guns from Miguel Dominguez's helicopter. They had triumphed in firefights, and they had held their slain brothers as the blood had flown from their bodies. Yes, soldiers, soldiers of any battle, shared bonds that could not be replicated in any other profession.

"So, my friends, what can I do for you?"

"Miguel has asked us to bring you to him."

"What does Miguel have in mind for me?"

"We do not know, my friend. Can you come with us tonight?"

"I am afraid that I have to fly into the jungle tomorrow. Perhaps we could go tomorrow night." Jorge and Emilio seemed pleased with the answer. They would have twenty-four hours in the city to spend some of their money.

"Okay, my friend. We will call for you at this time tomorrow."

"Finish your drinks. I have nowhere to go tonight."

"We are anxious to go into the city, Ben. I'm sure you understand. We have been in the jungle for too long."

"I understand completely. I'll see you tomorrow. Don't get arrested in the meantime."

The two men set out for Bonanza, and Ben finished his beer and went to bed. As he lay there, he contemplated what his friend, Miguel Dominguez, could possible have for him to do. Oh well, he probably just needed his airplane for one thing or another. At any rate, it could wait for tomorrow. Nearly anything could wait until tomorrow.

CHAPTER 13

The physician from Oregon arrived just as the sun was rising in the eastern sky. He knocked on the door of the Quonset hut and found a very hung over Ben Harris struggling to start his day.

The American physician had no idea of the background of the pilot who would be flying him to his gold mine. If he had known, while he may not have been frightened, he would most definitely have been concerned. The two men had not conversed much on previous flights into the jungle, and there was really no reason to expect that there would be a change on this particular trip.

Ben Harris was a cool customer. He never really just came out and talked about his history, but if you were to look into his eyes, you would know that his history had been substantial. He was the kind of man who bore the burden of every questionable act he had ever committed within his eyes.

"Mr. Harris, did you forget that I had scheduled your services for today?"

"Yeah, yeah, I remembered. Give me a few minutes to drink a cup of coffee, and I'll be right with you. Do you want some?" The physician surveyed the less than tidy conditions within the Quonset hut and opted not to accept the pilot's offer.

"No thank you, Ben." The bright sun shown through the open door, and the luminescence caused Ben Harris to squint and to use his forearm to protect his eyes from the brilliant but unwanted light.

"Hey, shut the darn door, will you?"

"Oh, certainly. I'm sorry," said the doctor who left the door open for several more tortuous seconds.

Ben Harris finished his coffee and filled his thermos. He didn't care if his client was wealthy, respected, or powerful. He was hung over, and he didn't feel like talking. He slowly sauntered out to the twin-engine Beechcraft that he had fueled the night before, climbed in through the door, and then slid into his seat in the cockpit.

The pilot started the engines, one at a time, and allowed the revolutions per minute to increase gradually as the engines began to warm up. He had not invited his passenger aboard, but had merely expected the man to follow him into the cockpit – which he did.

Harris checked his instruments and checked to make sure that his flaps and brakes were in working order. Only then did he begin to taxi down the runway in preparation for take off. Once he had reached the end of the runway, he applied the brakes and then revved the engines to near full power. Once the propellers were spinning fast enough to shake the aircraft about, Harris released the brakes, and the craft sprung forward with a lurch.

Soon they were airborne, and the lush green earth pulled rapidly away from them. Within minutes, the rugged mountains of the Cordillera Isabelia rose up beneath them. They were en route to the Diaz Brother's Mining Company near to the town of San Pedro Del Norte.

Ben had taken the physician to the same destination several times before, but he still didn't know the man's name. What the passenger was unaware of, however, was that Harris had mixed a goodly amount of bourbon with the coffee in his thermos, and after several cups, he wasn't feeling any pain.

"So where are you from, Doctor?"

"Up north. Why do you ask?"

"I make it a habit of knowing who it is that I am flying and for what purpose."

"Well, there's no need to worry about me, Mr. Harris. I'm only here to visit my gold mine."

"That's what you tell me. Just where up north are you from, Doctor?"

"Oregon." The physician acted as if he had just given away a national secret and seemed disgusted with the pilot for having asked the question.

"You know, Doctor, this is the fourth time that I've flown you down here to San Pedro Del Norte, and I don't even know your name."

"That's not something that you really need to know, Mr. Harris."

"This is my livelihood, Doctor. If I feel that I need to know your name, then you have got to understand that I've got my reasons."

"Well, Mr. Harris, if I choose not to tell you my name, then you will have to understand that I've got my reasons as well." The two men were nearly shouting at each other over the roar of the engines.

"Listen here, Doctor. Your ass doesn't mean a damn thing to me. Look out the window. You're flying over the Central American jungle. I could kick your butt out of this plane and you re-enter the food chain from the bottom end. Why don't you just tell me your name?"

"I've got my reasons."

Ben Harris pushed forward on his steering wheel, and almost immediately, the nose of the Beech pointed toward the ground below. He was very careful not to lose control of the craft and drift into a spin, but the physician didn't know that the pilot next to him was anything but crazy.

"Paponis! My name is Ike Paponis!" Ben Harris was laughing like a wild man.

"What was that, Doctor? I can't hear you." Ike began to look frightened. He had no reason to believe that this maniac wasn't about to crash his plane onto the hillside below. That was how people died, you know, freak accidents, natural processes, and lunatics flying airplanes.

Ben Harris retracted the steering wheel and slid the Beech out of its dive. He made a hard, banking, right turn very close to the ground. With the perfect look of calmness on his face, he turned and smiled at Ike Paponis.

"So, Dr. Paponis, how long will you need to be staying in San Pedro Del Norte this time?"

Ike was still struggling to regain his composure. He was upset that he had allowed the pilot to unnerve him as he had.

"Two days, I think. Maybe three."

"Then I'll be back at noon in three days."

"I think that two days will probably do it, Mr. Harris."

"If I come back in two days, then you'll leave in two days. Or you won't leave at all. I have no intention of waiting around for twenty-four hours for you to be ready to leave."

"Mr. Harris, if I'm delayed then I'll be happy to make it worth your while. Just be here in two days."

The pilot expertly maneuvered the plane to a very low altitude and made two passes over the Diaz Brother's Mining Company. He was immediately taken by all of the expensive heavy machinery that he saw within close proximity to the mine. Not only was there a lot of it, but all of it was brand new. He could not begin to assess the value of all of what he saw, but the physician from up north had obviously sunk a great deal of money into this place.

He spotted the dirt airfield on the northwest corner of the property and gently set the Beechcraft down. As he taxied the plane to a controlled stop, a military-looking Jeep came to a stop very close to the craft. A Spanish man was driving the vehicle, and he eagerly jumped out of the driver's seat and ran over to help the physician with his luggage.

"Dr. Paponis, it is good to see you." The English was heavily accented but understandable.

"Hello, Ernesto." The two men carried Ike's two suitcases away from the plane rapidly, and the physician turned and called back to the pilot.

"Two days, Mr. Harris." Ben just nodded his head, smiled, and revved the plane's engines. In what seemed to be no time at all, he was gone.

Jorge Delgado and Emilio Vega had experienced the kind of night that soldiers dream of. They had gotten drunk, had gotten laid, and had not been arrested or ripped off. Now they were laying in the shaded area next to the Jeep awaiting the arrival of Ben Harris. Despite their good fortune of the preceding night, they were both extremely hung over, and the heat of the sun rising even higher in the sky was adding to their already substantial discomfort.

They could hear the roar of the plane's engines before they could see it, and both men simultaneously raised their heads to scan the horizon.

Ben landed the Beechcraft on the runway of the airfield and taxied over to where the hot tin roof of his weather-beaten hangar baked in the late afternoon sun. He could easily see his two friends as they reached up to hold their hats on against the prop blast of the plane's engines.

The two Nicaraguans jumped to their feet and raced over to the hangar to pull the doors open so Harris could park his plane inside. After doing so, he shut down his engines and climbed out of the aircraft.

"Let's get a beer and go see Miguel." Ben's clothing was drenched with sweat, but without grabbing so much as a change of clothing, he jumped into the elevated rear seat of the Jeep. Emilio then sped down the runway toward the encampment of Miguel Dominguez and his men.

Miguel was growing increasingly impatient. It had been nearly twenty-four hours since he had dispatched his two men to Bonanza to retrieve Ben Harris. Dominguez was not a man who was prone to being nervous, but he was also not a man who was accustomed to being involved in the drug trade. To be killed in a battle while trying to liberate his countrymen would be a noteworthy end to his life, but to rot in prison until his emaciated body would succumb to one terminal illness or another would be a disgrace that he could not bear.

The Jeep rolled into the encampment and Miguel quickly realized that the driver and passenger were not Jorge and Emilio. The two men looked like rogues – poorly dressed and unkempt. But the weapons that they carried, U. S. Issue M16 assault rifles, were clean and well oiled.

The two men, obviously Colombians, got out of the Jeep and strolled into the midst of Miguel and his men.

"We have lost some valuable items, and we wonder if you know anything about them." The larger of the two men was speaking like a bully even though the two were clearly out- numbered.

"And what sort of items might you be referring to, my friend?" asked Miguel in his most patronizing manner.

"Airplanes," replied the larger Columbian.

"Did the airplanes have any cargo, or did you just lose the planes?"

"We did not lose the airplanes, Señor. They were destroyed by bandits. Do you know who would want to do such a thing?"

"I cannot even imagine such a thing. Who would purposefully destroy an empty aircraft that might be used more beneficially for some other purpose?" Miguel was becoming amused by the exchange, but clearly the visitors were not.

"I would not advise you to play games with us, Señor. There are many others of us who would gladly kill you even if you are not responsible for our loss."

"Those are brave words for a man who is as helpless as you are, my friend."

"Go ahead and kill us. That would only bring my associates swarming down on top of you. They know exactly where we are, and as I told you, they would not hesitate to kill you."

Miguel Dominguez, with his pronounced limp, walked directly up to and stood face-to-face with the larger of the two Colombians. The eyes of the experienced soldier bored holes into the younger and obviously weaker man.

"You are lying, Señor. Nobody knows that you are here, and nobody even cares. We could kill you now and burn your bodies, and there is no one who would be the wiser."

Miguel's speech had been slow and deliberate. With one short statement, he had completely destroyed the composure of the intruder who looked like he was about to urinate in his pants. The younger of the two men, however, remained defiant or at least that was his bluff. He raised his weapon with the barrel over his shoulder to a position that would allow him to use the butt of the weapon to strike Miguel Dominguez in the head.

Before he could get the weapon fully retracted, however, a machete came from behind him and removed his head neatly from his shoulders. The head fell to the ground and rolled to a stop at the feet of his partner. Blood spurted from the exposed carotid arteries of the decapitated man, and the headless body stood there for several long seconds before it realized that it was dead and fell to the ground.

In a move of desperation, the other Columbian started to raise his rifle. He too, was parted from his head. Miguel was quite anxious now, because despite his tough talk, he knew that what the strangers had told him was true. There would surely be others who would come, and they would probably be here soon – at least in a matter of days.

"Bury the bodies, but do it far from the camp. Camouflage the graves. From now on, we will have a twenty-four-hour guard schedule. I am sorry, gentlemen, but I am afraid that we may be involved in another war. And I am also afraid that this enemy may be far more ruthless."

The Jeep containing Jorge, Ben, and Emilio pulled rapidly up to the cluster of men.

"What the hell happened here?" asked Ben Harris as he jumped from the vehicle prior to it coming to a complete stop.

"This is why I wanted to see you, my friend. We must talk."

Miguel's men set rapidly about disposing of the bodies, and Ben and the elder rebel ambled toward a fire away from where the carnage lay.

"Ben Harris, first of all let me thank you for coming."

"It is nothing for an old friend, Miguel."

"You say that now, but after you hear why I have asked you to come, you may not be so sure."

"What is it, my friend?"

"Ben, I am sure that the drug trade is no secret to you. I am also sure that you are aware that the Columbian cartels use our land to refuel their planes before going to the United States."

"Yes, Miguel, go on."

"I hate the drug trade, Ben. But I hate the Colombians more. I hate that they are making billions of dollars and that they are using our land for their perversions. I hate that now that our country is free, there are no jobs and no money." Miguel paused and stared at the ground as if he were searching for words. Ben knew that the world was weighing heavily on his friend's shoulders.

"What is it that you are trying to tell me, Miguel?"

"I have confiscated four plane loads of cocaine from the Colombians."

"You did what?" Ben was incredulous.

"I have done what I have said. I have confiscated four plane loads of cocaine with several tons of the powder. At first, I considered destroying it. But me destroying these drugs would do nothing to halt the flow. I am a poor man, Ben. Here I have a chance to make my fortune, and if I can do it, I will."

"What did you have in mind, Miguel?" Ben's expression was dead serious.

"Ben, I didn't know if you would be inclined to help me. One deal and we can have all of the money that we will ever need. If your morality will not allow you to help me, then I will understand. I only hope that you will not expose me to the authorities."

"Miguel, my conscience will not prevent me from doing this. Unfortunately, I am not quite sure of how to go about it. I have no connections in the underworld, and I would have no idea of how to dispose of such a large quantity of the drug. Let me see what I can do. This isn't something that can be done too quickly. One word to the wrong person, and we will all be spending the rest of our lives in prison. You know of my history with the CIA. I don't doubt that movement of this quantity of drugs into the United States could be considered treason for me. With the new drug laws, I could even get the death penalty. No, I must move very carefully indeed."

"I appreciate the sensitivity of your situation Ben, but my time is limited. Those two men, whose bodies you saw when you drove up, were Colombians. I am sure that there will be more. My soldiers are good fighters, and we have effective weapons, but we are still in danger.

"Let me see what I can do, Miguel. I'll be back in touch with you in a day or so. Be careful in the meantime."

Ben jumped into the Jeep with Jorge and began the drive back to Bonanza. Thoughts were coursing through his brain at breakneck speed. He didn't have the slightest idea of how he was going to engineer a drug deal of this magnitude without getting caught. He knew that the stakes were enormous. To succeed in this endeavor would insure wealth beyond his wildest expectations. To fail would undoubtedly bring his destruction.

Ben and Jorge stopped at a bar in Bonanza. A few drinks, he knew, would help him put things into perspective. He had told his friend, a dear and trusted friend, that he would do whatever he could to find a solution to his problem. But where did he begin?

"That was quite a reception that we got today, eh Señor?"

"I thought that we were back in the war, Jorge. It was nice to see that our comrades are as ruthless as ever. The stinking Colombians, anyway... Who the hell do they think the are?"

"I know two of them who aren't doing much thinking, eh Ben Harris?"

There was a hearty round of laughter regarding the fates of the recently deceased men. But despite the laughter, which most probably was a defense mechanism, there was real concern in the hearts of both men. Take something of this magnitude lightly, and you would most assuredly end up a dead man yourself.

They drank heavily, and with each bottle of beer and shot of liquor, their thoughts grew further from the business at hand. They talked of conquests – victories in battles and successes with women. An enemy already conquered made for better conversation than did future potential skirmishes when one was drinking. Both men knew that pride precedes the downfall, and neither was willing to boast of destroying an enemy who had not yet been engaged in battle.

Both Ben and Jorge slept fitfully in the pilot's home at the airfield, and once again, the rising sun brought headaches and nausea for the two men. Jorge bid his friend farewell, and Ben then fueled the Beechcraft for his return flight to San Pedro Del Norte and the Diaz Brother's Mining Company.

Rarely did Ben fly when he was impaired by alcohol, but today would have to be the exception. A hangover like this one demanded some hair of the dog, and when the pilot boarded the plane, he did so with twelve bottles of beer in his portable cooler.

The roar of the engines made his head pound as he revved them just prior to taking off down the runway. Soon he was airborne, and only then did he open his first bottle. The pattern of his flight was somewhat less steady than usual, but he knew that after he had choked down a couple of beers, he would rectify that problem.

Ben loved these times more than any others. They allowed him to taste freedom more fully than any other activity. He was totally alone and flying over the rugged mountains and jungles of central Nicaragua. He should in no way have been drinking beer while flying, but even in the event of a disaster, he would hurt no one but himself.

A short time after crossing the Cordillera Isabelia, Ben was tilting his wing and looking down toward the area surrounding the Diaz Brother's Mining Company. He could see the forms of several men outside the entrance to the mine, and he tipped his wings first to the right and then to the left as the men below waved to him.

The pilot landed the Beech on the rocky runway with a few more bounces than were usual for him. He remained under control, however, and taxied over to where the men were standing. He could see the man that he had come to know as Ike Paponis sitting on a rock next to the entrance to the gold mine. Ike looked to be nursing a bottle of liquor.

Ben shut down the engines to the Beechcraft, popped open the door, and climbed out onto the wing. He had an unopened beer in each hand as he jumped to the ground and strolled over to where Ike was sitting.

"You're early," said the doctor without much emotion.

"I had nothing much else to do. Is it a problem?"

"No. It'll actually be good to have someone here who speaks English. You're not in any rush to go back, are you?"

"Well, I don't have to go back today if that's what you're asking. But I do have a commitment for late tomorrow or early the next day." Ben did not really relish the prospect of spending the next twenty-four hours here with the cocky heart surgeon, but the man was a paying customer, and he really had nowhere else to go right now anyway.

"I'm in a drinking mood today, Ben. I could sure use some company. There's a waterfall a short distance from here. Let's pack up some booze and head up there, if you don't mind."

"Lead the way, Doctor."

The pilot had noticed that the physician's speech was a little slurred and also that the man seemed to be a bit despondent. He had never really cared much for Paponis on the flights to and from San Pedro Del Norte, but there was something different about him today. He wasn't his usual arrogant self. Ike had always been so damned cocky – so hard to reach. He had actually acted as if he were too good to waste his breath talking to the pilot.

If the physician had known Ben's history, then perhaps, he would have shown some respect for the pilot. Ben had distinguished himself with the CIA in Viet Nam, where he had honed his counter-insurgence skills to a fine art. There had been other missions to Angola, and then the Middle East, and finally to Nicaragua. He had been an American hero, but there would never be any recognition. True patriotism, however, did not require accolades.

The truth of the matter was that Ben had enjoyed being a spy. He had also enjoyed meddling in the political affairs of other governments. He had done very well at his varying missions, primarily because he liked to kill, without having to face the traditional legalities associated with the act.

But the U. S. Government and the CIA along with it, had changed drastically in recent years. In short, Ben had outlived his usefulness. There was no longer much call for his talents, and he had recognized the changes as they had come along. He had not resented the altered methods of his government. He had always known that one day developing civilizations would find ways to stop killing each other. But all of these events had left him without much direction in his life. He had been flying these shuttle missions into the jungle for nearly a year and a half, and his contacts with the Agency had dwindled to nearly nothing. Ben liked his freedom, but the truth was that he was probably drinking himself to death, and he had nothing to bank his future on.

Perhaps this deal with his friend, Miguel, was something that he really needed to pursue. It was going to be tricky, and the degree of difficulty would only be exacerbated by the speed with which the transaction would need to be completed. He would have to think long and hard, but the benefits of a successful completion were obvious – wealth great enough for a lifetime… for several lifetimes.

The surgeon and the pilot began to slowly follow the trail that wound up through the lush green foliage of the hillside. The vegetation on either side of the trail was dense, but the path itself was relatively worn and easily passable. Ben was winded after only several hundred meters of climbing, and even Ike, who was well conditioned, felt the strain of the climb.

After nearly a half hour ascent, the men's clothes were drenched with sweat and both were nearly sober. After making a sharp turn to the left, Ben could hear the roar of a waterfall. Almost instinctively the men quickened their pace. They were not unlike other men – the lure of a waterfall was nearly undeniable.

The water rushed off of the rock ledge with great force and fell one hundred and fifty feet to the crystal clear pool below. Wild flowers, trees, and plants with large green leaves of differing hues, pushed all the way to the edge of the pool. The mist from the waterfall created the sensation of warm humidified air, and the two men followed the trail all the way to the under ledge where they could stay dry and yet still watch the water as it fell only several feet to their front.

They removed their backpacks and slumped onto the moss-covered rocks. Ben was quick to open his pack, and he withdrew two beers which he quickly opened. He handed one to the grateful cardiac surgeon, and both the hikers greedily swilled the entire contents of the bottles. Paponis then withdrew the new bottle of Jim Beam that he had carried along with them. He opened it and offered it to Ben Harris who took a long draw of the liquor.

"You know, sometimes I think I should just give up all of the crap up north and move down here." Ike had spoken just prior to chugging down a slug of the whiskey.

"It's not all that it's cracked up to be, Doctor. I've been down here for a couple of years now, and I'm really kind of bored. I like the freedom, but I'm not really getting anywhere."

Ben took out his pack of cigarettes and offered one to Ike, who accepted it. He liked to smoke when he was drinking, and the two men were definitely drinking. They passed the bourbon back and forth, chased their shots with swallows of beer, and in no time, half of the bottle of whiskey was gone.

Alcohol is a truth serum, and before long, the two men were sharing secrets that they never would have divulged under other circumstances. There was something about the tranquility of the setting, the numbing sensation of the alcohol, and both men's need to have someone to share their darker secrets with. These were unlikely allies, but then life sometimes takes strange turns.

"You know, Ben, sometimes I hate myself. From the very beginning, I have been motivated by money. I always wanted to be rich. I wanted to have nice things, But the whole thing just kind of snowballed on me."

"Sooner or later you realize that money doesn't mean anything, Doc."

"Don't you think that it's about time you started calling me Ike? After that stunt you pulled in your airplane. You wouldn't have crashed it, would you? You're not that crazy, are you?"

"I guess you'll just have to wonder about that, Ike. I probably don't even know myself. I was pretty ticked off, and some strange stuff happens when I get ticked off."

"Just who are you anyway, Ben? What brought you to Nicaragua in the first place?"

Ben had just about enough alcohol to tell the truth.

"What I tell you has to be kept in absolute confidence. If you ever tell anyone, I'll only deny it, anyway." He paused for a long moment and stared directly into Ike's eyes. "I know that you've probably heard this from drunk people before, but I'm an ex-CIA agent. That's why I'm here. I was assisting the Contras in their fight against the Sandinistas, and I just kind of stayed on after the war was over." The intensity and the depth of Ben's stare told the heart surgeon that what the pilot was telling him was the honest truth.

"What made you give up on the CIA? Or have you given up on them?"

"Probably a better question would be: what made them give up on me? I guess the bottom line is that I'm a dinosaur – a dying breed. The agency just doesn't have much use for what I do any more."

"What is it that you do? Or should I say, what is it that you used to do?"

"I kill, Ike. And I'm very good at it. When I wasn't killing, I was planning it. And when I wasn't planning it, I was teaching somebody else how to do it."

The matter-of-fact way that Ben had described his former occupation sent chills through the cardiac surgeon's spine. Ike had also killed, although not as directly as had Ben, but to hear Ben talk about it as if it were just another day at the office was frightening.

"What you were doing was in the service of your country."

"To say that killing rebel factions in third-world countries was in the service of my country is stretching it a little bit, don't you think?"

"Well, you were just following the orders of your government, weren't you?"

"Ike, I enjoyed the killing. And what is worse is that there really wasn't much challenge to it. Most of my victims were nowhere close to being in my league. It was more like a turkey shoot on a Sunday afternoon. Sure, the United States had political interests in these countries, but when it comes to assassinations and what not, the will of a government ends up being the will of just a few powerful men. In a powerful democracy, the names, faces, and ideologies change with a predictable frequency. People like me merely serve at the will and the pleasure of whomever happens to be calling the shots at any given time. Who's to say that the power brokers of any given moment are more moral, that their causes are any more just, than the targets that they choose." The words were flowing from Ben Harris, but his spirit seemed to be drawing even more inward. This was a man in conflict, a man who faced a continual internal struggle to come to grips with some of the deeds that he had perpetrated in his professional life.

"What do you mean when you say that you enjoyed the killing?" asked Ike. He had been listening intently and was attempting to make correlative links to events that had occurred in his own life.

"I don't know, Ike. I think it's some kind of adrenalin rush or something. Maybe it's the sense of power that I feel. To take a life that has the same value, the same worth, that my life has, means that in some way I have conquered life itself."

"That's a pretty weird way to look at things, Ben, but in an obtuse sort of way, I think that I understand what you're saying. I get the same thrill from doing open heart surgery. When I hold a human heart in my hand, that has been stilled by the drugs that I have injected, and knowing that my patient's life depends on my skill as a surgeon, I get a power rush myself."

"I'll bet you do." Ben's stare was distant. It was almost as if he were pondering what it would be like to play the role that the doctor had just described.

"I don't know if this will make you feel any better, Ben, but I have killed before, too." The alcohol was continuing to work its magic, and the more secret aspects of both men's lives continued to unravel.

"Oh? Where did you serve?" Ben presumed that Ike had been a soldier when he was younger and that he had been involved in a military conflict.

"That's not what I was implying. I was never in the service." As soon as he had made the remarks, a strange sense of remorse began to flow through him. It was not remorse at having committed the acts that he had perpetrated, but rather he was distressed that he had begun to share his secrets – secrets that he had always intended to keep to himself. But he had already crossed the line, and he was sure that he would soon be divulging the entire truth to the pilot.

"Well, if you were never in the service, then what do you mean when you say that you've killed before? Did you screw up an operation and now you're just blaming yourself to the point where your guilt has you convinced that you are responsible for the deaths?"

And then the big leap... "I intentionally botched a couple of procedures, and the people died – just as I knew that they would."

Now it was Ben's turn to be appalled. Sure, he had killed, but all of those deaths had been without pretense. He had merely been doing what had been expected of him. It was quite another matter for a physician, a man sworn to the healing arts, to make an admission such as the one he had just heard.

"What would make you do something like that? Were these people enemies of yours? But why would an enemy let you do open heart surgery on them?" The pilot's mind was racing, trying to find some sort of valid rationalization for what he was hearing – for what he thought he was hearing.

"It was all about what I was telling you before. It was about the quest for the almighty dollar, at least that's how it all started. You see, I've been involved in a private business venture with a couple of friends. We own a nationwide chain of private laboratories, and we got into financial trouble. One of my partners is a probate attorney who arranges wills for some of the wealthiest and most powerful men in the city where I live. I, along with my partners, also control and administrate a charitable foundation that is funded by a number of my partner's clients. It just so happens that, over the years, a number of these individuals have also been patients of mine. When we got into financial trouble, and I mean serious financial trouble, the temptation to orchestrate the premature demise of some of these people became a little too much to resist."

115

"So, let me get this straight. Your lawyer buddy got these guys to donate their fortunes to this charitable foundation, and then you waxed them in the operating room, collected their money, and used it for your own purposes." A small but incredulous smile began to form on Ben's face as he began to understand the overall concept.

"Well, Ben, it was a little more complex than that, but I guess that's a pretty good assessment of the situation."

"What I don't understand is how come you didn't get caught. I mean, you weren't the only one in the operating room, were you? There had to be nurses and an anesthesiologist. Didn't they notice what was going on? And what about the coroner? Didn't somebody do autopsies on these people?"

"Now it was Ike's turn to smile. "The county medical examiner is also one of my partners. He didn't like what I did, but he found a way to live with it. He's kind of a gutless guy, and he's really fond of his creature comforts. As far as the nurses go, what I did wasn't overt. A little snip here, a missed stitch there. These people didn't die for weeks or months after their operations. Nobody suspected a thing, except for my partners, and they're not about to blow the secret."

"That's pretty slick, Doc. But everything's squared away now, right? You've got lots of bucks now. You don't do this crap anymore, do you?"

"I wish that was the case, Ben. The sad fact of the matter is that my partners don't know a damn thing about this mine down here. I've been soaking millions of dollars into this place, and I haven't taken out the first nugget. My partners think that all of the money has been going to finance the labs. I control the books for the labs, so they really don't know what our financial condition is. But I'm just about tapped out. Before long, they're going to start asking questions. My men here tell me that we're getting close to hitting a strike, but they've been telling me that for several years. If something doesn't happen soon, my whole world is going to collapse around me."

"Now I see why you are thinking of moving down here. You may need some place to run to, huh?

"I don't know what the hell to do, Ben. Something's got to happen or my butt's going to be in the ringer."

"And all for a buck, eh Doc?" Through the haze of the alcohol, Ben knew that he was looking at a desperate man. For all of his poise and cockiness, Ben knew that Ike was no different than any other caged animal. Underneath the glossy veneer, the surgeon had the same basic instincts for self preservation that any other animal had – the same instincts that Ben Harris had himself.

Even though he was not too steady on his feet, the ex-CIA agent stood up and stripped off his clothing. The surgeon was still staring blankly – self absorbed in his own dilemma. After he was completely naked, Ben turned and executed a perfect swan dive through the falling water and into the deep and crystal clear pool some thirty feet below.

After passing through the falling water, the pilot was lost from Ike's sight. Such acts, however, among drinking comrades, demanded replication. Ike stood, stripped off his clothing as well, and dived off of the cliff.

The surgeon entered the water every bit as gracefully as had Ben, and when he surfaced, he saw that the pilot was swimming toward him. Soon the two men were treading water as they stared back at the peaceful magnificence of the falling water.

"It's beautiful, isn't it?" said Ben.

"I really think that I could live down here, Ben. This place is wonderful."

"Ike, what would you say if I told you that I had an answer to all of your financial problems? What if you never had to work another day in you life?"

"I don't think you know how much money that would take, Ben. I mean we're talking millions here."

"I had already presumed from what you had told me that it would take a large sum of money. If you are willing to become involved with me and my associates, there will be plenty of money for everyone involved. I'm talking hundreds of millions of dollars, Ike."

"What type of venture could possible generate that much capital in an impoverished country like this?"

"Well, it ain't legal. I can tell you that much."

"Drugs?"

"Drugs."

"Is that what you do with that airplane of yours when you're not flying me between Bonanza and San Pedro Del Norte?" The two men had been inching slowly toward the bank and were now seated in the shallow water along side it.

"Ike, you have to believe me. I have never had even the most peripheral involvement in the drug trade. If we decide to do this, then I will be a novice the same as you."

"That sounds like the makings of a dangerous situation. From what I hear, beginners don't fare too well in the drug business. How do you even propose to make the necessary arrangements to purchase the drugs, and then who are we going to sell them to? I certainly wouldn't know where to begin to complete such a transaction."

"The selling will have to be up to you, Doctor. As far as procurement, several associates of mine, former freedom fighters, have already confiscated four plane loads of cocaine from the Colombians. They are already being pursued by the cartel for their actions, and they are anxious to expedite matters. If we are going to do this, we will have to do it soon."

"How much money are we talking about?"

"Ike, I really don't know what kind of deal that we could strike with my associates. I have done some rough calculations, however, and as near as I can figure, this amount of cocaine would have a street value of between four and five hundred million dollars. I can tell you that my friends probably don't know how much their product is really worth."

"Why bring me into this, Ben? Why not use some of your own contacts to pull this off? I'm sure that sums of money such as these could seduce a fairly strong set of morals."

"I have no intention of going back to the States, Ike. I've got my reasons. From what you've told me, you're desperate for money – lots of money. If we can put this together, it might be a perfect marriage." Ike sat silently for a long moment considering all of the possibilities and ramifications before he finally spoke.

"How do we even go about starting something like this?"

"Then you're interested?"

"For the kind of money that you're talking about, yes, I'm interested."

"Well then, my newly found friend, let's go talk to my associates."

The two unlikely allies began the short walk up the path to retrieve their clothing and backpacks. They drank a toast by passing the bottle of bourbon between them, and each man silently hoping that they would soon be collecting their fortunes.

CHAPTER 14

Miguel appraised the visitor who had been brought to his encampment by his friend, Ben Harris. He looked at the man's hands, and he could easily see that they were not hands that had done much manual labor. The clothing was of a fine quality and was obviously very expensive. Miguel was not current on popular hairstyles, but this man, Ike Paponis, had every hair in place. He could easily have been a politician. He was not at all unlike any one of the many politicians who had met with the Contra leader in the many years of war against the Sandinistas. The three men isolated themselves from the rest of the group and began to discuss their plans.

"Miguel, this is Dr. Ike Paponis. He is a friend of mine who has extensive high-level contacts in the United States. I think that he can help us with our project."

"Tell me, Dr. Paponis, why would a physician be interested in smuggling cocaine into his own country? Doesn't that conflict with your oath as a healer?" Miguel was skeptical, even paranoid, but paranoia was not an altogether bad quality when the dangers were as significant as they were in a deal like this one.

"Very simply put, Señor Dominguez, I have financial responsibilities well beyond my ability to produce at the current time. I am heavily in debt, and this deal could change that."

Miguel liked the response. The physician's motivation to successfully complete the deal was debt. Certainly there would also be an element of greed, but, hopefully, that would be secondary.

"What makes you think that you can engineer a transaction such as this one? Do you have contacts in the underworld? You must understand that our time is limited. Can you move quickly?" Miguel was still sizing up his new acquaintance and potential business partner.

"I have contacts, Señor. I am not sure that they are what you would call underworld connections, but they are certainly individuals who could be well motivated by money."

"Can you mobilize them quickly? There are obvious hurdles in an operation like this one."

"What sort of time frame are we talking abut here?"

"One week, Señor." Miguel had stared directly into Ike's eyes and made his statement in such a way as to leave no room for argument.

"One week?" Ike restated the constraint with incredulity. "That isn't much time."

"I understand the difficulty, Doctor, but the Colombians are pursuing us aggressively. We have already had to kill two of their men and more will surely be following them. If you are not able to meet this schedule, then, perhaps, we should say our goodbyes. I will utilize other means to sell my product." Ike sat quietly for a long moment. His mind was racing. He had no idea of how he was going to pull this deal off in the first place, and he absolutely had no idea of how to accomplish it in one week's time.

"I can manage, Señor Dominguez." The physician had made every attempt at sounding confident even though it was not confidence that he felt.

Ben decided to enter the conversation before the former freedom fighter could voice his doubts.

"Then that settles it. We'll take possession of the cocaine within one week. Miguel. I'll coordinate the details with you in several days."

"Not so quickly, my friend. I will require a deposit of ten million dollars, American. I will also want thirty percent of the profits after the sale has been completed. It would be unwise for you to attempt to cheat me. I, too, have many high-level contracts in the United States, and there would be no place where either of you could hide."

"We have no intention of trying to cheat you, Miguel. You and I have been through too much together for that to even be a consideration." Ben made the response as Ike was once again frantic about this new requirement. How in the world was he ever going to be able to get his hands on ten million dollars in cash in one week?

"Yes, but your good friend the doctor and I have no such bonds. I hope that nothing happens to damage our friendship. That would be a tragedy." The implications were concrete. If anybody tried to screw Dominguez, blood would flow. Ike was no longer even sure that he could decline to participate in this deal and walk away. He had always had a firm will and feared no man. But these guys were every bit his equals and were maybe even his betters in affairs such as these.

"Then we are agreed." Miguel stood and offered his hands to the two men. His face became the picture of congeniality. The three men slowly walked toward the Jeep, and Ben and Ike climbed in for the return trip to Bonanza.

"I will look forward to hearing from you, Ben. And good luck to you, Doctor. Our fortunes depend on it."

The Jeep pulled away from the encampment, and Ike was silent for the first hour of the trip. His mind was cluttered with a mix of possibilities and consequences. He thought that perhaps his inexperience in matters such as these might actually be an asset. He was bound to consider options that others in the drug trade would never consider.

"Ben, what would be the chances of arranging a meeting with President Diaz de Santiago, if I was able to produce a powerful senator who just happens to chair the Appropriations Committee?"

"I'd have to say that they would be pretty good. Her economy is dying and so is her political support. A meeting like the one you propose would be very good for her politically. Talmadge Hyle heads Appropriations, doesn't he? How would you ever get someone like that to consent to a meeting with Diaz de Santiago?"

"That's the easy part, Ben. Hyle owes me. He owes me big. I have been his single-most largest contributor in the past several elections. He'll do it or I'll cut him off. And besides, it'll be good for him politically, too. The American people don't take kindly to our meddling in the affairs of a foreign government and then leaving the country to drown after we have helped to restore Democracy. Especially a nation that is in our own hemisphere. My problem is in the amount of time that your friend Dominguez has allowed us."

"Boy, you are well connected, aren't you? Miguel isn't trying to be unreasonable. He has always been very good at anticipating the moves of his enemies, and he knows that the Colombians will be closing in on him soon."

"I'm aware of his reasons, but that still doesn't make my task any easier."

"I know that, Ike, But the rewards could be enormous. You have to stay focused on that. Everything else will fall into place."

The two men drove the rest of the way to Bonanza in silence. Upon arriving at the airfield, Ben drove Ike to the terminal where the physician purchased a first class ticket back to the States. They agreed to speak again in three days. In the meantime, Ben would begin to arrange the meeting between Diaz de Santiago and Hyle. Miguel Dominguez had considerable clout with Nicaragua's president, and rightfully so. The meeting would be easily arranged on the Nicaraguan end.

Ike boarded his plane for the flight to Miami and then on to Portland, Oregon. He didn't know how he was going to explain to his new wife that he was going to be making a return trip to Nicaragua in less than a week. He was even less sure of how he was going to account for his whereabouts during the course of this entire transaction. But Ike had never been accountable to anyone before, and he had no intention of starting now.

Sharon Paponis waited eagerly at the American Airlines terminal at Portland International. She had only been married to the cardiac surgeon for several weeks, and already she felt estranged from the man. She had known that marrying a surgeon would entail making some sacrifices, but she never dreamed that she would see so little of her husband.

In addition to his responsibilities at the hospital, he also seemed to be very interested in the political goings-on both locally and in Washington. What all of this meant to her was that she was forced to spend a good deal of her time alone.

Sharon was much younger than her husband, and while she was reasonable, the separations were still difficult to tolerate. The plane landed and taxied to the end of the exit ramp. Sharon craned her neck for the first glance of her husband.

Ike was one of the first passengers to deplane. As he rounded the corner into the gate area, his wife was no longer able to contain her enthusiasm. Here was her Indiana Jones back from the jungle. She raced to meet him and wrapped her arms around him – expecting a strong embrace and a warm kiss. What she got was a quick peck on the cheek from a familiar figure who had barely slowed his pace.

"Come on, Sharon. Let's get out of here."

"What, no hello? No how are you? Just a let's get out of here? Hey, it's great to see you too, Ike." Her enthusiasm had been drained in a single moment of inattention.

"Come on, Sharon, I've got things that need to be done quickly."

"Whatever. I'm sorry that I'm cutting into your busy schedule." She disentangled herself from her husband and stoically, rapidly, exited the terminal building in silence. She had driven his Porsche to the airport thinking that he would enjoy driving it home, and as they arrived at the vehicle, she merely flipped the keys to him.

He quickly opened his door, electronically opened her door, got in and started the engine. The woman could see that her husband was preoccupied, but she still could not rationalize his blatant inattention to her. He was treating her like she wasn't even there. What was worse, he was treating her as if he didn't want her to be there. He operated his beloved Porsche down the highway toward their home, but still he remained silent.

"So, how was your trip?" She asked in an effort to stimulate conversation.

"It was okay." He offered nothing.

"That's it? Just okay? I've been living for the moment you get home, and you act like you could care less."

"I'm sorry, Sharon. I've got some things on my mind."

"Well, that's obvious. I had hoped that you would have me on your mind," she said as she snuggled more closely to him.

"Do you have any idea what my interests in Nicaragua are?"

"No, you didn't offer that information, and I didn't ask." She pulled away from him momentarily.

"What I'm going to tell you has to remain confidential between just you and me. Marty and Allan don't even know about this, and I don't want them to know either."

"I know that we haven't been married for too long, Ike, but that goes without saying. I'd never betray your confidence."

"I'm counting on that, Sharon. My interest in Nicaragua includes a gold mine near the city of San Pedro Del Norte, in which I am the sole stockholder. We haven't had a strike yet, but the geological engineers whom I have hired to evaluate soil samples, have encouraged me to be optimistic. They tell me that it's just a matter of time."

"That's exciting, Ike, but I don't see why you find it necessary to keep that information from Marty and Allan. I would think that would be something that you would want to share with them."

"Unfortunately, it's not that simple. Our business relationship is rather complex. S.P.S. has taken several rather large financial hits in the past couple of years, and I wouldn't want the guys to think that my efforts have been directed anywhere other than our corporation." Ike felt that he had skillfully explained why it was necessary to keep the matter strictly between his wife and himself. In addition, he had imparted a very private aspect of his life with his spouse, and she would treat the confidence with undying loyalty. And as a final bonus, she would understand why he would be so busy in the next several weeks.

"I guess that makes sense, Ike," she said grateful to have finally been taken into his confidence. She could handle almost anything as long as she knew what it was that she would be asked to deal with. It was the secretiveness that was so difficult to understand.

Ike activated his garage door opener and expertly navigated the car into his garage. He jumped out of the car, walked into the house, and went directly to the telephone. Sharon had been appeased, and therefore, was not put off by the continuing lack of interest.

"Talmadge, this is Ike. Do you think that we could meet tomorrow?"

"What's this about, Ike?"

"I've just returned from Nicaragua. Some of my contacts there suggested a meeting between you and President Diaz de Santiago."

"What kind of time frame are we talking about?"

"I was told that the meeting should take place within a week."

"That's funny, Ike. I've heard no rumblings about anything of this nature in Washington."

"This is strictly informal, Senator. My contacts know of my association with you, and they thought that perhaps I might be able to make his happen."

"Well, I'd like to hear more about this. Did you say that you wanted to meet tomorrow? Can you come to Washington?"

"It'll have to be late afternoon, if that's okay with you. I just walked in the door, and I've got to go to the office in the morning."

"About three p.m. then?"

"That'll be fine, Senator. I'll see you at three."

Sharon had been listening intently to the conversation but was also trying to avoid being obvious. She was standing at the bar mixing cocktails for both herself and her husband. The woman was quite impressed with how at ease he was with the power brokers in Washington. She was as of yet unaware of the large sums of money that he contributed to the varying campaigns, but if she would have stopped to think about it, she would have realized that it was the money that bought the power. Sharon took the drink to her husband as he hung up the phone.

"What was that all about, honey?"

"Are you familiar with the political situation in Nicaragua?"

"Well, I know that a few years ago they were governed by a Communist regime under Daniel Ortega. And that through the efforts of the Contras, with the aid of the United States, Democracy was restored, and the country is now governed by President Carmalita Diaz de Santiago."

"That's pretty impressive, Sharon, but what is really going on down there?"

"I guess I don't know."

"The bottom line is that the economy of the country is dying. We went to such great lengths to restore democracy, but now we're pretty much turning the cold shoulder on them, and Democracy is not turning out to be the Godsend that everyone once predicted that it would be. Talmadge Hyle heads the Senate Appropriations Committee. He controls the purse strings to a large degree, and he can assist in getting some much-needed financial aid to the Nicaraguans. This could help President Diaz de Santiago salvage what is left of her government."

"And with you having business interests there, the personal benefits of your being able to arrange a successful summit between Senator Hyle and President Diaz de Santiago are obvious."

"You got it, baby. Did anyone ever tell you how smart you are?" That was all that she needed to make her purr. Sharon sat on her husband's lap, and at long last, they were able to enjoy that warm kiss that she had so longed for.

CHAPTER 15

While Ike and Sharon made love in the warmth of their bedroom, Miguel Dominguez was meeting with Nicaragua's president in her private residence. Ben had done as he had promised. He had contacted Miguel, who had in turn contacted President Diaz de Santiago. Dominguez had not divulged the purpose of the request for a meeting to the president's aides, but rather had waited for the face-to-face and private meeting.

Miguel had always had a great deal of respect for Carmalita Diaz de Santiago and she for him. But beyond the respect was a true friendship. They had communicated often during the fight for freedom and had been endeared by each other's efforts to oust the Sandinistas. This evening, in the privacy of the president's receiving room, Miguel Dominguez and Carmalita Diaz de Santiago shared a warm embrace.

"Carmalita, you are looking better than ever. It appears as if presidential power agrees with you."

"You are too kind, Miguel. And ever the flatterer."

"Some things never change, Madam President."

"So what brings you to call under such pressing and secretive circumstances, Miguel?"

"Madam President, I have had a contact from a man close to the chairman of the United States Senate Appropriations Committee. It seems that Senator Hyle wishes to meet with you."

"Who is this man, and why have the usual diplomatic channels not been utilized? This is a rather unusual method of conducting the affairs of state."

"The man's name is Ike Paponis. He is a heart surgeon from the state of Oregon, and he owns a mining interest here in our country. As for the reasons for him requesting this meeting on behalf of Senator Hyle, I too can only guess. Perhaps his reasons are selfish. Our economy is suffering. I am sure that I don't need to tell you that. Maybe he fears a failing economy and is motivated by his own greed."

"The proposal is interesting at any rate. I am sure that there are concerns regarding our economy. There are problems there. But it will not fail. It cannot. Our people have fought too hard, too long, to allow that to happen. I cannot allow any measure of victory for the Sandinistas – moral or otherwise. For the most part, I am agreeable to a meeting such as the one that you have suggested. When would our friends in the United States like to see this take place?"

"I am told that it should be within one week."

"That isn't much time to make the necessary preparations. I wonder at the reasons for their sense of urgency."

"Again, my President, I can only guess. But there should be no need for lavish preparations. I am told that this is to be an informal meeting."

"This is all very confusing to me, Miguel. But you may tell your contact that I am amenable to such a meeting."

"That is good, Carmalita. I will make the necessary arrangements on my end, and I will be back in touch with you later this week."

"As always, Miguel, I am grateful for your patriotism."

"Thank you, Madam President. The freedom and prosperity of my country are my only goals in this life." Miguel was lying, but his statement had sounded convincing.

"Miguel, I wish you would consider accepting a position in my government. You, above all others, deserve it. And our country has a need for selfless individuals such as yourself."

"I appreciate your confidence, Carmalita, but I have never been one for politics. I am afraid that I am nothing more than a freedom fighter without a war to fight."

"Old warriors should learn to relax and enjoy the spoils of their battles."

"I am afraid that to enter politics would demean the depths of my struggle."

"I know you too well to be offended by your statement, Miguel. Go with God, my friend. I will look forward to hearing the details of the visit of the esteemed Senator from the United States. I thank you for your loyalty."

A handshake was the farewell chosen by the two friends after they had conducted their business. Although Miguel Dominguez had arranged the meeting at the bequest of Ben Harris, and on behalf of Ike Paponis, he still did not know what the heart surgeon was really up to. In reality, he thought that was probably better. He did not wish to elevate his profile and increase his culpability if something were to go wrong. No, let the surgeon and Ben Harris bear the brunt of the risk. A truly experienced soldier knew when to assault and when to keep his head down.

Carmalita Diaz de Santiago was secretly thrilled with the prospects for a meeting with the American senator. Her popularity was sagging as a direct result of her country's failing economy. She had been angry with the

Americans for quite some time as she felt she had been betrayed. There had been many promises for financial support, but the aid had been slow in coming. What was the use in restoring Democracy to Nicaragua if the new free market was to fail before it had a chance to succeed?

Talmadge Hyle had been one of the most ardent supporters of the new Diaz de Santiago led government. He had actually made more promises than any of the other American politicians. And Carmalita Diaz de Santiago liked Talmadge Hyle. She found him to be politically astute and well read on current issues. In addition to this, while his will seemed to be firm, he was not totally unalterable. Talmadge Hyle was a man whom the President of Nicaragua could deal with. At least she hoped that she could deal with him, because politically, she was in dire straits.

Ike was moving at warp speed. He had scheduled a meeting with Allan at ten o'clock that morning and had made plans to stop by his office prior to that. He also needed to be at the airport by one o'clock for his flight to Washington. There was no way that he would be able to meet the senator at three o'clock, but Hyle would just have to understand.

Lois was seated at her desk within the reception area of Ike's office when the heart surgeon walked through the door. There were patients in the waiting area, but the physician motioned to his receptionist to join him in his private office.

He stopped by the back counter in the treatment area, poured himself a cup of coffee, and then walked directly into his office. He sat in his comfortable swivel chair and put his feet up on his desk. He eyed his receptionist carefully.

"So bring me up to date, Lois. Any impending emergencies?"

"No, Dr. Paponis. Dr. Pifer has been covering your patient calls. There have been several calls from the hospital Board regarding some incident between you and Dr. Switzer. They didn't elaborate, but they're very anxious to hear from you."

"Screw them. Switzer got what he deserved. Anything else?"

"Mayor Cranston called. He wanted you to know that he's recovering nicely and he really appreciates what you did for him."

"So everything else is under control?"

"You're getting backed up on your office and surgery schedule. There are some cases that Dr. Pifer just doesn't want to get involved in. S.P.S. needs some attention, but all in all, things are holding their own pretty well."

"Good, because I'm going to be out of the country for the next ten days. I've got business in Nicaragua. I'm sorry, I know this makes things difficult for you, but I know that you'll manage admirably."

"Thanks for the confidence, Doctor." She had never heard the words "I'm sorry" voiced by Ike Paponis in all the years of their association.

"Well, if that's all, then I've got an appointment at Allan Spandell's office at ten. Thanks for everything, Lois." The surgeon rose and left his office as briskly as he had come in. The patients in his waiting room stared in wonder at his seeming inattention until Lois explained the Dr. Pifer would be in to see them shortly.

Allan was happy to meet with his partner. He had, in fact, seen very little of the man in the past several weeks. Ike was like that though. He came and went as he pleased, and he never divulged much regarding his whereabouts during the interim. That was just Ike's way, and the probate attorney had learned to live with it.

Paponis strolled into the richly decorated office as comfortably as if it were his own.

"Allan, how are you?" The surgeon walked over to the attorney's desk and extended his hand. Following a warm greeting, he took a seat facing Spandell.

"Where the hell have you been, Ike? I called your office and the only word I get is that you're out of the country. What the heck are you up to? When are we going to get together and play some golf? I'll tell you, between Marty and that darn Aid Clinic, and you and your travels, I'm pretty much left to myself these days. It's just not like it used to be."

"I know, Allan. And I know that you have been shouldering a large portion of the burden for S.P.S. I'm sorry, but I've been involved with a little something for Talmadge Hyle."

"What has Talmadge got you doing now?"

"I'm afraid that I'm unable to divulge the details, but in short, it's just a little emissarial work. No big deal."

"I wouldn't say that. You're hob-knobbing in the big leagues now, Ike." The statement had in no way been accusatory. Allan was just voicing the facts as he saw them.

"So where do we stand with S.P.S. right now, Allan? Are there any operational problems that I need to know about?"

"I've talked to Marty, and I think that the three of us need to get together and hash this thing out. We're losing money in Colorado Springs and Sacramento. I think we ought to consider cutting our losses and pulling out."

"What do you think the problem is? Our feasibility studies indicated clearly that both markets had adequate populations. What is causing us so much grief?"

"I'm not sure, Ike. I think the medical community in Colorado Springs is trying to put their own thing together. There hasn't been anything official out yet, but those guys aren't stupid. They can recognize a good thing when they see it. I think that they're just trying to choke us out and then they'll fill the void with their own deal. I think our failure in California is just a reflection of all the HMOs that have sprung up out there. Managed care doesn't have much concern for private doctors trying to earn a buck. What do you want to do, Ike?"

"We're not pulling out, Allan. I won't give the clowns the satisfaction. Okay, in Colorado, I want you to go out there, Allan. Take Marty with you if you want to. Wine and dine the bastards. Stroke them up one side and down the other. Do whatever you have to. They'll come around. If we end up having to cut them in somehow, then we'll do it. As far as Sacramento goes, I'll talk to Talmadge and see if he can't apply some political pressure. Those HMOs are already on the legal fringes, and they've got no business screwing with free enterprise. The only problem that I might face there is Gerry Abrams. He's the one who was giving us some crap over monopoly law awhile back. We'll just keep everything low key and see what we can do."

"Sounds good to me. I'll talk to Marty and see if he's interested in going to Colorado Springs with me. You know, you kind of created a monster with the Aid Clinic thing. Marty thinks he's a general practitioner now. He hasn't even been doing much pathology down at the morgue. He and Sally have been down at the darn clinic ten or twelve hours a day. All of the news stations have done features on the two of them."

"Do they mention S.P.S. in their stories?"

"Yes, Ike, they do."

"Then, it's good PR for us. Don't let him forget that we still have a business to manage and that he is still the county medical examiner. As long as he doesn't lose sight of what we're really all about, then I don't have a problem with it."

"So how are you, Ike? How's the new marriage? That's a beautiful woman that you married."

"Thanks, Allan. I'm fine. My marriage is fine. Things couldn't be better, really. How's the fund doing by the way?"

"Great. We're raking in the cash, and we're being very selective about what we do with the money. I've had Angelo Galafaro doing some investing for us, and it's really paid off. He's great. In addition to that, the man donated three million of his own money. Said he likes what we're doing with the local charities and that he wanted to be a part of it. You know him, don't you?"

"He's that securities broker from the club, isn't he?"

"That's the guy. Really big ticket. But I think he's into a lot more than just securities. I've even heard rumors that he has mob connections. I don't believe the rumors – just because he's got money and an Italian heritage doesn't make him one of the bad guys. I wouldn't have let him anywhere near the fund if I thought any of that crap was true."

"I've heard the same rumors, Allan. Be careful. About the last thing that we need right now is to be tied to the mob." Ike was once again playing patriarch, but his mind was already racing at the prospect that maybe, just maybe, Angelo Galafaro was his man for the Nicaragua deal. He hated to approach a man who he hardly knew to propose a deal of this nature. But time was short, and the potential rewards were far too great. He would have to do a little more checking, but, hopefully, Angelo Galafaro was his man.

"Allan, I need you to float me a loan for ten million bucks. I need it in cash, and I need it within four days."

"Holy shit, Ike! What do you need that kind of money for?"

"I can't tell you, Allan. All that I can tell you is that I'll have it back in the account within two weeks. Hell, I'll even pay interest on it if you want me to."

"Shoot, Ike, you know you don't need to pay interest, but it's absolute crap that you won't tell me what you need the money for. We've been friends for years, and we've been through plenty of stuff together. I'm having a hard time accepting all of this secrecy."

"Allan, this is for your own good. The less that you know the better. Really, I'm just trying to protect you."

"Why? Is the money going to be at risk? Are you involved in something illegal?"

"I wouldn't be being honest with you if I told you that there was no risk, Allan. But beyond that I'd really rather not say any more."

"Ike, I'm not sure that I feel comfortable with you risking ten million dollars that isn't really even ours to risk. I consented to this stuff when the corporation needed money, but I knew what was going on with that. To tell you the truth, I have a real problem with this. If you lose the money and we get audited, then we're screwed. I hope that you've thought about that."

"When have I ever steered you wrong? We've got a long history of making money together, Allan. I would think that you would trust my judgment by now."

"I do, Ike. It's just all the secrecy that concerns me. All I want is for you to be aware of the risks. That's all."

"I'm not a moron, Allan. I know what I'm doing. Trust me." Those last two words sent chills up and down Allan Spandell's spine. If it wasn't Ike who was making the request, the attorney knew that he would turn it down flatly. But it was Ike Paponis, and the surgeon's business instincts had always been phenomenal.

"Okay, Ike. I'll do it. But you've got to promise me that someday you'll tell me what this was all about."

"When we're old and gray, Allan. Trust me. It's better that way." There were those two words again.

"Don't get yourself in over your head, buddy."

"I won't, but I appreciate your concern. I also need another favor."

"My lucky day. What else can I do for you, Ike?"

"I want to play golf with Angelo Galafaro either tomorrow or the next day. Can you arrange it?"

"Probably. If he's in town, it shouldn't be a problem. In fact, I ought to be able to join you."

"I want it to be a twosome, Allan. I want to work this guy over a little bit. Find out what he's all about. If you were there, I'd probably be too much on my best behavior. This guy is getting pretty far into our operation. I'd just like to know a little more about him."

"I think you're being a little paranoid, but I'll set it up." Ike rose from his seat and once again extended his hand to his partner.

"Allan, thanks for everything. You're a true friend."

"No problem, Ike. I'll be in touch." Paponis turned to leave, and even though the two men had been friends for a good number of years, Allan felt as if he had just been raped.

The American Airlines 737 touched down smoothly onto the runway at Dulles International Airport. Ike Paponis grabbed his briefcase and exited the first-class cabin rapidly and moved down onto the concourse. A tall man in a plain blue suit strode up to him.

"Dr. Paponis, Senator Hyle has asked me to drive you to his office." The surgeon was impressed with the politician's sense of protocol. He had not even told the senator what flight he would be taking, but Hyle had managed to have him greeted at the airport anyway. This was traveling in style.

"Thank you, sir." The two men moved directly out of the front door of the terminal building and into the waiting burgundy colored Lincoln Town Car. The tall man in the plain blue suit opened the door to the rear passenger compartment, and the surgeon got in. He was getting the royal treatment, and he liked it.

Talmadge Hyle had cleared his calendar for the afternoon. The suggestion that Ike Paponis had made on the telephone last evening had been quite intriguing. Politics was a curious game, and Talmadge Hyle was an expert at playing.

Americans were, by and large, fed up with the funneling of billions of dollars to foreign countries. The average American citizen felt that it was about time that the federal government started using some of that money at home. But the citizenry of the United States was still not without a conscience – especially when it came to blossoming Democracies in their own hemisphere.

There was a sentiment of national regret that the economy of Nicaragua was failing so badly so soon after the Communist regime had been replaced by a free electorate. If American money was going to be spent in foreign countries, then Nicaragua was as good as place as any to spend it. There were certain elements of danger in participating in meetings with foreign heads of state, however. Talmadge Hyle would hear what Ike had to say, but he would move very carefully when it came to definitive action.

The door to Talmadge Hyle's office was opened by his secretary, and Ike walked briskly in carrying his briefcase. The senator rose from behind his desk and moved rapidly around to shake hands with the surgeon.

"Ike, how are you?"

"I'm good, Talmadge. Good to see you."

"Thanks for coming down, Ike. You look good. The last time I saw you was under considerably less-favorable circumstances."

"Oh yeah, Switzer. He was way out of line on that one."

"Well, at least Dick Cranston is doing well. That's what I hear from Portland anyway. What do you have for me, Ike?"

"Senator, I'm not sure whether you know this or not, but I have a mining interest in Nicaragua. At any rate, I have made several good contacts in the country, and somehow or another my association with you has become known. I was recently approached by another American who suggested that perhaps by arranging a meeting between you and President Diaz de Santiago, a fall of her government, which right now is a distinct possibility, could probably be averted."

"She has had a tough time of it, Ike. But this is very tricky business. For me to interfere in the affairs of State without the express approval of the President and the State Department could put me in a tight spot."

"What I'm proposing, Senator, would be very informal. I think that this would be more of an exchange of ideas than anything else. Perhaps it could lead to something more concrete in the future. But right now, just the publicity could positively affect President Diaz de Santiago's administration. That's all she's really looking for. There's no doubt that they need money, and there is definitely the perception that you could be the catalyst that could help to arrange funds for them."

"I don't suppose there could be any real harm in attending a meeting such as the one you have suggested. I'm just a little concerned about your motives though. It really looks like you're just trying to protect your investment down there."

"What the heck do you expect me to do? Do you really think that I would just be willing to stand by and let this government fail? Who knows what would replace it. The next thing you know, they go right back to some form of dictatorship, nationalize my gold mine, and I'm out millions of dollars. If you want to look at this as a personal favor to me, then so be it."

"Well, God knows that I certainly owe you a few favors. You've been a loyal supporter, Ike. And your contributions have seen me through some tough times. You make the arrangements, and I'll make the necessary alterations in my schedule to attend your meeting."

"I really appreciate this, Talmadge. I just can't afford to take a big financial hit in Nicaragua right now."

"I understand, Ike. Look, while I've got you here, I've got something else that I wanted to talk to you about. I talked to your partner, Marty Spencer, about this the last time I was in Portland. I visited that Aid clinic of yours, and Ike, I've got to tell you that's the darndest phenomena I've ever seen."

"Yeah, I noticed that it didn't take too long for you to get your picture taken down there."

"A good politician never misses a good photo opportunity, Ike."

"And you are definitely an astute politician."

"Anyway, my idea is for the same sort of thing. Only on a grander scale. What I have envisioned is a sort of medical response team. You know what I'm talking about. When there is some sort of natural disaster, we assemble a team of doctors, nurses, paramedics, etc., that rush to support the victims. We could finance it, in large part, with private donations. But I have talked to the President, and he thinks it's a great idea. He intimated that quite possibly there could be some federal funds available for a project such as this."

"It's an interesting concept, Talmadge."

"What do you mean by interesting concept? It's a great idea. The team will consist primarily of Oregonians. We'll base it in Portland. And can you imagine the publicity? I'll never have to be concerned about being reelected again. I don't know if you are aware of this, Ike, but I've been considering a run for the Presidency. Something like this could be my ticket to the Oval Office if I play my cards right. Heck, it could even get you elected to the Senate after I leave. That is if you are so inclined. It's a win-win proposition all the way around, Ike."

"Well I can certainly see that you've allowed yourself to get excited about this, Senator."

"Excited? How could I be anything else?" Ike was intently considering the politician's idea, and he too could see merit in the proposal.

"I know that my friend, Marty Spencer, would be interested in this project. I half way expect to see him give up his medical examiner's position before too long anyway. It's almost like he's forgotten that he's a pathologist and now he's out to save the world."

"In all honesty, Ike, in defense of Marty Spencer, I think that all of that death would really wear on a fellow after all of these years. It has got to be tough."

"You're probably right, Talmadge. And me in the United States Senate… I've never even considered it before, but now that you mention it, I really think that I could warm up to the idea."

"I knew you would, Ike. The fact of the matter is that I've had you in mind for quite some time. You'd be perfect. You're a political outsider, and the public wants political outsiders in government right now. I'm just not sure that you've got the temperament for the job. When I consider the possibilities, I sometimes wonder if perhaps your personality isn't a bit too unyielding. You have to learn to play people, Ike. You have to make them do what you want, and at the same time, make them believe that what they are doing is in their own best interest."

"Listen, Talmadge. You do this thing for me in Nicaragua, and I'll check into setting up this team for you. You might also want to talk to Marty Spencer about this again. Tell him that I'm for it, and he should start to make some informal inquiries with physicians and nurses."

"Just what I wanted to hear, Doctor. The President will probably want to meet with you and your associates as well. It's a sad fact, but everybody will want to cash in on the publicity that this project will generate." Ike rose from his position on the couch where he had been seated next to the senior senator from Oregon. There had been no overt indication that the meeting was over. It had been a subtle signal. Their business had been completed, and both men had other affairs to attend to. They shook hands, and the surgeon turned to leave.

"So you'll be in touch later this week, Ike?"

"Certainly, as soon as I've firmed up the details."

"Should I arrange transportation with one of our Air Force jets?"

"That won't be necessary, Senator. I'll take care of arranging transportation."

"You mean that you're willing to pick up the tab for an official government visit?"

"It's not exactly official, Talmadge. Remember that I've got a personal stake in Nicaragua as well."

"Still, it's damn decent of you, Ike. I could arrange for a plane."

"I'll take care of it, Senator. It's the least that I can do to thank you for your cooperation."

"I'll look forward to your call, Doctor."

The American Airlines jet touched down at Portland International. Ike rapidly deplaned and made his way to the parking garage where he found his car and drove home. A lot of thoughts were coursing through his mind in rapid-fire succession. His plan, as far as he could tell, was falling into place just as he had designed it. The missing link, at this point, was how he was going to dispose of the cocaine. Without that, he had nothing. He was certain that Allan would be successful at arranging for him to play golf with Angelo Galafaro, and this is where the big leap would come into play. If the man had no connections to the underworld, then his plan was finished. Maybe his entire future would be finished.

The surgeon parked his car in the garage and entered his house. He was immediately aware that the only lighting within the structure was that of numerous lit candles. He also heard the low sound of good jazz emanating from the stereo speakers in the living room. Sharon was nowhere to be found.

The physician walked to the refrigerator and pulled a cold green bottle of imported beer from the shelf on the door. He opened it with the metal opener that he found in the silverware drawer, and he sat down at the bar that was an extension of the kitchen counter.

The intact newspaper sat before him, and he paged through it quickly glancing at the front page of each section. When he came to the ACCENT section, he was immediately taken with the photo of Marty and Sally Spencer. They were standing in the treatment area of the medical aid clinic and were flanked by an apparent indigent person with a splint and sling on one arm. The article was titled *Coroner Gets New Lease On Life*. Ike Paponis rapidly scanned the article and saw mention of his and Allan Spandell's name several times. The article only served to cement Talmadge Hyle's supposition that these types of projects made for good publicity.

As he finished his reading, the surgeon raised his bottle of beer to take a drink, and out of the corner of his eye he caught a glimpse of his wife. He immediately noticed that she was wearing a sheer scanty negligee. What else Ike noticed was that she looked beautiful. One look at her had made him forget all of the stress of his recent difficulties. This was the way a marriage should be. This was what it was all about – having a beautiful woman to make you forget all of your troubles.

"Sharon, you look beautiful."

"Do you mean that I've finally gotten you to notice me? She moved out of the shadow and more closely toward him. The light from the candles accented the prominent parts of her perfect anatomy.

"I always notice you, honey. My mind is just going in so many different directions right now. I'm sorry that I haven't been more attentive. And what's worse is that I've got to go back to Nicaragua later this week." She was sitting on his lap now and gently kissing his neck.

"Why do you have to go back so soon?"

"I've been instrumental in arranging a meeting between Senator Hyle and President Carmalita Diaz de Santiago of Nicaragua. It would be in poor taste for me not to make the trip."

"What would be the possibility of me going with you?"

"I'm not so sure that would be a good idea, Sharon. This is an official State visit. I'm not even sure what my role should be." Ike was trying to find a way to tactfully deny the request. This whole venture was going to be extremely risky, and in no way did he want to endanger the safety of his wife.

"I don't see why I can't go with you. I can keep myself out of the way."

"Let me run it by Talmadge. If he doesn't have a problem with it, then I suppose it'll be okay."

The surgeon stood straight up and cradled his wife in his arms. He carried her back toward the bedroom and gently laid her on the bed. He kicked off his shoes, stripped off his suit, and turned to go into the bathroom that was adjacent to the bedroom. He wanted to climb into bed immediately, but the ardors of his travel and meeting with the senator from Oregon had left him feeling like he needed a shower.

The hot water bathed over his skin and soothed his tired body. His mind continued to race as he attempted to shore up all of the loose details that floated through it. Now was a time for relaxation, however, and he knew that his wife was waiting for him in the next room.

He stepped out of the shower, hastily dried his body, and quickly combed his hair. He stopped briefly to inspect his muscular form in the mirror. He was once again pleased to see that his advancing years had not exacted a too-telling toll on his body.

As he stepped back into the bedroom, he saw that Sharon had removed the negligee and was now laying totally naked on top of the comforter. She had struck her most seductive pose, and the effect on her husband was immediate.

He moved directly to the bed and covered her body with his own. She ignited with overwhelming passion, and the fierceness of their foreplay intensified their need. She rolled her husband onto his back and then straddled his waist. She urged him to enter her, slowly at first, and then she began to rock rhythmically back and forth.

The physician watched his wife's face as her position carried her far away and yet focused her intensely on where she was and what she was doing. He watched dreamily the rise and fall of her perfect breasts. He could sense her nearing completion as her entire body slowly approached a synchronized muscular spasm. It was at that moment he knew that if he could ever really love anyone, it was this woman. She was the perfect reflection of himself, so totally in control, and at the same time, so recklessly out of control. He joined her in her orgasm, took her in his arms, and fell fast asleep.

The phone that rested on the night stand next to Ike's head rang at precisely nine o'clock the next morning. He rolled over and absently picked up the receiver.

"Hello."

"Ike, are you still in bed?" It was Allan Spandell.

"Yeah. What time is it anyway?"

"Nine o'clock. I'm sorry. You never sleep this late. I was sure that you would be up by now."

"Don't worry about it. I should be up. It's just one of those rare mornings when I don't have to be anywhere early."

"Well, that's all changed my friend. You've got a golf date with Angelo Galafaro at eleven o'clock."

"You old dog… you were able to pull it off after all."

"Yeah, and you had better get up and get moving. Give me a call later this evening. I'll be interested in knowing what you think of the guy."

"No problem. Hey, I appreciate you putting this together for me."

"I'll talk to you later, Ike. Enjoy your round."

"See ya, Allan." Ike replaced the telephone, once again got out of bed, and headed for the bathroom. He brushed his teeth, shaved, and climbed into the shower.

As he was washing his hair, he suddenly felt his wife's warm hands encircle him from behind. In just a matter of seconds, she had aroused him and then spun him around to face her.

"Sharon, I'd love to but I've got a business meeting at eleven."

"Come on, you can spare ten minutes for me," she teased.

She turned away from him and bent over, using the porcelain corners of the bathtub to support herself. Her husband needed no more prompting as he stepped forward and entered her. Their movements became fierce, and the act culminated rapidly.

After they were finished, she turned to him once again, lightly kissed him on the lips, and exited the shower.

"You'd better hurry, honey. You've got a meeting at eleven." There was a satisfied smile on her face as she toweled off her body before going back to bed.

Dr. Ike Paponis, dressed in a pair of casual slacks and a comfortable golf shirt, navigated his Carrera from his home to the parking lot of the Lake Oswego Country Club. He had arrived nearly forty-five minutes early, and even though it was not yet noon, he went to the bar for a Bloody Mary.

His nerves had been calmed a great deal as a result of the interludes with his wife, but as the full impact of what he was about to do struck him fully in the face, his steely resolve began to waiver. After having two drinks, however, he was able to go to his locker to retrieve his golf clubs. Once again he began to feel in control.

Ike was hitting several practice putts on the green that served that purpose when he saw the man he knew to be Angelo Galafaro walking up to him. Mr. Galafaro was flanked by a behemoth of a man who had the same olive complexion as did his golfing partner for the day. The larger man bore Galafaro's clubs.

"Dr. Paponis, so good to see you. I don't think that we've been formally introduced. I am Angelo Galafaro." The man extended his hand, and Ike grasped it in a firm handshake. The eyes of the two men met, and the physician found nothing overtly frightening in those of his counterpart.

"Mr. Galafaro, the pleasure is mine. I've heard many good things about you from my friend, Allan Spandell."

"Please, call me Angelo. Yes, Allan is a good man. I'm flattered that he speaks so highly of me. This is my associate, Michael." The larger man stepped forward, and he too extended his hand.

"I had been under the impression that it would just be the two of us playing today."

"That is true, Ike. Michael will be acting as my caddy. We are rarely separated. Michael looks after me." So the guy had a bodyguard. That was a good indication that Angelo Galafaro was the man that the surgeon had thought him to be.

Angelo Galafaro had money written all over him. His clothing, while appearing casual, was obviously perfectly tailored. The watch was a Rolex. The jewelry was impressive. But the man was not ostentatious in his demeanor. He was low key and cordial, and he was a man that Ike Paponis thought that he could do business with.

"Well, Angelo it's just about eleven o'clock. What do you say we head over to the first hole and get underway."

"I'm ready. I hear you've got a five handicap. Is that true?"

"On a good day, Angelo. Only on a good day anymore." Ike invited his playing companion to tee off first. Michael handed his boss the Big Bertha from his golf bag as well as a ball and tee. Galafaro proceeded leisurely to the championship flight, inserted his tee into the ground, and placed his ball on top of it. He stepped back and took several practice swings, stepped forward and addressed the ball, and made a swing so fluid that even Ike had to admire the man's style. The ball was hit long and negotiated the dog-leg left, just as Angelo Galafaro had obviously intended for it to do.

"Nice shot, Angelo."

"Thank you." The Italian replaced the club in his bag in an unassuming fashion.

Ike stepped up to the ball and drove it nearly as far and every bit as neatly as had his playing companion. He too replaced his driver into the golf bag, but he had to carry his own clubs.

The two men started down the fairway while Michael lagged behind – giving the playing partners an approximate twenty yard head start.

"So why did you wish to meet with me so quickly, Ike?"

"I don't know. My friend, Allan Spandell, tells me that you have become quite involved with our administration of the Portland Fund. I just wanted to get to know you a little better."

"So this round of golf is to size me up… so to speak? I have to tell you, Ike, I'm not very used to this sort of thing. It is usually me who is doing the sizing up."

"I'm certainly not trying to be rude, Angelo. It's just that you have taken such an active role in the investment of our money that I thought that I should know you better." Angelo Galafaro stopped and looked directly into Ike's eyes.

"Come now, Ike. It's not really your money, is it?" The question had not been meant to be disarming, but it had the effect of unnerving the heart surgeon. Did this man know what Ike had done with the fund in the past and also what he intended to do with it in the very near future?

"You misunderstood what I was saying, Angelo" Ike stated dismissively. He had arrived at his ball, withdrew a five iron, and made a near-perfect shot that landed his ball on the green a mere fifteen feet from the cup.

"Marvelous shot, Ike!" Ike nodded his head to acknowledge the compliment and turned to take the few paces to where Galafaro's ball lay. Michael stepped forward and allowed his boss to choose a club. Angelo then made a shot to rival that of the surgeon's, and after doing so, he turned to Paponis.

"Ike, what did you really want to see me about?" There was now no doubt that this man was not being taken in by Ike's small talk. Galafaro had made his money by being an observant businessman, and he knew that the surgeon had more on his mind than just friendship.

The two men stopped in the middle of the fairway, and once again they stared directly into each other's eyes. Michael once again assumed his place out of earshot. Ike had hoped to have become a little better acquainted with the man before posing the potentially destructive question, but obviously that was not to be.

"Angelo, I don't know you very well. In fact, I'm afraid that I'm going way out on a limb here. What I'm interested in is knowing if you have any ties to organized crime?" Ike was now holding his breath waiting for Michael to pull a submachine gun out of the golf bag and fill his body with Mafioso bullets.

"Just go ahead and say what's on you mind, Ike." Angelo was smiling at the way the physician had just blurted out the question." If you are concerned about my involvement in the Portland Fund placing you and your friends in a compromising position, then the answer is no." Galafaro then turned and walked toward the first green as Ike followed him. Fortunately, on this day, there was no other group waiting to begin their round.

When the two men reached the green, Ike decided to press the issue a bit further.

"That wasn't the purpose of my question, Angelo. I have a personal need to know if you have underworld connections."

"Does it concern the ten million dollars that Allan is loaning you from the fund?" Ike was livid. He couldn't believe that prick Spandell would betray a confidence with this man whom he hardly knew.

"He told you about that?" Ike asked with incredulity.

"Allan and I have grown to be very close. We both respect each other's business judgment. I have been able to be of assistance to him, and he has likewise been supportive of me. Is there some way that I can help you too, Ike?"

Well, the man had in no way shown his hand, but he had certainly led the surgeon to the brink of playing his own hand. If Ike was to make the plan work, then he was going to have to bluntly ask the question.

"Angelo, what I'm about to ask you, I will ask you to keep in complete confidence. Marty Spencer and Allan don't even know some of my business interests, and for right now, I will expect it to stay that way.

"I have a mining interest, gold mining, in Nicaragua. On my last trip to that country, I was approached by a business acquaintance who put me in contact with a group of ex-Contra freedom fighters." Ike's heart was pounding in his chest, and he could feel multiple small beads of sweat forming on his forehead.

"The leader of this group informed me that he and his men had confiscated four plane loads of cocaine from Colombians who were refueling their planes in Nicaragua. He asked me if I could be of service by finding a buyer in America."

"And you told him that you could?"

"I did. I didn't have the slightest idea of how to go about it at the time, and in all honesty, my first reaction was to avoid this deal entirely. But the lure of profits in the several hundred million-dollar range was more than I could resist."

"Tell me, Ike, have you approached anyone else about this?" Galafaro's tone was speculative.

"No. No, I haven't."

"Why then did you ask me?"

"I was just taking a gamble. I suppose that I allowed the old stereotypes to come into play, as well. I wanted this deal to work, and given that I had my back against the wall..."

"This is a very dangerous move on your part, Ike. If I am not the man that you hope that I am, then you have made a reckless miscalculation."

"That is a risk that I felt I needed to take."

"Then in that case, I hope that you have been correct." Galafaro bent over his ball with his putter carefully grasped in both bands and effortlessly sank his putt. Paponis knew that the man was toying with him, or maybe he was just assessing his nerve. Paponis then sank his own putt which was of a slightly longer length.

"Nicely done, Ike." Ike, being away, should probably have shot first, but he was not about to trifle over minor details. The two men put their clubs back into the golf bags, walked to the next hole, and took seats on the bench next to the tee.

"Ike, normally I would have walked away from a deal such as this immediately. But I know a good bit about your history. In fact, I know all about the Diaz Brother's Mining Company. I have to tell you that I'm more than a little concerned about your willingness to be so out in the open about this, but I also think I know a little bit about desperation. I know that you have been siphoning funds off of S.P.S. for quite a few years. I also know that you need a big influx of funds. Yes, you're probably desperate, and that concerns me."

How in the hell did this guy know so much? Surely the trail to Nicaragua had been more concealed than that.

"Angelo, how do you know so much about me?"

"I make it my business to know about the people with whom I work closely." Paponis was openly worried now. He had thought that his business dealings in Nicaragua had been known only to him.

"Have you discussed any of these matters with Allan?"

"No, Ike. Your secrets are safe with me. I am interested in knowing, however, how you intend to pull something like this off. That is, if I were to be amenable to it..."

"Then you're interested?"

"I didn't say that, Doctor. I said that I wanted to know a little bit more about your plan." This guy was incredible. He was carefully gleaning every bit of available information without committing himself to anything. Ike had no choice but to divulge more of the details.

"As you probably know, I am closely associated with Senator Talmadge Hyle. He chairs the Senate Appropriations Committee. My contacts in Nicaragua are close to President Diaz de Santiago. I have managed to arrange a meeting between the two politicians. It is to be an informal meeting, and I also will be arranging a private charter to ferry the entourage to Nicaragua. It is my hope that I will be able to disguise the cocaine in boxes that will appear to be ore samples from my mine. It was also my feeling that an airplane that would be flying a United States Senator on a return trip from an official meeting would be able to avoid the usual scrutiny from the customs officials. I only need to find a buyer."

"Well, for a novice, Ike, I'd have to say that I am impressed with your plan. So you hoped that I would be your buyer?"

"Yes."

"In this particular instance, I am going to break all of my personal rules and allow you to do this business with me. I like your plan, but you must know that if you fail, I will disavow all knowledge of this. From this point forward, you and I will have no further contact. I will have an associate get in touch with you discreetly, and all future logistical affairs will be handled by him alone."

"How will I know who he is?"

"Not to worry, Doctor. You will have no doubts when you meet him."

"Then we're agreed on this?"

"We are. And now do you think we could play some golf?" Galafaro extended his hand, and the two men sealed their deal.

Ike was overtly relieved. The final piece of the jigsaw puzzle was now in place. He had always prided himself on being a good judge of character, and he felt that he could trust Angelo Galafaro. In one week, Ike knew that he would be rich beyond his wildest imaginings. The two men finished their round of golf without further mention of the deal that was to transpire in less than one week.

CHAPTER 16

The Boeing 737 touched down at the international airport in Managua, Nicaragua at the same moment that Richard Cranston was swimming laps at the health club that was operated by the Salesian Brothers of Don Bosco in Portland, Oregon. His recovery had been remarkable after having undergone open heart surgery.

The mayor had not been willing to endure a long period of convalescence as had been recommended by his physicians, Dr. Ike Paponis and Dr. Curt Pifer. He had worried that a prolonged absence from City Hall would weaken him politically, and he would not be able to tolerate that. So he had begun to exercise, slowly at first, and he was now confident that his recovery was complete.

In fact, he felt better than he had in years. Ike Paponis was a miracle worker. The mayor's energy level was already greater than it was prior to his heart attack, and he was not even in tip-top shape yet. He had also made alterations in his lifestyle. Gone were the booze and the cigarettes. He was also paying close attention to dietary considerations.

The mayor had been spending several hours in his office at City Hall following his daily swim, and he knew that within several weeks he would be back to nearly full capacity. He found the warm water in the Olympic size swimming pool to be quite soothing. Perhaps colder water would be more stimulating, but the warmth was so reassuring. He swam slowly, searching more for endurance than speed. He would take a stroke and rotate his head to the right to take a breath of air. If he tired, he would stop and rest. He was not out to break any records.

The pain arrived suddenly and it panicked the mayor immediately. He struggled to make his way to more shallow water, but his body would not respond to the will of his mind. In that instant, Mayor Richard Cranston knew that he was dying.

The pain in his chest was unrelenting, and he was unable to breathe. He felt the weightless sensation as he began to slowly, dreamily, sink under the surface of the water. His body was dead, but his spirit had not yet deserted him. As he expired, he was grateful for the way in which he was dying – it was peaceful beyond his ability to comprehend. But what could have gone wrong?

Clarence Edwards, whose job it was to hold the old building that housed the Salesian Center together, entered the pool room not fifteen minutes after Mayor Cranston had departed the world. He had become personally acquainted with the mayor in recent weeks and had come to like the man immensely. And this said a great deal, for Clarence Edwards had never liked a politician in his life. The mayor had shared his hopes and his fears with this gentle man and Edwards had enlightened the mayor with the wisdom of his years.

When Edwards saw the lifeless form floating in the water, there was no doubt in his mind as to whom it was. The maintenance man was trained in cardiopulmonary resuscitation, and he immediately plunged into the water and dragged the mayor, first to the shallow end, and then onto the hardened concrete deck that surrounded it.

He checked for a pulse and he watched for the rise and fall of the chest. Nothing. He delivered two quick respirations and then began to administer chest compressions. He relied on his training for the synchronization that was necessary for a successful resuscitation.

Clarence Edwards worked until he had dried his clothing with his efforts and had soaked them again with his perspiration. He breathed into the lifeless body until he no longer had any breath of his own. Father Bill O'Brien found him that way – collapsed over the lifeless body of the mayor of the city, unable to try any longer.

The medical examiner's office was summoned and arrived promptly, as did a representative contingency of police officers from the Portland Police Department. The group included two sergeants, a lieutenant, and a deputy commander.

It was clear to all of the trained investigative eyes at the scene that this death was clearly the result of natural causes. It was also obvious to all present that the efforts of Clarence Edwards had been valiant, albeit in vain.

The body of Mayor Richard Cranston was loaded unceremoniously onto the coroner's gurney and laboriously carried down several flights of stairs. It was then carried out into the bright midmorning sun and was placed in the rear of the waiting removal vehicle. The drive to the morgue was a short one, and within minutes the body was laying on the autopsy table, awaiting dissection.

As luck would have it, Martin Spencer was in the building. He was at his desk organizing the details of the medical response team that Senator Talmadge Hyle had proposed. Word had spread quickly that the mayor had died, and the phone was already beginning to ring with calls from the press.

From the moment that he had heard of the initial details of the death, Martin Spencer had known that he would be the medical examiner responsible for performing the postmortem examination. Dutifully he responded to the autopsy room.

Martin Spencer hated to perform autopsies on people he knew, and he especially disliked doing the posts on friends. And Dick Cranston was a friend. But this was nothing more than a task that required him to bear the responsibility that he had accepted a long time ago.

At times like these, he changed to a mode that was mostly mechanical and very methodical. The walls went up, protecting his emotions from the pain that he would surely suffer if he allowed himself to feel anything at all. Dr. Martin Spencer had been a survivor in the field of forensic pathology, and the reason had basically been because he knew his limits.

As he gazed upon the lifeless form of the mayor of Portland, he viewed the imminent task at hand as nothing more than a science experiment. This was the clinical side of his life – to determine the cause of death of a human organism – nothing more.

The external description of Richard Cranston's body was basically unremarkable. There was, of course, the healed surgical incision that coursed downward longitudinally across the sternum, from the sternoclavicular notch to the xiphoid process. This was the incision that had been made by Ike during the mayor's coronary artery bypass graft. The medical examiner also noted that the victim's skin was very pale. But this was not such an odd finding. Most dead people had pale skin.

He opened the body utilizing the usual Y-shaped incision. For speed, and speed was essential, as every media was more that adequately represented in the lobby of the medical examiner's office, he used the band saw to rapidly cut through the ribs. His first view of the organs of the chest was informative in itself. The lungs were characterized by what is known as visceral pallor – they were almost white. As he lifted them up off the floor of the posterior chest cavity, he immediately found out why. Dick Cranston had a chest full of blood.

Marty began to sweat, and he was sure that the blood had drained from his own organs as well. Had his friend, Ike Paponis, killed again? But to what end? Dick Cranston was a close personal friend of the heart surgeon, or at least Marty thought that they were friends. He also knew that Ike had fiercely defended his right to treat Cranston. No, if this had been a consequence or sequela of the bypass graft, then surely it had been nothing more than one of those unfortunate circumstances. A predictable number of people would die in the first six months following open heart surgery. Things just happened that way.

He removed the organs of the chest using the Rokitansky maneuver and began to closely inspect the heart and the major blood vessels arising from it. At this point, he began his dictation.

"Case number forty-three seventy six. Richard M. Cranston. They body is that of a normally nourished and developed adult male Caucasian appearing consistent with the reported age of fifty-four years. The head is normocephalic. The head hair is brown. The eyes are green. There is a healed longitudinal surgical incision in the midline of the anterior chest. The genitalia are adult male and circumcised."

"The body is opened in the usual fashion. The lungs are found to be atelectatic and quite pale. There is no fluid found in the tracheobronchial tree. The surface of the heart is quite disrupted. There is a large rupture of an apparent left ventricular aneurysm with evidence of exsanguination at this site. The margins of the aneurysm are quite well defined."

Marty Spencer completed his examination and dictation, but there were no further items of note. Richard Cranston had died as a result of the rupture of the aneurysm in his heart. The medical examiner was quite relieved. This was a cause of death that made sense and in no way implicated his friend, Ike Paponis. There was at least some comfort in these findings. The mayor had simply pushed himself too hard too fast.

The Multnomah County Medical Examiner responded to the lobby of his building where he immediately became the focus of bright lights, video cameras, microphones, and more screaming reporters than he had ever personally encountered.

"Ladies and gentlemen!" The noise did not abate quickly.

"Ladies and gentlemen!" Slowly the sounds quieted to a gentle roar.

"I have just completed the autopsy on Mayor Richard Cranston. I shall sign the cause of death as cardiac arrest secondary to the rupture of a left ventricular aneurysm with subsequent exsanguination."

Dr. Spencer, was this in any way related to the mayor's open heart surgery?" asked a finely coifed reporter hungry for information.

"In all reality, I would have to say that this is an unfortunate outcome to Mayor Cranston's heart surgery."

"Were there any signs of foul play?"

"None."

"Were there any mistakes made by the surgeon who performed Mayor Cranston's operation?"

"That does not appear to be the case. His bypass graft was intact."

"Had the mayor been drinking?"

"Come on, guys!" Marty Spencer was beginning to get angry. "I know that the mayor has been a prominent political figure in our community for a number of years – that's why I'm talking to you in the first place. But let's not forget ourselves, folks. Dick Cranston has a family, and they are entitled to our respect and courtesy."

"So then he was drinking?" a reporter yelled from the back of the crowd.

"That's all I have." Marty Spencer turned away from the ravenous crowd indignantly and retreated to the sanctity and security of his office before he could lose his temper and dishonor his office.

The television broadcast of Dr. Martin Spencer's statement had gone out live to all three of the local stations. Shelly Grayson had been eating a muffin and drinking a glass of orange juice in the nurses' lounge when her soap opera had been interrupted with the report. Her only comment was, "Oh Shit."

The intercom buzzed in Marty Spencer's office less than one half hour after he had retreated from the uncouth mob of reporters.

"Dr. Spencer, I have a Shelly Grayson on the phone for you. She says that it's urgent." The statement had been intoned by the medical examiner's secretary.

"Who is she? I don't want to talk to any more reporters."

"She's not a reporter. She says that she's an operating room nurse on the open heart team at Health Sciences Medical Center. She says that it has to do with Mayor Cranston's death." Marty Spencer could feel his breath being involuntarily sucked from his body, and the sensation was accompanied by an overwhelming feeling of impending doom.

"Put her through." There was a click on the telephone line. "Dr. Spencer here."

"Dr. Spencer, my name is Shelly Grayson. I'm an open heart nurse at Health Sciences."

"Yes, Ms. Grayson, how can I help you?"

"I just saw on television that Mayor Cranston died."

"And?"

"I was the scrub nurse for his open heart surgery."

"What is it that you're trying to tell me, Ms. Grayson?"

151

"Dr. Spencer, I'm at the hospital. I'd really rather talk to you in person, if I could. I know that you're busy, but..."

"Is it that important?"

"I think it is, sir."

"Do you know where O'Leary's Pub is?"

"The one on Burnside?"

"That's right. I can meet you there in half an hour if that's all right with you."

"I'll be there. My schedule's empty for the rest of the day."

"Okay, I'll see you in half an hour then."

"Thank you, doctor." The medical examiner and the operating room nurse hung up their telephones, and Marty knew that he had a problem. Sure, Ike had been a longtime friend, but how could the surgeon keep putting him in situations such as these?

The medical examiner didn't know if he hoped the nurse had evidence or if he wanted her to have some lame story that didn't make any sense. He did know that he had just lost a close friend, however, and if Ike had been in any way responsible for the death, then regardless of the eventual outcome, he would have to take definitive action.

The medical examiner navigated his Mercedes into the nearly empty parking lot of O'Leary's Pub and then reluctantly got out of the car and walked into the establishment. He stopped and stood just inside the darkened lobby and surveyed the few patrons who were seated at several tables and the bar. He heard his name being called out lowly from a nearby table, and he saw a pretty young blonde seated there.

"Dr. Spencer?" He walked over to the table and sat down.

"How did you know it was me?"

"I recognized you from the television."

"I'm not sure that I like having that kind of notoriety," he said pleasantly as he extended his hand to the woman. "Nice to meet you, Ms. Grayson."

"Please call me Shelley, Doctor."

"Okay, Shelley, what can I do for you?" A waitress arrived and took drink orders and both patrons decided on draft beer.

"This isn't easy for me. I'm not even really sure that I saw what I think I saw."

"But you obviously were confident enough to contact me."

"Yes, I guess I was."

"Go ahead, Shelley."

"As I told you, I'm an operating room nurse at Health Sciences. Several years ago I became concerned during an open heart procedure when I saw a technique being performed that I thought would be ineffective. I didn't say anything at first because I wasn't sure what was going on, but I made a mental note."

"What was the patient's name?"

"William Evans. A few weeks after that I saw in the obituaries that he had died."

"And now?"

"Well, the same surgeon who did Mr. Evan's surgery also operated on Mayor Cranston. Now the mayor's dead, and I felt like I needed to tell someone."

"What exactly did you see, Shelley?"

"On Mr. Evans, the surgeon did a straight stitch on the bypass graft. Usually they tie a series of knots to make the graft stronger or they use surgical staples. I didn't know if maybe it was some type of new technique or something, but when he died, I got really worried. On Mayor Cranston, I'm just about sure that I saw the surgeon make an incision on the wall of the left ventricle with his scalpel. I don't know if it was accidental or not, but this surgeon is usually very meticulous."

"You're referring to Dr. Ike Paponis, aren't you?"

"Yes. Do you know him?" The nurse had been surprised that the medical examiner had stated the name without her having told him who it was.

"Yes, I know him. In fact, he's a friend of mine. At least I think he's a friend of mine. Have you told anybody else about this?"

"No, Dr. Spencer, I came straight to you. I'm sorry. Maybe I shouldn't have said anything in the first place. But when both of these patients turned up dead, I got worried. I hope that I haven't put you in a tight spot by telling you." The nurse was becoming remorseful and a little bit frightened. If the medical examiner covered everything up and then went to Paponis about it, she would probably lose her job – or worse.

But Martin Spencer didn't strike her as being that kind of person. He seemed to be kind and gentle, and he was listening attentively to her concerns. She had seen him on TV and read about him in the newspaper, regarding both his duties at the medical examiner's office, and his volunteer work at the community aid clinic. No, she trusted this man.

"Don't worry about me, Shelley. It took a lot of guts for you to come forward like this and I respect that. I will ask that you not discuss this with anyone else for the time being. I don't exactly know what I'm going to do. It's a touchy situation and it'll be tough to prove. Let me look into this a little further, but you have my word that I'll get back to you on it."

"Thank you, Dr. Spencer. I also want you to know that I think what you're doing at the free aid clinic is great. I've seen the articles in the paper and I think it's wonderful."

"That's good to hear. In fact, right now I'm organizing a medical response team that would ostensibly respond to disasters anywhere in the world. Senator Talmadge Hyle asked me to put this together. I could sure use a few operating room nurses, too. Do you think that you'd be interested in something like that?"

"I'd love to. Would you really need somebody like me?"

"You bet, Shelley. I'll add you to my list if you want me to."

"Sure. And I could talk to some of my friends at work too."

"That'd be great. Listen, I've got to run, but I'll be in touch. Thanks for having the guts to contact me."

"Thanks for listening, Dr. Spencer."

The medical examiner left the tavern with the weight of the world weighing heavily on his shoulders once again. In his heart, he knew that what the nurse had told him was probably true. He also knew that, even if he were not personally involved, allegations such as these would be difficult to prove. All of this was coupled with his prior knowledge of various aspects of the death of William Evans.

In actuality, Martin Spencer had already falsified Evans's death certificate. His examination of Dick Cranston's heart had shown a medical cause of death that was an acceptable adverse effect in a measurable percentage of open heart cases. The only curious finding had been the well-defined margins of the ventricular aneurysm. As the physician reviewed the autopsy in his mind's eye, he could well see that the aneurysm could have been caused by the scalpel blade. Proving that it had been caused by Ike Paponis's scalpel would be quite another matter, however.

Almost without thinking, Marty realized that he was driving directly toward Allan's home. The probate lawyer lived close to the pathologist, and Marty knew that he needed somebody to talk to. Allan Spandell would be the only person who would be able to understand his dilemma. Maybe the attorney might have some ideas about what he could do.

He knocked on the front door of Spandell's house and within moments the heavy wooden doors opened. The entrance hall to the Spandell home was impressive. The chandelier itself commanded almost immediate attention. The lawyer had it custom made at a glass factory on Lido di Murano, a short way across the water from Venice, Italy.

Answering the door was Spandell's eldest son, Allan Jr. The young man was in his final year of law school at Yale University and was apparently home for a visit. He was strikingly handsome. He stood six feet four inches tall, had a lean yet muscular shape, and deep blue eyes that made women melt.

"Allan Jr., I didn't know that you were home. How's school going?"

"Almost done, Dr. Spencer." The younger man still hated being called junior."

"Is your dad home?"

"Yeah, he's back in his office. Go on back. I'm sure you know the way."

Marty walked down the long hallway that was tastefully decorated with expensive oil paintings and beautifully finished antique pieces. He walked into the office and saw that the lawyer was sitting in his favorite chair – a large comfortable lounge of rich black leather. He had his feet elevated on an ottoman of the same material.

"Marty, how are you? What brings you by?" asked the attorney as he raised his head and adjusted his horn-rimmed glasses.

"Allan, we need to talk." The medical examiner quietly closed the door to the study and took a seat opposite Spandell.

"What's on your mind?"

"I suppose that you know about Dick Cranston's death by now."

"Yes, I heard about it earlier today – terrible tragedy."

"That's not the half of it."

"Well, what did you find on his autopsy?"

"Ventricular aneurysm. Nothing shocking, really."

"Then what's the problem?"

"I got a call from this operating room nurse at Health Sciences. Nice gal. Her name's Shelley Grayson. At any rate, in no uncertain terms, she told me that she thinks Ike killed the mayor. She was there for Bill Evans's surgery too. Said the same thing about that case."

"Do you think she's on the level or do you think she's just trying to screw with Ike?"

"Nobody tries to screw with Ike, Allan. You know that. No, I think she's telling the truth. I liked her. And you and I both know what happened to Bill Evans anyway."

"Has she shared this information with anyone else?"

"She tells me that she hasn't. That's not to say that she won't. I got the distinct impression that she expects me to do something about this. Right now she doesn't know how closely Ike and I are associated."

"Why the hell would Ike want Dick Cranston dead? It just doesn't make good sense. As far as I could tell, the two of them were good friends. I think, on face value, I have some serious reservations about this gal's story." What Allan was saying was true, but it was also true that the attorney had some serious concerns about the ten million dollars that Ike had borrowed from the Portland Fund. If Marty went on a sudden crusade and made any loose accusations, then the fate of the ten million bucks could be in serious jeopardy. If anything happened to the money, then Allan Spandell would be in serious trouble as well.

"I don't know, Allan. It didn't make sense to me either. The only thing that is consistent with her story is that the margins on the aneurysm were fairly well demarcated. Physically speaking, the darn thing could have been caused by a scalpel blade."

"Even if that were true, Marty, the whole damn thing could still have been an accident. If Ike made an error in his procedure, it may be able to be construed as malpractice. But there is a big difference between malpractice and murder."

"Maybe not in Ike's view of things."

"You might be right there, Marty. My advice to you is to move slowly on this. Get all of your ducks in a row. Don't make any rash moves or you might end up paying a pretty high price for your impatience."

"I agree with you. Initially I thought that maybe I should get hold of the county prosecuting attorney. But now I think that I should look into it a little more closely myself. I suppose that perhaps even a medical examiner's inquest might not be such a bad idea. Heck, we haven't had one of those in years."

"Marty, for that very reason, I think that you should consider all of this very closely. The media would be all over a medical examiner's inquest. You'd have a circus on your hands. And from a strictly legal standpoint, you would have an obvious conflict of interest. No matter how straight you played it you would be accused of favoritism. If you end up exonerating Ike, nobody would ever believe that he wasn't guilty. I think that the best bet is to just wait until Ike gets back from Nicaragua and talk directly with him. Hell, make the conversation official if you need to. But don't jump the gun on this. I mean that, Marty. Our whole world could unravel if you do."

"I know that you're right, Allan. It's just a tough spot to be in.

Marty stood to leave. "I appreciate the counsel, as usual. I'll be in touch."

"No problem. How's the organization for the medical response team going?"

"Really well. We could probably go within the next couple of weeks if we had to. In fact, I signed up the OR nurse who called me about Ike. We've got ER personnel, medics, OR people, and a good contingent of physicians. Talmadge Hyle has managed to come up with some federal funds for us. It has actually been kind of fun putting this whole thing together."

"Keep up the good work, Marty."

The medical examiner exited the office and let himself out the front door. He had appreciated his friend's advice, but if anything, he only felt as if his hands were even more tied now. He understood Allan's trepidation about moving too fast. He felt it himself, but Ike Paponis, friend or no friend, could not be allowed to continue killing patients in the operating room.

But from a strictly prosecutorial standpoint, the legal issues would be intricate. These patients had not died for several weeks or months following their procedures. Attempting to formulate a case on the death of Dick Cranston would be next to impossible. Even based on the evidence, there was really nothing more than Shelley Grayson's accusations.

As Marty drove into his driveway, he could only mutter to himself, "Goddamn you, Ike Paponis."

CHAPTER 17

The Boeing 737 charter set down onto the runway at the Managua airport as scheduled. The plane was directed to the concourse area reserved for official visitors when extreme security measures were necessary.

Ike Paponis, seated in the first class cabin, looked out of the window to see a large contingent of security police armed with submachine guns suspended from their shoulders with black nylon slings. Probably Berettas, he thought. The khaki uniforms were all neatly tailored and the maroon-colored berets were smartly pulled to the side.

The plane taxied to a stop, and the rolling staircase was wheeled out to the halted aircraft. The front cabin door was opened, and the passengers within the jet began to gather their belongings as they prepared to deplane.

Ike had paid a pretty price to charter the craft, but he knew that if all went well, it would be a drop in the bucket when compared with the profits that he would realize. The ten million dollars in cold currency was neatly stowed in the cargo compartment beneath the passenger cabin. Ike had not expected to get much attention from the Nicaraguan customs officials, but he didn't want to take any chances either.

The surgeon had already informed the flight crew and airline personnel that he would be transporting soil and ore samples on the plane for the return trip to the States. There had been no problems and no questions. Ike had paid for the craft and the crew in advance, and the service had been impeccable.

Talmadge Hyle gathered his overcoat from the overhead compartment and retrieved his briefcase from under his seat.

"Well, one thing is for sure, Doctor. You certainly travel in style. Hopefully, things will go well, and then your country will be indebted to you," he said with a twinkle in his eyes.

"I'm glad to have the opportunity and the means to be of service, Senator. If we can somehow find a way to help the cause of Democracy here in Nicaragua, then it will have all been worthwhile."

The senator bent forward and whispered into the surgeon's ear. "And your little gold mine won't be in danger of being nationalized by a new government, either." Hyle winked at Paponis and then moved by him." Just keeping everything in perspective, eh Ike?"

Paponis knew that he wouldn't be able to pull anything over on the politician and that was just as well. Both men were well acquainted with each other's professional agendas. There would be no misunderstandings.

Hyle had introduced the physician to Jason Riley on the flight down from Dulles, and Ike had found the young reporter to be a bright young man. Riley had queried the surgeon as to his involvement in this whole affair, but the heart surgeon had been deliberately evasive. His own interests, he knew, would not be well served if he were to be given a high profile in the affairs of State.

Nevertheless, having Riley here to record the entire occasion would be of a profound political benefit for the senior senator from Oregon. And since Ike had arranged the whole affair, Hyle would be further indebted to him. It amused the surgeon that all of the political fanfare over this visit was really nothing more than a cover for his true purpose for the trip.

Sharon had made the journey with her husband. He had not been for the idea initially but had relented in the end. She was quite excited to be a part of the whole affair and had been impressed with the high caliber individuals who had made the trip down with her.

The occupants of the plane were ushered through customs without so much as a second look by Nicaraguan officials. There were six government vehicles waiting in front of the terminal as well as a bus for the press contingency. All of the vehicles were Mercedes, somewhat older than one might expect, but were shined to a glossy polish. The luggage was stowed in the trunks of the vehicles, and the short trip north to the Santo Domingo Hotel on Lago de Managua was made with no lack of haste.

The meeting between Senator Talmadge Hyle and President Carmalita Diaz de Santiago was to commence at ten o'clock the following morning, and a lavish reception had been planned for this evening. The visitors went to their rooms, some showered and changed their clothing, and before long the American contingency began to filter into the richly decorated convention hall on the first floor of the building.

One wall of the large room consisted of a huge plate glass window that overlooked Lago de Managua. Ike walked to the bar and ordered a scotch and soda. His wife would join him in a short while after she had herself exquisitely prepared. She wanted to look perfect for this reception.

Ike took his cocktail and stood by the window as he looked out over the lake. The sky was clear as the orange moon began to rise over the horizon. It would be a beautiful starlit evening, and he knew that the romantic atmosphere would not be lost on his wife. But Ike's mind was preoccupied with the logistics of the next twenty-four hours.

"Doctor Paponis." The surgeon turned at the heavily accented pronunciation of his name. He immediately recognized Miguel Dominguez, and he walked more closely to him. He didn't know if it was the worn facial features, the all-knowing look deep within the eyes, or the limp from the bullet wound in the leg from so many years ago, but the end result was unmistakable. The man left a lasting impression on all he met.

"Señor Dominquez, how nice to see you." The two men shook hands in the dignified manner of business associates. Ike tried to mask his surprise at seeing the rebel leader in this environment. The man was certainly dressed appropriately for the occasion but still managed to look oddly out of place.

"Ben Harris tells me that everything is going as planned. Ingenious, Doctor. I am impressed with how quickly you were able to pull together all of the details of our, shall we say, deal."

"The lure of such huge profits was too great for me to drag my heels, Señor."

"Indeed, Doctor. And I trust you were able to secure the funds for my down payment..."

"I was. I have the ten million here in Managua with me."

"How shall we complete the transfer?"

"The funds are on the plane. When you provide the product for me, I will gladly turn the money over to you."

"Do I sense mistrust on your part, Doctor?"

"Ten million dollars is a lot of money, Señor."

"Yes, it is."

"Is it possible that you will bring the materials here to Managua? Have they been packaged as I have requested?"

"Everything has been completed to your specifications, Doctor. I do not think it wise, however, that we make the transfer here in Managua. There are too many eyes in this city, and there is a great deal of interest in the visit of Senator Hyle."

"Where then? And how?"

"We must find a reason for you to land your craft at Siuna. They have a runway that is large enough to accommodate the Boeing 737 that you have come here in. Siuna is just south of Bonanza, and the back roads to that airfield will allow my men to transport the product without attracting too much suspicion. Perhaps you could attribute a stop in Siuna to wanting to show your gold mine to your traveling party."

"That could work, Señor Dominguez. This has been the only part of the plan that has been troubling to me." At that moment Sharon walked up to the two men. She was wearing a black sequined evening gown and had her long blonde hair pulled up on top of her head. Her make up was perfect, and the large diamond earrings that she wore drew immediate attention.

"Señor Dominguez, this is my wife, Sharon."

"You look elegant, Mrs. Paponis. You are a lucky man, Doctor." Miguel Dominguez bent forward and kissed Sharon's hand with all of the grace of a true gentleman.

"You are too kind, Mr. Dominguez," responded the surgeon's wife.

"I am only honest, Señora. Doctor, I will speak with you later this evening." Miguel Dominguez slowly limped off across the room, and Ike turned to his wife.

"You do look stunning, dear."

"Thank you, sir. Do you think a pretty lady could get a drink around here?" The physician escorted his wife across the room and secured a glass of champagne for her. They stood together and stared out of the window enjoying the tranquility of the evening until they heard an increasing chatter behind them.

As they turned to identify the commotion, they could see Senator Talmadge Hyle entering the room. There was a definite flurry of activity as various Nicaraguan government officials tried to get the senator's attention.

Ike Paponis could see that the politician was flanked by the young reporter, Jason Riley. The surgeon thought to himself that this was beginning to look like a very cozy relationship between the two men. In fact, he had noted that Hyle and Riley were sharing a suite within the hotel. He wondered about the exact nature of the relationship, but he didn't dwell on it for too long.

Hyle was in his element. He smiled, and he shook hands. He gave brief soliloquies, and he told humorous anecdotes. He was gracious when receiving praise, and he didn't miss an opportunity to place himself in front of a camera. And there were a lot of cameras in this room.

Jason Riley was taking everything in. Talmadge Hyle had been a great source of material for him over the past several months, but this was big news. He had been personally relieved that the subtle sexual suggestions had recently ceased. But there was still a strange undercurrent – the indication that if the reporter were to encourage the senator in any way there would be no turning back.

Jason had initially thought that exposing Hyle's sexual improprieties was a way to advance his own career, but he was no longer sure about that. He had become privy to some very good information from the senator, and his stock was already rising at the Post. This trip, however, was already the icing on the cake. There was the very good possibility that real news would be made in Managua tomorrow.

A hush came over the crowd, and the very absence of noise within the room heightened interest and anticipation. It was soon apparent that the change within the magnificent hall was due to the arrival of President Carmalita Diaz de Santiago.

She walked into the room flanked by her security personnel and exuded that sense of power that is exclusive to chief executives within their own countries. Deference was granted to her every move. She wore a gray business suit that was conservative in its cut, and her face, with that starkly drawn expression, bore evidence of her struggle. Like any good politician, however, she was able to light up the room with her smile when she chose to.

She and her entourage made their way directly to where Senator Talmadge Hyle awaited her. The two exchanged a handshake that was both warm and personal as well as diplomatically correct.

"Senator Hyle, I welcome you to Nicaragua as a representative of the government which helped to liberate my country from the oppression of the Communists. You are an honored guest here."

"You are too kind, President Diaz de Santiago. My visit is designed to express the continued support of the government of the United States to the people of Nicaragua and to other budding Democracies within our hemisphere and throughout the world. We are proud to be of service to the government of Nicaragua which is now directed by your very capable hands."

The official statements were out of the way, and the photo opportunity was quickly being exhausted. The flashes from all of the cameras had lit up the room like the Fourth of July.

Diaz de Santiago's security personnel appeared anxious as their president gently took the senator by the arm and led him off to a more private area of the room. Their president was not without her enemies, and with a meeting such as was to transpire the following morning, her political stature would only be enhanced. There were those who would like for that not to happen.

"So, Senator Hyle... What truly brings you to Managua?" There was the faintest hint of a smile on her face, and her eyelids were raised.

"Madam President, I am here on behalf of my government to express our continuing support for what you are attempting to effect here."

"Come now, Senator. This all happened far too quickly. What is going on here?"

"I was under the impression that it was you who requested the hastiness," stated the senator from Oregon.

"Senator Hyle, you know my political situation, and you know the state of our economy. Of course, I'm grateful that you've arrived so soon. My only hope is that our discussions tomorrow will be fruitful for the citizens of my country. We are in desperate financial straits, and it will take a good deal of economic support to keep us from collapse. I become increasingly concerned with each passing day that the Communists will once again gain political support and that this chance at Democracy will all be for naught."

"Rest assured that my government will not let that happen."

"I am counting on that, Senator. I cannot overemphasize our need," she stated earnestly.

"I am confident that we can be of assistance. Do you have a moment? There is someone I would like you to meet."

"Certainly, Senator. Lead the way." The President of Nicaragua locked her arm through that of the Chairman of the Senate Appropriations Committee and moved with him as would a bride being led down the aisle.

Ike and Sharon could see the couple moving toward them, and Sharon's heart quickened with anticipation as they drew more closely. She was accustomed to wealth, but she was truly impressed with her proximity to political power.

"Dr. and Mrs. Paponis, I would like to introduce the President of Nicaragua, President Carmalita Diaz de Santiago." The woman extended her hand first to Sharon Paponis and then to the heart surgeon.

"So this is the man responsible for our meeting. I also understand that you have a mining interest in our country, Doctor." She had caught the physician off guard, and she could see the surprise as it registered in his eyes.

"You have done your homework, Madam President," said Ike with obvious respect.

"One does not survive long in a volatile environment if one is not aware of whom they are dealing with. Since politics is always volatile, I always try to keep myself aware."

"Most admirable." Ike really did respect the woman's obvious toughness.

"So you think our economy might actually fail, Doctor?"

"My intentions were merely to see that it doesn't."

"Well, Dr. Paponis, we will accept you at your word, and we will graciously accept any financial help that we can get at this point."

"Mrs. Paponis, I am glad that you have accompanied your husband here. Perhaps we will get the chance to talk before you have to return to Oregon. I don't get much chance for girl talk these days."

"I would like that, Madam President."

"Please, my name is Carmalita. All of these titles tend to get burdensome. At any rate, it has been nice to meet the two of you, and I sincerely appreciate your intervention on behalf of my government, Dr. Paponis."

Hyle and Diaz de Santiago drifted away and across the room.

She had no intention whatsoever of meeting privately with Sharon, but the mere suggestion of such a meeting had elated the surgeon's wife. There just wasn't time for small talk – not in this lifetime anyway.

Ike was duly impressed with this woman whom he had never met. She exuded a sense of inner strength and power.

"She's marvelous, Ike."

"She's a strong woman. She has to be. Her opponents would eat her alive otherwise.

There was a great deal of celebrating that continued late into the evening. Jason Riley was careful not to consume too much alcohol. He was trying to collect as much data as possible for a series of articles that he hoped would run upon their return to Washington.

He had been quite relieved by the way he had been treated by the senior senator from Oregon on this trip. It was becoming quite obvious that Senator Hyle was utilizing him as a conduit to make sure that the media treated the politician favorably. In some ways, Jason was beginning to feel like the senator's private publicist rather than a newspaper reporter. But not so slowly, he was beginning to make his climb in the newspaper business.

The crowd began to thin out, and Talmadge Hyle made his way to the bar. He secured two servings of champagne and deftly and discreetly dropped an ample amount of methaqualone into one of the glasses. He noticed that his companion was now standing alone and staring out over the fully moonlit Lago de Managua. He casually made his way over to where the reporter stood.

"Jason, I think you would be quite safe to enjoy a cocktail at this point. I think most of the activity is over for the evening."

"Thank you, Senator," said Riley as he accepted the refreshment.

The two men sat on a couch near the window and were silent for several long moments.

"It'll be a big day tomorrow." The senator seemed distant and just a bit reflective.

"You have a very real opportunity to help these people, Talmadge. And from everything I've seen, they need it. You know, we don't do this sort of thing often enough. We're so darn anxious to bring down governments that don't conform to our philosophy, but we abandon the new Democracies that arise. There is something innately wrong with that."

"Jason, we do nurture developing Democracies. We can never do what certain segments of the population expect us to do, and we always do more than other segments of the population would have us do. You have to remember that these young governments, in a large part, attain their strength from the depths of their struggle. We try to be supportive but not overbearing."

"But there are starving children here, Senator."

"There were starving children before the revolution, Jason. There are starving children in the United States. We have only so much in the way of resources, and the demand certainly exceeds the supply."

"I suppose you're right, Talmadge." The reporter was barely able to speak through his yawn.

"Come now, Jason, let's go to bed. We'll need to be up early in the morning, and that is not so long from now."

The senator leaned over the couch and helped the young reporter bring himself to a standing position. Riley actually did fairly well staying erect, but he was definitely groggy. They moved slowly across the reception room floor toward the elevators.

"I'm sorry, Senator, I didn't realize that I was so exhausted. I've never had one glass of champagne affect me this way. I'm just so tired."

"You've been pushing yourself too hard, Jason. Couple that with jet lag, and you have your explanation." Hyle pressed the button in the elevator that closed the doors.

Talmadge Hyle had to drape the young man's arm across his own shoulder as they made their way the short distance from the elevator to the suite of rooms. The senator retrieved the key from his pocket and somehow managed to open the door with his one free hand.

The two entangled men staggered into the room, and Hyle managed to drag Jason to the bed where he rapidly began to undress the younger man. At first Jason seemed to struggle though his semi-delirium, but the drug-induced listlessness overtook him, and his motions became more uncoordinated and his speech became more unintelligible.

Inside of Jason's mind the world was spinning. He was terrified at the implication of what was happening to him, but he was powerless to stop it. The senator removed his clothing as well and joined the younger man on the bed.

Jason felt Hyle's hands begin to fondle him – felt the man's mouth and tongue on his neck. He was screaming inside for the humiliating abuse to stop, but he was unable to verbalize the words. The politician's pace was becoming more accelerated, and it wasn't long before Jason felt the statesman's mouth in an area where it never should have been.

As repulsive as the entire affair was to him, the reporter responded to the simulation in a manner that further offended him. All of those adolescent fears, all of those concerns about achieving a true masculinity were once again challenged while he writhed on the hotel bed with another man.

Hyle aggressively sought the younger man's satisfaction, but the effects of the methaqualone so disrupted Jason's concentration that climax would not be achieved.

Through the haze of the chemicals, the reporter felt the dulled and delayed sensation of pain. Over and over again the older man thrust against him until his body stiffened with orgasmic pleasure. Jason could feel the tears of humiliation. He had been wantonly raped by one of the most powerful men in Washington.

His mind raced, and the progression of his thoughts was such that they were incongruent with one another. But he tried to concentrate – tried to insure that his memory of the event would not be erased. Only a very brutal revenge could exact any measure of justice.

Jason could feel the bed move as Talmadge Hyle disengaged himself and rose to the floor. He could hear the senator moving about the room, and he was aware of the light being turned off. He was alone with his disgrace now, but he must remember. Remember. Remember. Remember...

Ike was a nervous wreck, and that fact was not lost on his wife. She attributed her husband's tension to the hoped for success of tomorrow's meeting between Senator Hyle and President Diaz de Santiago. She had donned her most seductive negligee and teasingly attempted to interest him in making love to her. But he was so preoccupied.

The warmth, the tropical plants and flowers, the beauty of the moon over Lago de Managua, and the close proximity of so many powerful people had ignited a fire deep within her that would be difficult to extinguish. Her husband, however, had seemingly not even noticed. He only sat in a lounge chair and stared out at the lake.

"Come to bed, Honey."

"I will in a minute. I've got other things on my mind right now."

"I hope that wasn't meant to make me feel good. Is it the summit meeting tomorrow that has you concerned?"

"That's at least part of it. If we can't get this economy turned around, I face the very real possibility that I'll lose my mine. I've got millions invested in that damn thing, Sharon."

"Relax, Ike. You've done everything that you can do. If this all works out, you'll be aiding an entire nation. That's got to make you feel good about yourself."

It was true. Ike Paponis felt good about himself, but the only reason was that he soon expected to be depositing one hundred million dollars into his bank accounts. Money was the best aphrodisiac that there was for a man like Ike Paponis. He turned out the light, went to bed, and did his best to extinguish the fire that was burning within his wife.

CHAPTER 18

The morning of the summit meeting dawned brightly in Managua, as if to foreshadow the hopes of great strides for the people of Nicaragua. The same room on the lower level of the Santo Domingo Hotel was being used for the discussions. The hall had been decorated far differently this morning, however. There was a long table centrally located within the reception hall that had been covered with a long white tablecloth. Chairs were neatly arranged around it, and every three feet there was a fresh pot of coffee and an iced pitcher of water.

Upstairs in the suite of rooms assigned to Senator Talmadge Hyle and Jason Riley, the senator was standing before a wall mirror, finishing the knot on the rich red silk tie that he had chosen for the occasion. After doing so, he put on the tailored pin-striped suit coat. It was his power suit and that was how he felt on this day. He knew that his actions of earlier that morning would never be remembered by his traveling companion. He had insured that the dose of methaqualone was sufficient to prevent that.

The senator rounded the corner and walked into the room where the young reporter was still sleeping. Such a beautiful man. He just stood and stared for a long moment and then walked over to the bedside and attempted to rouse him.

"Jason, wake up. Jason." He shook his friend's upper arm and shoulder, and all he got was a groggy response.

"What? Where am I?" Riley rolled over and opened his eyes. He looked at Talmadge Hyle's face, but recognition came slowly to him.

"We're in Managua, Jason. Remember the summit meeting?"

"What time is it?"

"It's eight thirty. I'm going to go ahead and go down. You should probably get up and get moving."

"Holy shit! Eight thirty? I don't even remember going to bed last night."

"You were very tired, Jason. You had one glass of champagne and nearly passed out."

"Gosh, that's weird. That's never happened to me before."

"International travel sometimes does that to you. Don't worry about it. I'll see you shortly." Hyle stood and exited the room while Jason stared at the ceiling.

He could not understand the haze in his brain regarding the end of the evening. Amnesia such as this was so uncharacteristic of him. And here he was, stripped naked in bed in a foreign country, sharing a room with a powerful political figure whom he strongly suspected of deviant sexual behavior. Not a pretty picture.

Jason got up and headed for the bathroom. He was immediately struck by a physical sensation that gave him an overwhelming feeling of dread. Had the senator drugged him and then violated him? Surely that couldn't have happened. He showered, dressed, and went downstairs to the summit meeting while his mind searched for some rational explanation for the unusual set of circumstance that had befallen him.

Talmadge Hyle joined his aides in the conference room as all of the participating parties began to assemble in the hall at the same time. There was no need for much conversation between him and his aides. This was not a bargaining session. He had come to Managua with authorization for a specific economic support package. Any other requests would have to be considered at a later date.

There was a good deal of fanfare, and everyone seated within the room rose as Carmalita Diaz de Santiago entered the room flanked by several members of her cabinet. She took her place at the table and invited everyone else to take their seats.

"On behalf of my government and the Nicaraguan people," the stately president began, "I would like to welcome Senator Talmadge Hyle and the other representatives of the government of the United States. We would like to express our friendship to your country, and we would also like to renew our vow of responsibility to protect Democracy in our hemisphere.

"I must also express my gratitude to Dr. Ike Paponis, whose role in arranging this meeting has been instrumental in bringing our two countries together.

"Nicaragua has been involved in the struggle to be free for many generations. We have faced many oppressors, and our victory alone is a testament to the validity that all people should be free to effect their own fates. The despots must not be permitted to control the masses.

"And so it is today that my country must rely on our friends in the United States to nurture our struggling economy. It is not our wish to become dependent upon the goodwill and generosity of other nations, but we are now like a young child who must be supported in order that we might grow strong. And with this support we shall eternally pledge our commitment to the principles of a free and Democratic Nicaragua."

There was applause from those seated at the table as President Carmalita Diaz de Santiago concluded her opening statement. When the applause began to subside, Talmadge Hyle took his cue to begin his statement. As he raised his eyes above the reading glasses that were riding low on his nose, he saw Jason entering the room. He glanced at the young reporter but received nothing in return but a cold stare.

"President Diaz de Santiago, esteemed members of your cabinet, honored guests, it is my distinctive honor to be sitting at this table today to represent my government, the government of the United Sates of America.

"The struggle of the Nicaraguan people to be free has been a long and arduous one. You have our respect. The battles that you have won, the sacrifices that you have made and continue to make, the ironclad resolve of your people to join the ranks of other free and democratic peoples in our world, demands that we aid you in your struggle for independence.

"It is not enough that you have defeated Communism. It is not enough that dictatorship has been replaced by an elected government. It is not merely enough that the will of the people has been realized. You must be able to feed and clothe your children. You must have schools that will educate those children in order that they might compete in a global marketplace. Your democracy must survive to be a beaming banner to other would-be democracies in our hemisphere and throughout the world.

"For these reasons, the government of the United States has a desire to assist your efforts to provide a stable economy for your people. We know that you are a proud nation, and therefore, we do not intend to dictate to you. We intend to provide both grants and loan guarantees that you can utilize as you see fit. I have prepared a list of specific proposals, and we have carefully detailed the full extent of what we have the opportunity to offer to your country. So let's get down to business."

Folders opened, papers were passed to the participants of the meeting, coffee was poured, breakfast rolls were eaten, and within just a couple of hours, smiles graced the faces of all who were seated at the table.

Jason was not seated at the table, and he was not smiling either. His gaze had met that of Senator Hyle several times throughout the three hour session, and the senator knew that obviously, the young reporter's memory had not been completely erased.

Jason, on the other hand, had no specific memory of the events of the previous evening. He had only a strong physical sensation that he had been raped. He was in Managua on official business, however, and he would do his job and keep his perspective until a later, more private moment presented itself.

Ike awakened on the morning of the Summit having his continuing bout with nervousness. He had made all of the necessary plans and preparations for the transaction that would take place later that same day. He searched his mind, trying to visualize any possible scenario, any possible complication, and then he would rapidly assimilate what he thought was the proper contingency. The process, however, was making him crazy. There were just too many things that could go wrong.

The surgeon and his wife had hastily packed their suitcases that morning, and he had then sent her out on an escorted shopping trip. He had found it unusual that one of the hotel services had been to provide bodyguards to those patrons who needed them. That fact alone had alerted him to just how perilous of an environment he was operating in.

Ike was busy attempting to make telephone calls. He called Ben Harris in Bonanza, he attempted to call Angelo Galafaro in Portland, but there was no answer, even after repeated attempts. Had something gone wrong already?

While the meeting between Talmadge Hyle and President Carmalita Diaz de Santiago was concluding, and while Ike was nervously pacing in his hotel suite, Ben Harris, Jorge Delgado, Emilio Vega, Miguel Dominguez, and a small complement of hired hands were on the road to Siuna.

The men had carefully packaged the cocaine in plywood boxes which were then stenciled with the logo of the Diaz Brothers Mining Company. They were then marked **CORE SAMPLES**. It had required a total of six five-ton trucks to transport the coke overland to the airfield at Siuna, and the whole group gave the appearance of a military convoy.

Miguel had obtained papers from his friend, President Diaz de Santiago, that would prevent the group from being questioned or inspected by any Nicaraguan government officials. He had told her the same story that Ike had told to Talmadge Hyle. These were soil and core samples from the surgeon's gold mine in San Pedro del Norte. There had been no questions asked.

In fact, Dominguez feared the Colombians more than he feared his own government. The packaging of the cocaine had been completed in a remote area, and he had complete faith in the loyalty of his men, but the road to Siuna was a long one, and a convoy across the mountains was bound to attract attention. Fortunately, the distance to be traveled had forced them to leave in the dead of night, and hopefully, they would be far from where the

Colombians were operating by first light.

It was early afternoon as the meeting at the Santo Domingo Hotel began to break up. The sun was shining brightly on Lago de Managua, and the American contingency rapidly collected their belongings and then returned to the hotel lobby.

The disaffected stares of Jason throughout the morning had informed the senator that now was not the time to be alone with this man. It was for this reason that he kept one of his aides with him at all times. No overt remarks had been made by the young reporter, but his mood was strikingly cool.

"How did it go, Senator?" The voice had been that of Dr. Ike Paponis, and Talmadge Hyle turned toward it.

"Splendidly, Ike. I couldn't have asked for anything more. You did a fine job of organizing the entire affair. I'm sure that the President is going to be quite proud of both of us."

"That's good to hear, Talmadge. Are we just about ready to go?"

"I think so, Ike. I've been told that the motorcade is standing by. Now we have a stop to make for you on our way out of here, don't we? It won't take too long, will it?"

"No, Senator. No longer than half an hour. All of the security arrangements have been made as well. So you have nothing to worry about there either."

"You are quite the planner, Ike. You'll make a wonderful Untied States Senator someday."

"And judging from what you've managed here today, you'll make a fine president too, Senator."

"Let's get the stuff loaded and get out of here. I'm anxious to get home." Talmadge Hyle picked up his briefcase and checked to make sure that his other baggage had been loaded.

The Americans loaded into the five black Mercedes and the one tour bus and began their trip to the Managua airport. Word of the success of the Summit must have spread quickly because the streets were lined with the citizens of Managua. They ranged in age from infants in their mother's arms to the emaciated elderly. The casual observer would have identified hope in eyes where none had existed only several weeks before.

The motorcade made its way down the crowded streets, and Talmadge Hyle smiled and waved as if he were a conquering hero. Jason Riley sat stiffly by his side in the back seat of the luxury sedan.

"It looks like you're quite the hero, Senator." There was just the slightest hint of sarcasm in the reporter's voice.

"This is all certainly more than I expected. It is just a bit overwhelming, isn't it?"

"Yes, I'd say it's certainly a bit overwhelming, Senator," said the journalist referring to items other than crowded streets.

He remembered. Dammit, he remembered. Hyle could feel the air within the sedan begin to get close. He could also begin to feel the beads of sweat as they formed on his brow. What would Riley do with the information? Suddenly, Talmadge Hyle knew that he needed to get out of the car.

"Stop the car!" Hyle's request had been just a bit too desperate, and it startled the driver, who was quite fluent in English.

"But Senator, we have no stops scheduled."

"I said, stop the car." More controlled this time. More in control.

The Mercedes came to a halt, as did the others in the convoy, after receiving the radio message from the senator's vehicle. Ike turned in his seat to see Talmadge Hyle and Jason Riley exiting the rear door of their car. He could also see that the crowd was going nuts. In a matter of seconds, the two men were completely engulfed in a sea of people.

"What the hell is he doing?" Ike could see his plans going up in smoke with the senator's efforts to get a photo worthy of the cover of a national magazine.

"That looks dangerous, Ike. Why is he doing that?" Sharon sounded totally befuddled.

"It's a fool's move, Sharon. God, it's not like Talmadge to take chances like this. He's been around too long to pull a stunt like this."

"Should you get out and help him?"

"No way. Look at that crowd. They're out of control. I only hope that he can manage to get back into the car." Ike had been talking to his wife, but now he directed his attention to his driver. "Get on the radio and have them get the senator back in the fucking car!"

"Right away, Doctor."

Ike felt almost as if he were watching a movie – so helpless was he to change the event that he was watching. The crowd was becoming wilder, fueled with the opportunity to touch this man who had surely changed their fates.

In the bell tower of the Catholic church that was diagonally across the street, a singular figure watched the activity below him. There were others like him, strategically placed along the route that the motorcade would take.

But is was his good fortune that the motorcade had stopped directly in front of him. His shot would be the one that would kill the senator. His would be the act that would renew the hostilities, would restore the Sandinistas to their rightful place of power in Nicaragua. He would be a hero for generations to come and all of this was nothing more than his fate – nothing more than blind luck.

He raised the M16 rifle that he had acquired from one of his victims on the battlefield. He had equipped the weapon with a high-powered scope, and within seconds he had the cross-hairs trained on the neck of Senator Talmadge Hyle. This would be the shot that would change his world – would change the direction of his country.

The gunman could feel the adrenaline as it surged through his body. He could feel the perspiration as it seeped through his pores. He tried to steady himself, but there was the slightest tremor in his usually still hands. He knew that he must squeeze the trigger gently while he kept the sights trained on his target. To jerk it would cause an errant round, and the opportunity would be lost.

Ever so slowly he began to squeeze the trigger. Any second now the firing pin would fly forward within the bolt, the round would be discharged, and the foreign politician would be dead. Then the money would not come, and the government of Diaz de Santiago would collapse.

The pigeon came from nowhere and flew directly into the side of the sniper's head. The bird had lived in the bell tower for quite some time and had never encountered a human there before. It was not the bird's fault. The gunman was the intruder here.

The man was startled as he squeezed the trigger, but the mission was more important than his own safety. For all he knew, he had just been struck by a bullet from the rifle of a soldier or a policeman. He continued to squeeze the trigger, but he had been unnerved enough that the bullet did not strike the designated target.

Talmadge Hyle felt the impact in his left shoulder at the same time that he heard the collective gasp from the crowd. It was as if time froze. He did not feel pain initially – just the sensation of falling as the force of the round slammed him into the ground. So helpless was the feeling. Will I die here? Has it all come down to this?

Jason was frantically calling for help, but he could not be heard above the din of the national police returning fire to the bell tower. Nothing survived in that bell tower– not even the pigeon whose home it had been.

The crowd hit the streets amid the gunfire, and Jason found himself on all fours above Talmadge Hyle. He could see the blood as it rapidly soaked the politician's shirt and suit coat. What a pitiful figure the man had become.

"Hold me, Jason. Please? I need you to hold me. I'm so afraid." As Hyle spoke, the words and events of the previous evening were startled into Jason's consciousness.

"Hold me, Jason. Just hold me." The senator's naked body on him. Kissing him. Caressing him.

Jason started to rise to his feet. He could feel the vomit welling up within his stomach, and he tried desperately to hold it back. He looked Talmadge Hyle directly in the face and spit directly where he was looking.

"Help yourself, you fucking bastard!" The emesis followed his words and soon the powerful politician was bathed in a mixture of blood, vomit, and saliva. Jason turned and forced his way through the bodies that were lying on the street. He had to get to the car. Let the faggot die on these Godforsaken streets. He didn't give a rat's ass.

Ike was rapidly losing his composure within the vehicle in which he was seated. He now knew that he was in the midst of a combat zone, and what was worse, he was unarmed and had his wife sitting next to him.

"Get the cars moving! We've got to get the hell out of here. Get to the airport. We're going to have to count on the Nicaraguans to take care of Senator Hyle. There's nothing that we can do for him now."

"Ike, are you sure? We can't just leave him here. We've got to do something – anything."

"What we've got to do is to get moving. Look around you. If there are more snipers out there, it's going to turn into a turkey shoot for them. I'm not going to tell you again, get this car moving, and get on the horn and get the rest of the motorcade doing the same thing."

Ike could see his chances for completing the deal that would give him his fortune going down the tubes. This was one scenario that he had never even considered. Wasn't that just the way of the world? The one thing or event that you expected least was exactly the one that you got.

The Mercedes began to force its way through the crowd as the masses parted, allowing the vehicle to pick up speed. The driver of Ike's car was on the radio as he drove, and soon the other vehicles within the motorcade were following him – all except the vehicle that had been carrying Talmadge Hyle.

"Doctor, they tell me that the senator has been shot in the shoulder. There is no way of knowing where the bullet went once inside of him, but there is a lot of blood." The driver was relaying information that he had just received on the two-way radio.

"He's going to need a hospital. It wouldn't have done any good to pull him into the car and head for the airport. He's definitely going to need medical attention in a controlled environment. We've got to get that damn jet off the ground before any terrorist group can get to it. How is security at the airport?"

The driver turned his head over his shoulder to speak to the physician. "Security is very good, Doctor. It would take a well-organized effort to wrest control from the national police."

"Good. How long until we are there?"

"Fifteen minutes, Doctor."

Ike's thoughts were racing with incredible incongruity. He tried to force them into cohesion, but there were so many factors to consider. His primary goal at this moment was to get to Siuna and load the cocaine. But he also knew that he was going to have to be able to explain every move that he made. He was going to have to explain why he, a practicing surgeon, had left Senator Hyle behind, and that was not going to be easy to do.

"Driver, call ahead to the airport and advise the pilots to get the engines fired up. We're going to have to be able to get off the ground quickly. We'll reassess just exactly what the hell is going on after we have gotten airborne. After you do that, call the other vehicles, and inform them that everyone is going to have to be responsible for their own luggage. What they can't carry gets left behind."

The driver did as he was instructed, and as the crowds began to thin out, he was able to accelerate to speeds that began to scare Sharon Paponis. No matter how fast the man drove the car, however, they would never be able to outrun a bullet.

The motorcade arrived at the gates of the Managua airport to armed and uniformed sentries waving them through with white-gloved hands. Ike, by virtue of his position in the lead vehicle, could see a flurry of activity around their airplane. The cars pulled rapidly alongside the aircraft, and the exodus from the vehicles commenced with haste.

Within what could have only been moments, the passengers were boarded, the doors to the aircraft were closed, and the Boeing 737 was taxiing to the end of the runway for takeoff. There was a sudden increase in the sound level as the engines revved, and the passengers could feel the craft tremor ever so slightly.

The plane lurched forward and in a very short time was airborne.

"What the hell is going on?" Talmadge Hyle's chief assistant was struggling against the steep incline in the ascending aircraft.

"Look, we don't know what's going on down there. We were scheduled for a stop about an hour away from here anyway. We'll just go ahead and set down in Siuna until we know what the heck is going on." Ike was trying to be the voice of reason in the midst of all the confusion.

"But you just can't leave a United States Senator stranded in a foreign country after he's been shot."

"I have no intention of leaving him here. We're just getting the rest of us and this plane off the ground before we're all taken hostage. There was nothing that we could have done for Senator Hyle back there. He needed to be taken to a hospital where he could be stabilized for transfer."

"But you're a doctor, aren't you?"

"I'm a doctor, but I've got no supplies to work with. I'd like to be able to work miracles, but unfortunately, I'm not trained in that art."

"So we'll go back and get the senator before we leave the country? I've got your word on that?"

"Absolutely."

The aide returned to his seat in the rear passenger's compartment as the plane began to level off at cruising altitude. Ike got out of his seat and walked the short distance to the cockpit.

"Are you guys picking anything up on the radio?" He had directed his question to the pilot.

"Whatever the hell is going on down there sounds pretty organized. They've got firefights in the streets of downtown Managua, and there was an assault on the airfield. So, it's a darn good thing that we got out of there when we did."

"So right now we're on course for Siuna."

"That's correct, Doctor."

"Okay, we'll set down there and load my cargo as previously arranged. In the meantime, we'll try to get a handle on what's going on in Managua. We're going to have to go back there to pick up Senator Hyle. There's no two ways about that. Hopefully, this will give us some time for the situation to stabilize."

"I hope you're right, Doctor. I sure as hell don't like the idea of setting this bird down on a hot landing zone. I haven't had to do that since Viet Nam, and I don't care if I never have to do it again."

"That's why I thought the best solution for right now was just to get the hell out of there."

"I think it was a good move, Doctor. We'll get you to Siuna, and then we'll take things from there."

"Thanks a lot." Ike made his way back to his seat. His wife could see the stress lines on his face, and she knew that he felt personally responsible for what was going on.

"Don't worry, Ike. Everything will work out just fine." Her husband looked directly into her eyes, but he didn't speak. What his wife didn't know was that the safety of Talmadge Hyle was the last thing that he had on his mind.

The Boeing 737 touched down uneventfully onto the runway at the Siuna airport and taxied to the cargo loading area as previously planned. As Ike looked out of his window, he could see the five-ton trucks parked neatly in a row awaiting the arrival of the American jet.

When the plane came to a stop, Miguel and his men navigated the portable conveyor system under the jet and began to load the crates into the cargo compartment of the airplane. The men worked quickly and efficiently, and within twenty minutes Ike Paponis's fortune was neatly stowed and secured within the bowels of the giant aircraft. Ike then made his way outside of the plane where he met Miguel.

"Señor Dominguez, are you aware of what is happening in Managua?" Ike had dispensed with all pleasantries, and his question took Miguel Dominguez, who had been on the road for hours, completely by surprise.

"No, Doctor, I haven't been told of anything."

"Look, Senator Hyle has been shot. There are firefights in the streets, and the airport has been assaulted."

"The Sandinistas?"

"I can only presume."

"Those bastards. I had feared that something such as this would happen. It was too perfect of an opportunity for them to disrupt the government. How large of an insurgence are we talking about?"

"I have no idea. I only know that Senator Hyle was shot after he got out of his car in downtown Managua. We were in our motorcade en route to the airport, and he just couldn't resist the temptation to get out and have his picture taken with the people. He is still in Managua." Ike's dejection was obvious to the rebel leader.

"And now you have a planeload of cocaine, and you must fly back into hostile territory to rescue your senator. Not an enviable position to be in,

Doctor."

"Do you have any suggestions, Miguel?"

"My helicopter is only an hour's drive from here. I would like for you and two of my men to go there with me to get it. Keep this craft on the ground for several hours until we have a chance to get close to Managua, and then we will radio them to rendezvous with us there."

"Why do you need me to go with you?"

"You are a doctor. If those stinking pigs have the hospital sealed off, we may need to get you in. You are just going to have to trust me on this, Doctor. By the way, I am still looking for my ten millions of American dollars."

"Just give me a minute." Ike went to the cargo compartment of the airplane and returned the cash to Miguel Dominguez. He then climbed back into the airplane and informed the pilot of their plans. Having done so, he went back out onto the tarmac and got into the passenger seat of one of the five-ton trucks. Miguel was in the driver's seat and Jorge and Emilio Vega took their places under the olive green canvas cover in the bed of the truck.

Dominguez navigated the vehicle northward toward a small village west of the town of Tunki. It had been months since he had flown the helicopter – longer still since he had been involved in a firefight. Now his blood was boiling at the possibility of getting into a skirmish. The money had changed nothing for him. He still hated the Sandinistas and nothing in the world would ever change that.

He had the five ton going as fast as it would go on the bumpy unimproved dirt road that was heavily littered with potholes.

"So just what is it that you plan to do, Miguel?"

"We have to get the senator out, Doctor. If we are unable to accomplish that task then all is lost. My country is desperately in need of the aid that your country has been willing to provide. If the senator is killed or even held hostage, then the money will not come. I cannot let that happen."

"But Miguel, you are a rich man now. Why not just let it go?"

"Some things are more important than money. This is my country. I will fight to the death to save it."

"This may be a fool's journey, Señor Dominguez."

"Then so be it. I will make it anyway."

They traveled along in silence after that exchange, and Ike wondered what role he would be playing in all of this. He was not, and had never been, a combat soldier, and he had no inclinations in that direction. He wanted no part of the rescue operation, but at this point, he had no choice.

They arrived at the village and then veered off onto a road that was even worse than the one on which they had been traveling. It was here that Miguel Dominguez kept his largest stores of weapons and equipment. The villagers had been fiercely loyal to the Contras and the fight for freedom, and they continued to protect Miguel's cache of weapons as if it were an insurance policy against the tyranny that had beset them for so many years.

The sun was beginning to set on the horizon, brilliant hues of oranges and deep purple, as Miguel brought the truck to a halt and turned off the engine. Ike began to feel a bit nervous. He could see no helicopter, and the memory of the two Colombians, in their decapitated state, was all too close to his consciousness. Now that Dominguez had his money, Ike wondered if he had become expendable.

As soon as the vehicle came to a stop, however, Delgado and Vega hopped out the back and ran toward the tree line. They began to fold back a large camouflage drape, and within seconds the form of a large UH-1H combat helicopter came into view.

"This is my baby, Doctor. Do you like her?"

"Pretty impressive, Señor Dominguez. There aren't too many guys that I know who have their own military helicopter. Do you know how to fly it?"

"You insult me, Doctor. I could fly my baby when I was sleeping." Miguel began to limp across the field toward the chopper. He had adopted the same persona that one would expect from a teenager who had just waxed his prized Camaro.

Miguel pulled back on the sliding door to the rear of the front passenger seat and locked it open. He then climbed into the craft and opened the door on the other side. He was crouched down, a position that was difficult for him, as he moved up and into the pilot's seat and donned his green flight helmet. Within moments he began to warm up the engines and check his instruments.

Meanwhile, Jorge Delgado and Emilio Vega were busy transporting weapons from a large metal container nearby. They mounted M-60 machine guns on swivel mounts in the rear compartment and packed hand grenades, assault rifles, C-4 plastic explosives, and light anti-tank weapons into the center of the craft.

Soon Miguel had the rotors turning slowly, and Ike began to climb into the ship. He could see that Dominguez was shouting into his helmet-mounted microphone, and he presumed that the soldier was getting a condition update on the situation in Managua. Ike was glad that his fears of being killed by Miguel were proving to be unfounded. He was troubled, however, that his prospects of being killed by the Sandinistas were very real.

They were in the air now, hovering until they had attained a sufficient altitude. Miguel then dipped the nose of the chopper and set a heading of west by southwest.

He was contour flying – keeping the helicopter just above the treetops and other prominent terrain features. The speed was fast enough to tighten the sphincter muscles of even the most stout-hearted individual. Jorge and Emilio were manning the machine guns and scanning the earth that was rapidly passing below their ever-vigilant eyes.

Ike had wished that Ben had been with them, but Miguel had designated the mercenary to fly aboard the 737. Ike knew that he was way out of his territory, his area of expertise, and he longed for some other familiar faces. In some ways, however, he was glad that Ben was in a position to guard his shipment of cocaine.

The time passed quickly but took forever doing so, and soon the lights of Managua began to come into view. Ike could hear the conversation between Dominguez and someone else, presumably within the city. The dialogue was entirely in Spanish and its meaning was lost on the heart surgeon.

"Doctor, the resistance is more organized than we had expected, but the forces are small. They have taken the terminal building at the airport, and they have the hospital surrounded."

"So what do you propose that we do, Señor?"

Miguel looked over at the physician with a half-crooked smile.

"We will land at the airport and retake the terminal building. Then, we will fly to the hospital, destroy every last Sandinista pig, and then we will transport your senator back to the airport for a safe trip to the United States."

"You make it sound easy."

"I have been fighting these bastards for more than ten years. If this battle is concluded tonight, then yes, it will have been easy."

As soon as Miguel had finished speaking, the first tracer round left the ground in search of the helicopter. It looked like a fine bright red laser beam streaking across the sky. Tracers were only loaded every third or fourth round, and the bullets that were unseen caused the most concern.

"Get ready, Doctor, we're going in."

"You're out of your mind!" screamed Ike. Miguel only laughed a wild possessed laugh as he zigzagged his way toward the parking lot outside the terminal building.

Firing tracers worked both ways, and Jorge and Emilio were able to identify their targets from the points of their origin. The M-60 machine gun to Paponis's rear laid down an almost constant steam of fire, and soon the ground fire had been effectively suppressed.

Miguel cruised along the front of the terminal building, barely ten feet away from the structure. He then executed a hard bank to the left, quickly leveled off, and gracefully set the bird on the ground. With a quick move upward, both Vega and Delgado disengaged their M-60 machine guns from their mounts and jumped out of the door.

It appeared as if all of the resistance had dispersed by the time the two men hit the front door to the terminal building.

"Where are the bastards?" screamed Jorge as he burst through the glass doors.

"They were all outside, Señor."

"Then they are all dead."

Running as fast as they could, while carrying the machine guns, the two freedom fighters reassumed their positions on the helicopter, as Miguel lifted off before they were even completely settled.

The Santo Bernadetto Hospital was a mere eight minute flight from the Managua International Airport.

"Doctor Paponis, I am going to set the ship down on the top of the hospital. Jorge will go with you, but the two of you will be responsible for getting the senator out of the hospital and back up to the roof. You must move as quickly as possible. I do not know how big the resistance force will be, and I do not know how long we will be able to keep them at bay."

Dominguez sat the Huey down on the hospital roof amidst a frightening flurry of both incoming and outgoing rounds. Ike bailed out of the door as did Jorge and his machine gun. The two men ran to the only door on the roof. After they realized that it was locked, Jorge fired a short burst into the lock, and the door exploded open.

The surgeon and the soldier began to rapidly descent the multiple flights of stairs, and at each floor Jorge opened the door with his weapon at the ready position. When they reached the fourth floor, they realized immediately that this was where the bulk of the patient population was housed. A number of people in the hallway were startled as the two men exploded through the doorway.

"Donde esta le Americano?" Jorge's voice was booming.

As soon as he had finished speaking, two men down the hallway turned and revealed assault rifles. Delgado's finger was already on the trigger and the two Sandinistas died before they were able to fire their weapons.

Ike was the first to enter the room, and he was surprised to find Talmadge Hyle sitting in a lounge chair calmly gazing out of the hospital room window.

"Are you my conquering hero, Ike?"

"For God's sake, Talmadge. What the hell happened down here?"

"Just another of many coup attempts"

"Well, Senator, there's a helicopter on the roof, and I think we ought to get the hell out of here. Are you okay to travel?"

"You would probably know more about that than I would. I feel comfortable in your very capable hands though, Ike."

The senator was wearing a sling, and his shoulder was heavily bandaged. But he appeared to be surprisingly well to the physician's appraising eye.

"Well then, Senator, let's go." Jorge had been standing guard in the hallway, and when Hyle and Paponis came through the door, he led the way back to the stairwell.

"Rather distasteful business, Ike," said Hyle as he looked at the two dead men laying on the hallway floor. He found it remarkable that none of the health care workers seemed interested in tending to the two men.

The surgeon supported the senator with a hand under his good arm, but Hyle ambulated without apparent difficulty. As they neared the top of the building, the three men could hear the chatter of gunfire outside of the building. Miguel had kept the rotors on the chopper moving, and Jorge, the senator, and Ike boarded rapidly. Within seconds they were once again airborne.

Talmadge Hyle now occupied the front copilot's seat, and Ike was in the rear with Emilio and Jorge. The rounds were dispersed all around them as they lifted off, but Miguel did not rise very far vertically, but rather dipped the nose and sped off laterally toward the airport.

Just as they cleared the edge of the building, Emilio was thrown backward into the center of the helicopter where he landed on Ike. A quick inspection by the physician revealed a rapidly expanding blood-moistened area in the center of Vega's chest.

"Emilio's been hit," Ike screamed into his mike. "Get us the hell out of here!"

Miguel banked the helicopter back around and began to dive the craft toward the source of the gunfire.

"What the hell are you doing, Miguel? Ike sounded nearly hysterical.

"You'd better man the machine gun, Doctor. The bastards will pay for what they have done to Emilio.

Ike was reluctant, but the speed of his motions did not reveal it. He was at the back of the gun and looking through the sights as if he was a trained soldier. The tracers were rising from the ground, and Ike was firing back at where they were coming from. The bullets fed through his machine gun as they rose from the ammo box at his side, that was secured to the floor of the helicopter.

To the surgeon, the scene was surreal. If it wasn't for Emilio's dead body laying next to him, it would have felt a lot like game of war that he had played as a child. But this was no game, and the bullets were very real.

In minutes, that seemed an eternity, the ground forces had been neutralized. Miguel once again banked the helicopter toward the airport.

Eight minutes later he set the Huey down within yards of the Boeing 737. Hyle and Paponis removed their helmets and began to exit the chopper. Miguel met them on the ground and escorted them to the portable staircase below the door to the jet. Ike offered his hand and then grasped the soldier's forearm with his other hand.

"Thank you, Miguel. I'm sorry about Emilio."

"Emilio has died a hero's death. You are a friend to my country. I'll look forward to hearing from you soon." And with his comment, Miguel winked his eye.

"Good luck to you, and I hope you heal quickly, Senator."

"Thank you, Señor Dominguez. I think, with all things considered, I have been pretty lucky already."

The Sandinistas never could shoot straight. You had that in your favor."

Paponis and Hyle ascended the steps while Miguel returned to his helicopter and rapidly lifted off. He was a rich man now, and once again he would be a hero for having squelched yet another coup attempt.

CHAPTER 19

As Talmadge Hyle bent over and entered the door of the aircraft, the passengers on the plane rose and applauded – all except one, and that was Jason Riley. Immediately, the senator's aides were all over him like nervous mothers.

"It's okay, boys. Nothing more than a flesh wound." The senator was reveling in the attention, and he knew that his popularity at home would skyrocket. Yes, he might be able to ride an incident such as this one right into the White House. And Ike would be the big hero – manning a machine gun in the rescue effort that had clutched the senator from the hands of the Communists. This would certainly make for good press.

"If everyone would please take their seats and fasten their seatbelts, we'll get out of here before anything else goes wrong." The pilot's voice coming over the loudspeaker sounded like God, and it had the desired effect.

The occupants of the airplane had never taxied more quickly, but the pilot had trained in the military, and he was familiar with exiting hostile airfields in a hurry. The plane rolled and then flew.

"I need a drink," said the senator once the plane was airborne.

"Me too, Senator," answered Ike.

Soon the booze was flowing and the stories of their trip to Nicaragua were being embellished. The reporters interviewed Hyle and Paponis and carefully recorded the details of the rescue.

Sharon could not have been prouder of her husband than she was at that very moment. As he recanted his tale to the press, only then did she realize how much danger he had been in. She would have been very satisfied to have been married to a heart surgeon, but her husband was a hero, and he was now helping to effect international policy.

The more alcohol that was consumed, the livelier the crowd became. But there was one passenger who kept completely to himself. Jason had been treated like a stepchild after the senator had been shot. Nobody could understand how he could have returned to the vehicle while leaving the bleeding senator laying on the crowded streets of Managua. They would all know soon enough. Jason would keep his mouth shut for now, but he had every intention of slaying the senator in the press when they returned.

In at least one way, Ike was glad that the coup attempt had occurred. It had created the perfect diversion for the trip to Siuna. No one would ever question the cargo in the hold of the plane. For American officials, the truly precious cargo being returned to the United States was seated in the first class compartment. The crates that bore the stamp of the Diaz Brothers Mining Company would never get a second glance.

All of this did not entirely put Ike at ease, however. The very last facet of this operation was close at hand, and that fact alone served to make him increasingly more nervous. So he treated his anxiety with alcohol and hoped that his ability to reason would not suffer too greatly.

The Boeing charter touched down uneventfully at the Portland International Airport and taxied to a stop at gate ten on the main concourse. It was a rather inebriated crowd that deplaned shortly thereafter, to the near-constant flashes of cameras, and the bright lights that illuminated the area for the video units.

Senator Hyle was inundated with questions as soon as he stepped into the gate area. The news of what had happened in Managua had obviously preceded them.

"Tell us what happened, Senator. Were you in fear for your life? Who were the aggressors? Is it true that Dr. Paponis was involved in the rescue effort?"

Talmadge Hyle was blasted, and he had every right to be. He had been shot and held hostage by terrorists and had literally had the piss scared out of him. His aides were well aware of his condition and rapidly intervened on his behalf.

"The Senator will answer all of your questions, but not tonight. He has been through a tremendous ordeal and needs medical attention." The aide took the senator by the arm and quickly led him through the crowd which reluctantly parted in deference.

Ike was the next target of the media. The surgeon kept looking over his shoulder at the crew unloading the cargo from underneath the plane. He hoped against hope that they were Angelo Galafaro's men.

Ike could see Galafaro standing against a wall across the walkway that traveled down the center of the concourse. He could also see Marty, flanked by two Portland policemen, and looking rather somber faced.

"Dr. Paponis, tell us about the rescue. We hear that you participated in the shooting. Did you have to kill anyone?" Ike had his beautiful wife on his arm, but the surgeon looked haggard, and he too was drunk.

"I'm afraid I'll have to defer questions for this evening as well, folks. It's been a long day." Sharon and Ike slipped through the crowd of reporters, and Ike whispered into his wife's ear. "Go ahead, honey. I'll catch up to you in a few minutes. There's somebody I need to talk to."

Dutifully, his wife moved on toward the main part of the terminal without question. It had been a long day, and she was tired.

The surgeon started toward Angelo Galafaro but was intercepted by Marty Spencer. The police officers stayed close behind.

"That was quite an act you pulled down there, Ike."

"Thanks, Marty. I never expected you to meet me here at the airport. Believe me, it's great to see you. What's with the police officers? Is there something going on that I don't know about?"

"I'm afraid I'm here on official business, Ike. I need you to come down to the office with me to answer some questions."

"Come on, Marty. It's three o'clock in the morning. I've had a helluva day, and I need to get some sleep." The reason for Marty's statement had totally averted Ike's cognition.

"I'm afraid I'm going to have to insist, Ike. We need to have a serious heart-to-heart.

"What's this all about, Marty? And what's with the police officers? You and I are friends. You should know that all of this isn't necessary." Ike was pleading.

"I'm afraid it is necessary, Ike. I need to talk with you about the death of Dick Cranston." The surgeon kept redirecting his glance toward Angelo Galafaro who allowed no change in his demeanor. In fact, he was pretending to ignore what was going on with Paponis and Spencer.

"For Chrissakes, Marty, Sharon is going down to collect the luggage, and we need to get home. Couldn't we do this in the morning?"

"I'm afraid not. One of the officers will insure that Sharon gets home okay. Don't make this any tougher than it already is. Do you think this is easy for me? This is the last thing in the world that I want to be doing right now."

"Okay Marty. Let's go talk and get this over with. Tell this officer to go ahead and get back to what he was doing. You don't need the police to have a conversation with me." The physician was already verbally disarming the medical examiner. After what he had been through in Managua, he knew that Marty could not pose much of a threat to him.

The police officers were discharged to find and escort Sharon. The surgeon and the medical examiner made their way to Marty's waiting Mercedes.

"Where are we going, Marty?" Ike asked as they pulled away from the curb in front of the terminal building.

"I thought we'd go to my office."

"Why not just come by the house. I could fix you a drink, and we could talk this thing over."

"You've had enough to drink, Ike. And what I've got to talk to you about is serious business."

"What's this about anyway? I did Dick Cranston's bypass. You know that. Everything should be okay."

"Ike, Dick Cranston is dead." Spencer was driving down the road, but he was looking directly at Ike – looking for any sign of emotion – looking for guilt on the man's face.

"Dead? What the hell happened?" After everything that had happened to the surgeon that day, acting surprised was no difficult task.

"A ruptured ventricular aneurysm." By this time, they had reached the medical examiner's office, and Marty parked directly across from the front door and got out of the car. Ike did likewise, and the two men crossed the street and entered the building.

The apparent seriousness of the situation had sobered the surgeon rapidly, and his mind was working overtime trying to prepare his explanation. He had never expected any repercussions regarding the death of Richard Cranston. He had especially not expected any flak from Marty Spencer. But here he was, and from all appearances, this was no joke.

They walked across the lobby and into Martin Spencer's office. The medical examiner then closed the door, moved behind his desk, and took his seat. Ike had already slumped down on the couch against the far wall.

"Marty, you know as well as I do that ruptured ventricular aneurysm is a potential complication following any open heart procedure. It's a damn shame, but it happens."

"I know it happens. In fact, I never even gave it a second thought until I got a call from your scrub nurse."

"Shelley called you?"

"She did. And we met later. She suspected that something was amiss clear back when you did Bill Evans' procedure, and we both know what happened there. So when she came to see me regarding Dick Cranston, and as you can probably guess, I had to take her seriously."

"She's just got an axe to grind, Marty. Sometimes I ride those people a little hard. She just got it in her head that this was a good way to get back at me."

"Darn it, Ike. Quit trying to bullshit me. We both know that there's more to this than some scrub nurse trying to play games with your reputation. This is a level-headed professional. Even knowing what she knew, having seen what she saw, she was still apprehensive about coming to me with it. So why don't you just tell me what the heck is going on, or I can just get an officer down here to read you your rights, and we'll just take all of this one step further."

"Settle down, Marty. Dick Cranston was my friend. About the last thing in the world that I would want to do is to in any way be responsible for any harm coming to him. What would I have to gain? This is ridiculous. What did she say that she saw, anyway?"

"She said that you made a deliberate incision into Dick Cranston's left ventricle before you closed him."

"Give me a break. It was a ventricular aneurysm. Ventricular aneurysms happen without any help from anybody in a predictable number of cases. You know that."

"Ike, I'm going to be honest with you. The margins of that aneurysm were too well defined to have been caused by anything but a scalpel blade. I thought that was unusual when I first did the autopsy, but like I said, I never really gave it a second thought. But after Shelley Grayson contacted me with her story, all the pieces fell into place."

"So you're not really looking for any answers from me. It sounds like you've got your tight little scenario put together already. What do you want from me, a full confession? Okay, I screwed up. I had that deal with Paul Switzer, and I'm afraid I let myself get a little rattled. Shelley was telling the truth. I did slit the wall of the ventricle, but it was definitely not on purpose. I made a technical error. What else can I say?"

"I think this is the first time in all the years that I've known you that you have ever admitted to making a mistake. I appreciate your honesty, but we still have the problem of what to do about this. Ms. Grayson seems to believe that you did this deliberately. She acted as if she expected something to be done. How can we handle this?"

"Do you mean that you're satisfied with my explanation?" Ike seemed surprised that the whole affair could be resolved so easily.

"I'm satisfied with your explanation, Ike. Shelly Grayson, however, may be quite another story. I think that we're going to have to do something, and I want to know what it is that you want me to do."

"Don't worry about Shelley Grayson. I'll take care of her."

"I'm afraid that I can't let you do that, Ike." Marty was in charge for the first time ever in any interchange that he had with Ike Paponis, and while he was trying not to gloat, he was certainly enjoying the moment.

"What do you mean you can't let me do that? She works for me. The accusation that she made involves my professional reputation. I can handle it."

"No, you can't. You've got to remember that she cited the Bill Evans case as well. If she raises a ruckus over that one, I could be implicated too. I gave her my word that I would investigate her charges, and I have to be good to my word."

"Well, what do you plan to do?"

"I think the best way to handle this is to conduct a Medical Examiner's Inquest. That way, I maintain control, and it would be more in your favor than a grand jury would be."

"No way, Marty. That would destroy my reputation and standing in the community. Talmadge Hyle was talking to me about a possible run for his senate seat. This kind of publicity would ruin that. Don't do this to me."

"This is the best I can do, Ike. If you think about it, you'll see that I'm doing you a favor."

"Well then, don't do me any favors. Let this go, Marty. The Bill Evans thing is bound to come out, and then you're screwed too. You could squelch this if you really wanted to."

"I can't, Ike. Too many people know about this."

"Who else knows?"

"I had to talk to somebody so I told Allan. Miss Grayson told me that she thinks the anesthesiologist and another nurse probably made similar observations to hers. I think you're just going to have to face this because the inquest is going to happen."

Ike stared directly into Marty's eyes and delivered the coldest bone-chilling glare that he could muster. And after what the surgeon had been through in the last twenty-four hours, the look was nearly sufficient to unnerve the medical examiner.

"If you do this, Marty, you'll live to regret it. I promise you that."

"Then so be it. My hands are tied."

Ike rose from his chair and spun around to leave the office. He had opened the door and was starting to walk out when he heard Marty's voice to his rear.

"Don't go too far, Ike. I'll be in touch."

"Screw you, Marty." Ike slammed the door and walked outside where he realized that he had no transportation home.

The night was cool and crisp, but clear. The black limousine pulled forward and stopped next to the curb directly in front of the medical examiner's office. The rear electric window on the passenger side came down, and Ike immediately recognized Angelo Galafaro as the occupant of the limo.

"Can I give you a lift, Ike?"

"Hell yes." Galafaro opened the door, and Ike got in.

"Can I get you a drink?"

"A glass of Scotch would be nice, if you've got any." Galafaro poured the liquor and offered it to the surgeon.

"It should make you breathe a little easier knowing that everything came off without a hitch. The transfer was made, and there was no suspicion by any of the customs officials as far as I could tell. That was an impressive act that you pulled down in Nicaragua. It's been all over the television news. You have my respect. That took a good deal of courage."

"I didn't really have much choice. Those bastards had pretty poor timing when it comes to making a political statement, though."

"I guess that would depend on your perspective. At any rate, you are a hero, and that can only be good for business."

"Well, it's the only thing that is going smoothly for me right now."

"You're referring to the charges regarding Dick Cranston's death. He was the mayor of our city, Ike. There were bound to be questions."

"How the hell did you know about that?"

"I told you when we first met that I make it my business to know my associates' affairs."

"This hasn't exactly been common knowledge."

"I'm not a common man, Ike. I thought that you knew that. What do you think will happen now?"

"Marty is threatening to hold a medical examiner's inquest."

"That still sounds better than a grand jury."

"That's what he said. I hope you'll pardon me if I don't agree with you."

"Don't even worry about all of this, Ike. You're a rich man now. The fight is over. You can do whatever you want."

"How exactly am I going to be paid now that the merchandise has been delivered?"

"Approximately one hour ago, I made a transfer of funds to the Bonanza,

Nicaragua branch of the Banco Natzionale. That is, I believe, where the affairs of the Diaz Brothers Mining Company are conducted. The transfer was in the amount of three hundred million dollars."

"Holy shit."

"Holy shit indeed, Dr. Paponis. This business with Marty Spencer will blow over. Don't trouble yourself any further. You are a rich man." The limo came to a stop in front of the Paponis residence, and the surgeon got out.

"Thanks for playing it straight with me, Angelo."

"That's the only way I play it. I'll be in touch. Be sure to give me a call if you need my help." The physician closed the door, and the limo sped off down the street.

CHAPTER 20

Jason Riley was in his editor's office making every attempt to effectively plead his case. This was no longer an effort to gain notoriety. It had become much too personal for that.

He had not said one word to the senator on the return flight from Managua, and it was all that he could do to keep from physically assaulting the man. His only regret now was that the sniper's bullet had not been more carefully aimed.

"He's a homosexual, Mike. It's time to break the story. I've been working on it for months. I know for a fact that he's homosexual, and it's one of those right-to-know issues. If he had been up front about it, that would be one thing. But he's been masquerading as an arch-conservative, and that's bullshit."

"What's your proof, Jason?"

"This is extremely embarrassing for me to tell you about. While we were in Managua, Talmadge Hyle drugged me and then raped me. I'd like to kill the sonofabitch, but I'll settle for ruining him politically."

"Do you have any corroborating witnesses?"

"To my particular incident?"

"In anything, Jason. What have you got on Hyle other than what specifically happened to you?"

"I've got two senatorial aides who told me that the senator coerced them into having sex with him."

"Coerced? What do you mean by that? Were they forced?"

"They were led to believe that their jobs would be in jeopardy if they didn't relent."

"And these guys are willing to go public with this?"

"No, but they don't have to. I'm willing to put my name on it."

"It'll be your word against his, and his will carry more weight. I can understand that you would be incensed by what has happened to you, but from a legal standpoint, you don't have a leg to stand on."

"But Godammit, I was raped by a United States Senator. There's got to be something that I can do about it."

"Try to get your personal emotions out of this. You're a reporter in a foreign country. You were covering a diplomatic visit by a highly ranked U. S. Senator whose sole purpose for visiting that foreign country was to endow that government with millions of U. S. Dollars. You had no witnesses. You have no evidence. You have no proof. I hate to tell you this, son, but unless you can get those two aides to come forward, you don't have a story either. I wish that I could be of more help, but I can't. Deal with this the best way that you can, but from the paper's standpoint, you're on your own."

"Let me go to work on those two aides. If anything new happens, I'll be in touch."

"Jason, I feel terrible about this, but my best advice to you is to cut your losses, and let this thing go. This is not a battle that would be easy to win. If we broke this story based on your word alone, then Talmadge Hyle would own this newspaper. We just can't allow that to happen."

"Thank you for your time, sir." Jason had been intensely angry, but now he was merely hopelessly dejected. Since he now knew that he would not be able to publicly humiliate Hyle, his only recourse was to confront the man.

Talmadge Hyle had required surgery to rebuild his left shoulder joint after returning to Oregon. There was much associated publicity during his convalescence, and he was riding high politically.

The coup attempt in Nicaragua had been effectively put down by Miguel Dominguez and others of the Nicaraguan Militia, and already funds were being channeled to Managua. Talmadge Hyle was a hero in both Managua and Washington. Americans were glad to see their tax dollars aiding a fledgling democracy in their own hemisphere.

Hyle had used his convalescent period to tend to details in his home state that he had never seemed to find time to deal with before. One of these details was his involvement with the Medical Response Team. He had used his influence and connections to attain medical supplies and food. There were contingencies for aircraft, and field tents were already in storage to be used as portable operating rooms.

The senator had met frequently with Marty Spencer and Ike Paponis to shore up the details for possible emergency response. He had attempted, during these meetings, to mend the apparent rift that had developed between the two physicians, but for the most part, his efforts had been unsuccessful. The medical examiner had not been amenable to the senator's propositions. He held no malice toward Ike, but he definitely felt that the duties of his office required him to take some definitive actions regarding Shelley Grayson's accusations.

Ike had not moderated in his opposition to a medical examiner's inquest. It was a seldom used and antiquated method of obtaining information. As a result of its sheer infrequency, it was bound to attract a lot of media attention. Ike did not hold with Marty's contention that some sort of action was necessary. Give him fifteen minutes in a private room with Shelley Grayson and the entire affair would be permanently laid to rest.

Marty, on the other hand, was bound and determined to see the proceeding through to its natural conclusion. He alone would make recommendations as to whether or not an indictment should be handed down, and he had no intention of making any such recommendation. This was merely his way of making a statement to Ike.

In the medical examiner's mind, the heart surgeon was out of control. The inquest would serve notice to him that his actions would not henceforth be without ramifications. Marty saw it as a tidy little was of making his point without exacting too high a price on anyone. Shelley Grayson's accusations would be answered, Ike would be heeled in, and Marty's stature within the community would not be in any way diminished.

The only person who had been truly concerned about the potential long-term conflicts had been Allan. The attorney had the luxury of being on the outside looking in, and he didn't like what he was beginning to see. Marty was getting a little lost in his power play, and Ike, if pushed much further, would explode. For this reason, Allan had also tried to mediate a reconciliation between the two men.

The medical examiner and the probate attorney had met for lunch in a small restaurant in downtown Portland. They had opted for sandwiches only, and Marty had been on the defensive from the outset.

"So I suppose that we're having this lunch so you can get me to take the heat off of Ike. That seems to be everybody else's priority these days."

"Marty, you're paranoid. We haven't gotten together for lunch for awhile, and I just thought it was about time."

"I'm sorry, Allan. I guess I have been getting a little paranoid about this whole thing. You wouldn't believe the heat that's been coming down on me over this."

"Yes, I would. This is an unusual way to conduct a potential criminal case, and it was bound to attract attention. You knew that going in."

"Yeah, but I never expected all the crap I've gotten over this. Talmadge Hyle has been calling me nearly every day. The reporters are all over it. The county prosecutor has been dragging his feet the whole way. He wants a grand jury and thinks it's foolhardy to do the inquest in the first place."

"Malcolm's concern, and it's a legitimate one, is that evidence obtained in an inquest might not be admissible in a future criminal proceeding."

"There aren't going to be any future criminal proceedings, dammit. That's the whole reason I decided to do the inquest in the first place."

"Then what the hell are you doing, Marty? You're going to open a can of worms. You know Ike. He's coming apart at the seams over this thing, and heads are going to roll. Shoot, Marty, we're in business together. Our fortunes are all tied together in one tight little bundle. If you mess with him, he's liable to screw with us ten times worse. He's a vindictive sonofabitch. Why don't you just back off of this thing?"

"I can't, especially not now. I would be accused of a cover-up and maybe even complicity. Too many people have got their claws into this, and they're not about to turn loose of it now."

"Haven't you considered that you're bound to take some heat when you don't recommend a criminal indictment?"

"You're probably right. But the fact of the matter is that there isn't enough evidence to indict. Look, I'm the medical examiner. It's within my jurisdiction to conduct an inquest. That's what I've decided to do. Ike is just going to have to learn to live with it."

"I hope you're right, Marty. Because if you're not, there's going to be hell to pay." The two men finished their lunches in relative silence. It was clear to the probate attorney that the medical examiner's mind was made up regarding the issue, and further pressure would not be productive.

Ike had been acting like a caged animal. He could barely tolerate the fact that all of his financial dreams had finally been realized, and Marty had him stuck in Portland where he couldn't get his hands on his money. Spencer and his principles had become absolutely insufferable. The surgeon now had more money than he could have ever hoped for. He also had a great deal of power at his fingertips. In fact, the funds that he had reaped from the Nicaraguan deal would be more than sufficient to buy Talmadge Hyle's senate seat when the politician finally abdicated.

But now the damn county medical examiner, a man that Ike had counted among his few close friends, was poised to ruin everything. In many respects, none of it really mattered anymore. Ike was wealthy beyond his dreams. But money alone, he knew, would never serve to occupy his sensibilities in the years to come. He had to find a way to come out of this unscathed.

The surgeon had retained the services of the best malpractice attorney that money could buy. Allan had put the two men in contact with one another. It had also been Allan's counsel that had persuaded him to hire a malpractice attorney rather than a criminal defense lawyer in the first place.

There had been several considerations that had gone into the decision. First of all, to have hired a criminal defense lawyer would have suggested that the surgeon was concerned about criminal culpability. By hiring a malpractice attorney, it lent a civil tone to the whole affair that, it was hoped, would assuage the media into complacency.

Ike didn't really care either way. To him, any suggestion of malpractice, and certainly under these conditions, would be as damaging as would be the suggestion of criminality. All that he could feel was betrayal by a man that he had called his friend.

Sharon had shared her husband's outrage. The man that she was married to was a powerful and gifted surgeon, and the accusations that had been bandied about were nothing short of slander. She had done everything that she could do to be supportive, but in the end, her efforts had done little to comfort her husband.

Ike was intense. As far as Sharon knew, all heart surgeons were intense. But there was something very different about his mood recently. He was threatening and ruthless. He was frightening.

The surgeon had talked about the retribution that he would exact against his enemies when this whole affair was over. But his tone was violent rather than legal. He wasn't threatening lawsuits – he was threatening physical harm to anybody that was not in his corner on this issue.

Allan had proven his loyalty, but the attorney had also expressed concern over the ten million dollars that Ike had borrowed from the Portland Fund. The surgeon was more than a little pissed over that fact too. As unlikely as it all seemed, the only two people that Ike seemed to be able to trust were Talmadge Hyle and his wife.

He had tried to make a transfer of ten million dollars from his account at the Banco Natzionale in Bonanza, but there had been some sort of red tape that would require him to sign for the funds initially. He didn't exactly understand the difficulty, but he was also quite familiar with the many bizarre governmental regulations of the country of Nicaragua. The bottom line was that it was just another aggravation that was causing him grief.

The morning of October tenth dawned brightly with the full glory of yet another Indian summer day. Ike awakened early, showered, and dressed. He was in no mood for conversation, and his wife was able to discern that fact early on.

The two had not been married all that long, but already she was becoming quite adept at reading the sometimes subtle signals that her husband exuded. If he had never mentioned a thing to her regarding the inquest, she still would have known that he was facing some sort of crisis of great personal import.

The inquest had been a headline story every day for the previous week and intermittently for the past month. It was a process that the media types were unfamiliar with, and therefore, it had aroused their curiosity. There had been research done into the history of the coroner's inquest, and the whole archaic process had lent to visions of inquisitions and guillotines.

The editorial on the evening news the night before the inquest had been delivered by the station owner and that was an oddity in itself. His speech had not been in the American tradition of innocent until proven guilty. He was ready to hang the heart surgeon for murder most foul.

"And it should be clear to the citizens of this county, that if guilty of nothing else, Dr. Ike Paponis is certainly guilty of the most grievous violation of the Hippocratic oath, that he, like all other physicians throughout the civilized world, must swear to upon becoming a medical doctor. Ladies and gentlemen, physicians are sworn to do no harm. How then can Ike Paponis look himself in the mirror and say, 'I have done no harm?'."

The nurses from the cardiac care unit at Health Sciences had all been interviewed, and they had detailed the incident of Dr. Paponis punching Dr. Paul Switzer. The cardiologist, being the gentleman that he was, had declined comment.

The end result was that Ike had been tried and convicted in the media, and despite the fact that he would probably never be criminally prosecuted, his medical career was over and his political career would never begin.

"Honey, it's eight thirty. I think we ought to get going." Sharon was making every attempt to remain cheerful amidst the stressful conditions.

"Sharon, I don't want you to attend this farce." The surgeon's tone had been dismissive, but his wife had forced herself not to be offended.

"Ike, I'm your wife. I have every intention of being with you through this thing. I know that it must feel like the world is closing in around you right now. And I know it also must feel like you're being deserted by your friends. I won't desert you. If that is the only constant that you have in your life then, hopefully, it will be enough. I love you. I hope you know that."

"Sharon, there will be all sorts of lies told about me during this proceeding. I've got more than a few enemies, and they're all lined up for their chance to take a pot shot at me. I don't want the way you feel about me to be affected by those lies."

"I don't know if I should feel loved that you want to protect me or offended that you don't think I'm astute enough to recognize a political railroad job when I see one. You know, Ike, I had a life before I married you. I'm able to make up my own mind about things, and the one thing that I'm sure of is that you are a good man and a skilled surgeon. I don't know why all of this is happening, but I intend to see it through with you."

The beleaguered surgeon cradled his wife under his right arm and rested his chin gently on the top of her head. For the briefest of moments, he felt secure. He felt that eventually he would be able to put all of this behind him and get on with his life.

"Okay, let's get this over with." They put on their jackets, went to the garage, and got into the Porsche. Ike, feeling more confident, navigated the vehicle downtown to the Multnomah County Justice Center.

As was expected, the media vans were everywhere. After all, this was a case involving the death of a beloved mayor, and a prominent local heart surgeon had been accused of having caused it. News just didn't get any better than that.

Ike parked his car in the garage across the street from the courthouse, and with an air of authority, strode with his wife toward the front steps of the edifice.

The picture of the couple on the sidewalk was that of privilege. Both Ike and his wife were poised and well dressed. It didn't take long before they had been identified by the news teams, and were inundated with microphones in their faces, and video cameras trained on their forms.

"Dr. Paponis, do you have a statement for us?"

"Doctor, what of the allegations against you?"

"Why did you feel the need to kill Mayor Cranston?" The question raised the hair on the back of the surgeon's neck. He stopped, faced the microphones, adopted his most personable posture, and began to speak.

"I was advised by my attorney not to talk to the media. I value that advice, but the allegations that you are making are outrageous. I played no role in Dick Cranston's death. In fact, he was my friend, and I have been suffering a great deal of emotional grief as a result of my not being able to have extended his life further. This whole process has gotten away from you, ladies and gentlemen. I am a healer, and I resent the implication that I am anything else."

"Why then were you betrayed by your own surgical nurse?"

"I have no idea what Ms. Grayson's agenda is. Perhaps she is mentally ill. Maybe she is doing the bidding of some unknown enemy of mine. The bottom line, folks, is that I expect to be fully exonerated when we have finished with this process."

"Why a medical examiner's inquest, Doctor? Isn't it true that there hasn't been a proceeding such as this in Portland in more than 30 years?"

"I know that inquests are not common, but I truly do not know how long it has been since we have had one here. The obvious answer to your question, however, is that the officials of this city and county are conducting an inquest merely to address Ms. Grayson's spurious allegations. If there was any real evidence, then this would be a criminal trial. They obviously can't indict, but the case has a high enough profile that they feel like they need to do something. I don't know. I suppose that you would have to ask Dr. Spencer or our illustrious prosecuting attorney, Malcolm Barnes, why I am being persecuted in this fashion. I'm sorry, but I'm afraid that we had better get inside or I will be late to my own inquest."

Ike and Sharon took the elevator to the eighth floor and then strolled nonchalantly into a crowded courtroom The medical examiner's office, not having adequate facilities, had made arrangements to utilize one of the chambers of the Multnomah County Superior Court. Sharon took a seat next to Allan and his son, Allan Jr. Ike made his way to the front of the courtroom and was seated next to his attorneys, Sean Merrick and Kurt Krieger.

Merrick and Krieger were the finest malpractice attorneys that money could buy. Their track record was a nearly unblemished slate of wins, and their schedule of fees conversely reflected that record.

Merrick was the ebullient one, lambasting opposing witnesses and coddling judges and juries. Krieger was the antithesis, a scholar of the law who won cases based on meticulous fact finding and an almost mechanical delivery of those facts. Together they made a formidable team.

The two lawyers had never defended a client who was facing a medical examiner's inquest, but this was otherwise the type of case that they actively sought – high profile, high stakes, and a wealthy client paying exorbitant fees.

During a medical examiner's inquest, the medical examiner himself sits as would a judge in most other types of legal proceedings. The examination is conducted by the county prosecutor, and the rules are not so well defined as they would be in a formal trial.

Malcolm Barnes was the Multnomah County Prosecutor, and he would be personally handling the case. Generally, his role was to administer his office and utilize assistant prosecutors for the actual courtroom cases, but he occasionally did some trial work himself. He had several reasons for involving himself in this affair.

First of all, this was a high-profile proceeding and his was an elected position. It was necessary to prove to the public that he was doing his part to keep the community a safe place to live and work, or in this case, to be operated on. Secondly, he had been a close personal friend of Dick Cranston. And he had always felt that Ike Paponis had wielded a disproportionate amount of authority in government, considering his station in life as a local surgeon. But most influential in his decision to handle the case, was the fact that he despised Sean Merrick, and would take every available opportunity to oppose the man.

Barnes felt that Merrick represented everything that was wrong with the law. The malpractice attorney had gotten rich suing physicians and hospitals for cases of neglect or wrongful death, and now he had turned his coat to defend a physician who was probably guilty of that very thing. Merrick had no principles, and Barnes would have loved to embarrass the man.

The prosecuting attorney had no such feelings regarding Merrick's partner, Kurt Krieger. He respected Krieger's mastery of the law and personal integrity. He knew that Merrick and Krieger had grown up together, but he had never been able to understand how Krieger had been able to tolerate Merrick's arrogance as an adult.

There were a good many similar dichotomies when it came to Sean Merrick. He was married to his high school sweetheart, herself a lawyer, and now a well-respected family lawyer. He enjoyed the friendship of many prominent people within the medical and legal communities, and the man seemed well liked. But to Malcolm Barnes, the man was an asshole.

Included among the interested crowd of observers in the courtroom was a young homicide detective by the name of Mitch Petrowski. Petrowski too had been a childhood friend of Sean Merrick and Kurt Krieger, and now he was beginning to prove himself in the homicide division. He had been quite taken with the total lack of interest in the Paponis case at the police department. If the allegations made by Shelley Grayson were true, then this was most certainly a case of homicide.

Petrowski figured that this case was just so unusual that his associate detectives didn't know how to deal with it. He was an innovator in the homicide division, and he enjoyed cases that the traditional criminal justice system didn't understand. So during this inquest, he would make himself a casual observer in the courtroom, and if there was any truth to the charge, he would be informed enough to begin his own investigation.

Marty Spencer walked into the courtroom from the judge's chambers and took his seat at the bench. He was dressed in a business suit but seemed comfortable in the role that he was about to play. Ike stared at the medical examiner as if he were an enemy that he had never met. And in many ways, Ike did not know Spencer as he now was.

The medical examiner tapped the judge's gavel several times, and the courtroom became quiet.

"I want to thank you all for coming today. As you may know, there has not been a proceeding of this kind in Multnomah County for more than thirty years. This is not a criminal trial. If anything, it is a fact-finding mission that will allow me to put all of the facts of this case into some sort of order so that I can make a determination in the death of Mayor Richard Cranston.

"The rules for the coroner's inquest are not well defined. Therefore, I am going to conduct this affair as informally as possible, while still trying to adhere to some sort of judicial format that will allow for an orderly progression.

"Since both sides of this issue are represented by counsel, I think we'll have the attorneys make brief opening statements to kind of set the stage before we start interviewing witnesses. Mr. Barnes, would you like to do the honors and get us rolling here?"

"Thank you, Dr. Spencer." Malcolm Barnes rose from behind the table where he was seated and walked toward the bench. After doing so, he turned to the audience of observers in the courtroom and slowly began to speak.

"Ladies and gentlemen, as Dr. Spencer here has been good enough to point out, this is not a criminal trial. In fact, I have been against conducting a proceeding of this nature from the outset. It has been my contention all along that if we had enough evidence to indict Dr. Paponis for murder, then that is what we should do. If not, we should leave it alone. But there have been some very serious allegations made in this case, and I agree with Dr. Spencer that they need to be addressed. He chose this forum to conduct this task, and that is certainly within his rights.

"Normally at this juncture, I would be telling you that I intend to prove that the defendant is guilty of a crime. But at this point, I can't do that. I can't even call Dr. Paponis a defendant.

"This case is cluttered with problems. First of all, from a prosecutorial standpoint, Dick Cranston lived for a full month following his open heart surgery. Is it possible that his death could have been engineered by Dr. Paponis in such a fashion that our former mayor would not have any symptoms for an entire month following surgery and then spontaneously and tragically die? I don't know. Hopefully, we'll be able to gather the necessary information to clear up these problems and questions for all of us." Malcolm Barnes shrugged his shoulders, looked quizzically at the crowd, and walked back to his seat.

"Thanks, Malcolm. Mr. Merrick? Mr. Krieger?" It was Sean Merrick who rose to make the opening statement on behalf of Ike Paponis, and he did so by first disarming the crowd with his smile.

"Ladies and gentlemen, no offense to Dr. Spencer or to Malcolm Barnes, our esteemed prosecuting attorney, but this proceeding is ludicrous. Our criminal justice system has been neatly and constitutionally arranged to bring to trial those individuals accused of a crime. It is then up to a jury to determine guilt or innocence. No crime has been committed here. If Dr. Paponis had killed anyone then he would rightfully stand accused of murder."

"All of this has been brought about as a result of the spurious and unfounded accusations of a single operating room nurse who, for some unknown reason, has it in for Dr. Paponis. My client, by his own admission, is a difficult taskmaster. He depends a great deal on his staff, but he asks no more of them than he does of himself. Open heart surgery is no cakewalk. I don't know if you are all aware of this, but the human heart is completely stopped during an open heart operation. The patient, for all intent and purposes, is essentially temporarily dead on the operating table."

"Dr. Paponis is a driven man, as well he should be. He's demanding, he's obsessed, and occasionally he is unforgiving. Again, all of this by his own admission. But he is also very good at what he does."

"I can understand the emotional duress of an operating room nurse having to work under these conditions. The stress must be enormous. I can even understand that his same nurse would be resentful of a man like my client. She has many of the same pressures without nearly the professional clout or financial rewards that my client enjoys. I can further understand that all of this stress could lead her to believe that she saw something that she did not see. What I cannot understand is that she would take these hallucinations to the authorities in our community in an effort to destroy the professional reputation of a man who is so respected in his field."

"I also cannot understand how the county medical examiner and the prosecuting attorney, in the absence of one iota of evidence, have allowed a carnival like this to take place. There are rules of evidence, but in this case there isn't even any evidence. If there was, my client would be standing trial for murder. This is a dangerous charade aimed at ruining the reputation of a giant in the field of cardio-thoracic surgery."

"I guess we have no choice but to play out this charade, but let me tell you this ladies and gentlemen, we fully intend to expose it for what it is - a blatant and total miscarriage of an antiquated law." Merrick tilted his head downward in deference to his audience and returned to his seat.

"Thank you, Mr. Merrick. I hope that I am not the villain that you have just portrayed me to be, but I think I understand your intentions, and I want you to know that I do respect them." Marty was smiling sheepishly as if he had just been blind-sided by a blitzing linebacker whose skill he had respected.

"Mr. Barnes, if you would like to call your first witness, then we'll get this thing under way. I fully intend to complete this proceeding today."

"Dr. Spencer, I guess the only way to get started is to start at the beginning, so we would call Ms. Shelley Grayson to the stand." The operating room nurse rose from her seat in the audience and made her way to the witness stand. It was obvious that the nurse had made every effort to mask her physical attributes for this affair. She wore a conservative brown business suit, and her long blonde hair was pulled into a tight bun at the back of her head. Her judicious use of makeup and lipstick were toned down but could not totally obscure her beauty.

"Ms. Grayson, I'm not going to swear you in, but I will ask that you be as accurate and truthful as you can be when answering the questions that you will be asked."

"I will be, Dr. Spencer."

"Mr. Barnes, you may proceed with your questioning of the witness." Malcolm Barnes rose from his seat and strolled closely to the witness stand.

"Ms. Grayson, would you be so good as to tell these folks where you are employed and give them a brief description of your duties?"

Her words were halting at first, but slowly she gained confidence. She was careful to avoid looking at Ike Paponis for fear of once again being intimidated by the surgeon.

"I am employed as an operating room nurse at Health Sciences Medical Center. I am on the open heart team, and I serve as both a scrub nurse and a circulating nurse."

"So it has been in this capacity that you have come to know Dr. Ike Paponis, is that correct?"

"Yes, it is."

"And how long have you been working closely with Dr. Paponis?"

"For approximately ten years."

"That's a good long time, isn't it? I would imagine that after ten years you would become quite familiar with the work habits of a surgeon, wouldn't you, Ms. Grayson?"

"With Dr. Paponis, you had better be familiar with what he expects."

"What do you mean by that?"

"Oh, nothing really. Dr. Paponis is a perfectionist, and he doesn't tolerate anything less than perfection from his crew, that's all."

"And you don't agree with his methods?"

"I didn't say that. Most surgeons are intense. You just sort of learn to live with it."

"Okay, Ms. Grayson, let's get to the reason that we're all gathered here today. You approached Dr. Spencer here with some alarming information, didn't you?"

"Yes, I did."

"And what was the nature of that information?"

"I expressed some concerns that I had regarding the coronary artery bypass graft that Dr. Paponis performed on Richard Cranston."

"And exactly what were those concerns?"

"I felt that I had seen Dr. Paponis make a small incision into the outer wall of the left ventricle of Mayor Cranston's heart."

"And this is something that would not normally be done during a procedure of this kind? You'll have to forgive us. This is all pretty much foreign material for us lay persons. I apologize for our collective ignorance."

"No, Mr. Barnes, the incision that I saw Dr. Paponis make was not typical of any open heart procedure that I have ever seen."

"Did you say anything to Dr. Paponis at the time? Did you confront him about this deviation from standard procedure?"

"No, I didn't."

"Why not?"

"Well, Dr. Paponis is not really very approachable. He is famous for his outbursts in the operating room when…"

"Objection!" Sean Merrick was on his feet. "Not relevant."

"Mr. Merrick, we are not in a court of law. I'm afraid your objection won't really gain you very much here. We'll let Ms. Grayson answer Mr. Barnes' questions. Believe me, Mr. Merrick, you'll get your chance, and we'll afford you the same courtesy that we're allowing Mr. Barnes right now."

"But, Dr. Spencer, this is a public forum, and my client's professional stature is being openly attacked. I hope you are prepared for counter litigation."

"I hope that won't be necessary, Mr. Merrick. Look, we're just trying to establish the facts here. It is my hope that these facts will speak for themselves in the end."

"In the meantime, Dr. Spencer, my client's reputation is taking some serious heat, and let the record show that we do not appreciate it."

"I'll note your concerns, Mr. Merrick, but this is my proceeding, and I will conduct it as I see fit. Now please sit down. As I said, you'll get your chance. Go ahead and finish what you were saying, Mrs. Grayson."

"Let me just say that Dr. Paponis does not restrain his aggravation when things don't go as he has planned." Sean Merrick's objection had obviously had the desired effect on the witness, and she had somewhat curbed her remarks.

Malcolm Barnes still wanted more from his witness. "So what you are trying to impart to us is that Dr. Paponis is prone to temper tantrums in the operating room, isn't that correct?" For the first time, Shelley Grayson allowed herself to look directly at Ike.

"I think I'll just let my statement stand as it is." Malcolm Barnes had seen the exchange of a glance between his witness and the surgeon, and he had no doubts that the nurse was feeling a bit intimidated. Years of experience had taught him that it wouldn't do any good to pressure her for more information in this particular vein. The prosecuting attorney deftly changed his tack.

"Ms. Grayson, are there any other, shall we say, unusual habits that Dr. Paponis has when it comes to his professional practice?" Barnes was away from the stand with his back to the witness now.

"He operates in the middle of the night."

"What do you mean? Is this unusual?"

"He's the only one that I know who does it. He starts his procedures at three or four o'clock in the morning."

"Do you think that this presents any problems?"

"Other than scheduling problems, no. I think it's a control thing. I think Dr. Paponis enjoys making people jump through hoops for him in the middle of the night."

Sean Merrick was once again on his feet. "Come on, Dr. Spencer, this is ridiculous. You stated that we were going to gather facts. Let's gather facts. This is not pertinent, and we're now engaging in wild speculation."

"I'm inclined to agree with you, Mr. Merrick. Let's get on with it. Mr.

Barnes."

"Getting back to the procedure that Dr. Paponis performed on Richard Cranston, Ms. Grayson, was it your impression that this incision that you describe was made intentionally?"

"Gosh, I don't know. Dr. Paponis is usually so meticulous about what he does in the OR. I guess I had put it out of my mind until the mayor died. That's when I got concerned."

"Are you aware of an alleged altercation between Dr. Paponis and a cardiologist named Paul Switzer that occurred just prior to going to the OR that morning?"

"Yes, I heard that there had been an argument and that Dr. Paponis had hit Dr. Switzer in the face."

"Were you surprised when you heard what had supposedly happened between the two men?

"Not really. Dr. Paponis can be pretty high strung when it comes to his patients. No, I wasn't surprised."

"Do you think that the altercation could have in any way negatively impacted the doctor's ability to operate that morning?"

"I'll have to say no again. If anything, he seemed calmer than usual. It was really pretty weird. I had expected him to be angry, but he wasn't. I do remember that."

"I don't need anything more from this witness, Dr. Spencer. Thank you, Ms. Grayson."

The operating room nurse nodded her head demurely. She had gotten through the first half of her testimony relatively unscathed. She had never had to testify before, but she had been told that cross examination would be much tougher.

"Mr. Merrick? Mr. Krieger?" It was Sean Merrick who rose from his chair and walked directly toward the witness stand.

"How are you, Ms. Grayson?"

"Fine, thank you."

"Ms. Grayson, you are a very pretty woman."

"Thank you again."

"Have you ever been romantically involved with Dr. Paponis?"

"No, I have not."

"Was it ever your desire to be romantically involved with Dr. Paponis?"

"I suppose that I was interested in him in that way a few years ago."

"Did Dr. Paponis return your affection?"

"No."

"Being a beautiful woman, like you are, how did that affect you?"

"It didn't affect me one way or the other."

"Come on, Ms. Grayson. Do you mean to tell me that you didn't even feel the slightest bit of rejection?"

"Okay, I was disappointed, but it was no big deal."

"Big deal as in wanting retribution against Dr. Paponis – as in wanting him to pay?"

"That'll be enough of that, Mr. Merrick." Marty Spencer made no effort to conceal his displeasure.

"So, Ms. Grayson, was it your perception that this little extra incision that you spoke of was made intentionally?"

"I've already answered that question, sir. I really don't know."

"So, based on what you think you saw, but you're not even really sure about that, you took this whole story of yours to the medical examiner. You knew full well that you would be damaging the career of a respected open heart surgeon whom you describe as skilled and meticulous. And yet, even knowing all of this, you did it anyway. Did you have any other reason to do this? I mean, had there been other cases of improper procedure that had alerted you to poor surgical technique. Was his practice so poor that you would run directly to the authorities based on something you think you might have seen, but that you aren't really sure about?"

Whistles and sirens were going off in Marty's head. He couldn't allow Shelley Grayson's concerns about the Bill Evans case to come out or he could be implicated.

"Let me just interject here that we are only conducting this inquest to determine the cause of death of Richard Cranston. I'm afraid that any references to other cases are not pertinent and will not be allowed."

"If that is to be the case, Dr. Spencer, then I have no further questions."

"You are excused, Ms. Grayson. Thanks for your time."

Shelley Grayson left the stand feeling like a fool. Sean Merrick had manipulated her testimony to make her accusations look like the unfounded ravings of a jealous, would-be lover whose affections had been spurned. Oh well, she had only been doing what she thought to be right.

Malcolm Barnes rose from his chair. "Dr. Spencer, the rules of this proceeding are so contrary to what I am accustomed to that I am having a difficult time deciding what is acceptable and what is unacceptable."

"Just ask, Mr. Barnes. We'll see if we can help you out."

"Well, Doctor, you performed the autopsy on Richard Cranston. But you are also the presiding authority at this hearing. I would like to ask you several questions for the record, but since you are the person who will ultimately render a decision in this case, I wonder how productive questioning you would actually be."

"I don't really have any objection to that. I would hope that any decision to proceed beyond this inquest would be made in conjunction with your office. I also think that the people here, and that includes the media, are entitled to know the cause of death as I have determined it. After all, it is a matter of public record. So fire away, Mr. Barnes."

"Thank you, Doctor. Exactly what was the cause of death as you saw it?"

"Richard Cranston died as a result of a ruptured left ventricular aneurysm."

"Could you please explain that for the non-medical people here?"

"There was a weakened area on the lateral aspect of the left ventricle that created a balloon-like structure that ruptured under the somewhat higher than normal pressures that were created while Dick Cranston was swimming."

"If my understanding is correct, then this would prohibit the heart from delivering oxygenated blood to the other vital organs of the body."

"Very good, Mr. Barnes. You've obviously done your homework. In effect, Mayor Cranston bled out into this chest."

"As a forensic pathologist, was this a result that surprised you in a patient who had recently undergone open heart surgery?"

"Not really. This is an expected outcome in a small but measurable percentage of patients undergoing coronary artery bypass graft."

"So, it wasn't until you were approached by Shelley Grayson that you developed concerns about this case?"

"That's correct."

"Was there anything in your findings that correlated with Ms. Grayson's story?"

"Maybe. Maybe not. The margins, the edges of the aneurysm itself were sharp and well demarcated. Her story was plausible given the findings but certainly not conclusive by any stretch of the imagination."

"But it concerned you enough to pursue it further didn't it, Doctor?"

"Yes."

"And you are a close personal friend of Dr. Paponis aren't you, Doctor? In fact, you are a partner with Dr. Paponis in a long-term business venture, isn't that correct?"

"Yes, it is."

"So you must have really had some major concerns that prompted you to pursue this even though the possibility existed that it would negatively impact a longstanding friendship and business arrangement?" Malcolm Barnes was confident that he had just made a powerful point in implicating the surgeon, but the medical examiner was not going to be led into this trap.

"Quite the contrary, Mr. Barnes. I was trying to avoid even the suggestion of impropriety. I did this primarily because Dr. Paponis and I are friends. I felt it necessary to conclude beyond the shadow of a doubt that no wrongdoing had occurred."

"Do you think that you have managed to do that, Doctor?"

"I'm not sure. I just don't know."

"So what I think you are trying to tell me is that this entire scenario could have been played out just as Ms. Grayson has described it?

"Yes, I suppose it is conceivable."

"I don't have any more questions."

Ike was livid. All along Marty Spencer had defended his actions by stating that he was doing all of this in the interest of clearing the surgeon's name. But he had just delivered a crushing blow, and there would be hell to pay for that.

"Mr. Merrick, do you have any questions of me?"

"Just one or two, Doctor. What was Richard Cranston doing when he died?"

"Swimming laps."

"Wasn't it just a little soon after such a complicated surgical procedure to be performing such strenuous physical activity?"

"Yes, it was. But Dick Cranston was determined to get himself back into top physical condition as quickly as possible."

"But isn't it true that during strenuous physical exercise the blood pressure elevates, and the heart rate accelerates."

"Yes, that is true."

"So isn't it conceivable that with this elevated pressure and rapid rate that a weakened ventricular wall could spontaneously rupture in such a way as to give these sharpened demarcations that you have described?"

"Yes, it's completely conceivable."

"No further questions."

Marty Spencer was stunned. This Merrick guy was good. He was so good that he had just made the county medical examiner, a man with more than twenty years as a forensic pathologist, look like a bumbling idiot.

But Sean Merrick's questioning had also served to further enrage Ike. The points that Merrick had made were factors that Spencer should have considered before going off half cocked into a public hearing. At any rate, things were going as the surgeon had hoped, and that was good.

"Dr. Spencer, I have only one additional witness that I would like to call, and then I'll turn this over to Mr. Merrick and Mr. Krieger. The prosecution would call Dr. Paul Switzer."

Paul Switzer arose from his place in the audience and made his way to the witness stand. Ike was immediately concerned, as was Sean Merrick. If anybody had an axe to grind with Ike, it was definitely Paul Switzer. The man could, and most probably would, impugn not only the surgeon's clinical practice, but also his personal behavior.

"Dr. Switzer, I understand that you had temporarily assumed the care of Mayor Richard Cranston while Dr. Paponis was out of town. Is that correct?"

"Yes, that is true. Richard Cranston suffered a rather large myocardial infarction, a heart attack, while he was entertaining guests at his home. He was transported to Health Sciences, and an effort was made to contact Dr. Paponis. When he could not be located, Mayor Cranston requested that I assume responsibility for his medical care."

"Had you treated the mayor prior to this occasion?"

"No."

"Were you socially acquainted with the mayor prior to this?"

"Acquainted... yes. Were we friends? I would have to say the answer to that questions would be no."

"Why then do you think the mayor requested you personally?"

"He told me that it was because he had heard that I was good at what I do."

"Incidentally, Dr. Switzer, I have heard the same thing. But specifically, what you do is different from what Dr. Paponis does, isn't it?"

"Technically, yes. I'm a cardiologist, and Dr. Paponis is a heart surgeon. Invasively, the only thing that I do is cardiac catheterization and balloon angioplasty. I do have the ability to open occluded arteries in the coronary circulation with a very small balloon, but if I am unsuccessful, then I must refer my patients to a heart surgeon such as Dr. Paponis for coronary artery bypass graft."

"And you did perform one of your balloon angioplasties on Mayor Cranston following his heart attack, did you not?"

"Actually, it was during his heart attack. But yes, I did."

"And what were the results of that procedure?"

"I was able to open the left anterior descending coronary artery with the balloon and to restore circulation to the portion of Dick Cranston's heart that had not been receiving oxygenated blood. I was, in effect, able to stop Mayor Cranston's heart attack."

The miracles of modern medicine…" Malcolm Barnes took a long pause for effect. "But something went wrong, didn't it, Dr. Switzer?"

"Yes. Mayor Cranston's left anterior descending coronary artery re-occluded."

"And what was your plan of therapy after that happened?"

"I wanted to take him back to the cath lab for a repeat angioplasty."

"What stopped you from doing just that?"

"Very simply, Dr. Paponis. He had just returned from out of town, and he became aware of what was happening with his patient. He responded immediately to the hospital and made the decision to take Dick Cranston to the operating room for bypass graft."

"And did you agree with his decision?"

"No. I felt that I could reopen the vessel without surgery. I was also concerned because the mayor had been given TPA, tissue plasminogen activator, a clot-busting anticoagulant that could have caused the patient to have severe bleeding during any type of surgical procedure."

"So I can assume, that being two professional medical men, you were able to sit down and resolve your differences and come up with a mutually acceptable therapy for your patient?"

"Not exactly."

"Not exactly?"

"Dr. Paponis was not to be deterred that particular morning."

"So you relented and allowed Dr. Paponis to reassume care of the patient?"

"Not exactly."

"Why don't you just tell us what exactly did happen, Dr. Switzer?"

"In short, Dr. Paponis punched me in the face and took over by force."

"He did this in the hospital? In front of witnesses?"

"Yes."

"And did you file charges?"

"No."

"Why not?"

"I felt that there were better ways to resolve our differences. Some things are better left alone."

"Are you afraid of Dr. Paponis, Dr. Switzer?"

"Ike Paponis is a powerful man."

"Are you afraid of him, Dr. Switzer?"

"Yes."

"So then, given the right circumstances you would tend to believe that Dr. Paponis is capable of the very act which we are investigating today."

"It's conceivable."

"No further questions." Malcolm Barnes took his seat. He had failed to prove anything in this case beyond supposition, but he had certainly managed to cast doubt on the character of Ike Paponis.

"Mr. Merrick?" Sean Merrick rose from his chair and walked deliberately and rapidly toward the witness stand. The mere pace of his stride served to unnerve the cardiologist.

"Let's have the truth here, Dr. Switzer. You've never liked my client, have you?"

"We've had our professional differences."

"Come now, Dr. Switzer, it's been far more than that, hasn't it?"

"I don't know what else to say to you beyond that, sir. We don't exactly see eye to eye on a good many professional issues."

"Dr. Switzer, isn't it true that in the past, on a number of occasions you have attempted to deliberately undermine my client's professional ability with other medical staff members at the hospital?"

"I know that is Dr. Paponis's impression, but it is my contention that this is not the truth. We have differing opinions regarding the treatment of various types of heart disease, but as far as I'm concerned, that's the extent of it."

"So you have never discussed Dr. Paponis's professional practice with colleagues that the two of you have in common?"

"I have, but it has only been to stimulate an academic discussion."

"Why don't you just be honest with this gathering, Dr. Switzer, and save us all a lot of time. I can subpoena additional witnesses if I have to. Isn't it true that you have accused Dr. Paponis of doing unnecessary procedures? Isn't it true that you think that you can cure nearly every cardiac malady without surgery? Isn't it true that you have made these statements to colleagues, thereby undermining Dr. Paponis's professional practice?"

"As I said before, Dr. Paponis and I differ on a great many professional issues."

"I think we've got the picture, Dr. Switzer. Let's see if we can clarify at least one other issue, though. You were aware, as you previously stated, that

Dick Cranston was Ike Paponis's private patient. That is correct, isn't it?"

"Yes."

"And you were also aware that Dr. Pifer was taking Dr. Paponis's calls while he was out of town, weren't you?"

"Yes."

"So the ethical thing to do, in a case such as this, would have been to refer the case directly back to Dr. Pifer?"

"As I previously stated, Mayor Cranston asked for me specifically. He had the right to make decisions regarding his own care."

"But you knew that you were out of line, didn't you?"

"I had some concerns."

"That translates to me that you knew you were out of line."

"I suppose that's your prerogative, sir."

"What bothers me most about all of this, however, is that after Dr. Paponis arrived at the hospital, you continued to contradict his professional judgment. You did this in front of witnesses, and during a time when Mayor Cranston's condition was in a severe state of medical crisis. I want to ask you to try to think about how you would have felt under similar circumstances had the roles been reversed."

"That's difficult to do, but in all honesty, I would have to say that I would have found the entire situation to be aggravating as well."

"At last, a forthright answer. You see, Dr. Switzer, a great deal has been made regarding this altercation between you and Dr. Paponis. I think that my client is getting a bad rap over this. You aggravated him during a very stressful time. I'll admit that what happened probably shouldn't have, but I think that you have to share some of the responsibility here. No further questions."

"Thank you, Dr. Switzer. I hope that we haven't inconvenienced you too much, and we do appreciate your participation here today." Marty's words brought the cardiologist back to reality and liberated the man from his bondage. Switzer left the witness stand and the courtroom as rapidly as possible. He felt as if he had just been raped, and what was worse, he had been raped in front of a crowded courtroom.

It was now Sean Merrick's turn to present witnesses, and he was eager to do so.

"Mr. Merrick, I presume that you would like to present some witnesses."

"Thank you, Dr. Spencer. We would first like to call Dr. Gregory Stevens."

Marty had a stunned expression on his face. Greg Stevens was his chief deputy medical examiner. The pathologist had been waiting in the hallway, and when summoned, he strolled casually into the courtroom and up to the stand.

"Good morning, Dr. Stevens."

"Hello, Mr. Merrick." Both Merrick and Stevens had gone to high school together, and the young forensic pathologist frequently offered expert testimony for Merrick and Krieger in many of their malpractice trials. The formal courtesy was nothing more than theatrics.

"Dr. Stevens, are you familiar with the post mortem examination that Dr. Spencer performed on the body of Mayor Richard Cranston?"

"Yes, I reviewed the report."

"'Was there anything of note in any of the materials that you reviewed?"

"No, it was a rather straightforward exam. Cause of death was cardiac arrest secondary to a ruptured left ventricular aneurysm."

"Now, Dr. Stevens, there has been some rather lengthy discussion regarding the margins of this aneurysm. In fact, this would, if anything would be, the only physical evidence of this alleged incision that Dr. Paponis supposedly made. What are your feelings on these findings?"

"I believe these findings to be rather nondescript. In fact, there was no mention of any unusual variances in the official report that Dr. Spencer dictated. I did review the microscopic slides of the aneurysm and found nothing noteworthy."

"So, in your professional medical opinion, there was nothing to support Ms. Grayson's allegations?"

"That is correct. There was nothing to support Ms. Grayson's allegations."

"Thank you, Dr. Stevens. I have no further questions."

Marty was incensed with his chief deputy for involving himself in this affair without giving him prior knowledge. But his outward demeanor did not betray this sentiment.

"Mr. Barnes?"

"I have no questions for this witness."

"You're excused, Dr. Stevens." Marty was beginning to regret having insisted on holding this inquest. It wasn't like he hadn't been warned. Ike, and a score of his own associates had all advised against doing it. But the medical examiner had insisted on it, and now he was being undermined by his own employee. He had wanted to complete the process to clear the air regarding the death of Dick Cranston, but all he had really managed to do was to alienate a man who had been a close friend for many years and to make himself look like a complete fool.

CHAPTER 21

As Martin Spencer ruminated about the error of his decision, Miguel Dominguez sat in a comfortable lounge chair next to the pool to the rear of his large new hacienda that overlooked the lush green valley east of Bonanza. Finally, after all of these years of fighting for the independence of his country from the rule of the hated Sandinistas, he was able to relax and enjoy the fruits of his labors.

The sprawling stucco ranch sat on a hill that was immune to clandestine entry. There had not been, and never would be, any questions as to how Dominguez had financed his newly found opulence. He was a national hero, and there would be nothing but good feelings from his countrymen that he was now able to live in the style he so richly deserved.

It was just after noon and the sun was stifling. Even though there was a slight haze high in the sky, it only seemed to magnify the ultraviolet rays. Dominguez was darkly pigmented, and he was even more so at this time of the year. After years of acclimation, he found that he was easily able to enjoy the heat, the thick humidity, and the privacy that his new home afforded him.

The sensation that he experienced next was one that was totally foreign to him. The ground beneath his feet began to rumble violently and soon felt as fluid as the ocean waters. His pool looked like a large aquarium that had been rocked by a playful dog. The outer walls of his beautiful new home began to shift, crack, and shatter like the shell of an egg.

Miguel looked through the giant window at the rear of his house as it exploded outwardly toward him. He became almost instantly captivated by the chandelier, within the room behind the window, as it swung back and forth like a huge pendulum. The soldier had never been afraid, but now he was struck with that very emotion at the core of his being.

Miguel had always been able to count on the earth beneath his feet being stable, even if the rest of his world was a whirlwind of turbulence. But now, his one constant in life had failed him. Within seconds his new home had collapsed into a pile of rubble.

The epicenter of the earthquake was a mere eight miles west of Bonanza on the fault line that ran beneath the Cordillera Isabelia. The tremor measured seven point four on the International Richter Scale and was sufficient to nearly level the entire town of Bonanza.

In the streets of the city, there was a near total bedlam. Women wailed as they searched for their children under the heavy piles of wood and concrete that had been their homes. An emergency alert siren screamed out across the sky, and the echoing sound of a barking dog could be heard like an aberration in the flattened city.

Bonanza was not prepared for what had befallen them that day and neither was the entire country of Nicaragua. Help would have to come from the international community, and it would have to come quickly.

Sean Merrick had just finished calling and interviewing his last witness, Dr. Able Samson. The open heart team's anesthesiologist had been unable to corroborate any of the allegations that had been made by Shelley Grayson. Now that the inquest was drawing to a close, it was clear to everyone in the crowded courtroom that there was virtually no evidence against Ike Paponis. The overwhelming conclusion was that Shelley Grayson's allegations had been the result of vindictiveness spawned from being a rejected would-be lover. There would be no grand jury and no indictment.

A medical investigator from the county medical examiner's office entered the courtroom and walked directly to where Dr. Martin Spencer was seated. The medical examiner turned the microphone away from himself and shielded it with his hand.

"What's up, Mike?"

"I'm sorry to interrupt you, Doctor, but we've had a call from Senator Talmadge Hyle's office. It seems that there has been a huge earthquake in Central Nicaragua, and he wants you to activate the Medical Response Team."

Marty's heart began to race with anticipation. This was the moment he had been waiting for. All of the planning would now pay off.

"Ladies and gentlemen, we are at the end of this inquest, and it is my conclusion that no negligence, nor any overt act allegedly perpetrated by Dr. Paponis, contributed in any way to the death of Richard Cranston. Therefore, my office will make no recommendations to the county prosecutor's office for any further action against Dr. Paponis. This case is closed."

There was a great deal of excitement within the room as the reporters scrambled out of the chambers to insure that their stories would make the deadline. Ike and Sean Merrick shook hands. Malcolm Barnes placed his briefs into a folder, and Shelley Grayson sat stunned in her seat. Marty rapped his gavel several times to restore order.

"Ladies and gentlemen? Ladies and gentlemen? Could I have your attention please? There has been a large earthquake in Nicaragua, and the Medical Response Team has been activated. The protocol is now being enacted, and for those members now present, we will be meeting at Portland International in two hours."

The two C-141 Starlifters sat side by side on the tarmac at the airport as several forklifts busily loaded medical supplies, tents, and vehicles onto them. The night was already dark, but the lights at the airfield cast a futuristic, almost surreal, glow on the scene.

Already, members of the response team had begun to assemble at the airfield. It would be an unusual crowd making the trip to Nicaragua this night. Ike had arrived with Allan, and Shelley Grayson had come with several other operating room nurses. Marty had been picked up by the senator and his driver, and he and the senator had shared their visions of what the team would accomplish, on the way to the airport. Talmadge Hyle, by all rights, should not have even been making the trip to Nicaragua, but he was not going to miss the opportunity to see his brainchild in action.

There were anesthesiologists, surgeons of every specialty, paramedics, nurses, and a complement of general volunteers. All were keyed up regarding what they were about to do.

After the supplies and equipment had been loaded onto the planes, the personnel had begun to load. These were not luxury accommodations. The seats were woven of red nylon material and spanned longitudinally along both outer walls of the aircraft. The vehicles and supplies were loaded into the center of the two jets, with the Jeeps and trucks being secured with large chains at all four corners.

It was loud in the cargo compartments of the planes as the jet engines roared in preparation for take off. Seat belts were secured in place, and the planes taxied quickly to the end of the runway.

The elite crowd that comprised the Medical Response Team, were accustomed to traveling with all of the frills, but there was something to be said for flying on an Air Force jet to perform a truly humanitarian task.

The first C-141 leapt forward down the runway, gathering immense momentum very rapidly. The plane shook, rattled, and soon left the ground. If there had been any thoughts about this trip being similar to commercial travel, they were soon erased, as the jet began its climb toward cruising altitudes. The pilots had the plane performing what felt like an almost vertical climb.

There were looks of astonishment exchanged among the passengers, and several tried to speak to one another. But the roar of the engines drowned out any and all sound save for themselves. The vehicles pulled at the chains to their front as the sheer force of gravity pulled them toward the rear of the craft.

Within moments, the other 141 was also airborne, and the two planes began their southwesterly journey toward Nicaragua and the Bonanza airfield. They soon leveled off at approximately thirty-two thousand feet and the passengers in the cabin were alerted that it was permissible to move about.

The engines were not nearly as loud as they had previously been, and it became possible to hold a conversation without screaming against the background noise. Marty sought out Ike and found him standing near the jump doors at the rear of the plane.

"Ike, I'm glad that you were able to find it within yourself to make the trip with us. I hope there aren't too many hard feelings."

The surgeon didn't even turn to face the medical examiner. He merely continued to stare blankly out of the window. His inattention began to make Marty feel just a bit nervous.

"Come on, Ike. We've been friends for far too long to let something like this ruin it for us. Our professional careers just got in the way of our personal relationship. It was bound to happen sooner or later."

Paponis turned slowly and stared the medical examiner down. The intensity was that of molten steel – an iron resolve.

"Don't even bother trying to lay your rationalizations on me, Marty. You fucked up, you screwed me over, and trying to pass it all off as being your professional responsibility is not going to cut it. Everybody and their brother tried to warn you not to do it. And what did you accomplish? Just what the hell did you expect to accomplish?"

"Ike, I had to do something. Shelley Grayson came to me with her allegations, and she had the right to expect me to investigate."

"So why don't you tell me why you don't do an inquest every time somebody else comes to you with a hair-brained accusation. Darn it, Marty, you haven't held one of these things in all the years that you've been medical examiner. And now you're trying to tell me that it was all just your professional responsibility. That's crap, and you know it."

"I don't know what you're so upset about. You were totally exonerated. We accomplished everything that I set out to accomplish."

"Come on, Marty. I know that you can't be that stupid. And even if you are, don't expect me to play stupid along with you. My career as a heart surgeon is over thanks to you, my friend."

"I think you're blowing this way out of proportion, Ike. I think you came out of the whole thing looking pretty good."

"The only way that I would've looked good is if the whole thing had never happened in the first place. But you made sure that it all did happen, didn't you? You made your choice, Marty. Don't come crying on my shoulder now."

"Don't be like this, Ike."

"Just leave me the hell alone!" Ike turned away from his former friend and resumed his vigil staring out into the blackness beyond.

Marty was rattled and wasted no time seeking out Allan.

"Have you talked to Ike?"

Allan looked up from the magazine that he was reading, and much to Spencer's chagrin, the attorney had a stone-faced expression as well.

"What are you talking about? Of course I've talked to Ike. We rode to the airfield together."

"He's really ticked off."

"What did you expect, Marty? Everyone warned you about the inquest. To be perfectly honest with you, I would have been ticked off too. Don't let it bother you too much, though. He'll get over it. He has to. We're in business together, and you know that nothing takes precedence over making money with Ike."

"I wish that made me feel better than it does."

"Don't worry. I'll talk to him."

"Thanks, Allan."

Spandell walked to the rear of the plane where Ike continued to stare out of the window. The surgeon looked up as the attorney drew closer.

"Can you believe that sonofabitch? Does he think that he can just do whatever the hell he wants to and have me think nothing of it?"

"Come on, Ike. You know Marty. I really think he believed he was doing the right thing. Heck, he would've had to since everyone was telling him not to do it. Marty probably truly thought he was doing you a favor."

"He's got to know better than that now."

"I'm sure he does. But I'm also sure that he thinks your making this trip is a good sign too. I guess he must think that you're not too far gone if you're willing to participate in a humanitarian effort like this."

"Allan, I hate to burst your bubble, but I'm probably doing this a lot more for Talmadge than I am for Marty."

"Be honest, Ike. You're doing it for yourself, and you know it."

"What, did you get wind of the senate thing?"

"I heard something about that. President Talmadge Hyle and Senator Ike Paponis. I also heard a little bit about the Diaz Brother's Mining Company."

Ike felt his stomach muscles constricting. He knew that Allan was no dummy, but he thought he had covered his tracks better than that. The realization that his partner knew of Diaz Brothers made him wonder just what else the attorney knew. He redirected his gaze back out the window.

"How did you find out about that, Allan?"

"That's not important. I know, and I promised that I would not divulge my source."

"Is that why you've come along on this trip?"

"Partially."

"Does Marty know?"

"I haven't said a word to anyone, Ike."

"So then, you've come along to retrieve the ten million dollars that I borrowed from the Portland Fund?"

"Let's just say that I know that the money is in Nicaragua. I didn't doubt that you'd repay it. I think my real concern is over this mining company of yours. Have you been using S.P.S. funds to support it?" Allan's stare nearly matched that of the surgeon. The ex-prosecutor was quite diplomatic, but he could also be unnerving when he wanted to be.

"It seems that you know a good deal more about my business dealings than I thought you did. Yeah, I'm afraid that I've been doing that for quite some time. I expected to get a return from this a lot sooner than I did. It was a gamble that I thought would pay off. I still expect it to pay off big."

"So what was the big deal, Ike? Why did you feel like you had to keep this a secret from Marty and me?"

"This was my project – my thing."

"But you were using our money. What made you think you had the right to do that?"

"Listen, Allan, I've had enough stuff going on in the past several weeks. I don't need this crap from you."

"Don't get self righteous with me. I know what happened with Bill Evans, and I've got a pretty good idea what happened with Dick Cranston. I know about Diaz Brothers, and I know about your little deal with Angie Galafaro. I can live with all of that, but don't pretend that you didn't bring any of this on yourself."

"So Angelo told you the whole story?"

"Wrong. I told Angelo most of the story. You sell me short, Ike. I've known about the Diaz Brother's Mining Company for quite some time. You don't think I'd just give you ten million dollars without question, do you?"

"I guess I thought that was exactly what you were doing."

"You know, for supposedly being so slick, you're pretty damn naive. And that's where you've gone wrong. I would have been with you on most of this stuff, but you have dug your deepest holes trying to cover your tracks."

"Look, Allan, I think I understand what you're trying to say. I just don't want to talk about it right now."

Ike once again went back to staring out across the blackened horizon, and Allan, realizing that further attempts at making conversation would probably be futile, returned to his seat.

The attorney had made his point. He had been the silent partner for far too long. If Ike ran into trouble with his medical practice, or in his bid for political office, he would have nobody to blame but himself.

Talmadge Hyle was in the height of his glory. He moved about the cabin shaking hands with the volunteers and stopped to pose for pictures with the various people who wanted them. He had brought the usual entourage of reporters and photographers along with him, and his aides were busy scurrying about making sure that no photo opportunities were lost.

This was the very best of the American spirit of volunteers at work. These were definitely "points of light," highly skilled medical professionals, giving freely of their time to help those in need.

Jason was doing his best to make the most of this trip. He was certain to get a front page story out of this excursion, and for that he was glad. He had not breathed a word of his suspicions, or of his anger regarding those suspicions, to Talmadge Hyle. But the senior senator from Oregon was a people watcher with a very good capacity for discernment. He knew that all things were not well with the young reporter.

Hyle took a moment to rest on the isolated seat near the rear of the plane. He was convinced that this trip was going to provide him with that last needed shred of national publicity that would give him the recognition that would easily propel him into the White House. The developments of the last several hours could not have been better if he had written the script and orchestrated the events himself.

Certainly it was too bad that hundreds of people had died. And he could not enjoy the fact that many thousands more were injured and homeless. But to have a situation develop that would allow him to appear as the white knight, riding in to save the day, was almost too good to be true. In addition, he was also obviously so forgiving and compassionate, that he would return to help the citizens of a country where he had so nearly been killed by a rebel's bullet, only a few short weeks ago. That was the very type of commitment that the citizens of the United States looked for in their elected leaders.

Out of the corner of his eye the senator could see Jason approaching him. It was not the stride or the facial expression of an angry man. It was the composed demeanor of a man with a purpose – a purpose that he would be patient enough to see through to fruition. Talmadge Hyle was immediately on guard.

"Well, Senator, once again you are seizing the day. Going to be the big hero all over again, aren't you?"

"Just a bit sarcastic, eh Jason. Do you mean to tell me that you don't approve of our humanitarian mission?"

"Oh, I approve of the mission. But just how will the ledger read when it's over? Who will have benefited more, the victims of the earthquake, or Senator Talmadge Hyle?"

"Such cynicism from a man of your tender years is unbecoming, Jason."

"You know how it is, Senator. You get fucked up the ass a few times and your whole perspective changes. It tends to make a man bitter."

"If you're speaking figuratively, then I understand what you're saying. If you are speaking literally, then I'm afraid that we may be seeing things from a different point of view."

"So the truth is finally out. You've finally admitted that you're nothing more than a faggot masquerading as a well-adjusted family man."

"I would never have denied it, Jason. Not to you. You just never had the courage to speak to me about it, did you? And that, my young friend, brings us down to the essentials of our relationship. Do you think I was unaware of your intentions? I have known what you were trying to do all along. I probably would have never given you the time of day, but Jason, I do find you so attractive."

"You make me sick."

"And that is such a loss for both of us. I could have enhanced your career – like I have already done. It's a trade off, Jason. Everything in this life is. You have gotten what you wanted, and I have gotten what I wanted. And it's such a shame. We could have done so much more for each other."

"Oh, I intend to do plenty for you. If I have my way, you'll never spend a night in the White House. Every intimate detail of your sordid sexual preferences will be known in every household in America. You'll be ruined." Jason had spoken in a softened voice, and he was making every effort at maintaining his composure, but the desperation was beginning to become more obvious.

Hyle, on the other hand, was well schooled in the art of diplomacy, and he was nowhere near being rattled.

"You know better than that, Jason. There won't be a publication in the entire United Sates that would touch a story like this one. A man's sexual preferences are his own business, and nobody is going to want to be labeled as being anti-gay. And me, with my sterling record and adoring family... You'll look like a fool, and I'm sure you don't want that."

"You raped me, you sonofabitch, and I'm going to make you pay for that."

"Watch yourself, Jason. Don't do anything that you'll regret."

"Don't tell me what to do!"

"Always remember that discretion is the better part of valor."

Jason managed to walk away from the senator without telegraphing his disgust. He was still at a loss about what to do about all of this, but he had certainly resolved to do something.

The pilot announced that they would soon begin their descent into Bonanza and advised everyone to take their seats and fasten their seat belts. Five minutes later, they began to drop altitude with all of the gentility of a fighter pilot on a strafing mission. Several minutes later, both jets were on the ground, enduring a particularly bruising trip down a runway that had been disrupted by the earthquake. The jets came to a halt after taxiing to a group of aluminum Quonset huts, one of which was the home of Ben Harris.

Deplaning commenced rapidly, and the gear and vehicles were backed down the ramps at the rear of the craft. There was a large contingent of Nicaraguan Nationals waiting for the medical team, and among them were Miguel Dominguez, Jorge Delgado, and Ben Harris.

Ike stopped briefly after exiting the plane, and in the waxing light of dawn, he made eye contact with Shelley Grayson, standing a mere twenty feet from him. The stare of the nurse was unabashed and somewhat disconcerting.

Grayson did not know what to think of Ike's presence here. She knew why she had come – a love of humanity and a strong desire to exert a positive influence in her world. But for Ike to be here was so out of character for what she knew about the man. She had no knowledge of the Diaz Brother's Mining Company, but in her heart she knew that the surgeon was not in Nicaragua as a result of any love of mankind.

"Doctor Paponis, once again you come to the aid of my country."

"Miguel, it's good to see you. How can we be of service? Ben, how are you?"

"I'm good, Ike, but the city is a disaster area. We've got a lot of dead bodies and a lot more who are injured and dying. This place just doesn't have the resources to deal with a situation like this. We're really glad that you came."

"Doctor, it would be too difficult to move you into the city. The streets are covered with debris and are for the most part impassable. We have cleared one of the hangars here, and we have enough generators to provide power. I am sorry to say it after your long journey, but there are already injured waiting for you. Many of them are gravely ill."

"Well then, we'll get started with what we came to do."

The Air Force personnel rapidly moved the gear into the hangar, and within an hour, several makeshift operating rooms were ready for the team. They had set up the green military tents inside of the hangar itself and thus had provided a semi-sterile environment that would allow them to safely perform surgery.

Dominguez, Harris, and the other members of Dominguez's team busily transported the patients to and from the operating areas and assisted the U. S. Military personnel with preparing additional surgery suites. The work of caring for the wounded escalated to a near-frenetic pace within hours.

Most of the injuries were orthopedic. There had been many broken bones from the collapse of the buildings. But there were also a good number of blunt trauma cases with significant injuries to the internal organs of the abdomen and chest.

There were collapsed lungs, ruptured spleens, lacerated livers, and contused kidneys. It was a cornucopia of surgical pathology, and the surgeons embraced their tasks with a zeal that most of them had not felt since early in their careers.

Even Ike was enjoying the challenges of operating on the victims of this disaster. It was so unlike his practice in Portland where he knew ahead of time what he would find. Here, it was a total crapshoot. The best that he could do was to try to make an educated guess as to what the surgical problem was and then try to fix it.

They didn't have elaborate laboratory facilities, nor did they have the advanced technologies of CAT scanners, or magnetic resonance imaging. It was fly by the seat of your pants medicine, and it was invigorating to all of the participants.

Marty even tried his hand at several minor surgical procedures – something that he hadn't done since his days as a medical resident. Mostly, however, he was relegated to the task of triage, making decisions regarding the severity of the varying injuries, who was most critical, and who would have to wait.

The operating suites were kept busy twenty four hours per day for the first three days of the relief effort. The physicians and nurses slept in shifts and ate meals prepared for them in a military-style mess tent.

Ike had demanded that Shelley Grayson serve as his personal scrub nurse. His argument for doing so had been her familiarity with his professional needs. Grayson had balked at first, but she soon found that the surgeon's arguments were persuasive ones.

Ike watched the woman closely, looking for some indication of what had prompted her brutal frontal assault on his professional reputation. He saw nothing. She was composed, deliberate, and skillful in everything that she did.

The reporters and photographers chronicled the devastation in Bonanza. Hunger and homelessness were beginning to play a large role in their coverage, but the efforts of the Medical Response Team continued to be their primary focus.

Jason stayed close to the converted hangar. He was becoming increasingly consumed with his struggle to deal with what had happened to him in Managua. He found himself shadowing Talmadge Hyle and began to feel like a stalker. It was his sense of helplessness that threw him further and further into his irrational behavior.

Hyle was acutely aware of the constant attention that he was receiving from the reporter, and it was making him increasingly nervous. The inappropriate behavior was not lost on other members of the team either. Jason's affect had become almost psychotic, and trained physicians did not have a difficult time recognizing it.

Ike needed a break and a cigarette. Over the years, he had come to realize that he was most vulnerable to his old habit when he was fatigued, and the strain of recent days had tired him greatly. He left the operating tent and hangar and went out into the stifling midday heat.

The surgeon was surprised to see Talmadge Hyle sitting on an empty fifty-gallon drum outside of the hangar. There had been little use for a United

States Senator in the midst of a medical relief effort, with the notable exception of answering questions during the twice daily press conferences. Hyle had circulated as much as possible, trying to boost morale, but his left arm was still in a sling, and he had been unable to physically assist with anything.

Ike withdrew a cigarette from his half-empty pack. He lit it, took a long draw, and held the smoke in for an extended period. Out of the corner of his eye he could see Jason standing approximately fifty feet away, and his gaze was directed on Talmadge Hyle.

"Ike, good to see you old man. Tremendous job you folks are doing down here."

"Thank you, Senator. Are we making any headway?"

"Oh, Lord yes. They're having a difficult time locating victims in the city right now. I have heard that they could use the services of some of your folks over in Tunki, though. I guess that city got hit really hard by the earthquake too."

"Well, as soon as we get caught up here, I'll see about sending a contingent down there. The whole crew is pretty exhausted right now though."

"And well you should be, my boy. This has been a Herculean effort, and I have to tell you, I am proud of all of you. You're doing a great thing here, Ike. Great things. It humbles me to see you folks at work. Tremendous skill. Tremendous effort.

"Thank you, Senator. But this was really your idea, and you have to take a good deal of the credit. Without your support, we wouldn't even be here."

"I'll hear nothing of it. This has been your baby all along. And tell me, son, what good is an old crippled politician during something of this magnitude. Not much, I'd have to say. No, you doctors and nurses are the real heroes here."

"Don't sell yourself short, Talmadge. You've done a great deal for this country, and I know the entire nation feels indebted to you. I can see how you would feel useless with that bad shoulder of yours, but it's healing nicely. Before long you'll be back to your old self."

"I hope you're right, Ike. But I'm beginning to feel a lot like an old man, an old has been."

"You've got a good many great things yet to do, Senator. Don't even think it's time to start slowing down."

"Thank you for that, Ike. I hope you're right."

Ike finished one cigarette and lit another. He could not help but notice the reporter sitting in the hot sun staring at him and Senator Hyle. The whole scene reminded him of a time when, as a young man, he had hiked to a secluded lake high in the Rocky Mountains after an early autumn snow.

It had been morning, just after daybreak, when he and his companion had started out on the trail that was barely identifiable in the fresh snow. He remembered how quiet the forest had been that morning. Every potential sound had been muffled by the newly fallen snow.

After walking almost a mile, they had begun to see the footprints of a large cat. Immediately, they had realized that they were probably the tracks of a mountain lion. The urge to turn back had been enormous. But there had been something challenging in those tracks as well. Something that forced them onward.

As they had continued their hike through the woods, they began to realize that the tracks, the trail of the lion, was paralleling their own. They had begun to imagine sightings, and their senses had been keenly heightened. There had been fear, but they had found the sensation to be invigorating.

When they had finally reached the lake, they had found the scene to be overwhelming. The black waters were as calm as a plate of glass. The limbs of the fir trees were heavily laden with the weight of the bright white snow. They had thought that they were totally alone and had found peace in that realization.

But soon, as they continued to scan their surroundings, they had found their mountain lion. He was perched on a large rock that jutted out slightly into the stilled waters of the lake, a mere fifty yards from them. And his gaze had been trained directly on them.

Jason Riley reminded Ike of that cat – poised, vigilant, and waiting to strike.

"What's with that guy, Talmadge?"

"It's a personal matter. It seems that he's got it in his craw to destroy me. I don't think that he'll be able to accomplish it, but he has certainly gotten my attention."

"One of your many dalliances, Senator?"

"I'm afraid so."

"What do you intend to do about him?"

"I don't know just yet. I had hoped to ride it out. But he seems so determined, so vindictive."

"Do you want me to handle it for you?"

231

"What did you have in mind?"

"It's better that you know nothing of it."

"I suppose you're right. But I'm concerned about the bad press if anything happens to that boy."

"From the sounds of it, Senator, you should be concerned about the bad press that will be generated if you don't do something about him."

"Maybe. I've just never had to consider anything such as I think you are proposing. It worries me."

"Put your mind to rest. Nicaragua is still a hostile environment in many ways. Many things can happen here, and very few questions will be asked."

"Well, you handle it, Ike. I don't want to know anything about it."

Ike now had the blessing that he needed to perform his true mission in Nicaragua. He took one of the Jeeps from in front of the hangar and made his way toward downtown Bonanza. He was impressed with just how fast the roads were being cleared.

There were large bulldozers and front loaders clearing the streets of debris, and within moments, and only a couple of short detours, he was able to park directly in front of the Banca Natzionale.

Ike was marginally surprised that the bank was operating, but power had been restored to the central portion of the city, and apparently the bank had been one of the most sturdily constructed buildings. It appeared to have only suffered minimal damage.

After identifying himself, Ike was treated like royalty. The bank manager escorted the surgeon back to his large desk where he immediately began to exercise his marginal command of the English language.

"We are honored, Doctor. How can I be of service to you?"

"I would like to make a withdrawal."

"Certainly, sir. I hope that you would not be withdrawing all of you money, however. Under the circumstances, I am afraid that might be difficult to accomplish."

"No that isn't my intention at this time. I will be keeping a large portion of my funds here in Nicaragua for quite some time."

"That is good to hear. How can I help you today?"

"I need two cashier's checks. One will be in the amount of thirty million dollars and the other for ten million. You may make the necessary conversions to Nicaraguan currency, but this is all that I will require of you today."

"For such a valued customer, we can accomplish this task rather quickly."

"Thank you. I would appreciate that."

"No, Doctor Paponis. For all that you and your friends have done for my people, it is we who appreciate you."

The bank manager scurried off, and within fifteen minutes, Ike was leaving the bank with the checks in his hand. He enjoyed the celebrity that his wealth and position were providing for him in this country. He left the bank smiling.

After arriving back at the airfield, the surgeon summoned Ben Harris and Miguel Dominguez and asked the two men to take a walk with him. They strolled out onto the runway and away from the converted hangar. When they reached a distance where he felt that their activities could not be observed, Ike removed the check for thirty million dollars from the pocket of his scrub shirt.

"As you had probably guessed by my presence here, our flight back to the United States was a success. Here is your percentage of the profits, Miguel."

"You are good to your word, Doctor. That is a quality that I respect in a man."

"And here's a little something for you, Ben," said the surgeon as he withdrew the check for ten million dollars.

"Holy shit, Ike. I never expected this. Out of the ruins come my riches." Ben looked like a kid at Christmas.

"Gentlemen, what I have to ask of you now is a favor that goes beyond friendship. It is something that I never thought I'd have to ask of any man."

"We owe a great deal to you, Doctor. What favor can we do for you?"

"I will be dispatching a team to Tunki later this afternoon, and I would like for you to insure that they do not arrive there."

"These will be some of the people who have come to the aid of Bonanza?"

"Yes."

"This is indeed a delicate matter, Doctor. What is the reason?"

"They are people who are not my friends. They are people who have tried to destroy me. I would not ask this of you were it not absolutely necessary."

"Then I will ask no more questions. We will serve your wishes, but I must say that it makes my heart heavy."

"Thank you, Miguel." The three men walked somberly back toward the hangar and another word was not spoken among them.

Upon his arrival back at the hangar, Ike formulated a list of the people who would be making the trip to Tunki. On that list were the names of Martin Spencer, Allan Spandell, Shelley Grayson, and Jason Riley. He also included others so as to not unduly raise suspicion, but he was surprised when there was minimal dissention among the participants.

Allan was the only individual who had a hard time figuring out why he had been asked to go.

"What's this all about, Ike?"

"Allan, I was hoping that you could coordinate this little excursion for me. You're the best mind that I've got down here, and no doubt there'll be a need for somebody who can think on his feet. And besides, Marty needs some company. You know how spastic he can get. Listen, if you don't want to go, I'll understand. But I'll consider it a personal favor if you do go."

"I guess I wouldn't mind getting out of here for awhile. I've been feeling kind of useless."

"Thanks, Allan. I won't forget this."

The Tunki rescue party departed the Bonanza airfield at four o'clock p.m. The heat was nearly unbearable, and the humidity raised the level of discomfort exponentially. Two five-ton trucks and one Jeep transported the personnel and their supplies.

The road to Tunki skirted along the base of a mountain ridge, but for the most part, the terrain was flat as it coursed through the lush green valley. It was only as they neared their destination that they began to climb higher into the rugged mountains.

The quality of the road began to deteriorate rapidly as dusk began to fall. Progress became slow as the vehicles climbed even higher onto the mountain.

Just as the two trucks and Jeeps reached the summit of the ridge line, the gray sky erupted into a fiery scene that mimicked the flames of hell. Machine gun fire could be heard sporadically, as could the explosions of the incendiary devices that were used to destroy the vehicles and equipment. People jumped from the trucks and Jeeps and ran quickly to the tree line. The entire incident had been carefully choreographed prior to the staged attack, so that inhabitants of the nearby hills would witness the mayhem, but not the escape of the men and women who were on their way to rescue the people of Tunki.

EPILOGUE

Mitch Petrowski quietly surveyed the murder scene. To be able to do so amidst the surrounding bedlam was an exhibition of his practiced art. The Secret Service was there, as were the Bureau boys, in their expensive and well-tailored suits. There were uniforms from the Portland P.D. who had cordoned off the area surrounding the body. The State Crime Lab officers scurried about collecting blood, fiber, and photo evidence. Forensic science was the discipline of the day.

A large crowd had already formed beyond the police barrier, and the media was everywhere. Several helicopters hovered overhead, and cameras were jacked up on the backs of the television station vans. As the stylish reporters began their soliloquies, Mitch drew further into himself. Before him lay the body of a United States Senator. This senator, Talmadge Hyle, was also the Republican front- runner for the presidential nomination.

The candidate was flat on his back with his right leg drawn up until it was nearly beneath him. There was a singular gunshot wound to his right temple, and the left side of his head was gone. A river of blood flowed from the senator's head as it began its arduous journey down the steps that led up to the Justice Center.

Mitch was focused. The Justice Center was virtually surrounded by sites that would provide ample concealment for a sniper, as well as a good line of fire, but the shot had come from only one of these, and it was his job to pinpoint the exact firing location.

He was looking for that one item of evidence that nobody else would see. This was why he went into this nearly trance-like state of mind when he approached a homicide scene. The practice had served him well. He had the best closure rate of any homicide detective in the Police Bureau. Mitch knew that the federal boys would take control of this case. But the murder had taken place in his backyard, and he would not give it up easily.

"So what do you think, Herb?" Mitch had rejoined the natural world and was addressing his long-term partner, Herb Adams.

"This is an assassination, Mitch. Who the heck knows what the motivations might be. Hyle had a lot of enemies. We've got a single shot from a high-powered rifle that could have come from any one of a hundred locations around here. But don't worry about it, this case will be yanked from us before we can get back to headquarters."

"Greg Stevens will have custody of the body. They can't take that away from him. Maybe the feds will get the case eventually, but I think we'll at least have the chance to open an investigation."

Mitch and Herb had been partners for nearly five years, and in that time, they had come to know each other well. Herb could almost see his friend locking his jaw, and he knew that tremendous investigative mind was already formulating a plan of action. He also knew that this was just the kind of case that would torment the detective. Mitch would never be able to tolerate the killing of a United States Senator on his turf. Somebody would have to pay.

* * *

Allan Spandell Jr. was in his hotel room that overlooked the Multnomah County Justice Center. He stood in the middle of the room transfixed on the television. The local reporter was speaking from just outside the Justice Center, directly below the room where Spandell was staying. And he was detailing the assassination of Senator Talmadge Hyle. How could this be? He knew Hyle, at least casually, and the thought of the man being killed right outside of his hotel room was nearly inconceivable.

He heard the lock to his hotel room door turn, but he was not alarmed. Within seconds, a beautiful blonde entered the room and tossed her purse on the dresser.

"Sharon, look at this," said Allan Jr. as he motioned her toward the TV. She moved toward him and watched the newscast with interest.

"Senator Hyle was just assassinated right outside of our hotel. Can you believe it? A United States Senator and presidential candidate gets waxed on the Justice Center steps in broad daylight. I guess there isn't anyplace safe anymore.

Sharon watched the newscast in silence, and then walked quietly over to the window, where she had a bird's eye view of the events below. She studied the scene carefully before turning to address her companion.

"Talmadge Hyle was nothing more than a slick talking bastard. That's all we need, another silver tongue with a load of empty promises in the White House. Ike told me that he was gay, too. I lost my faith in Talmadge Hyle at the same time I lost my faith in Ike - and you know when that was," Sharon stated with an averted glance.

"When Dad and Marty Spencer disappeared," Allan Jr. replied.

"You've got it. It's been six months, and I know the official investigation didn't turn anything up, but it just doesn't feel right to me. Fifteen bodies just don't disappear from the face of the earth without a trace."

"That never made sense to me either. But they didn't work too hard or too long on the investigation."

"Hyle shut the investigation down. That sends up some red flags for me. There's got to be more to it," said Sharon circumspectly.

Allan Jr. just looked at her. He knew that he was falling in love with her. He had never been able to see her and Ike together. The surgeon was so much older and so unfeeling. And as of late, Sharon seemed to despise the man. That had made an affair with her that much easier to rationalize.

Sharon left her position overlooking the Justice Center and silently moved across the floor to where Allan Jr. was standing. She embraced him from behind as he continued to stare at the television. Soon she had freed the tail of his shirt from the waist of his pants, and slowly, teasingly, began to undo buttons.

Allan Jr. feigned disinterest in her activities, but as her hands caressed his chest, lingering at the nipples, he was soon unable to maintain the charade. He turned to face her and kissed her fully on the lips. His tongue explored her mouth for several long moments before he directed his attention to her neck and ears.

Her breathing became more rapid and shallow as she undid the zipper on his pants and took his fully-erect penis in her hand. The two then simultaneously undressed each other as they moved slowly toward the bed. As they tumbled into the bed, the intensity of their fondling increased. This was not the usual routine. More often they both remained in control.

Her hips rose forcefully to meet his thrusts, and her fingernails dug deeply into the skin of his buttocks. She urged him on with the sounds of her passion as she became lost in their lovemaking. The time that it took to reach satisfaction was short, but the pleasure was complete.

Allan Jr. rolled over onto his back and stared at the ceiling. He had enjoyed their lovemaking but could not turn his thoughts from the assassination of Talmadge Hyle.

"I still can't believe that it happened."

"Put it out of your head, Allan. Talmadge Hyle was a bastard and no doubt got what he deserved. Come on, you're not that naive, are you? I can't even imagine how many people he must have had to walk on to get where he is."

"I suppose you're right. Do you think this will affect Ike's chances for the Senate?" the young lawyer asked.

"Ike doesn't know it yet, but he's in for a bumpy road anyway," said his wife, with some measure of disdain.

"You don't really care much for him anymore, do you?"

"All Ike ever wanted was an ornament on his arm. I'm sure he was a little disappointed when he found out that I came with a brain too."

"Do you think he ever loved you?"

"Ike Paponis is not capable of loving anyone, unless of course loving himself counts. You wouldn't believe some of the stories that I could tell you, Allan. But I wouldn't want to burden you with the responsibility of having knowledge of some of the stuff he has pulled."

"Come on, Sharon. Ike's a respected surgeon. Surely he can't be as bad as all that."

Sharon had gotten up from the bed and was already starting to get dressed.

"I'm telling you, Allan. Ike is a dangerous man. Don't kid yourself and don't get in his way. If he knew what was going on between you and me, he would probably kill you, or at least have you killed. And if anybody else were to find out and embarrass Ike with the information, he would surely kill you."

"How can you still live with him? How can you remain his wife?"

"I don't have a choice right now. You may not understand that, but very simply put, that's the way it is. Ike is going to get what's coming to him, Allan, just like Talmadge Hyle. But for right now, I need to stay put," she said as she gathered her things to leave.

"Why do you have to rush off? It's still early afternoon."

"With Talmadge Hyle getting killed, you can bet that Ike is going to want to make some lame statement. And of course he'll want his loving wife close by. I'll give him that for now. Bear with me, Allan. Everything is going to work out for us. I promise."

* * *

Mitch Petrowski and Herb Adams walked hurriedly into the office of the Medical Examiner for Multnomah County.

"You are aware of what's been happening this morning aren't you, Greg?" said Mitch to the Multnomah County Medical Examiner.

"I'd have to be blind and deaf not to know what's going on. I can't believe that all of this happened just a few blocks from here."

"Greg, I gotta' believe that this case is going to be pulled from us by the Feds. What do you think?"

"Well, there's a precedent for this sort of thing. When Kennedy was shot in Dallas, that's exactly what happened. And look what a fiasco that turned into. It's taken thirty years to get the records of that investigation released into the public domain, and some things we'll never know. I don't know how you feel, but I don't want to face that kind of scrutiny. If there's a conspiracy, then the feds can investigate that end of it. As for the autopsy, we can do that right here. Hell, I do them every day. I don't want to be involved in a media circus. If we simply do our jobs then nobody will be able to criticize our actions."

As Greg finished his statement, the door to his office burst open. Within a fraction of a second there were three suits abreast.

"You're the county medical examiner, I trust?"

"I am. Just who the hell are you?" Greg was composed and stayed seated behind his desk.

"Barry Guyton. Secret Service. These are my partners, Rod Hamilton and Red Langdon."

"And you are here to…?"

"We intend to assume control of the senator's body," said Guyton as if there were to be no opposition.

"And what would make you think that I'm willing to relinquish jurisdiction here?"

"This is big, Doc. Really big. We have more resources than you do. We're willing to take this off your hands. All you have to do is give us the word."

"Well then, Mr. Guyton, I'm sorry. Because the word is that we're going to do the autopsy ourselves. And my friends here are going to be opening a homicide investigation. Of course, we will appreciate any assistance that you can give us."

"You're out of your league, Doctor," said Red Langdon, the appropriately named agent with the carrot colored hair.

"That's a subjective assessment, Mr. Langdon. And you have no idea what I'm capable of."

It was Barry Guyton's turn and the tone of his voice bordered on being threatening.

"Look, Doctor, we came in here and made every effort at being polite. We didn't want you to feel like we were stepping on your toes. But make no mistake about it, we are taking jurisdiction of this case. Quite frankly, we don't give a damn what you intend to do. This matter is closed."

Mitch Petrowski locked his jaw, and this, coupled with his flat-top haircut, gave the appearance of a bulldog ready to strike. But Greg Stevens interceded before the detective could speak.

"Gentlemen, I'm sorry that you feel the need to use your collective muscle to wrest this case from us. The bottom line is that by law I have legal jurisdiction over Senator Hyle's body. I intend to execute my right to perform a postmortem examination unless you can obtain a court order to the contrary. And gentlemen, by the time you get that order, I'll be done with my examination."

"You'll regret this decision, Dr. Stevens," said Guyton.

"Not half as much as I would regret turning the body over to you and neglecting my sworn duty. Now get the hell out of my office, and let me do my job." With looks of disgust, the three agents turned and left the office without further comment."

"Mitch, you and Herb get over to the scene and help my people get the body over here as soon as possible. I don't want to underestimate those fools' ability to get an injunction. I'll be waiting for you in the dissection room."

Ike was in Lincoln City for a Rotary Club luncheon when he received the news of Talmadge Hyle's death. He was not normally capable of genuine emotion, but to the casual onlooker, he did appear to be visibly shaken by the news. He took a few moments to collect himself and then began to address the audience.

"Ladies and gentlemen, I have just been informed that Talmadge Hyle has been assassinated in Portland. I don't have many details, but I was told that it was a fatal gunshot wound. This luncheon is important to me, as is your support in the Fall, but I'm afraid that my place is in Portland with Senator Hyle's family."

Surrounded by his handlers, he exited down the center aisle of the banquet room and out to the waiting limo in front of the hotel. The limo took the candidate to a small airfield about twenty minutes out of town where a helicopter was waiting. The rotors were already turning rapidly when Ike and his people ran at a half crouch to board the chopper. Within minutes, they were settled and airborne.

"Give me details," Ike shouted over the moan of the engines.

"The media is all over it, sir. But even with all of the exposure, there *aren't* many details. Apparently the Senator was making a speech on the steps of the Justice Center. It was a kind of "when it all began" kind of thing. It was a single gunshot wound to the head."

"I know all of that. What I want to know is why!"

"I think you'll have to wait awhile on that one. Senator Hyle had plenty of enemies. Shoot. Anybody at that level has enemies. It goes with the territory. And you can never rule out a lone crazy. We all know how often that happens."

The helicopter began to descend on Portland International where a limo was waiting.

* * *

The Federal Express envelope stamped **URGENT,** in bright red letters, was handed to the receptionist at Secret Service Headquarters in Portland, Oregon. The woman tried to detain the young man who was obviously a courier, but he was gone before she could question him.

She took the envelope to Barry Guyton's office immediately. Guyton carefully opened the flap and removed the single typewritten page. The expression on his face could only be described by one word. Barry Guyton was stunned.

* * *

Jason Riley watched CNN on the personal television on the adjustable arm of his chair in the waiting area at Portland International Airport. Of course, the only thing being covered was the assassination of Senator Talmadge Hyle, and the young man watched the reports with a mixture of satisfaction and regret. He had certainly grown to hate the man on a personal level, but there was also a tinge of respect for many of the good things that Hyle, the statesman, had been able to accomplish.

He pulled out his ticket and studied the flight information. He was still unaccustomed to the name of Jon Morrison, unaccustomed to *BEING* Jon Morrison. But, of course, his death on the road to Tunki had prohibited him from carrying on as Jason Riley. Fortunately, Ben Harris had been able to fit him with a new identity. He had also taught him to be an expert marksman with a high-powered assault rifle.

Boarding began for the flight to Houston and on to Managua, and Jon Morrison left the city of Portland, as the live images on the television showed the body of Talmadge Hyle being bagged and removed by officials from the Multnomah County Medical Examiner.

* * *

The receptionist at the Multnomah County Medical Examiner's office recognized Ike as he came through the door with his entourage. And that recognition didn't trigger any endearment, either. Greg Stevens was now the M.E., but that business with Dr. Spencer down in Nicaragua had never set right with the receptionist. She didn't like Ike Paponis, and she didn't trust him.

"I would like to speak with Dr. Stevens. Can you tell me where I might locate him?"

"Dr. Stevens is in the autopsy room. I would be happy to let him know that you're here."

"That won't be necessary, I know where the autopsy room is. I'll let myself in." The bully was back in action.

"I'm afraid he can't be disturbed, sir."

"Nonsense, I'm a medical man. There's nothing going on in there that I haven't seen before."

"That's not the point, sir. He specifically stated that he did not want to be disturbed." Ike waved her off with the brush of his hand and started down the hallway. The receptionist was on the intercom to warn Greg Stevens that Paponis was on his way to the autopsy room.

"Don't worry about it, Millie. We'll handle it down here," said the pathologist as the door to the autopsy room came flying open.

"What is the meaning of this? How dare you refuse me entry to the autopsy room? Hell, I built this place."

Greg Stevens rapidly pulled the white sheet up so it covered the senator's lifeless body, and Mitch and Herb moved toward him to further obscure his view. Just as the pathologist moved to address Ike, the doors flew open once again.

Barry Guyton had handcuffed Paponis before the door had swung shut.

"What the hell is going on here?" Ike appeared perplexed.

"Dr. Paponis, you are under arrest for the federal charge of conspiracy to commit murder in the death of Senator Talmadge Hyle. You have the right to remain silent. You have the right to an attorney..." Guyton continued to Mirandize Ike as the surgeon tried to fathom what course of events had lead to his arrest. Surely this was all a mistake.

Later that evening he was permitted the opportunity to make one phone call. He decided that he would call his wife, Sharon, and that she could coordinate lawyers, private investigators, and anything else he might need.

The phone rang twice before she picked up. "Hello."

"What the hell are you doing at home? Don't you know I'm in jail? They think I killed Talmadge. Can you believe that?"

"Oh, Ike baby, it's you," she cooed.

"It's so good to hear your voice. You've got to get me out of here. Call Sean Merrick and get him down here right away. He's got to get me bail. I can't stay in this place."

"Oh, baby, that's it," she moaned softly.

"What are you talking about?"

"Oh, I'm sorry, Ike. Allan Junior was just screwing me and I forgot I was on the phone with you."

"Allan Junior is doing what?"

"He's screwing me, Ike. I know you weren't aware, but he's been screwing me for a long long time. I sometimes forget that you don't know. Everybody else does."

The blood drained from Ike's face as the reality of his situation began to become clear.

"Well, I'll deal with that later. For now just get a hold of Sean Merrick and get him down here to get me out this hole!"

"I'm so sorry, Ike. Nobody is coming to get you out. In fact, nobody could get you out if they wanted to. You see, Marty, Allan, that young reporter, Jason Riley, and your old nurse, Shelley Grayson, they're all alive, Ike. They're alive and they've all given depositions of all your nasty little deeds. The authorities know about Bill Evans and Dick Cranston, and all of the others, dear. I don't think you're ever going to get out of prison, that is if you don't get the death penalty. And since you hired somebody to kill Senator Hyle, because he knew about that little mess in Nicaragua, well, Ike, they just might give you the death penalty."

"I didn't have anything to do with Talmadge's death. You've got to believe me," said Ike desperately.

"I'm sorry, Ike, but I just don't think anybody's going to believe that. Oh, baby, that feels so *goooood*. I'm sorry, Ike, but Allan and I have to go. We've got a flight to catch to Nicaragua. There are rumors that there is about to be a big strike at the Diaz Brothers Mining Company."

* * *

The crowd outside the entrance to the main shaft at the Diaz Brothers Mining Company was a happy one. The Big Bad Wolf was not going to blow the house down. The Wicked Witch of the West was about to be melted, and the evil heart surgeon was not going to hurt anybody ever again.

It was a good crowd of good people. And they were all ever so rich. A government dictum out of Managua had transferred the vast sum of money in the Banco Natzionale, under the name of Dr. Ike Paponis, to Sharon Burch, his soon to be ex-wife. Sharon had, in turn, divided the money equally among all those who had been used or harmed by her ex-husband. The Spencers were here, as were the Spandells. Jason Riley, *A.K.A.* Jon Morrison, was also here, and his demons were now gone. Ben Harris and Miguel Dominguez were also here, and they, along with Jorge Delgado and Emilio Vega's oldest son, were on the verge of being blissfully drunk.

These were good people who had been united by a common enemy. And now they had all joined together to work the mine. Why not, if Ike Paponis had his way, most of them would be dead. Maybe someday they would go back to the States, but for now this would do nicely. It was so peaceful here, so green, and so relaxing.

That is until Allan Junior stood at the mouth of the mine opening and screamed, "Eureka, we've hit the mother lode!"

The End